Culmination (Dragon Diar
Copyright © 2019 by Selen

MW01173335

The "fiction dragon" logo is a trademark of Drake Books & Media.

Book design copyright © 2019 by Drake Books & Media
Cover design by Selena IR Drake
Author photo by Robert Berry.

Drake Books & Media
901 62nd Avenue NE, Suite B, Minot, ND 58703
Visit us online at www.DrakeBooksMedia.com

Published in the United States of America

First published: October 2013

ISBN: 9781708971021

PUBLISHER'S NOTE

Other books by Selena IR Drake

Dragon Diaries:
Ascension
Culmination
Return of the Dragon Keepers

The AEON Files:
The Archfiend Artifact
The Lycan Pharaoh
The Lullaby Shriek
The Bone Prophet
The Sovereign Flame

WEIRD Chronicles
Episode One

Available on Amazon and at DrakeBooksMedia.com

Previously...

Shortly after the start of a new year on Ithnez, a young girl named Xyleena – Xy affectionately - began having strange dreams. The phoenix form of the Spring and Fire Goddess, Zahadu-Kitai, appeared in these dreams and forewarned Xyleena of dangers to come. Strange things began to occur in the days that followed, most notably was the sudden appearance of an ancient-looking book in Xyleena's hip sack.

While Xyleena and her friends tried to figure out the meaning of the book, a man claiming to be High Prince Valaskjalf Za'Car arrived at the Temple of Five Souls. He was there for the Festival of the Phoenix, but his intentions laid elsewhere. In truth, his name was Dimitri DéDos and he was after the hand-written diary of Amorez Renoan, the Legendary Dragon Keeper.

Unable to locate the diary, Dimitri blew up the festival with a massive fire spell. He managed to spot the book he was after when Xyleena tripped and spilled the contents of her bag. He immediately sent his two Dákun Daju cohorts after Xyleena. A battle ensued in which Xyleena's friend and first love, Ríhan, was murdered. Xyleena fainted after casting a massive spell and was sent adrift on the Anakor River.

While Dimitri and his cohorts continued to search for the girl and the diary, Xyleena was discovered by Teka Loneborne. Pulled from the water and nursed back to health, Xyleena accepted Teka's help in finding a path to take with her life. Teka sailed Xyleena to the Sorcerers' Isle to get Amorez's diary translated.

While on the Sorcerers' Isle Xyleena was introduced to Thera Onyx, the daughter of the Necromancer who helped create the Dragons of Light. Thera managed to translate a portion of the diary that included a complex riddle to unearth the twelve dragons. Xyleena, Thera, and Teka set out to find the first dragon, Vortex, whose lair was nearby.   Meanwhile, Dimitri and his team were able to find the Sorcerers' Isle. They wove a series of lies and managed to turn the Feykin against Xyleena. Thera's younger sister, Pox, fell under Dimitri's mind control and led his team in pursuit of Xyleena.

After battling Dimitri and his team in Vortex's Sky Castle, Xyleena obtained the first dragon. She, Teka and Thera then set out to find the second dragon, Kkaia. Weeks went by at sea and Xyleena's team finally landed on the Shaking Isle. They were ambushed by Dimitri's team and the fight ended only after Kkaia herself appeared and killed one of Dimitri's team members, Luna.

Dimitri's team retreated to Zadún, the capital city of Arctica. While dealing with his teammate's death, Dimitri stumbled upon Xyleena's team. He followed them as they teamed up with a Fox Demon named Kitfox Latreyon, who led the team to the third dragon, Atoka.

Once Xyleena obtained Atoka, she and her team set out for Kamédan to team up with Shazza Hoshino, the Dákun Daju Queen of Katalania. Shazza led Xyleena and her team to the Tomb of the Lost where they faced many perils and barely managed to acquire the fourth dragon, Helios. Upon leaving the tomb, Xyleena and her team met Kkorian McKnight, a pirate who wasn't trusted by Kitfox.

Xyleena's team returned to Kamédan to rest and to translate the next portion of the riddle in the diary. A few days later, the five of them set out for the next two dragons believed to be hidden beneath the Dragon Head Bay.

With an alien sky overhead, we had decided to create some new constellations by which to navigate. It took over a year to observe the stars and pick out these constellations. Eventually, we created a long list that included Seraph the Slayer, Camena the Muse, and Lisica the Fox. Finally we could find our way at night.

– FROM "THE CHRONICLES OF ITHNEZ, VOL. II" BY ADJIRSÉ DÉDOS

D imitri shielded his eyes from the late afternoon suns as he peered out across the Dragon Head Bay. The water was as calm and pristine as a sheet of glass; its mirrored surface broken only by an occasional insect daring to land. He could see the world around him reflected upon the tranquil surface, so at peace. So quiet. So beautiful. He felt its serenity wash over him, soothing his troubled soul and quieting his rampant thoughts. He found himself wishing that he could stay here forever, just enjoying the peace. But he was on a mission and knew he could not afford to falter from the path before him.

I have to find the Shadow Dragons. He thought, fighting to stifle the mix of emotions that swelled within him as he focused upon his goal. I have to avenge my mother. I promised her I would make all these retched Humes pay for the blood they cost us. A terrified scream ripped from a memory long thought naught but a ghost echoed through his mind. In that instant his serenity was forgotten, and he was back home in Drún F'Zrahl-Tokai. Strange how clearly he could remember things from centuries so long ago, almost as if those tragic events had happened only just yesterday. And even when he longed to forget every last detail and pain the memory wrought, he only remembered it all that much more clearly....

It was late summer of his twelfth year. Life so far had not been easy for him. Being the half Dákun Daju bastard son of a Hume, he was constantly harassed by the purebloods and treated worse than the lowest slaves. His dear mother, Solahnj, was not immune to the abuse, but being a pureblood meant even she was treated better than he. But things were beginning to look up. This day was to be the day he became a M'Ktoah, a proud and honorable standing amongst all Dákun Daju and the first step to becoming a true warrior. If he could become one, he would restore his mother's honor and he would finally be counted as one of the clan. He had spent every waking minute over several years refining himself and mastering the techniques his mother drilled into him. All of his strength, his wits, his endurance, everything would be tested during the Sango Tuurik – the Blood Hunt – this day. He had everything to prove, and he'd be damned if he failed.

So it was that long before first light this morning, when the sky overhead was bejeweled with stars and moons, Dimitri found himself seeking out Viktohn, the teacher, and other M'Ktoah disciples that were to be tested. He knew the designated meeting place, and walked briskly over the ancient stones that formed the many bridges and platforms of the cliffside city known as Drún F'Zrahl-Tokai. He listened to the enormous Thundering Falls, which surrounded the city and kept it partially hidden in its mist, and took comfort in the familiar sound as he navigated the maze of unlit walkways by memory. It took him only a handful of minutes to find Viktohn and the potential M'Ktoah, all gathered around the shrine at the heart of the city. Realizing he was not the last to arrive, he took it upon himself to utilize the shrine and quietly pray to his ancestors for guidance and strength. For once, the others did not ridicule him for his actions, and remained silent. When at last the final disciple arrived, Viktohn called for them to move out. Dimitri lingered at the shrine just long enough to fall at the far back of the progression, as was proper for one of his standing. As the group moved northeast, towards the bridge that connected to the mainland where the hunt would begin, Dimitri studied each of the disciples.

2

Féca, though only in her tenth year, was the strongest and fastest of the six potential M'Ktoah. Dimitri had always thought that her spiked, sunset orange hair and golden eyes were attractive. He knew better than to tell her so, for she was the daughter of the clan's Zoloekuhl – the Elder. His compliment, though expressed with innocent intentions of admiration, would be taken as an insult, and she would have the right to kill him for it. And if she didn't kill him, the Zoloekuhl would. It was not Dimitri's place to say such things. Féca's place, however, was right behind Viktohn, leading the potential M'Ktoah on the Sango Tuurik, a fact that made her father very proud.

The second in command of the potential M'Ktoah was Pikal. He was a strong, proud, and tall for being in his twelfth year, standing at just under two meters in height. His hair was pine green, worn long and tied in multiple, thin braids adorned with hand-carved beads made from the bones of Humes and Wakari. Pikal already wore scars from his many scraps with the other Dákun Daju children. He was looking forward to winning a few more during the Blood Hunt, and did not care who or what he would have to sacrifice to win those scars.

The other three M'Ktoah disciples were Venli, Temala, and B'Lenditonair, who preferred to be called Bone. The three of them were triplets, girls all. They could all be easily mistaken for Humes due to their chocolate brown hair, but their brilliant turquoise eyes and lust for battle betrayed their true heritage. Though not as strong or proud as Féca or Pikal, the triplets were formidable in their own right. They specialized in group tactics, and seemed to have developed their own hand and body language for use in choreographing their attacks to bring down foes. Dimitri had actually spent some time watching the trio in their training, and had managed to memorize some of their signals; an advantage he knew he would utilize later.

Dimitri knew all of this about his fellow M'Ktoah, yet they knew nothing of his strengths or weaknesses – and he had several surprises in store for them once the hunt began. He also knew that they would probably use him as bait, a fact that he was prepared to exploit to his advantage to make the first kill. After all, it was

3

the first kill of the Sango Tuurik that won the most glory for the M'Ktoah.

So Dimitri and the other five disciples followed Viktohn across the long, stone bridge that stretched over the Thundering Falls, connecting Drún F'Zrahl-Tokai to the northern mainland. There, a small group of Dákun Daju greeted them with weapons of their choice to use on the hunt. Dimitri waited his turn while the others had their pick of the weapons. When at last it was his turn to chose, he went straight for the one weapon he knew no one would bother with – the beat up, old double-edged swords that had been fused at the hilts. He referred to the odd weapon as the dual sword, and was quite fond of it. His choice earned him a few snickers, but the group was otherwise quiet.

Viktohn ordered them onwards.

They marched through ever-thickening woods for nearly an hour, until Viktohn pulled them to a stop in a small clearing. There, the teacher looked to Féca, who nodded and promptly took command. Dimitri listened closely to her instructions as she divided up the team. As expected, he was to wait in the middle of the clearing to act as bait while the others vanished into the trees to drop in on the kill at the perfect moment – probably when the beast was distracted by tearing him to pieces. So Dimitri calmly walked past the other disciples and sat upon a boulder situated near the center. He watched as the others took up their positions in the surrounding trees, making sure to memorize their locations for the future. He had to be prepared to defend himself from them, for he knew his plan would throw them into a fury once it was revealed.

Silence spread through the clearing.

They waited.

Hours crawled by as if they were days.

Morning turned to afternoon.

Leaves rustled.

Every muscle in Dimitri's body tensed in preparation. His hand gripped the hilt of the dual sword laid by his side. Féca suddenly dropped down from the canopy to land on a low branch. He had to force himself not to glare at her in his

4

frustration. She ordered him to venture further into the woods in search of the appropriate prey. Dimitri sighed, nodded. He took a minute to stretch before hopping down from the boulder. He got his bearings and then started walking northward, towards the foothills of the mountains where he was sure fierce predators like wyverns gathered for their own hunt.

He could not tell how long he had been walking before he heard strange noises coming from the forest further ahead. Carefully, silently he made his way towards the noise. The forest came to a sudden end, and Dimitri tucked himself behind the thickest tree trunk he could find in order to observe the area beyond. Countless trees had been cleared away, leaving only stumps or deep ruts in the ground. Several meters away from the tree line stood the beginnings of a stone wall. Within the infant barrier sat many small houses built from the felled trees. It took Dimitri only a moment to realize that Humes had moved into the area, and they were hard at work building their own village. It disturbed him that their settlement was so close to Drún F'Zrahl-Tokai, for Humes had been known to lash out at Dákun Daju without provocation. Should this band of Humes stumble upon his home, he was sure there would be a battle. Knowing that he should alert the Zoloekuhl about the encroaching Humes, Dimitri made a mental note of the town's location. Then, like a creature of the wilds, he vanished into the shadows of the forest.

He skirted the Hume town, travelling further eastward, towards the mountains. The shadows of the forest were beginning to grow long, and he knew he would soon have to turn back or face the wilds of the forest after nightfall. He did not want to return to the others without prey for the Sango Tuurik. If he did, the other disciples would be scathing mad at his failure and see fit to kill him for slowing them down. Driven by his hatred of failure, he pushed on.

When at last the sky overhead turned deep blue, and twilight reigned over the land, Dimitri finally gave in. With a frustrated sigh, he turned to make his way back to the waiting M'Ktoah. As he walked along, he prayed to his ancestors for help; begging them to give him a worthy challenge that would bring him much honor as a M'Ktoah. For such a gift, he was willing to do almost anything.

It wasn't long before he came across the Hume settlement again. He lingered in the trees, eating some of the wild berries that clung to the low branches and watching the Humes as they retreated into their wooden houses for the night. He mused at how easy it would be for him to destroy the whole settlement singlehandedly. Perhaps he could use knowledge of the village as his savior for failing to bring worthy prey for the Sango Tuurik. With that thought in mind, he moved on. As before, he skirted around the village, this time heading south, to where the M'Ktoah would be waiting in the clearing.

A twig snapped.

He froze.

A low growl betrayed a presence.

He smirked.

Slowly, he turned to scan the trees. To his left, golden feline eyes seemed to glow in the dark. His hand calmly moved to grip the hilt of his dual sword. Before he could draw the weapon, the wildcat pounced and Dimitri darted away. It roared in frustration, and immediately took up pursuit. Dimitri dared a glance back at his hunter, noting the dagger-like incisors that ended with a sharp tip below the cat's chin, the scrolling and spiny horns that swept back over its sleek head, and the inky splotches on the pale pelt. It was a large, male Amber Crested Lion that had seen at least seven years; a predator worthy of the hunt. Dimitri whooped, both in delight and to alert the M'Ktoah disciples of his success in finding prey, and put on a bit more speed. The cat was fast and agile, and he had to make sure to stay just ahead of it long enough to draw it into the clearing else it would give up the hunt.

Trees whipped by and branches grabbed at Dimitri's skin and clothes. He fought his way through them, ignoring the painful scratches and somehow managing to stay just out of reach of the furious lion. Ahead several meters, he heard the sound of an obvious struggle. The voices of Féca and Pikal called out commands in a frenzy, and he knew something else of worth had stumbled upon the hunting M'Ktoah. With no chance of jumping in to the midst of the others to claim their kill, Dimitri knew he had no choice but to face the cat alone or he would never become a M'Ktoah.

Dimitri had only seconds to come up with a plan. He knew his dual sword was much too big to draw in the tight spaces between the trees, especially on the run. That left him with only the small bone dagger that he kept hidden in his boot, but to draw it would require a mix of agility, dexterity, and absolutely perfect timing. If he could pull it off, it would be a splendid kill that would win him much honor.

With the lion hot on his heels, Dimitri burst into the clearing. He sped towards the boulder in the middle, and leapt upon it. He landed on one foot, jerked the bone knife from its hidden sheath, and before gravity could take over, leapt again. The lion snarled as if to announce its victory, and bounded after him. Dimitri twisted his body around to face the cat in midair and let loose a fierce roar of his own. The duo crashed to the forest floor, locked in an embrace.

All was still.

The lion trembled awkwardly and suddenly lifted, then slumped sideways. Dimitri kicked its lifeless body off his legs and got up. Féca's voice released a victorious ululation, and the other M'Ktoah joined in. Dimitri yanked his knife free from the cat's chest before adding his voice to theirs. Viktohn clapped him on the shoulder in congratulations. He was a M'Ktoah. He could now be counted as one of the clan.

Dimitri looked around the clearing as he set about the chore of claiming the head of his kill. The ground had been chewed up, and several branches lay broken and splintered. Dark stains on grass and leaves betrayed spilled blood. It was then that he realized a large, bull wyvern had made its way into the clutches of the awaiting hunters. Féca was bent over its corpse, knife in hand to claim the head of her kill. As if feeling his gaze, she looked up at him. He exposed his throat to her as a sign of respect and congratulations to his fellow hunter. She hesitantly returned the gesture, and he fought the urge to smile.

7

With the heads claimed and the kills prepared for the glorious feast that would honor the new M'Ktoah tomorrow, Viktohn ordered his students back home. When Dimitri tried to take his place at the back of the progression, Bone and Venli pushed him up the line. Pikal frowned as he made way for Dimitri to stand in front of him, right behind Féca. Dimitri hid his elation of the new ranking, lest they call him out as being nothing more than a weak Hume. He could not wait to get home to tell his mother of all that happened this day. She would be so proud of her son, and have her full ranking and status as a Dákun Daju assassin restored.

The group of hunters made their way home, traveling swiftly as the late evening sky betrayed a growing storm. Dimitri sniffed the air, loving the scent that signaled the coming rain. Something else tainted the smell. He inhaled again, long and slow, and detected a faint hint of blood and smoke. Panic gripped his heart and he rushed forward, ignoring the calls of his fellow M'Ktoah. He hollered back to them, warning them of the threat carried on the wind. They did not hesitate to chase after him.

In mere moments they were upon the bridge that ran over the Thundering Falls, sprinting towards the heart of their burning city. Corpses of Dákun Daju and Hume alike littered the walkways, and blood slickened the old stones. Ferocious fighting could still be heard in a few sections of the city, and Viktohn freed the M'Ktoah to spill the blood of those who dared attack their brothers and sisters. Dimitri raced over the bridges as fast as he could, heading towards his home in hopes of finding his mother. He was still several meters away when the soft call of his name stopped him dead in his tracks. He found his mother in a pile of rubble, run through by a Hume's blade and barely clinging to life. It was then that she told him of his birthright and gave him the diary of his father. He vowed to avenge her, and, as she slipped from the world forever, told her that he was now a M'Ktoah. She was dead with her honor once again intact. She had smiled.

Slowly, the memory of the day that had changed his life forever melted away and Dimitri returned to himself. Tears stung at his eyes, but he refused to let them fall. His hands had turned to fists at his sides, clenched so hard his nails pierced skin and droplets of blood broke upon the emerald grass where he stood.

He sighed to dispel the last remnants of the memory, and slowly shifted his crimson gaze upwards. The Pekkuli-Orsahn Mountains rose high above the fruit-heavy whisker palms on the distant shore. The lovely visage created a living, breathing curtain that shrouded the dead and barren desert that lay to the northeast. Though the mountain slopes were thick with the emerald green foliage of the subtropical climate, their sheer height meant that their caps remained dusted with snow. That perpetual source of moisture ran like wild rivers down the southern sides, pooling in the lowlands at the feet of the mountains thus forming the bay. Almost no water was drawn northward, and no one had even been able to discover why. Perhaps that was why the Ancients named the mountains 'strange ones' and cursed the desert hidden behind their peaks. Dimitri suddenly wondered if the desert was the hiding place of his dragons.

It couldn't be that simple, could it? A frown broke across his lips.

"You have that look again, Dimitri." Said a voice as soft as a kiss of wind.

He smiled inwardly, loving her voice, and looked sidelong at her. She sat just meters away, perched upon a boulder nestled amid the waters of the bay. Due to the balmy, late-summer heat, much of her armor had been removed, revealing tawny skin marred with old scars and a blood red spider tattoo that graced the side of her hip – her Dákun Daju assassin guild mark. He traced her taught muscles with his gaze as she bent over her swords to clean and sharpen them.

"What look, Godilai?"

She looked up from her work; her icy cyan eyes locking upon his crimson ones. The way she looked at him, he could tell she was reading his being all the way to his inner core. That gaze of hers affected him in ways he could never have imagined. It was so intense and so chilling that he shivered, and was ultimately forced to look away. Had she been the gloating kind, he was sure she would have smirked in victory before chastising him for being a weak Hume-aju.

"You were wondering if the dragons we seek were hidden right in front of you."

He scoffed. "Am I that transparent?"

"To me, yes."

Silence fell like a curtain between them. Then the gentle scrape of Godilai's honing stone against her blade began again. He watched her work as if with interest, but his mind filled with questions. The most troubling of which played at the forefront of his mind: how she could read him so easily? In fact, over the course of the last few weeks, it was as if she could read his mind. She knew precisely when he wanted to make or break camp, when he was hungry or thirsty, and what he was going to say before he said it. It had become almost like a game to him, to see if she could guess what he was going to do next. But something about her intricate knowledge of him worried him.

Finally, he dared to ask, "So you spend a lot of time watching me?"

"It is not a compliment." She said coldly. "I am an assassin. I merely watch to learn. What I learn, I utilize against my targets."

He suddenly found himself frowning at her. "But I am not your target."

"You could be."

His heart skipped a beat as icy cold fear gripped him, but he made sure to betray no emotion lest she see. Troubled thoughts raced through his mind as he pondered her words carefully. *How could someone have out-bidded me? I promised her satisfaction against the Humes she so despises as well as a place at my side as High Queen. No one on the whole of Ithnez could have beaten that! Unless...*

Godilai sighed. "You are yet safe, Dimitri."

"What?" Though he tried to hide it, he could still hear the distress in his voice, and he cursed himself for being weak.

She stood, sheathed her swords. "I said you are safe." She leapt down from the boulder with such ease and grace it could easily have been mistaken for flight. "No one has made a purchase of my skills against you."

Dimitri silently thanked the Gods.

"Pox and the ugly Hume come."

"About time." He softly muttered.

It was there, in the vale and beside the Mirror amid wildflowers and dragon eggs, that Djurdak asked for my hand in marriage. I was stunned to a tearful silence, and all I could do was nod. He chuckled as he took me in his arms and kissed me.

— FROM "THE DIARY OF AMOREZ" BY AMOREZ RENOAN

D imitri watched as a petite, charcoal-haired, Hume girl in a black dress made her way towards him. Her face was stoic mask; a blank canvas for even a ghost of an emotion. Even her soft green eyes seemed distant and lifeless. She was pale of skin with great muscle tone, and moved over the uneven earth with grace and poise. She would have made a fantastic Dákun Daju. But hidden beneath that Hume-like exterior beat the heart of the Feykin, Piper Onyx – Pox. And, as she drew nearer, the magic veil melted away to reveal her true self. Her hair turned to silver; her eyes violet. Even the simple Hume dress transformed, turning back into her favored, Feykin smock. Great wings, as black as coal, swept back with a thunderous flutter. They came to rest in such a way to frame her small form with the pearlescent feathers. She was a deadly beauty, and one that could have been mistaken for a goddess of the night.

An arm's length away from the Shadow Keeper, she stopped. Dimitri waited with baited breath for her to reveal her findings. She was about to speak when a loud curse caused her to pause. She sighed in frustration and sent a venomous look over her shoulder. Dimitri followed her gaze, spotting Vincent meters away. The bulbous and aged Judge had stumbled over the uneven ground and fallen. Now he lay sprawled in the mud, struggling to right himself, but only succeeding in digging himself further into a hole.

Pox muttered a string of nasty insults in Kinös Elda, which made Dimitri smirk, and turned her back on the old Hume. "A villager told me of a long-abandoned house on the far edge of town."

"Oh?" Dimitri's attention returned to Pox. "And what is the significance of this old house?"

"There is a story that in ages long past, a volcanic eruption rocked Nemlex one early morn."

"That is odd." Said Dimitri. "There aren't any volcanoes amongst the Strange Ones."

Pox nodded.

Vincent cried out for help.

The Feykin whipped around, a spell on her lips and her hand poised to execute the magic. A look of sheer terror crossed Vincent's red and muddy face. Pox hissed two words of Kinös Elda, and the old Judge was launched skywards. Pox shifted her weight to the other foot, pirouetting to face Dimitri again, and bringing her hand down in a rapid but fluid motion. Vincent screamed as the magic forced him deep into the waters of the bay.

"I hope he drowns." Muttered Godilai.

Pox exhaled a calming breath, then continued her tale. "When the villagers went out to investigate the cause of the eruption, all they found was the charred remnants of a house that had belonged to a woman known only as Azreom. No remains of the woman or her belongings were ever found, and no one has ever been able to explain the strange eruption."

"Sounds a good a place as any to begin our search." Dimitri looked to Godilai. "What do you think?"

The assassin dipped her head in the smallest of nods. "Let's go."

Dimitri looked back to Pox. "Lead the way."

Dimitri looked around in silent wonder. Remnants of blackened lumber and shards of hand-crafted bricks lay strewn about the ground. A thick layer of ash had long ago turned to fertile soil, and life sprang forth anew. Vines, wildflowers, and other untamed vegetation clung to every surface, splitting wood and cracking stone. It was hard to believe that a house had ever existed here. Had it not been for the stone fireplace, which stood like a gravestone to watch over the silent remains, Dimitri and his team would have walked right passed, oblivious to its presence.

"Do you see anything peculiar here?" Godilai asked as she looked around.

Dimitri nodded. "The debris pattern suggests that an explosion came from below, and it was strong. It sent these heavy rafter beams sky high, which is why they're only charred instead of ash like the rest of the house."

"My thoughts exactly."

"So," Dimitri kicked at the young soil, "we're looking for a fissure buried beneath the rubble."

"I'll take a look from the air," said Pox. Without waiting for a response, she leapt into the sky and flapped her wings hard to boost herself higher and higher. Then she leveled out to hover several meters over the gravestone fireplace.

With Pox already occupied on the task, Dimitri ordered Vincent to go around the opposite side of the house and begin the search over there. He and Godilai would rummage around at this end. Before Vincent had gone three steps, Pox called from overhead. She dove at the ground, and landed heavily in the middle of the remains. Dimitri and Godilai joined her in moments, and Vincent scuttled over the heaps of overgrown debris as fast as he could in hopes of to catching up. Pox used a spell to shove aside one of the foliage-leaden beams, revealing a deep void in the earth.

She smiled. "Found it."

Dimitri thanked her. Then, with a glance at Godilai and an apprehensive breath, he dropped into the gaping maw. His crimson eyes adjusted to the shadows quickly, revealing a marvelous, undersea tunnel. Varying shades of blue shimmered and swayed all around them. Fish of all kinds and colors danced and darted just out of hand's reach. He could almost touch them if not for the clear, crystal walls that held the water at bay.

With a quick glance back at the other three members of his team, he finally began the trek through the winding tunnel. The slightest sound echoed off the moist walls. Light from the two suns overhead pierced through the water and refracted off the jewels and coins that packed the corners of the tunnel, accumulating into a mirage of dancing lights. It was beautiful.

But Dimitri had not come to admire the place. He was here solely to find the next key, for all twelve were required to unlock the route to the Dragons' Gate. Once he had found them and the gate, he could unleash the Shadow Dragons and finally take his revenge upon the people of Ithnez.

With a heavy sigh, he pushed his sloppy, ebony bangs out of his eyes and continued down the tunnel, wary of any traps that might have been left by its creator. Behind him, the old and fat Judge, Vincent, wheezed as he tried to keep pace with Dimitri. Pox, the young Feykin Mage who had been proselytized by Dimitri's trickery, mumbled something inaudibly. Dimitri figured she was casting spells to protect the team. Smart girl.

And bringing up the rear of the team was the beautiful and deadly Godilai, a talented Dákun Daju Assassin. She had spent the last month brooding over the death of her clansmen, Luna. Dimitri could tell she was eager to exact her revenge on Xyleena, the one ultimately responsible for Luna's murder. But it would have to wait. The keys were more important at this point.

Pox's quiet mumbling suddenly stopped with a gasp. Dimitri froze and instinctively grasped the hilt of his dual sword. He waited, silently, for anything to jump out at him from the swirling blue mist emanating from the room ahead. When nothing happened, he gestured for Pox to precede him. She quietly cast a spell, forming a lighted ball in the air and throwing it into the room ahead.

"It's clear." Pox whispered minutes later, when the glow of her light orb faded away. She waved for Dimitri and the others to follow her. One cautiously slow step at a time, the young Feykin entered the room and was washed in the shimmering, cerulean light. "Wow."

Dimitri rushed forward, eager to see what lay beyond. The room was round and unlit except by the filtered sunlight. A great, crystalline pillar stood at either side of the room. Both were scoured from top to bottom with ancient runes. And a skeleton rested on the floor beside each.

Dimitri quickly spotted the two black marble dragon statues. One statue stood guard beside a wall of gently swirling, sapphire water. The other statue stood opposite, watching over a dull grey and smoldering pit. When he was satisfied that no enemies were present, Dimitri scoffed and set about collecting the keys from the two statues.

"These are Dákun Daju remains." Godilai whispered quietly as she knelt beside one of the skeletons. "Why would they be in a place like this?"

"It looks like this Kkorian character you hired really did come through for us." Vincent said between pants. "'...Beneath Dragon Bay....' Ingenious!"

"This place is teeming with magic." Pox whispered as she gently touched her fingers to the water wall. She shivered at the contact and watched as ripples danced over the surface. "I've never seen anything like this."

"Here, Pox." Dimitri handed her a scrap of parchment with the keys written on it. "Translate those for me."

Pox nodded and studied the runes Dimitri had copied from the two statues. "'...Above a small world...' '...Dusted and grey...'"

Dimitri quickly removed his father's diary from the bag on his belt and scribed the translations into the pages. "So the clues we have so far read: 'The greatest secret lies; Just beyond human eyes; On an isle moving by day; Above a small world dusted and grey'. Any ideas on what in the names of the Five Souls these keys are talking about?"

"This might seem a bit strange, but it sounds as if the clues are pointing to another planet." Vincent shrugged at his own idea.

"As far as anyone knows, Bedeb is the only other habitable planet in the Rishai System. No one on Ithnez has been there since it was abandoned by the Feykin in AR 79, 491 years ago."

"Who said it had to be a habitable planet, Pox?" Vincent wiggled his bushy eyebrows at her. The young Feykin scoffed and rolled her eyes.

"The abandonment of Bedeb happened only thirty-four years before Amorez was born. It might have been possible to warp safely back to the pla..."

"Bedeb isn't grey, Dimitri." Muttered Godilai. Dimitri sighed and looked at her over his shoulder. "Look up at Bedeb in the night sky. Beyond the double rings, you can see blue oceans, green and brown continents, and white clouds and ice. Nothing is grey and dusty."

"Maybe the isle the keys are talking about is dusted and grey." Suggested Pox. Godilai rolled her cool, cyan eyes.

"Believe what you want to. We probably won't know exactly what these keys are pointing to until we obtain the other six."

"Agreed." Dimitri sighed. "Of course that plan would proceed much faster if we could actually steal Dragon Diary from that brat, Xyleena."

"Speaking of the brat, Dimitri," Vincent smirked and pointed his thumb to the wall of water. "Since this place looks untouched, I think we may have beaten her and her team here. What do you want to do about that?"

Dimitri was quiet as he thought things over. He sighed and glanced sideways at Godilai. "How do you see another ambush working out for us?"

"Given the outcomes of the previous attempts, dismally." She answered crossly. "Why?"

"Because that is what we're going to do." Dimitri sneered. "Pox, I need you to mask our scent so Xyleena's Demon friend doesn't smell us. Also, if you could set up some kind anti-magic ward, that would be great. Vincent, go with Pox as back-up in case Xyleena is close. Godilai, you and I will set up the trap in here to catch the brat's team."

"You really think your idea is going to work this time?" Godilai sighed and watched as Pox and Vincent left to start their tasks.

"I can only hope. After all, we desperately need Amorez's diary." Dimitri muttered. He sighed and finally turned to fully face her. "Have you thought about my proposal?"

17

She was quiet as she thought back. "You still want me to marry you?"

"Of course." He smiled.

"I still don't see why I should." Godilai stood and turned away to scan the chamber. She growled in annoyance when Dimitri's strong arms gripped her around the waist.

"You would be High Queen of Ithnez." He whispered in her ear. "Subject to no one. Think of all the Humes you could kill or enslave for any reason."

"Enticing offer, I will admit." Godilai broke free of his grasp. "I will think on it a while longer."

Dimitri frowned. "Why won't you just say yes?"

Godilai flipped her white hair over her shoulder as she met him with an unreadable expression. "Because I'm not yet sure if it is a wise union."

"You want me to prove that I am a strong and capable mate? Haven't I done that already?"

"You are still part Hume." Godilai turned away from him again. "You are weak and you have lost more battles against Amorez's heir than I care to count." She sighed. Dimitri's hands turned to fists as he fought to control his rage at her words. "You are not a worthy mate."

"What would make you change your mind about marrying me?" He was surprised how even he kept his voice despite his boiling rage.

"If you really want to claim me for yourself, you will figure it out." Godilai said as she walked away. Dimitri growled through his teeth.

I finally got to see the woman the whole camp was abuzz about. I thought, how could this no-name peasant woman be given command of the entire army? Then she did something and a wild flurry of colors and shapes burst forth, and suddenly we were in the presence of dragons. It was amazing, Mom!

– FROM "A LETTER HOME" BY PG. VELARD R. MARTKEIN

I whooped as the wind rushed passed me. I felt almost weightless as Helios dipped in time to catch the next air current. The ride had my head spinning and my stomach turning, but it felt so good. My dragons were right; flying was so exhilarating that no words could adequately describe the feeling.

Glancing downwards, between Helios' wing and neck, I watched as the lush, emerald forests whipped passed. The deep, blue-green water that marked the Dragon Head Bay came into view moments later. We had made excellent timing on this leg of the quest. The distance would have taken over a week by wyvernback, but four dragons covered it in just over a day.

I smiled and leaned back in my seat. The last six months had been like living in a nightmare. I was amazed that I was still alive. Hopefully soon, I would have half of the Dragons of Light collected. Quite an accomplishment. However, I couldn't escape the feeling that things were about to get extremely complicated.

"There! I see Nemlex!" I barely heard Kkorian's shout over the rush of wind. The dragons banked slightly left and I once again looked earthward. Half a heartbeat later, the trailing edges of the fishing town, Nemlex, came into view. Built upon the shores of the Dragon Head Bay, it sat at the heart of the Eastern Trade Routes. Though it was not the largest city on Ithnez, Nemlex held the record for the world's most expansive open-air market, which included over one hundred kilometers of shopping stalls collectively known as Centre. Being the height of the summer trade season, Centre would be swarmed with people from all over the world. I could only pray that Dimitri was not among them.

"Helios, land at the outskirts of the town." I said as I thumped him on the neck to get his attention. The white dragon looked back at me and nodded. He led the other three dragons in a dizzying, downwards spiral. A few stomach-turning minutes later, all four dragons back-winged and poised their hind legs to take the impact of their landing. They touched down on the rocky beach in-sync, with barely a hands-width between their outstretched wings.

Kitfox immediately jumped down from Atoka's shoulder and sprawled out on the ground. I laughed as I watched him. "Ugh! All that spinning made me sick."

"Yeah, it didn't sit too well with me either." Muttered Thera as she used her ebony wings to drift down from her spot astride Vortex. She stuffed Dragon Diary into her pack and glanced around.

"This Hume seemed to have enjoyed the entire ride." Shazza said as she dropped Kkorian on the ground before gracefully hopping off Kkaia's back.

Kkorian shrugged as he smoothed his wind-licked, blonde hair. "What can I say? The ride was fun."

"Sure. If you don't mind the whiplash from the wind or the sickening spiral descent, the ride was great fun." Kitfox muttered and finally got to his feet.

"Perhaps you should look into obtaining some gear for when we fly you." Said Vortex as he sat on his haunches. "Something to cut the wind down."

"And some sort of device to communicate between team mates." I replied. "I barely heard Kkorian's shout."

"I might be able to rig some kind of communicator. It would require some sort of catalysts though." Thera explained.

"Lemme know what you need to make the coms. I can get it." Kkorian winked at her. Thera rolled her eyes.

"I am more than capable of acquiring my own items."

20

Kitfox crossed his arms and frowned. "Must you hit on every woman you see, Kkorian?"

"Cark it, Kitfox. I'm not going to have another blue with you."

"Knock it off, both of you." I sighed. "You act like such children sometimes."

"What in the--?!" A stranger's voice shouted from a little ways away. I looked over my shoulder at the owner of the voice. It was a middle-aged fisherman and he wasn't alone. In fact, it looked as though half of the town had come to see us. I was surprised to see that they weren't cheering the appearance of the dragons like the people of Kamédan had. "Who are you?"

Helios turned to face the villagers and crouched low to the ground. I finally dismounted, ran a hand through my tousled hair, and greeted the townspeople. "I am Xyleena, Daughter of Amorez and the new Dragon Keeper. These are my friends: Kitfox, Thera, Shazza, and Kkorian." I pointed at each of them respectfully. "And these four are the Dragons of Light."

"Well met, Villagers of Nemlex." Helios said, nodding his great wedge of a head in greeting.

"What are you doing here?" Asked a woman from the crowd. It still wasn't the reaction I had been expecting, but I could see the excitement on her face.

"We are here to find two more dragons. We believe they are hidden somewhere beneath the bay." Kitfox explained as he and Thera moved to stand beside me.

"You mean our town is the home to two dragons?" Asked another face in the crowd.

"That is what we're hoping." Kitfox smiled.

"How will you find these dragons?" The first man inquired.

"We're not totally sure yet, but I will personally guarantee that no harm will come to anyone or anything in Nemlex." Shazza announced, finally stepping forward. Several people in the crowd recognized her as the Queen of Katalania and bowed.

"Miss Shazza! Miss Shazza!" A young girl ran right passed everyone and glommed onto Shazza's leg, taking the Dákun Daju by complete surprise. "Miss Shazza, can I help you find the cave?"

"Er...What cave, child?" Shazza said awkwardly.

"The one the other people were looking for." The girl looked up at Shazza with big, blue eyes. I shivered. Shazza sent me an unreadable look.

"'Other people?'" Kitfox quirked an eyebrow and looked at me. "Dimitri?"

"Feels like it." I muttered. With a sigh, I stepped forward and knelt beside the child. "Do you know where the other people went?" The girl nodded vigorously. "Can you show us?"

She beamed and released Shazza's leg. "Follow me!"

"Hold up, child." Shazza caught up to the girl in a few quick strides and took her hand. "Are your mom and dad in the crowd?" The girl shook her head. "Where are they? I have to tell them about—"

"Mellyn's mother is busy at the Widwe Wiccan." Said a soft-spoken boy in the crowd. Shazza glanced at him as he walked closer to us. "I'm supposed to keep an eye on her, but she keeps running away from me."

Shazza nodded. "I see. And who might you be?"

The boy flushed bright red. "I'm Jox. Mellyn is my cousin."

"Would you accompany her and us to the cave?" Thera asked gently. "It wouldn't be safe to have her with us while we're searching the cave and we certainly can't leave her all alone."

"Anything to help the Queen and Dragon Keeper." The boy said with a bow.

Shazza and I thanked him. Then I turned to face the four Dragons of Light. "Will you be staying here and enjoying the sun and water or coming with us?"

"We will come, Hatchling." Vortex said. I watched as he and the other three faded into their elements. Earth, wind, light, and ice swirled around me before shooting into the Dragon Eye Amulet. The jewels marking their presence flashed with their powers.

"Alright. Let's find this cave."

"This way! This way!" The girl called Mellyn cheered in a sing-song voice. I chuckled as I watched her grab Shazza's hand and lead her along the beach at a brisk, child's pace.

Death and disease were everywhere. In the trees. The land. The people. All due to that damned dragon and the man who had unleashed it. It? No. Them. I counted them as they perched on the courtyard walls and circled overhead; fifteen in total.

We are doomed.

— CARVED INTO THE PRISON WALL IN ARCADIA BY AADRIAN ZA'CAR, FIRST KING OF THE SECOND AGE

The five of us and Jox followed Mellyn as she skipped along the beach. The town of Nemlex was now about a quarter of a league behind us and still growing further away. The girl finally stopped and pointed.

Just ahead of us stood the remnants of a house. The blackened lumber lay collapsed and strewn over the ground. Wild vegetation had begun to reclaim the area, creeping over the wood and climbing its way up the only thing that still stood: an old, stone fireplace. I frowned as a feeling of familiarity washed over me. I had been here before.

"Mellyn, that isn't a cave." Jox muttered as he came to a stop beside his cousin. "That used to be someone's house."

"Not that!" The girl frowned and pointed again. "That!"

All I could see was what remained of the abode. Kitfox clicked his tongue and stepped passed the kids, gesturing for them to stay put. I watched as the Fox Demon sniffed the air as he drew closer to the house. He frowned and sent me a look before continuing on. A moment later, he stopped and waved for us to come.

Upon joining him, the first thing I noticed was the gaping crater cut in the ground. Rocks, charred wood and other debris lined the area around the hole. It was almost as if something had exploded outwards from the depths with tremendous force. That must have been the cause of the house's demise. Odd. There wasn't anything even remotely volcanic in the area that would cause such an explosion.

"Some of the debris has been moved aside." Shazza said. She knelt to take a closer look and nodded. "Looks like there is a hole just big enough for someone to slip through."

"What do you think?" I muttered, looking at Kitfox for an answer.

"Something doesn't smell right." The Demon frowned. "I caught trailing edges of Dimitri's scent, but it keeps fading in and out. Either it is a few days old or someone is trying to mask it."

"I'd bet a bundle that it's the latter." Kkorian muttered. His hand instinctively found its way to one of the pistols on his hip as he looked at the surroundings.

"Mellyn, how long ago were the other people looking for this cave?" Shazza asked, looking sweetly at the child.

"Lunch time." She said as she sucked on her thumb. Shazza turned a frown on me and I nodded.

"They're trying to ambush us to get the diary again."

"You'd think they'd give up on that idea after a while." Thera chuckled and knelt beside the crater.

"So, what's the plan?" Kkorian asked, crossing his arms.

"We spring the trap." Thera grinned up at him, mischief teeming in her violet eyes.

I whistled a happy tune as I strode confidently down the crystalline tunnel. Though I knew of the danger present, I couldn't help but smile at the good mood Thera's mischievous and ingenious plan wrought. Not to mention, the cavern was an absolutely splendid sight! Try as I might, I couldn't remember how it had been created, though I was sure I had played a part in it.

Kkorian stopped frequently to stuff his pockets with the gold and gems that lined the tunnel. I frowned and promptly smacked him soundly on the head. He flashed me his best innocent look, but I wasn't fooled in the slightest. So, with a groan, he emptied his pockets.

Kitfox chuckled and gently grasped my hand, effectively averting my attention from the pirate. I shot him a look, and stole my hand back. He frowned and crossed his arms with a sigh. We walked on in silence.

I knew Kitfox had only the best intentions in mind, but I couldn't afford to let myself get attached to him any more than I already was. I don't know what I would do if I lost him. And who knows how long it would take me to recover from his death so shortly after Ríhan's. It was better to just keep my distance... even if I did feel guilty about hurting him.

"We've finally reached the end of the tunnel." Thera announced much louder than she needed to. She winked at me and cast a spell as quietly as possible. I stood back and watched as the spell went to work. A few moments later, the Feykin led the way into the room beyond. I hesitated only a moment before following.

Once all five of us were in the room, we surveyed our surroundings. Nothing jumped out at us right away like I had been expecting. But Dimitri was clever and his Dákun Daju friend was even more so.

Kitfox sniffed the air and coughed. "Smells like sea water and smoke."

"Interesting perfume, hey mate?" Kkorian jabbed the Demon in the ribs with his elbow. The act earned him a menacing growl. I chose to ignore the two of them, focusing instead on locating the two dragons.

I had only taken two steps passed the boys when a voice echoed throughout the cavern. Half a heartbeat later, an opaque dome ensnared all five of us. Violet and crimson lightning crackled and danced over the surface of the trap, effectively dissuading any attempts of breaking free.

My gaze fell on Dimitri as he stalked out of his hiding spot, laughing like a madman.

There were many nights when I had watched Amorez from afar. She would spend hours staring into her fire, oft until it had turned to ghostly embers. I always wondered where she went during those times. Now, looking at Xyleena as she does the same, I realize, they are lost in dreams of happier times.

– FROM "THE SECOND KEEPER" BY THERA ONYX

"I finally have you, Xyleena!" Dimitri's cries of triumph echoed in the room. He turned slightly to face the three members of his team. "I told you this plan would succeed."

"Oh, shut-up." Muttered Godilai darkly. "Just grab the damn diary and step aside so I can kill the wretch who stole Luna's life."

"All in good time, Godilai. All in good time." Dimitri smirked. "First, I want to revel in my good fortune at capturing Amorez's heir." He turned to sneer at me, choosing to ignore Godilai's mumbled string of insults. "So, how does it feel, little girl, to be caught by your nemesis?" He stepped closer, barely avoiding contact with the dome's electric wall. "I can tell you, as your nemesis, it feels great to actually defeat you. And now I will make you wish you had given up your futile attempts to thwart my plans of revenge."

I stared back at him, completely disinterested. "Are you done yet, or would you prefer to soliloquize a little more?"

All smugness instantly evaporated from his face. "Do I bore you?" Dimitri scowled. "You seem to forget, little girl, that I currently hold your fate in my hands." He made a show of clenching his fists. "I could kill you right now, if I wanted!"

"So what's stopping you?" Kitfox smirked. Dimitri growled fiercely, making the Demon laugh. "I'm guessing you are too feeble to even attempt to end her life." Kitfox strode right up to Dimitri until the only thing between them was the crackling dome wall. The two of them stared each other down. "Make no mistakes, Hume-aju, she will beat you."

Dimitri roared. In uncontrolled rage, he pierced through the dome to land a punch to Kitfox's face. Dimitri's fist went right through the Demon as if he were air. Kitfox smirked before fading with a puff of smoke.

"What?!" Dimitri retracted his fist from the sphere as his other captives vanished in swirls of smoke. Behind him, Godilai swore loudly and unsheathed her weapons.

"Now!" Simultaneously, all five of us launched from our hiding spots. Thera led the offense, hurdling spell after spell at our opponents. Kitfox tackled Godilai to the ground. The two of them wrestled while Shazza and Kkorian went head to head with Vincent and Pox.

I faced Dimitri alone. He glowered at me as I flared my tessen fans. I sunk into my Demon-modified Dákun Daju fighting stance and smirked. "I can't believe you fell for the same trick you used on us during the race to Atoka's island."

"Mirages..." Dimitri scoffed and sunk into his own stance. "I should have known better."

"You should just give up, Dimitri. All of your attempts to kill me and steal Dragon Diary have proven futile." He snarled at that and swung his dual sword in a feral sweep. It was an easy block, but that didn't stop him from attempting the same maneuver again and again.

I closed one of my fans as I spun away to chuck it at Dimitri's head. He narrowly dodged in time to avoid the hit. My war fan sunk into the wall of swirling water behind him causing it to bow and flex. I was mesmerized by the effects wrought by the piercing and narrowly avoided Dimitri's next attack.

"Eyes on your opponent, girl." Dimitri jeered.

I snorted. "I'd hate to have to burn my eyes out for looking at you."

Dimitri frowned but made no verbal retort. Instead, he took a few slow steps towards me before making a rapid lunge and sweeping the blades of his sword from side to side. At the last minute, I somersaulted beneath the outstretched blades. I recovered faster than he did and spun to kick him between his shoulder blades.

While he toppled to the ground, I retreated to retrieve my tessen from the wall. It broke free with a loud slurp. Water began to drain into the room from the hole. Thinking nothing of the meager amount of water, I turned to survey the room.

Kitfox and Godilai were still at each other's throats, fighting as fiercely as expected of either race. Thera once again faced her younger sister, casting a rapid succession of spells while trying to convince her that Dimitri was the Keeper of the Shadow Dragons. I didn't have time to find Shazza and Kkorian before Dimitri launched himself at me.

I danced out of the way, leaving Dimitri to collide head-long with the wall. An angry roar followed the hard slap, and all activity in the room halted in an instant. The wall of water wobbled, waivered, then exploded. The sea surged into the room unabated, toppling both me and Dimitri.

Kitfox forgot his opponent and braved the torrent to rush to my aid. He yanked me out of the mad rush of water and dragged me back to the safety of the other members of my team. We watched for scarcely a moment as the water filled the room before we had the sense to start evacuating.

Just as we reached the exit to the tunnel, the water shrunk back. My heart skipped a beat and I quickly turned around. The water sloshed and gelled, forming a familiar shape. With a roar, the water solidified into a dragon with deep aqua scales and ivory, hair-like spines.

"Riptide!" I exclaimed in time with her roar. I ran up to hug the dragon's foreleg. Riptide snorted and moved her head so she was eye level with me.

"Xyleena Renoan, Keeper of the Light, you have not changed much in three hundred years." I smiled and thumped her neck. Kitfox and Thera laughed in relief and moved to join me beside the Dragon of Water. "Though, your hair is much shorter than I remember."

And then there were five. Helios' voice echoed in the back of my mind. I didn't even notice he was following the events. But where is Wildfire?

"Wildfire is here, too, right?" I looked at Riptide for the answer. She seemed to frown at me in response.

"Do you not reca—"

"She lost her memory." Kitfox replied. The dragon stared at me for a long minute, then nodded in understanding.

"No wonder it took you so long to return." She unfolded one of her wings and pointed to the smoldering pit of ash with her wing claw. "Therein lays Wildfire, Dragon of Fire."

"'Riptide the Torrent points the way; To fire beneath Dragon Bay.'" Shazza chuckled. "Literally."

Thera frowned and looked up at the Dragon of Water. "How do we release Wildfire?"

Before Riptide could answer, Godilai exploded from the spot Dimitri's team had holed up in. She held her deadly blade poised for a killing stroke, but never got close enough to deal it. Riptide shoved me and the others out of the way with her wing and took the hit. With an angry hiss, the dragon's eyes flashed white. Massive globes of water formed in the air and were instantly launched at the Dákun Daju and her teammates. They fled from the room in a ruckus as the balls of water chased them.

Riptide snorted. She glanced at her wound; a small cut in the membrane of her wing. Without a word, the dragon walked over to the smoldering pit and stood with her wing poised over it. A few moments of silence followed, and then a drop of blood hit the ashes. In a heartbeat, the grey ashes turned into a raging inferno. Riptide backed away as the blaze swirled and danced. With a roar, the ruby-scaled Dragon of Fire leapt from pit to stand beside her sister dragon.

Six have been found at last! Save six more to be amassed! I laughed at Helios' excited rhyme and repeated it aloud for all to hear.

"You have only found six of us?" Wildfire was aghast at that revelation.

"It is a long story that not even I know all the details to." I muttered apologetically. Both dragons stared at me as if waiting for me to go on. I sighed and prepared to tell the story again. "All I know so far is that about four years ago now, I fell from the Dragons' Gate and woke up in the Infirmary of the Temple of Five Souls. I had no knowledge of who I was, where I was from, or what year it was.

"Shortly before starting this quest, I had dreams where Zahadu-Kitai appeared and warned me of things that were about to happen. I had obtained Amorez's Dragon Diary somehow. Anyway, a few days after that, Dimitri blew up the Temple and I barely escaped with my life." I purposely neglected to mention Ríhan's murder, but glanced sideways at Kitfox. He quirked an eyebrow, before I turned my attention back to the dragons. "When I arrived in Thorna looking for a path to take, I didn't even know how to fight or use magic and I didn't know a word of Kinös Elda either. Then, slowly, with Thera's teaching, everything started coming back.

"With each dragon I collect, a little bit of my past comes back to me in dreams or visions. And Vortex told me that Zenith of Space and Time can fill in all the gaps once I find him. But, so far, none of the dragons I have collected know where he is because he was hidden after all of you."

The twin dragons exchanged a look. Then Wildfire moved her great wedge of a head to look me in the eye. I could feel the heat radiating off her as she spoke. "All which you have spoken of is very troubling, Xyleena. If you cannot remember your own past, I fear this quest may end your existence."

"Just what I wanted to hear." I muttered.

"She won't die." Kitfox stated fiercely. Both dragons snorted and looked at him. "With the four..." he smirked and glanced at Kkorian, who glared back. "...well, three and a half of us to protect her, she'll succeed."

"How can you be so confident, Demon?" Riptide inquired, stepping closer to Kitfox. His resolve never wavered, even as both dragons stared him down menacingly.

"I just am." That response earned him a sort-of laugh from the twins. Kitfox growled. "Would it kill you dragons to put more faith in your own Keeper's abilities? You always doubt her!"

Both dragons instantly quieted and met him with an unreadable stare. Kitfox only stared back at them, anger teeming in his amber eyes. I had never seen him so adamant about my abilities or his faith in me. Thera moved to his side a moment later, staring back at Riptide and Wildfire with a cool expression. Shazza soon followed, then Kkorian. The twins exchanged another look before turning to me.

"We like the team you've acquired, Young Keeper." Wildfire nodded.

Riptide agreed. "They are equally brave and have strong hearts. They will assist you well in the future."

"Especially the Demon." Added Wildfire with a quick glance at Kitfox. I smiled both in relief and at the sight of Kitfox's embarrassed blush.

"So what do we do now that we've run off Dimitri's team and collected these two as planned?" Thera looked to me for the answer. I could only shrug.

"The same thing we always do, I guess."

"Find an inn and solve the next portion of the riddle." Kitfox replied. I nodded before turning to my two new dragons.

"Are you walking out with us?"

"Regrettably, no. We do not fit in the tunnel beyond this room." Riptide replied.

"We shall join the others in the Eye."

"Before you go, can you tell us what happened to the house at the end?" Shazza pointed her thumb at the tunnel.

"I thought it was obvious." I said and pointed to Wildfire. "Her power of fire is what created the quartz walls of this tunnel. Unfortunately, Amorez's house didn't stand a chance once the jet of flame erupted through the only weak point in the tunnel. Just lucky for us, we anticipated such an event and removed all the artifacts we had collected."

The others gawked at me and I couldn't suppress a laugh. Kitfox looked defiantly up at the dragons. "Told you so!"

"What about them?" Thera gestured towards the two pillars in the room. More accurately, the skeletons that rested at the base of each.

"Moonwhisperer and Artimista have watched over us for centuries." Wildfire bowed her head in respects.

"They will be sad to see us leave, but happy in the knowledge we go with our Keeper."

"They are Dákun Daju?" Shazza looked surprised, and then saddened when both dragons nodded affirmative. "You guys go. I will catch up in a little bit."

"Are you sure?" Kkorian asked, daring to lay a hand on the small of her back. Shazza only nodded.

"As you wish." I whispered. Riptide and Wildfire faded into their respective elements. Fire swirled around me, blasting me with hot air. Water chased it, instantly washing me in a cooling sensation. Both elements joined the Dragon Eye Amulet simultaneously and two new jewels flashed with life.

The Dragons' Gate. That was what I called the doorway that kept the Shadow Dragons from returning to our dimension. Beyond it... a world incomparable to our own, discovered by mistake during my venture into Havel. I would hope never to see the Gate open again.

– FROM "THE DIARY OF AMOREZ" BY AMOREZ RENOAN

I recalled the team to the remnants of the house after verifying Dimitri had retreated from the area. While we waited for Shazza to surface, I studied the stones in the fireplace. Long ago, the tapestry I saw in "Zamora's" office at the Temple graced the surface. I remember it hiding something though. One of the rocks was fake and removable. And behind that rock was a treasure long forgotten. If only I could remember which stone...

"You okay?" I glanced back at Kitfox as he approached. I nodded and returned my attention to the fireplace. I heard him sigh before he moved to stand beside me. I knew he yearned to say more, but he didn't. Instead he just stood still, content with being so close.

With a click of my tongue, I stepped right up to the fireplace and tapped one of the larger rocks. I smiled at the hollow sound it produced and quickly removed it like I had hundreds of times before. I turned the rock over in my hands and freed the metal box from the compartment. I tossed the rock aside; it had served its purpose.

The box was slightly rusted and dented, but otherwise undamaged. A complex locking mechanism on the front prevented the lid from opening prematurely. With a simple spell, I unlocked it and slid the lid open.

"Now this is old." I laughed. I gently removed a strange, metal cylinder from the box and looked it over. It was about the length of my hand and as wide as two of my fingers. It had been made of an unknown metal that gleamed in the light of the setting suns, but it weight about the same as a leaf of parchment. No marks were on its surface, making it appear as just a simple metal dowel. "Good. Not a scratch."

"What is it?" Asked Kitfox. Thera, Kkorian, and the kids soon joined us.

"In all honesty, I have no idea. I've never known." I looked up at all of them as I answered. "My father, Djurdak, removed it from the Rare Books Room of the Grand Palace Library before it was leveled by Agasei in the first battle. No one then knew what it was either, but they all knew it came from Earth."

"Earth?!" Everyone chorused. I chuckled as they all surged forward to get a closer look.

"Father said it was brought to this planet by the children of Noralani Ithnez, the First." I went on, holding the cylinder for them all to see. "Though the Ithnezes descended from the man ultimately responsible for saving the Hume race, and were, therefore, greatly respected, they did not want to rule the planet that bared their name. But they stressed the importance that this cylinder never be lost or destroyed."

"But no one knows what it is?" I shook my head at Jox's inquiry. The boy looked flabbergasted at the answer. "Why keep it then?"

"How long has it been here?" Kitfox looked back at the fireplace with its removed false stone.

I shrugged. "I don't remember how long ago my parents hid it here. I do remember sneaking out of my room when they were sleeping to try time after time to figure out what it was, but I never could. And the fire that destroyed the house happened long after Father died."

"And you just now remembered the bloody thing was here?"

"Obviously, Kkorian." Shazza stated matter-of-factly as she pulled herself out of the crater. She glanced at the cylinder and clicked her tongue as she adjusted her sleeves. I caught a glimpse of crimson running her arm before it was covered. I held her gaze. "So, what are the plans for tonight? Or has everyone been too enthralled with that thing to think that far ahead?"

"Mister Kkorian said you guys needed a place to rest tonight." Mellyn said merrily. "Mommy owns the best inn in town! Want to stay there?"

Shazza finally looked away from me to smile at the young girl. "That sounds perfect. Can you lead the way?"

With a vigorous nod, Mellyn grabbed Kkorian's hand and led the way back to Nemlex. Kitfox, Shazza, and I lingered a few moments. I took the time to safely pack the cylinder away in my hip sack.

"Has your bloodletting done anything to ease them?" Kitfox muttered, rubbing his nose. I looked from him to Shazza, whose face was a stoic mask. "They've been dead for centuries and you don't even know them."

"It is none of your concern, Demon." With that, Shazza walked off. Kitfox merely watched her go.

"It is her way." I said plainly. He looked back at me, his expression one of mixed feelings. Choosing to avoid speaking about it further, I shrugged and strode passed him. He caught up to me moments later. Together, the two of us followed the rest of the team back to Nemlex.

Though Mellyn's mother, Shawdra, had offered us room and board free of charge, Shazza insisted on some form of payment. After things had been worked out between the innkeeper and the Dákun Daju Queen, each of us were shown rooms. The five of us agreed to rest and clean up before meeting in the downstairs tavern for dinner.

In my own privacy, I trimmed my sable hair up to shoulder length again before sinking into a hot bath to relax. Several long minutes passed before my mind began to wander, inevitably finding its way to Kitfox.

I frowned as an image of his amber eyes flashed in my mind. I felt incredibly guilty for giving him the cold shoulder, but it was necessary. With as much as I had grown to care for him, I feared losing him would be the end of me. I could not afford to be so weak when the balance of power was shifting more and more away from the Light.

You are right to worry for his safety, Hatchling. Vortex's gentle statement echoed in my mind. Some of the other dragons began to filter into the back of my mind. *But for your own happiness, please, move on from that which haunts you so.*

I growled at that. I can't just forget about Ríhan! We've been through so much that I'd feel like I'd be betraying him if I moved on to Kitfox so soon after... after....

Ríhan is dead, Xyleena. Riptide spoke her two-bits. *You need to get over it.*

"No!" I shouted and burst out of the tub in a fury. The dragons continued to harangue me about moving on until I forced them from my mind. I barely dried myself off when there was a loud knocking at the door. "Yeah, who is it?" I demanded rather sharply.

"Thera." It was as simple of a response as I'd expect from the Feykin. I sighed and donned a robe before answering the door. Thera simply quirked a silver eyebrow at me.

"I couldn't get the dragons to leave me alone." I explained as I opened the door wider for her to enter. She made a face at my answer and strode passed me.

"What could they be accosting you about that gets you so worked up that you turn bleary-eyed and red-faced?"

"Please don't tell anyone else?"

Thera turned to look directly in my eyes. "Eo rité res meo ligto." As she spoke, she touched her hand to her heart and bowed slightly. I nodded in acceptance of Thera's promise and moved to sit on the bed a few steps behind her.

I'm not sure what compelled me to confide everything in Thera. She just stood there, listening attentively, as I divulged everything to her. I spoke of my feelings about losing Ríhan and my unwillingness to let him go. Then shifted into my issues regarding Kitfox and how much I found myself wanting to be with him, but being afraid to, lest I lose him like I did Ríhan.

"...And I have no idea what to do about any of it. I feel guilty for pushing Kitfox away and feel like I'm betraying Ríhan for having Kitfox so near." I blinked to clear the tears that welled in my eyes. "What should I do?"

The young Feykin sighed and finally moved to sit beside me. "I do not know how Humes handle a situation like this. We Feykin accept the death of our friends and family, satisfied in the knowledge that they will be reborn one day.

"Xy, as a Priestess of the Five Souls, you are intimately knowledgeable about the workings of the Gods and Havel. By all accounts, you should be able to say farewell to Ríhan, and not feel guilty about moving on. Yes, you loved him and he loved you enough to die saving you.

"Now you have another man in your life, which you do care deeply for, willing to fight to the death for you. I can see where your uncertainties about a relationship with him rise.

"The only advice I can offer is this: Tell Kitfox everything. He needs to know the reasons why you need your space for the time being. He will support you all the same."

I was quiet as I mulled everything Thera said over in my head. She patted my shoulder and, with a smile, got up to leave. I watched her go; stopping her would have been an attempt made in vain. I sighed when I felt cool, liquid presence of Riptide brush against my mind.

Rather insightful, your Feykin friend. Have her words given you a respite from your worries?

I scoffed as I got to my feet. *She gave me something more to consider. That is all.*

Better than nothing. The Dragon of Water seemed to hesitate at her next words. *I apologize for how harshly I spoke to you. I was merely trying to get you to forget...*

You don't need to explain, Riptide. I know why you did it. Relief washed through my mind from the dragon. I smiled and sought fresh clothes.

~~~~ * ~~~~

I found Shazza, Kitfox and Thera at one of the larger, corner tables on the main floor of the Widwe Wiccan. Thera was so busy with working on the translation of the riddle that she did not react when I sat beside her. Kitfox, on the other hand, poured me a glass of whatever wine had been ordered. Kkorian joined us just as a wench appeared with a large tray of food. She skillfully set it on the table before striding away.

"Sorry I'm late, mates." The Pirate smiled roguishly.

"And here I thought the smell of the wine would have had you running to join us about an hour ago." Kitfox smirked when Kkorian made a face.

"Finally!" Exclaimed Thera as she dropped her quill on the table and leaned back in her seat.

"The translation is done?" Kitfox leaned forward to sneak a peek and frowned at the words. "'Kúskú of Illusion now sleeps; On isle hidden in Mysty deep.'"

"The 'Mysty deep' part has me worried." Thera said with a sigh. "If this next dragon is hidden in the Myst, we're in for heaps of trouble."

"I'll say." Kkorian paused to take a long draft of wine. "Magnathor patrols those waters. She'll sink any ship that even thinks about sailing close to her Myst."

"So we don't sail there." I smirked. "We fly."

"I'm not so sure you can see through the Myst from the air." Muttered Shazza. "No one has ever flown over it before to know."

"The big question is, how does Xy direct us to Kúskú's island? We might not be able to see it if it's hidden like the other islands." Thera chuckled at Kitfox's question and dropped five strange-looking wands on the table.

"I made the communicators."

"How do they work?" I asked as I picked one up to look it over. It was a simple wooden shaft with a raw, uncut crystal at one end and a smooth, round crystal at the other. Given the shape of the crystal at the bottom, I suspected both were made of quartz. The whole thing was held together with intricately detailed, metal filigree.

"Simply say the words 'Dasum meo...' and the name of the person you want to speak to. If you want to speak to everyone at once, say 'Dasum meo nishi.' An image of whom you want to speak to will appear in the orb after the citation."

"When did you have time to make these?" Asked Shazza as she looked over the one she chose. Thera simply shrugged in response and took a swig of wine.

"Okay, so we have the communication problem taken care of." I said as I tucked the wand into my hip sack. "Now the important question is..." I paused to meet the gaze of each of my teammates. "How do we deal with Magnathor?"

I had asked the dragon what he saw; how the battle would play out tomorrow. Zenith just looked at me and said, "Even if you knew the world would fall to pieces tomorrow, would you still fight? Do not dwell in the past and do not dream of the future. Concentrate instead on the present moment. Plant your jávi tree."

– FROM "CONVERSATIONS WITH DRAGONS" BY DJURDAK ZA'CAR

Crimson eyes gazed out over the moonlit water of the bay. Waves gently lapped at the soft sand of the beach. Birds chirped as they settled in for the summer night. Stars flickered to life in the growing darkness overhead. There was once a time when Dimitri would have stopped everything and enjoyed the beauty of the world around him. Now his mind, it seemed, was far too occupied to allow even a moment's respite.

His major concern, apart from finding the Dragons' Gate, was convincing Godilai he was, in fact, a worthy mate. Wooing a Dákun Daju female was not something he had learned before his mother was murdered. And everything he hoped would work was proving to be nothing more than a disappointing waste of time and energy.

There was only one person he knew he could turn to. But he was in Monrai, all the way on the other side of the planet. There was no way he could go to him for advice without earning suspicion from his teammates.

He sighed and turned away from the serene view in time to see his newest lackey dragged out of the woods by Godilai. A frown quickly spread over Dimitri's features as the blonde was dropped unceremoniously at his feet.

"What's the deal, mate? That bloody hurts!."

"You should have thought about that before that wretched Xyleena got the better of us in that last fight!" Godilai hissed.

Kkorian growled and quickly got to his feet. "What the blinkin' hell did you want me to do about it?" He shouted, waving his arms in frustration. "If I had warned you that they knew of your ambush, they would have killed me!"

"How did they know about it?"

Godilai grabbed the pirate's arm and jerked him so hard he was sure she'd break it. "You told them we were there?!"

"No!" Kkorian tried to fight her grip, only to fail. "That stupid, bloody mongrel picked up your scent!"

"Impossible." Dimitri muttered and crossed his arms. "I had Pox clear the area."

Kkorian gave up fighting Godilai's grip to glare at Dimitri. "Apparently not or Kitfox wouldn't't've smelled ya!"

Godilai threw Kkorian into the sand and faced Dimitri. "You are losing your grip on her. You should kill her and be done with it."

"What're you talking about? I thought she was on your side." Kkorian said as he rubbed his sore arm. Dimitri chose to ignore him.

"Don't worry about it, Godilai. It will be taken care of."

"Yeah, right." She muttered and strode away. Dimitri scoffed and watched her vanish into the forest.

"Do you still want the next clue or should I just keep it to meself?" Kkorian got to his feet and dusted himself off. He didn't really need to ask; he already knew the Hume-aju wanted the clue. Still, it was fun annoying him.

"What is it, already?"

"'Kúskú of Illusion now sleeps; On isle hidden in Mysty deep.'" Kkorian watched as Dimitri's expression changed from annoyance to curiosity. "They're headin' into the Myst of Mekora Lesca. My advice; stay away unless you want to take on Magnathor."

Dimitri grinned. The perfect opportunity to visit his old friend had just arrived. He tossed Kkorian a bag of coin. "That's for the clues to the two dragons beneath the bay. I trust you will get the runes found on the black dragon statue while you are in the Myst?"

42

"Sure thing." Kkorian said as he tied the pouch to his belt. "Where do you plan to meet up next?"

"Get them to rest in Monrai once you've made it out of the Myst. I will expect you at The Sign Out Front."

"The Sign Out Front in Monrai. Got it." The pirate nodded and turned to leave. After only a few paces, Dimitri called his name. Kkorian glanced over his shoulder.

"I'll triple your current price if you survive Magnathor!"

The pirate grinned and walked away with a wave.

The first crack woke me out of a stone dead sleep. The second had me running to the eggs as fast as I could while screaming for the others. After what felt like a lifetime, all of our hard work was finally paying off; the dragons were hatching.

— FROM "THE DIARY OF AMOREZ" BY AMOREZ RENOAN

"I had the weirdest dream last night." I heard Kitfox's cheerful laugh all the way across the bustling room. I paused at the foot of the stairs to listen. "We were all in this underground cave and these fuzzy, little things swarmed all over us like we were the strangest things they ever saw. Then they took us to this place and forced us to worship a big rock."

"Yup. You're one weird puppy." Thera jested. I couldn't help but smile as I finally made my way over to them.

"Kahs gözandí, Xy-sortim." Shazza dipped her head in greeting. I returned the greeting and took a seat next to her.

"You're just in time for breakfast." Kitfox grinned and wiggled his eyebrows. I couldn't help but laugh at him.

"Why are you weirder than normal today?"

He shrugged. "Why shouldn't I be?"

"Because we are about to face a big, ugly sea monster and brave the Myst of Mekora Lesca to find a dragon while defending ourselves from whatever plan Dimitri has next."

His ears drooped along with his expression. "There goes the good mood." He muttered. "Party pooper."

I shrugged. "Sorry, but it's true."

"I don't suppose anyone has actually come up with a plan to defeat Magnathor." Shazza said in between bites.

"There's only been one person in history to beat that monster; Amorez herself. And even she barely managed to pull it off." Thera sighed.

"Does my mother say how she did it in Dragon Diary?" The Feykin shrugged and removed the ancient, leather diary from her bag. With a quiet spell, the diary opened and flipped through pages of its own accord.

"Has anyone seen the Magnathor since Amorez beat it?"

"She nearly sunk me ship while I was en route to Fisherman's City to restock." Kkorian said, dropping like a lead weight into a char. I quirked an eyebrow as I took a good look at him. There were bags under his eyes and scrapes and bruises were clearly visible all over him.

"What happened to you?"

He flushed. "I... uh... I fell outta bed."

"Moron." Kitfox muttered and rolled his eyes.

"Mutt."

"Bastard."

"Inbreed."

"Shut-up, both of you." I sighed. "Kkorian, can you tell us anything more about Magnathor?"

He shrugged. "All I know is she's bloody hard to see coming through the Myst and she likes to hit ships just right to make them roll. Nearly sent mine to the bottom doin' that."

"Good thing we're not going by sea, then." Shazza muttered.

"The only thing Amorez says about Magnathor in her diary is that she barely got a fang from the beast." Announced Thera as the book closed.

You do not need to worry about Magnathor. The voice of Riptide echoed in my mind. I frowned at her tone and lack of worry.

What do you mean?

Mother will not attack daughter.

"Magnathor has a daughter?" I thought aloud. The inquiry earned several surprised and confused expressions.

"I don't think anyone can know that for sure." Replied Shazza.

"Riptide said 'Mother will not attack daughter' and told me not to worry about Magnathor."

"That makes about as much sense as a lizard drinkin'." Kkorian mumbled.

"Actually, it makes perfect sense." Thera chuckled. "Riptide was born from Magnathor's fang. That makes her the daughter."

"How did you deduce that?" Kitfox quirked an eyebrow at the young Feykin.

"My mother was the one who brought the Dragons of Light to life. I remember her mentioning a huge fang used to make water, which didn't make much sense at the time. Now it does."

Magnathor is your mother, Riptide?

Yes. I could hear the pride in her voice. And she will not attack so long as I am present.

Good to know. I smiled. "So Riptide has Magnathor covered. Now all we need to do is locate Kúskú's island."

"That, in itself, is going to be rough." Muttered Kitfox. "You are the only one that can actually see the dragons' islands, so..."

Not true! I flinched at Wildfire's shout and rubbed my ear.

Kitfox quirked an eyebrow at me. "What did the dragons say?"

"I think they can see the islands, too."

It is true! We all have dragon eyes.

You don't need to shout it, Wildfire. The others can't hear you, but I can just fine.

Sorry. I forgot about that.

She's so easily excited. Vortex made a sound like a laugh.

"Well, that helps immensely. With seven pairs of eyes that can see the hidden islands, finding Kúskú should be easy."

Thera nodded in agreement. "So the question remaining is, how do we want to approach the Myst?"

"The mountain range known as the Eyes of the Ages lie directly east of the Myst. They are so tall I doubt the dragons could fly over or between them." Kitfox glanced at me for confirmation. Hearing nothing from the dragons, I could only shrug in answer. "I think our best bet is to overnight in either Monrai or Fisherman's City before sweeping out over the Myst."

46

"If we go to Monrai, I can get a mate to give us a discount at his inn." Kkorian flashed a crooked smirk.

"Sounds like a plan to me." I nodded.

"We need to gear up for this one, I think." Thera muttered, staring at the hand drawn map in Dragon Diary. "Monrai is a long ways away from Nemlex."

Shazza nodded. "We should stop in Pletíxa for a night before going out over the ocean. I'll buy the supplies there."

"Even Pletíxa to Monrai's not within cooee." Kkorian added with a whistle after glancing at the map. "Hope the dragons can handle flying that far without landing."

We dragons can fly a few days on end without tiring. Kkaia said brazenly. We would be more worried about the five of you.

About how long would it take for you guys to fly that far?

Helios chuckled. No idea.

We are not familiar enough with your cities to estimate a time table for you, Hatchling. Added Vortex.

"They can fly it, but they don't know how long it would take." I announced. "They are more worried about us holding up against the flight."

"Since we won't be able to land, we should probably get some sort of straps to lash ourselves to the saddles so we don't fall off when we fall asleep adragonback." Thera suggested. Shazza nodded in agreement and wrote down the suggestion on a napkin.

"Food. Water. Warm clothes. Medicinal herbs. Anything else we need?"

"Muzzle." Kkorian chuckled as he looked Kitfox in the eye. The Fox Demon growled.

"Blunt object."

"How about you two torture and kill each other after we've beaten Dimitri?" They both shot me innocent looks.

"Alright. Let's get out of here. The sooner we collect the rest of the dragons, the better." Shazza stuffed the napkin in her pocket and stood.

Minutes later, the five of us had collected our belongings from our rooms. We made our way to the outskirts of Nemlex where I summoned all six of my dragons. With a fond farewell to the villagers who had gathered to see us off, the dragons took a few bounding steps and launched skywards in a close formation.

They circled the town once... twice... thrice... before turning eastward, towards the rising suns and Kúskú.

It took the wretched alchemist so many attempts to get the correct formula that I had lost count. He never gave up though; he was bound and determined to earn the money I had promised him, and to make a name for himself in the world. Little does he know that I have had every alchemist hunted down and killed lest they too discover the secrets to what I am about to see born.

– FROM "THE DIARY OF AGASEI" BY AGASEI DÉDOS

It was the third time the suns had set since we left Pletíxa, and the dragons still flew on. Land had yet to be spotted on the horizon and the orange and violet ocean spread out beneath us, stretching as far as the eye could see. Stars flickered to life in the quickly darkening zenith above. Their sparkle reflected off the mirrored surface of the ocean like diamonds nestled in velvet.

Usually I could appreciate the beauty of a sunset such as this one, but I had quickly become too irritated with this portion of the quest to care. My legs were stiff. My back ached. And my head wouldn't stop pounding. I couldn't wait to set foot on solid land and enjoy a nice, long rest.

With a weary sigh, I resigned to lean against Helios' neck. I let my eyes drift shut and slowly breathed the salty, ocean air. I felt Helios' neck constrict and knew he was checking to see if I was alright. I gently thumped his shoulder in reassurance and smiled. He looked away. I let sleep claim me.

"Xy! Xy, wake up!"

I groaned and ignored the voice calling to me. A moment later, someone was shaking me. I bolted upright in the saddle, narrowly avoiding smashing Kitfox's face. He blinked in surprise and smiled sheepishly.

"She sleeps like the dead." Helios chuckled. Kitfox agreed wholeheartedly. I frowned at the Dragon of Light and noticed we were still flying.

"How did you end up on Helios?"

Kitfox quirked an eyebrow. "I jumped. How else?"

"Are you insane?" I shouted, suddenly furious that he would do such a thing. "A stunt like that could kill you!"

"Sheesh! Will you relax?" He shook his head. "Look, I jumped over here to wake you up because you weren't answering the communicator. I thought you would want to know that I spotted land on the horizon." I eagerly looked beyond Helios in hopes to see it myself. The world was too dark now for Hume vision to discern anything. "There's a... small problem."

I frowned and met Kitfox's dimly-glowing gaze with my own. "What problem?"

"We've flown too far east. Monrai is about a half a day's flight northwest of here."

"What?!"

He flinched and rubbed his ears.

"How did we end up so far off course?"

"I can't say for sure." He shrugged. "But the dragons are landing to give us all a much needed break from the flying. I don't know about you, but my legs could really use a stretch."

As much as I was eager to be on land, I didn't like the idea of having to back track our steps by half a day. I sighed and tried to find my teammates in the dark. Thera was easy to find as she had lit an orb to continue her work on the translation of the Riddle of the Twelve. I found Wildfire by the perpetual flame that engulfed the tip of her tail; Kkorian would be riding her. Shazza, on the other hand, was too faint to see in the night.

I sighed and returned my gaze to Kitfox's face. He was as weary as I had ever seen him. Maybe a day's rest was in order before facing Magnathor and finding Kúskú.

"How long until we're able to land?"

The Fox Demon smiled and glanced over his shoulder. "I'd say about half an hour or so."

"Good. I can't wait to stretch."

"Same here." Kitfox turned and crouched low, pausing as if gauging a distance.

"What are you doing? Don't even think about jumping back over to Kkaia!" He blinked at me in surprise. "You're tired enough that you could miss the landing, so just stay here."

"I didn't want to make you uncomfortable again."

"What do you mean?"

"Never mind." He sighed and hopped over me, landing as gracefully as ever, before sitting down just behind me in the saddle. Instead of wrapping his arms around me like I expected – maybe even hoped – he crossed them over his chest and closed his eyes. We flew on in silence.

The six dragons landed on a sandy beach in a tight formation. I heard Helios' wings creak in protest at being folded after so long, but the dragon did not complain. Like the others with riders, he knelt down so that stiff legs didn't have such a large impact to absorb upon dismounting. I could barely move as it was, but thankfully Kitfox was there to help be down from the saddle.

"How long have the suns been down?" I asked Thera as I took a few awkward steps in hopes of loosening my muscles.

"Only a couple of hours for us, but they have been down longer in this region since we've been flying away from the sunset."

"In other words, it is about midnight here." Interjected Shazza. "We should eat and sleep."

"I vote we just sleep." Kkorian said through a huge yawn. "I'm all tuckered out, mates."

Kitfox nodded. "We all are."

"Nest for the night, Hatchlings. We dragons will watch over you."

I didn't need to be persuaded. As soon as I had my sleeping skins unrolled from the saddle bag, I was fast asleep.

I awoke to soft conversation. I opened my eyes only to realize I was in a protective cocoon made of Riptide's wing and the Dragon of Water was still asleep. Too comfortable to move for the moment, I elected to just lie there and listen.

"This Dragon of Illusion has me worried."

"How so?"

"I heard stories about his powers from Mother. He has the ability to see into your very soul and bring to life your greatest fears. He used it once in a battle against Wyrd, the Shadow Dragon of Undeath. Mother said it terrified even her to watch the horrors of Wyrd's soul brought to life before her very eyes."

"Handy trick, but I don't think the dragon would use it against his own Keeper or her friends."

"I would hope not. Still, it has me worried."

"What has me worried right now is those two boys. They went out hunting almost three hours ago. They should have been back by now."

I found myself frowning at that revelation. I wasn't sure about Kkorian, but I knew Kitfox was too skilled a hunter to take three hours to catch something to eat. What if something happened to them? Were they lost? Injured? Worse; what if they were...? No! I couldn't think that. I knew Kitfox was alright. He just had to be.

"Shazza! Thera! Gimmie a hand here, please. This moron slipped and nearly cracked his skull open!"

I sighed in relief. Kitfox was fine. I threw my sleeping skins off and rolled out from under Riptide's wing. I found Kitfox in an instant; a large boar in one arm and Kkorian slung over his other. Shazza was already tending to the large contusion on the pirate's head.

"Thanks, sheila." To everyone's amazement, Kkorian actually kissed her on the cheek. Shazza growled and promptly slapped him as hard as possible without killing him. While she fumed and he regained his senses, the rest of us just about died laughing.

The rest of the day passed without a care. We all ate heartily and bathed in the sea until it turned into a water war between us and the dragons. Naturally, the dragons won. So we gave their scaly hides a well-deserved scrubbing.

We all turned in early that night. In the morning, we would once again be on our way to face Magnathor in the Myst.

Dawn. The interlopers were at the gates. This did not seem to affect our new High King. "They are no threat. Let them break upon the walls," he calmly said. Then he cast his gaze skyward and cursed. There, in the early light of the rising suns, twelve shadows were flying in formation towards the city. I could scarcely believe my eyes. Twelve more dragons had been created!

Agasei briskly strode away, disappearing into the keep. I never saw him again. I was gladdened by this.

– FROM "UNTITLED" BY LD KNT YUE VERSAHN

I awoke with a start as a loud crack of thunder died away. I sat up and looked around in the dark. A heavy rain pelted the membranes of Riptide's wings. Beyond that, I could hear rough winds pummeling the trees and stirring the ocean into great waves.

"I was beginning to think you'd sleep through the whole thing." I turned at the voice and barely made out Kitfox. His eyes were closed as he leaned against Riptide's foreleg. As if sensing my gaze on him, he opened his eyes. He found me in the dark and smirked.

"How long has it been raining like this?"

"Few hours." He shrugged. "Riptide told me to keep you company because she remembered you were afraid of storms."

"I was?" I chuckled. "I don't remember that."

Kitfox grinned and closed his eyes again. "Silly thing to be scared of, really. Not like a little bit of thunder could hurt anyone."

"Are you scared of anything?"

Kitfox frowned and shivered but did not bother to look at me when he answered. "No."

It was a lie, but I let him think I believed it. I clicked my tongue and gathered my sleeping skins before moving to his side.

54

I draped the skins over both of us and rested my head on his shoulder. He sighed and wrapped his arm around me.

"I'm scared of losing people." I heard his breath catch, but he said nothing. "Especially people I love. It scares me so much because I don't know if I can handle living without them."

"Is that why you've suddenly been keeping your distance from me? You're scared of losing me?"

My throat constricted. Tears stung my eyes. I forced myself to calm down enough to finally admit the truth. He really deserved to know. "I was terrified out of my wits when the dire wolf nearly killed you. I hadn't even realized how much you came to mean to me until then. And as you were lying in my lap fighting for your life, I realized that if I lost you, it would be the end of me. I just can't handle another death so soon after..."

He hugged me closer and whispered in my ear. "After?"

"Ríhan, a boy from the Temple, was murdered by Godilai while he was trying to protect me." I choked on a sob. "I... I..."

"You loved him." There was a pain in Kitfox's voice. Too confused and miserable to speak, I nodded. "I'm sorry."

About hour before the suns rose, the storm finally blew itself out. Kitfox and I emerged from beneath Riptide's wings to see the beach littered with branches and debris. Hand in hand, he and I walked down to the water's edge and watched as a pod of eterfish played nearby.

The little talk we had last night had actually done wonders for the tension that had grown between us. He was no longer trying so hard to earn my affection and I found I could actually relax in his presence and not fret about hurting his feelings.

I turned and bade good morning to Wildfire as she rose from the ditch she had dug to nest down in for the night to shake the water and debris off her. She suddenly burst into flames, making me and Kitfox jump in alarm. A moment later, the inferno was extinguished and steam rolled off her ruby scales. She yawned to the tune of our relieved laughter.

"What a way to dry off!"

Wildfire shrugged. "I hate water." That earned a disgruntled snort from Riptide. The twin dragons argued loud enough to rouse the others from their slumber. They were only quieted after Atoka froze Wildfire and Kkaia smothered Riptide with sand.

Thera greeted Kitfox and me as she joined us at the water's edge. "Some storm last night, huh? It's a good thing we weren't flying through it."

"No kidding." Kitfox snorted.

I nodded in agreement. "Speaking of flying, how soon were we going to leave for Monrai and the Myst?"

"I'd like to leave as soon as possible so we can do a few flyovers. If we don't find Kúskú's island by nightfall, we can rest in Monrai and pick it up again in the morning."

"I agree with Kitfox. The sooner we start looking for the island, the sooner we'll find it."

"And Magnathor." I wanted to smack Kitfox for turning the conversation so gloomy by mentioning that monster. Even with Riptide's reassurances that no harm will befall us upon meeting Magnathor, I still had my doubts. Who could blame me? We've all heard the nightmarish stories of the Monster of the Myst coming out of Fisherman's City and Monrai. I shuddered.

"Well, we had better get started on packing up and breaking fast so we can be off." Still holding my hand, Kitfox escorted me up the beach to begin the chores. I barely caught Thera's delighted smile before it was erased.

Aruvan was just past the midpoint of its daily arc when the trailing edges of Myst were spotted. Helios and the other five dragons fanned out as they made a slow descent towards the thickening, perpetual fog. I barely made out the visage of a small town as it whipped by below and figured it must have been Monrai. Why anyone would build a town so close to this dangerous place was beyond me. Not only did the inhabitants have Magnathor to deal with, but strange and violent monsters frequently appeared in the area.

I pushed those thoughts aside and stared into the scenery below. I could barely discern rocky, lifeless islands through the thick Myst. Any one of those could be Kúskú's nesting place. How was I going to know which of these many islands truly was his?

Helios dipped lower. I watched as the Myst curled around his form, leaving an angry wake at his passing. Water sloshed somewhere to my right. I told Helios to circle back. Just as we passed the spot again, the Myst thinned. I caught a glimpse of a very large tentacle vanishing into the water without a trace.

I launched a light orb skyward as I clutched the communication wand. "Dasum meo nishi." The round crystal at the end began to glow in varying colors.

"Who launched the orb?" It was Shazza speaking.

"It was me." I replied. "I think Magnathor was just here so watch out if you come towards the orb."

"It was she." Helios confirmed. "I could smell her."

"Be careful over there, Xy."

"Will do." I nodded though no one could see me and tucked the wand away. I sent a prayer to the Gods to get us safely through this before returning to the task at hand. My breath caught as the roar of a dragon echoed all around us.

"I've found the island!" Kitfox exclaimed through the communicator. "Head towards Kkaia's roar!"

I sighed in relief and held tight to the saddle as Helios quickly pulled a sharp turn and ascended through the Myst. Once clear of its suffocating tendrils, he flared his wings to slow himself before searching for Kkaia's presence. Upon locating her, he tucked his wings and dove towards her at breakneck speed. At the very last moment, he flared his wings again and caught an updraft to nearly stop himself completely. He landed like a feather right next to the Dragon of Earth.

"Ugh! Were you trying to kill me or just make me sick?" I muttered as I slumped in the saddle.

Helios chuckled and crouched low to the ground. "I apologize for scaring you."

"You okay, Xy? You look like you're going to be sick." Kitfox said as he approached to offer assistance in dismounting.

"Oh! I'm just peachy!" I said as I dropped from the saddle and into his arms. Kitfox laughed and supported me while I regained my senses. "How did you find the island?"

"Simple. I couldn't see it, but Kkaia could." As he spoke, three out of the four remaining dragons descended from the skies above, landing in a way similar to Helios.

"Gods! Get me off of this crazy thing!" Shouted Kkorian, who promptly fell out of his saddle. He lay sprawled on the ground and whimpering for several minutes despite being teased by Kitfox and Shazza.

While the pirate recovered, Thera and I evaluated the area around us. The island was rocky and covered in moss and lichens. Everything was covered in a thick layer of moisture, courtesy of the Myst. Further in, the landscape grew too shrouded in the perpetual cloud to discern any features.

"Nevoa cäipe!" Thera was trying to dissipate the fog with a spell, but nothing happened. "Just what is this Myst?"

"No one has been able to figure that out." I said with a shrug. "Some believe Magnathor produces the Myst as a means to hunt and others believe it's just a strange weather phenomenon."

"This Myst has been here long before the Earthic Landings." Shazza explained. "Magnathor has been here just as long. And no one can explain the presence of either."

I nodded and turned to check on Kkorian. The pirate was finally returning to his senses and Kitfox actually helped him to his feet. As I moved to give them a hand, my gaze fell on the water not far from where they stood. A trio of beady, yellow eyes followed their every movement.

My breath caught.

Something was watching us from the watery depths; unblinking. I knew in an instant it was Magnathor; and she was hunting. She silently crept ever closer to shore, matching every step Kitfox and Kkorian took. Reason gave way to panic and I screamed. "Run!"

With an angry roar, the sea monster exploded from the water, drenching all of us in cold sea water. Kitfox shoved Kkorian away just in time to avoid getting caught in Magnathor's massive jaws. She crashed to the ground and rolled out of the water. All of us couldn't help gawking at the ghastly beast she was.

She was even larger than my dragons! Several gigantic tentacles and fragile-looking legs squirmed this way and that as she fought to right her long and sleek, eel-like body. Huge crab claws smashed into the rocks, easily reducing them to rubble. Finally, she was able to right herself. She freed her grotesque head from the rubble and hissed, revealing several rows of long, needle-like teeth. A split second later, she launched herself after Kitfox with astonishing speed. He yelped in surprise and took off in a full sprint, transforming into his fox form on the run to lead the colossal beast away. The dragons roared in synch and quickly took to the air to aid the Fox Demon.

Kkorian swore venomously as he freed his pistols from their holsters and took aim. "Never knew that bloody thing could run on land!"

"Daréta esso!" I launched several sizes of my favored spell after Magnathor. Thera lent her power, combining each of my thunder balls with her powerful fire. Even the combined powers of Helios, Vortex, and Atoka weren't enough. Each spell and bullet bounced off of Magnathor's thick hide like rubber balls, leaving her unscathed.

Wildfire appeared from murky skies above, diving so low and fast I thought she was going to crash into the sea monster. The Fire Dragon pulled up just in the nick of time to sweep low over Magnathor. As Wildfire passed overhead, she opened her jaws and spewed forth a liquid inferno. It rained down on Magnathor and the beast screamed as she rolled into the water. Great clouds of steam billowed off the surface and all was quiet.

"Cooked lobster, anyone?" Kkorian snickered at his own remark as he holstered his pistols. Shazza promptly smacked him upside the head. "No? How about surf and turf?"

"Shut-up."

"You're no fun, Shazza." Kkorian pouted. She ignored him and greeted Kitfox as he trotted up to us.

"Are you okay?" I asked, looking him over for injuries.

He nodded and quickly transformed back to his normal form and wiped sweat from his brow. "That was not fun."

"You're bloody quick though, mate. I didn't know you could do that."

The Fox Demon smirked. "I'm full of surprises."

Wildfire landed behind us with heavy thuds and folded her wings. "Do not let your guard down just yet. I don't think I defeated Magnathor; just made her mad."

As if taking a cue, Magnathor burst from the sea with an enraged roar. Wildfire bellowed a threat and took flight to continue the battle. The sea monster snarled at the dragon as she prepared to dive again. Magnathor snapped her great claws hard enough to send a shockwave through the air, causing Wildfire's flight path to hiccup and sending her spiraling out of control. Helios and Vortex rushed to aid their sister before she crashed into the sea. Atoka faced the sea monster alone, diving at her and biting at her tentacles.

Magnathor ignored the dragon and launched herself at us like a bullet. She was upon us before anyone could react. Her massive form was so close I could smell the harrowing stench of rotten fish and decay. Just when I thought it was the end of us, the ground exploded. The chunks of dirt and rock culminated into the form of Kkaia, who promptly clamped her jaws on the sea monster's throat. Magnathor was sent reeling with a horrid cry. While the beast was occupied, the five of us retreated further away from shore.

I listened to the sounds of the battle raging on behind me as I kept pace with the others. A pained scream echoed in the fog all around me and I froze. Another scream went out a second later. Momentarily forgetting the urgent need to escape, I ignored the calls of my friends and ran back to where I had last seen the sea monster and the Dragon of Earth. Peering through the Myst, I realized Magnathor had caught Kkaia in her claws and was squeezing her ever tighter.

"Kkaia!" My scream distracted Magnathor long enough for Kkaia to fade into a cloud of sand and rocks. The sea monster hissed in anger and bolted towards me. I was so terrified couldn't even force myself to run away.

A huge globe of water suddenly slammed into Magnathor's head, sending her flailing backwards and away from me. The enraged beast managed to right herself quickly and snarled viciously before launching after me again. Another huge mass of water hammered her. This time the sea monster turned her gaze skyward. She quieted in an instant and slowly sunk to the ground in submission.

I dared to look away from the sea monster, towards my savior. The shadow of a dragon hovered in the Myst overhead. I sighed in relief and returned my attention to Magnathor. The beast sent a look my way before slinking away to the depths of the sea with as much dignity as she could muster.

Riptide landed like a feather in front of me and folded her wings with a snort. She turned her aquamarine gaze to me and nodded in respect. "I apologize for being late, Keeper. I was speaking with Mother."

"Mother?!" I balked and looked towards the retreating form of the Magnathor that had just been scared away. "I thought that was your mother!"

"No. That is Little Brother. Mother makes him look like a shrimp."

"You've got to be kidding." I heard Kitfox mutter as he and the others rushed over. Riptide shook her head and calmly led the way towards the beach. Helios, Atoka, and Vortex stood guard over the wounded Kkaia and Wildfire, occasionally hissing a warning at the water each time a suspicious wave drew too close.

"Kkaia, are you alright?" Kitfox rubbed her snout affectionately, earning a happy sort-of purr. I smiled at the scene, remembering how they used to not get along so well.

"Mostly bruises. They should heal quickly." Thera announced after a quick assessment of Kkaia's injuries. "It doesn't look like anything is broken, but there is an ugly puncture in her left wing membrane."

"It is nothing a little mud won't fix." Kkaia replied.

"Why don't you all rest in the Amulet while we find Kúskú?" I suggested, feeling immensely guilty for putting my dragons in such a terrible predicament.

"What if that monster comes back?" Kkorian shivered at the thought.

"He won't." Riptide said with great fervor. "He wouldn't dare to anger Mother by going against her will."

"I hope you're right about that." Muttered Shazza.

After some further persuasion, all six dragons returned to the Dragon's Eye Amulet. My team and I set out to find the entrance to Kúskú's lair. The task proved to be more complicated than usual due to the thickening Myst combined with the waning light of the suns. There were times I couldn't even make out my hand right in front of my face. Though I stumbled a few times on hidden rocks and slick surfaces, Kitfox was always there to catch me.

Finally, a call from Kkorian rang out. We carefully made our way towards his voice and found him by a dragon statue just as the remnants of sunlight were sucked away. I lit an orb so Shazza and Thera could find us. Minutes later, the five of us were together again, looking down into a deep ravine.

I closed my eyes and focused on the pull I felt from the dragons yet to be collected. The closest and strongest one was pulling me downwards. I nodded and dropped the light orb into the chasm. I watched as it fell for ages and finally stopped when it was about the size of a pin prick.

"That is a long way down."

"Thanks for stating the obvious, Kkorian." Kitfox muttered. "The question is; how do we get down?"

I lit another orb and peered over the sheer edge. A ledge barely wide enough to stand on the very tips of my toes wound its way downwards. As I cautiously led the way down the ledge, I hoped it widened the further we found ourselves in the hole.

Our progress into the depths of the ravine was agonizingly slow. Almost two hours had gone by, and we had only crept a few meters from the top. My arms and legs burned with the effort to stay balanced on the dangerously narrow ledge. I was very tempted to simply let go and fall before catching myself with a spell. But I wouldn't leave my friends hanging like that. Nor could I summon a dragon now; there simply wasn't the room. If only the ledge would widen...

Rocks crumbled. A yelp echoed. My breath caught. I looked back at my teammates in time to see Shazza pull Kkorian back onto the ledge.

"You okay?"

"Y-yeah. Just s-slipped." He was visibly shaken, but didn't look injured.

"This is ridiculous." I heard Thera mutter. The Feykin shoved herself away from the ledge and dropped a few meters before she was able to take flight. "I'm going to take a look around and see if I can find a safer way down."

"Wait, Thera!" I called after her as she nose-dived.

"Don't think she heard ya, Xy." Kkorian replied. I sighed and returned to the agonizing task of slowly making my way down the ledge.

I didn't want to admit it aloud to anyone, but I felt greatly disturbed at Thera's sudden abandonment. Here I was, choosing to stick with everyone through this challenging descent even though I could pull the same stunt as her. And she just flies off! Gods, I was so angry I just wanted to punch something.

My anger ceased instantly when my hand brushed against something sticky. As much as I tried to wipe it off on the rock face, I still felt the stickiness clinging to me. With a sigh, I moved on and tried to ignore the strange sensation wriggling up my arm.

I couldn't take it anymore! I paused so I could balance myself on the ledge. Kitfox asked what was up, but I chose not to answer. With the utmost care, I slowly moved enough to produce a light orb. It seemed to explode into existence and blinded me with its brilliance.

When at last I could see again, I looked my arm over. Tendrils of silk-like thread clung to my finger tips. I sighed and cautiously moved to pluck them away. Just as I wiped the last of the thread clumps on the rock face before me, countless black shadows swarmed out. Intrigued, I moved the light orb to get a closer look. Thousands of little spiders scampered everywhere!

I screamed. In my panic, I lost my footing and dropped from the ledge. Kitfox barely managed to grab my hand before I was out of reach. The jolt forced him to lose his balance and we both plummeted into the jet-black chasm.

Shazza swore and punched the rock wall hard enough to leave a deep imprint. Kkorian tore his gaze away from the depths of the chasm to look at her. Had he been able to see in the dark, he would have witnessed the tears and the look of mourning in her sunset orange eyes. The pirate exhaled slowly and gently laid a hand on the small of her back.

"They'll be alright, Shazza." He murmured softly. "There's no way that dumb bitzer would let anything happen to Xy."

Shazza scoffed to hide how much she truly hurt at the thought of losing her friends and looked Kkorian in the eye. She read the emotions there; worry, fear, and strangest of all, love. She found it hard to believe that such a Hume like the one before her could betray that much weakness. She was unaccustomed to such displays. It made her feel...

"What do ya say we keep going?" She had to agree with him on that. There was no point in mulling about where they were. Without saying a word, the Dákun Daju Queen took Kkorian's arm and, ignoring his yelp of surprise, slung him over her back. She glanced downwards and clicked her tongue.

She jumped.

Thera folded her ebony wings with a sigh. Having been unsuccessful in finding a safer route down, she decided to land at the very bottom of the ravine to begin a new search. Hopefully this time, she could actually find what she sought.

"Luminös!" She was blind for a moment while her eyes adjusted to the sudden appearance of the orb. Once her vision returned, she glanced about. She found herself standing upon an overgrown, cobblestone walkway. It disappeared into the darkness beyond the orb's range a scant few meters away.

Thera summoned her Ribbon Staff and began to follow the cobblestones for some paces, only to come to the rock face with the narrow ledge. Apparently there was no other way to scale the sheer drop. With a defeated sigh, she turned and followed the cobblestones the other way.

After countless paces, the path was crossed by a magnificent, silver gateway. Just beyond the gate, Thera could make out a shadow against the darkness. She wasted no time in hurling the light orb towards the silhouette. She stood in awe as her single orb turned into many, completely illuminating a huge castle.

With a prayer to Régon and a final glance upwards at the rim of the chasm, she turned and strode through the open gate.

A breath of cool, moist air filled my lungs. Feeling slowly returned. I groaned and forced my eyes to open. Kitfox had me cradled in his arms ever so gently. Upon seeing my return to consciousness, he exhaled a worried breath and held me tighter to his chest.

"Thank the Gods! I thought you drained yourself completely with that spell."

Spell? I tried to recall what happened after I had caused both of us to plummet from the ledge. I must have acted on instinct as I couldn't remember a thing.

You used a levitation spell to break your fall and lower the two of you to safety at the very bottom of the ravine. Explained

Vortex. Very quick thinking, Hatchling, but it drained you substantially to maintain it as long as you did.

"Are you alright?"

Unable to find my voice for a moment, I nodded. Kitfox didn't fall for my bluff. With an understanding smile and shake of his head, he lifted me up as if I were his bride. I tried to ignore the butterflies in my stomach while he took a moment to get his bearings. Why does this feel so... right?

Thankfully, the dragons didn't offer an answer.

"I think Thera was here a few minutes ago." Kitfox said softly, finally taking the first steps towards a destination. "She lit up an entire castle with those light orbs you guys summon. I'm guessing Kúskú is sleeping within and she went to find him so he could help us."

We lapsed into a comfortable silence. While he strode along in the dark, I snuggled into his embrace and listened to his heartbeat. I hated to admit it, but I absolutely enjoyed this and even wished it to last.

"What are you thinking?" I looked up at him. His amber eyes were locked on mine, betraying a fear and a doubt. I smiled and reached up to gently stroke his cheek. He closed his eyes at the caress and walked on.

Several minutes later, we found ourselves just outside a beautiful, silver gateway. Kitfox gently set me down and supported me until he was sure I had regained my strength enough to stand on my own. The two of us gawked at the splendor of the illuminated castle before us.

Slowly, but surely, I led Kitfox up the pathway to the castle. As we drew closer, we noticed another couple walking towards us. Hoping it was Shazza and Kkorian, I skipped a few paces ahead of Kitfox only to stop short when I realized I was seeing a reflection of myself and him in the castle walls.

"I never would have suspected that!" Chuckled Kitfox. I nodded, suddenly overcome by a terrible feeling. I wanted so badly to tell him, but my voice still wouldn't work. "Come on. We'll take this slow."

He took my hand and cautiously led the way into the castle.

Shazza landed without a sound and finally dropped Kkorian. The unsuspecting pirate yelped as his rump hit the cobblestones. With a muttered oath, he stood and dusted himself off. Shazza ignored him and scanned the darkness around them. Xy and Kitfox were nowhere to be seen. She truly hoped they were okay.

She froze as she caught sight of something in the distance. When at last her eyes focused, she smirked. A castle was illuminated by light spheres several hundred paces ahead. Surely, Xyleena and Kitfox would be there!

Without bothering to tell Kkorian, Shazza took off at a slow run. The pirate yelled after her in a panic before he had the sense to join her. She hated to admit it, but Kkorian sure was fun to be around.

She laughed as they raced towards the castle.

Thera cursed her rotten luck and once again found herself wishing she had gone back to get the others. She really could have used their combined intellect and skills to navigate the maze of mirrors that made up the interior of the castle. She was too far inside now to even attempt to return.

With a defeated sigh, she turned and faced one of her many reflections. She made a face at herself and walked on. She paused at an intersection and muttered a spell. Once again the magic failed to work in this place.

"So far the only good thing about being lost in this place is the fact that Kúskú has yet to take notice of me." As she muttered to herself, she dropped her staff. It landed with a metallic clang. "Left. So be it."

Retrieving her staff, Thera turned down the path to the left. She prayed to Régon that the route she followed was actually leading her towards the dragon and not in circles.

Another intersection, another direction. Thera sighed and meandered along, pausing occasionally to entertain herself by making faces in the many mirrors.

"If the others saw me now..."

The floor suddenly gave way and she screamed. She plummeted several meters before striking ice cold water. Thera sunk to the bottom of the chamber and kicked off, surfacing minutes later with a huge gasp of air. She coughed and sputtered and tried desperately to remain calm.

She had to figure a way out of this, and quickly! She knew right away that any spells she would usually try wouldn't work in here. There was neither the room nor the leverage to use her wings to fly out. And, gazing at the smooth walls around her, there was no way to climb out.

She was trapped and she would drown.

She cried out.

Kkorian sighed as he followed Shazza. Neither of them had expected the maze of mirrors to be so difficult to navigate. At first, they had eagerly pushed on, expecting to stumble upon one of the others quickly. Alas, they only found themselves completely lost to its enigmatic puzzle with nary an idea as to where their comrades were.

He couldn't complain though. Being trapped in this place with Shazza was a darn far sight better than being stuck with Kitfox. And though she was trying to hide it, he could tell Shazza was glad to be with him, too.

"Damn. Which way?" Shazza stared down all three corridors of the intersection they had come to.

"It all bloody looks the same." Kkorian muttered. "If only we had a way to tell whether or not we were goin' in circles..."

Shazza smirked and punched one of the mirrors, putting a large starburst pattern in its otherwise flawless surface. "How's that?"

"Dontcha know breaking a mirror's bad luck?"

She laughed. "Right. If that is bad luck, I'm cursed for the next twelve lifetimes."

Kkorian frowned and followed after her as she started down the corridor to the right. "If you're really so cursed, how come you're a Queen and traveling with such great people?"

She shrugged. "You tell me, then we'll both know."

Their conversation lapsed into silence after that. Kkorian watched Shazza closely as she led the way through the maze. He had to admit, her intense and analytical gaze, cat-like grace, amazing strength, and even her ability to captivate him with every little move she made really intrigued him.

"What are you staring at?"

Kkorian felt the heat rush to his face and was grateful she hadn't turned around to look at him. He cleared his throat, apologized quietly, and stared at his boots as he walked on. "I was just admiring you."

He hadn't even realized she stopped until he bumped into her. He apologized profusely and backed away, hoping he hadn't angered her. Shazza cocked her head to the side.

"What exactly are you admiring?" Her tone was even; neither angry nor shocked as expected. Kkorian found it rather unnerving and thrilling at the same time.

He blushed as he answered. "E-Everything."

Shazza turned to face him. He cowered under her intense gaze and winced when she moved to put a hand on his shoulder. When nothing happened, he slowly opened his eyes to look at her again. To his utter amazement, she smiled! Actually smiled! He couldn't believe it.

Before either could react, the floor gave way and Shazza plummeted. After several meters, she landed in a pit of sand with a grunt. Shazza swore and looked around her prison. The walls were as smooth as glass, providing no means of climbing out. The floor panel that had given away beneath her was far too high to jump, even for her.

She was trapped.

And to make matters worse, the sand was rising.

I sensed Kitfox's unease as he led the way around another corner. He had picked up the scent of Thera when we first entered the maze and had followed it, but had lost it in the middle of this empty corridor. Now, like me, he was quickly becoming disturbed in this castle of mirrors and was desperately looking for an escape.

He paused to sniff the air again. A smile graced his lips and he took off at a faster pace. I was obliged to follow.

"I've picked up Shazza's and Kkorian's scents." He explained. "They're up ahead."

Still unable to speak, I nodded. That was another thing that was plaguing my mind. Why couldn't I speak? I've never had a spell affect me in such a way, even if it completely drained me. And my dragons had yet to provide any answers. In fact, they hadn't spoken to me since Kitfox and I started towards the castle.

I gasped as realization sunk in. Kitfox froze and wheeled about to look at me. Ignoring his concerned look, I walked up to one of the countless mirrors that made up the walls of the maze and exhaled on the surface. With a finger, I wrote in the fog:

Kúskú stole my voice and silenced the dragons!

Kitfox sighed in relief. "I was so worried it was something else." I nodded in agreement. "Come on. Let's find the others and collect that dragon so we can get the heck out of this place. It's giving me the creeps."

I smiled and closed my eyes to focus on the pull from Kúskú. Following the trail to a source close by, I clapped my hands excitedly. I opened my eyes again to find myself standing alone. I instantly knew something had happened to Kitfox. There was no way he would leave me...

Or would he? I forced myself not to panic. But alone in this terrible place, where every which way I turned looked exactly the same, it was hard to not to. I swallowed past the emotions and pushed myself away from the mirrored wall.

If finding Kúskú was the only way to end this nightmare, then so be it! I let my eyes close and focused on the pull of the Dragon of Illusion. Once again finding it not far away, I took off in the direction I hoped would not lead me astray.

"Help me."

Kkorian gasped as the whimper echoed up from the depths of the hole that had swallowed Shazza. He dropped to the floor

71

and called out to her in desperation, praying that she wasn't hurt by the fall.

"Kkorian, help!"

"I'm working on it, Shazza!" The pirate retreated from the opening just enough to give himself room to work. "Keep talking to me so I know you're alright!" He listened for her responses as he dumped the contents of his pack on the floor and rummaged through everything. Finding the things he would need, he began piecing everything together.

"The sand won't stop."

His heart skipped a beat at her tone. Never once had he heard a Dákun Daju sound so desperate and terrified. He cleared his throat and tried to calm her down. "It's gonna to be okay, Shazza. I'll have ya outta there in two shakes of a tail feather."

"Make it stop! Please! Just make it stop!"

Kkorian found himself wiping away tears. "Hang on, Shazza!"

The last piece clicked into place. He secured a length of rope to the rudimentary hook and glanced about. He silently swore when he realized there was nothing for the hook to grab on to.

Another desperate cry from Shazza echoed up from the hole. Kkorian cursed his luck and pulled a pistol from its holster. Shielding his eyes, he fired a round into the wall. Several mirrors fell away leaving a metal frame. He quickly tossed the hook to the frame and jumped down.

Kkorian fell for only a moment before the hook took hold on the frame. Glancing down, he was still several meters from the pinnacle of the sand. He couldn't see Shazza. Swearing, he forced himself to let go of the rope.

He landed with a loud crack and ignored the searing pain in his ankle. Desperately, he scoured the sand, pushing this way and that as he searched for Shazza. Seconds ticked by like hours and still no sign of her. He desperately called her name over and over. Finally, he unearthed her hand. Wasting no time, he dug in deeper and deeper until he had freed her head.

Kkorian patted her cheek to rouse her, praying that he wasn't too late to save her. "Shazza! Shazza!"

Her eyelids fluttered open. She looked at him with such emotion that he was left breathless. With his help, she finally managed to pull herself free from the sand. She clung to him and cried openly, thanking him over and over. He rocked her gently, whispering that everything was alright as he dared to kiss her forehead... her cheeks... her lips.

When at last Shazza had calmed down from her panic, she helped Kkorian climb back up the rope. Upon learning the pirate had broken an ankle in his rush to save her, Shazza tried a spell to heal him. When it failed, she helped him pack up the things he had dumped on the floor before picking him up and carrying him off.

Kitfox snarled violently and pounded against the mirror. When it didn't give way like he expected, he turned his claws upon it. Every scratch he made in the pristine surface immediately vanished, leaving the mirror unscathed as ever. He swore and touched his forehead to the mirror's cool surface.

"I'm sorry, Xy." His voice was strained and tears threatened to fall from his eyes. "I swear; I only took my eyes off of you for a second! Then this damned mirror stole you away." He suppressed a sob and let his hands drop to his sides. "I've failed you."

"Help!"

Kitfox's ears perked up.

"Someone!"

"Thera?!" Kitfox pushed away from the mirror and quickly scanned his surroundings. It wasn't until another cry for help later that he discovered the source was beneath the floor a few meters away.

He called out to Thera again, hoping she would hear him where ever she was. Nothing. With a look of concern back at the mirror hiding Xy, Kitfox moved to help the Feykin.

"Shield your eyes, Thera! I'm breaking the floor!" He gave her a moment to get ready before slamming his foot on a particular mirror. The mirror cracked, shattered, then drifted away. Water gurgled as it surged over the floor. Kitfox swore and reached into the hole he made in hopes to find Thera.

The Feykin burst out of the depths, nearly sending Kitfox reeling in fright. He recovered quickly and helped her to her feet, patting her back as she coughed up water.

"You okay?" Thera only smiled weakly in answer and hugged herself in a vain attempt to warm back up. Kitfox stripped off his tunic and gave it to her to dry off.

"Wh-where are the oth-others?" She asked through chittering teeth.

"I'm not sure about Shazza and Kkorian, but Xy is trapped behind that wall." He pointed to the mirror he tried to break.

"Kkorian and I are fine." Kitfox jumped in alarm at the Dákun Daju's sudden appearance. He glanced at the end of the corridor to see Shazza cradling Kkorian in her arms. The pirate looked like he was torn between pain and pleasure.

Kitfox so desperately wanted to breathe a sigh of relief. But with Xy still trapped alone and facing who-knows-what, he found he couldn't just yet. He stared over his shoulder at the mirrored wall and silently prayed she was still alive. There had to be a way to break her free.

"What's that noise?"

Kitfox's ears twitched at Shazza's inquiry. "I don't hear..." There! A rumble, as soft as a whisper, broached the outer range of his senses. He moved to see around Kkorian and Shazza. "What is that?"

"The dragon?" Offered Thera.

"No way." Kitfox shook his head. "Not unless this one has about a thousand legs."

"In that case, we'd better not stick around here to find out what it is." Shazza shifted Kkorian's weight in her arms and took off at a brisk pace.

"I'm not leaving Xy."

Shazza reeled around to glare at the Demon. "You don't have a choice."

He scoffed. "Yes, I do."

"Whatever's coming could kill ya, mate! Don't you..."

"I don't care what's on the way!" Kitfox growled and clenched his fists so tight he was sure his claws broke skin. "I'm not going to abandon Xy!"

"Then we'll leave without you." Shazza turned her back on him and once again started away.

"Coward!" The Dákun Daju froze at Kitfox's furious shout. "Running away and abandoning your friends because you're scared! What about them?!"

Shazza's heart skipped a beat. "K-Kitfox..."

The Fox Demon didn't fight to hide his emotions from any of them and let his tears fall unabated. With an enraged howl he rushed the mirror that held Xy captive, slamming into it as hard as possible. When it still refused to shatter, he roared and tried again.

"Stop it, Kitfox!"

"No!" He slammed his shoulder into the wall again. "How can you tell me to abandon her?!" Another slam. "What do you think Xy feels right now, all alone in this god-forsaken place?!" Another slam. Another. Again. Over and over.

Blood ran down both mirror and arm.

"Xyleena!"

A silver gateway stood before me. It guarded over a cobblestone bridge that spanned a deep, sapphire pool. Beyond the bridge, atop a mound of jewels and shattered mirrors, a silver dragon slept on. I shoved the gate aside and stormed right up to the dragon.

Still unable to speak, I picked up one of the many jewels and hurled it at his head. The dragon stirred, but did not wake. Frustrated, I picked up several more jewels and tried again and again. Still, Kúskú slept on.

"Xyleena!" Panic washed over me as Kitfox's anguished cry echoed over and over. I ignored the pain of impact as I fell to my knees. I couldn't help thinking he was badly hurt and calling out to me with his last breath.

Kitfox! I cupped my face with my hands and bawled.

"Do not cry, Little One." A liquid voice from above made me gasp. I looked up at the silver dragon as he lifted his huge head from his forelegs. His amber eyes seemed saddened by the fact that I was reduced to weeping by the nightmare he wove. With measured delicacy, he moved his tail to gently wipe away my tears. "Everything is all right now."

With his words, the nightmarish castle of mirrors melted away as if it never existed. The instant the walls vanished, Kitfox spotted me and took off for me as fast as he could. Ignoring the fact that he was shirtless and bloody, I threw myself at him. We toppled to the ground and I hugged him tightly. I wept on his chest and thanked the Gods that he was alive as he wrapped his good arm around me.

When the others joined us beside Kúskú some minutes later, I peeled myself away from him and set about healing his wounded arm.

Shazza sat Kkorian on the ground beside me and shot daggers at Kúskú. "What in the names of the Five Souls was all that about, Dragon?"

Kúskú stood and stretched before stepping off of the rocky shelf that had been mirrors and jewels only moments ago. "It was a series harmless illusions designed to test you."

"Harmless?!" Shazza exploded at the word. I did nothing to curb her rage at the dragon. Instead I focused on healing Kkorian. "I was nearly buried alive in a sandpit and Kkorian broke his ankle jumping in to dig me out! How is that harmless?"

Before Kúskú could explain, Thera interrupted. "I nearly drowned before Kitfox broke the mirror and let me out! And please explain just how all of that," Thera gestured to the now dark and empty ravine bottom, "tested us!"

"My Mirror Castle and the illusions within were designed to test the trust you all must place in each other, for it is a

76

necessity in what lies on the road ahead." Kúskú kept his voice even, which only made Thera and Shazza all the more furious with him. As if detecting their growing anger, the dragon sighed. "Before your rage boils over, please hear me out."

"Speak quickly, Dragon." Shazza crossed her arms.

"Thera, on the way to the bottom of the ravine, you took flight and abandoned the others on the ledge." The Feykin blinked in surprise. "Then, instead of returning to them to offer aid to the bottom, you entered the castle alone.

"Shazza, you didn't care whether Kkorian was afraid of heights or not; you just threw him over your shoulder and jumped to save time instead of creeping along the ledge. And yet he braved both of his fears by jumping into a deep, dark hole to save you from your greatest fear." Shazza met Kkorian's bewildered gaze with an unreadable look. "Then both you and Thera argued with Kitfox about his refusal to abandon Xyleena behind the mirror, even in the face of unknown danger."

I looked Kitfox in the eye and he blushed with embarrassment.

Shazza sighed. "So, what you're saying is that Thera and I have issues with depending on the others for help?"

"Not just the two of you." Kúskú gazed at Kitfox and Kkorian. "Xyleena managed to find me before I could test those two."

"Wha-?" Kkorian gawked at the Dragon of Illusion.

Kúskú's eyes flashed white. "Kitfox does not trust Kkorian simply because he is a pirate who was once spotted in the company of the Shadow Keeper." Kitfox's ears drooped in guilt. "And Kkorian doesn't trust Kitfox because of his guild affiliation."

The Fox Demon looked at Kkorian in surprise. "Really?"

"Er..." Kkorian cleared his throat. "I've had... trouble in dealings with the Tahda'varett."

"What kind of trouble?"

"That is not important right now." Kúskú said with a sigh. "First and foremost, you all must work on learning how to trust each other."

"Kúskú?" The silver dragon looked at me in interest, "Why do I have to continue on this quest? I have seven out of twelve dragons and Dimitri has yet to obtain anything relevant to freeing the Shadow Dragons. Why not just destroy the Dragon Diary to keep it out of his hands?"

"Please give me Amorez's diary." Thera quickly removed the book from her pack and extended it to the dragon. Without warning, he took the ancient book in his maw and ripped it to shreds. I watched as the scraps of ancient parchment fluttered to the ground. The edges of each scrap glowed brilliantly as they hit the ground. A moment later, all the pieces were fused back together and the diary looked as though it had never been touched. "You see? The Dragon Diary is protected by several layers of magic and cannot be destroyed until the Light has been completely gathered. The only way to prevent the Shadow Keeper from obtaining the keys to unlocking the Dragons' Gate is to finish the quest and unite the hearts of Twelve."

"Well, it was worth a shot." I muttered. Kitfox rubbed my shoulders in attempt to ease the weariness away.

"I can't speak for the rest of you, but I've had just about enough of this place." Thera replied. She looked at me as she bent to pick up the diary. "What do you say we get out of here?"

"Gods, yes!" We all laughed at Kkorian's exclamation. Without further delay, I released all six of my dragons from the amulet. We flew out of the ravine in a tight formation, bound for the outskirts of Monrai.

Dawn had come and gone before we reached Monrai's borders. We touched down in a part of the surrounding fields and I dispersed the dragons. As we followed a limping Kkorian along the muddy road, I observed the quaint village.

The Myst shrouded Monrai in perpetual gloom, giving the town a ghostly appearance against the gray. Stakes topped with remains of twisted creatures lined the main road; a warning to monsters born of the Myst. A high wall of ragged river stones and iron secured the buildings and villagers within. Even in this early daylight, countless lanterns were lit. Their flickering glow gave everything a strange, yellow-orange aura. Buildings of stone and wood lined the streets and half vanished into the thick cloud.

Crows complained and took flight as we drew to a stop by the gate. A scraggly guard with a patch over his eye and a missing arm blocked our way. "What is your purpose here?"

"We seek to rest at the Bird in Hand." Replied Kkorian. The guard nodded and gave a shout for the gate to be opened. We thanked him and quickly ducked into town.

"I don't like the smell of this place." Kitfox muttered, blocking his nose with his hand. Shazza agreed with him.

"It is an incense designed to dissuade monster attacks." Explained the pirate. "Unfortunately, it doesn't always work."

"You sure know a lot about this place." I said as I looked around. It surprised me to see so many villagers out and about despite the never-ending gloom and threat of attack.

"I consider this place me home." Kkorian replied, leading the way down a side street. "After me mum died, pa dropped me off here and ran away with a piratin' crew. Pulled in a mighty haul 'fore Magnathor got him."

"Sorry to hear that." Kkorian shrugged off Thera's sympathies and strode up the stone steps of a small inn. Uproarious laughter and cheerful music could easily be heard from within.

"Sounds like a party in there." The pirate smiled as he pulled the door open and led us inside. As we neared the long desk in the lobby, Kkorian called a name which I figured belonged to the innkeeper. We waited barely a moment before a door was opened and a woman walked out to stand behind the desk.

I gasped at the sight of her. She was a Demon of the likes I had never seen. Long and thin horns grew from the top of her head beside elongated and furry ears. Brown and black hair fell in dreadlocks down her shoulders, half-hiding her angular face. Her sharp, almond-shaped eyes were painted, as were her lips and cheeks.

"Rhekja?" To my surprise, it was Kitfox who spoke. The Demon behind the counter looked at him. Recognition flashed in her dark eyes and she smiled.

"Kitfox, you scoundrel! Where have you been keeping yourself?" She skipped around the desk to greet Kitfox with a tight hug and I gawked at her even more. Rhekja was almost Hume from the waist up, but the rest of her was completely animal! Her sleek and muscular body was similar to that of a deer, complete with four cloven feet and a short tail.

"I was wondering where you disappeared to, Rhekja." Kitfox's voice yanked me out of my stupor. "What on Ithnez are you doing in Monrai?"

"Running the best inn in town, silly!"

"Wait a tick!" Kkorian took a few uneven steps towards the Demon duo. "You own the Bird in Hand? Where's Eri?"

Rhekja nodded. "I took over ownership of the Bird in Hand when I purchased it from Eri two years ago."

Kkorian paled. "And... uh... what happened to Eri?"

"He moved out of the Myst, but I have no idea where." She turned her attention back to Kitfox and poked him in the chest. "You owe me an explanation, fox boy."

"What explanation?" He grinned coyly.

"Freya came calling about a month ago. She was talking about gathering Demons to battle against the greatest threat ever to arise in centuries. What was she talking about?"

Kitfox looked at me. "You see that lady there?" Rhekja followed his gaze and nodded. "Her name is Xyleena Renoan. She is the new Dragon Keeper."

"I see." Rhekja was quiet as she stared at me.

"We are in a race against the Shadow Keeper to collect the Dragons of Light before he can free the Shadow Dragons. If he beats us, a great battle will ensue and all of Ithnez will plummet into chaos.

"Freya, a Dákun Daju named Zhealocera, and a few others have gone to the four corners of the world to gather an army. Together, we hope to prevent a destruction similar to the one Agasei wrought nearly 500 years ago."

"Kitfox makes it all sound so poetic and beautiful," I said quietly, "but in reality, it is terrifying and evil. And we desperately need all the help we can get."

Rhekja nodded. "I shall join your cause and do my best to help gather Demons for the battle you speak of."

I thanked her for her vow and felt enlightened by her words. When we inquired about rooms for the night, Rhekja said it would be a bit of a wait while they were cleaned. While we waited, we sat in a quieter portion of the attached tavern to discuss the next clue.

"'Dear Thedrún of Thunderous crown; Sleeps beneath Lescan harbor town.'" Thera read her translation aloud again and slammed the Dragon Diary shut with an annoyed sigh.

"It has to be referring to Vronan." Kkorian muttered.

"There are several harbor towns on Mekora Lesca alone." Kitfox growled and counted off each one on his fingers. "Why would it be Vronan? I still think it could be Harbor Town. "

"Have you ever been to Vronan?" Kitfox shook his head at the pirate's inquiry. "There are over one million citizens in Vronan and the port has room to house ninety ships for weeks on end. And that doesn't include the fifteen docks used for repairs. That makes it the largest and busiest port in the whole of Ithnez! And let's not forget the fact that it was one of the first cities inhabited by Humes after the Earthic Landings."

"He makes a good argument, Kitfox." Interjected Shazza.

"Not to mention, the 'harbor town' referred to in the riddle isn't capitalized; meaning it isn't a name. Therefore, it can't be Harbor Town."

"Okay! Okay! It's Vronan." Kitfox finally surrendered with a sigh. "I still don't see how anyone could hide a dragon under a town that big though."

"Magic; just like all the others were hidden." I replied. "Now, the main question is; how do we get beneath Vronan to actually search for Thedrún?"

"We'll discover that once we get there." Said Thera. "Right now, we need to focus on resupplying and getting all the rest we can before we set out for Vronan."

"I hope the dragons are willing to fly us again." Shazza glanced at me. After a moment to speak to the dragons regarding the request, I nodded; of course they were willing to fly!

"Monrai to Vronan is nearly triple the distance between Nemlex and here. We'll be flying much longer this time." Kitfox's ears drooped at that thought.

"With land beneath us the whole trip this time, we'll be able to take more breaks."

"I shall stock up supplies accordingly." Shazza declared.

We all pitched in to develop a list of what supplies were needed until Rhekja approached. The Gazelle Demon explained that our rooms were ready and we were welcome to stay as long as needed without fear of cost. I thanked her and the five of us departed for our rooms.

You were right, my love; These Dákun Daju are a rather peculiar lot. I have been among a few of them for a full seven-day now, and am no closer to understanding why they value the weapons they wield so highly. It is almost as if they worshiped them, or something within them. Everyone back home says they are violent and savage, yet these few have allowed us 'Humes' in their village to care for one of our men who had taken ill on ....

– FROM "AN UNFINISHED LETTER TO AGASEI" BY RAYNELIF DÉDOS

T he little house was dark and unlit. A fine layer of dust blanketed everything in sight, giving the impression of abandonment. The air was stale and unmoving. Thankfully, the stench of Monrai's warding incense had not penetrated the dingy walls.

Dimitri wiped the lingering stink away from his nose and silently made his way down the hall. A floorboard creaked and he froze. The air whistled a warning. In a flash, he turned and caught the dagger meant to end his life. He scoffed and let the blade fall to the floor with a clang.

"Never could get you with that one after the first time." Came a raspy voice.

Dimitri smirked and allowed his guard to relax. "Still playing games with me, huh, Nír'l?"

"No, boy," an amused cackle echoed down the hall, "I am still teaching you."

Dimitri tracked the voice further into the house, to a room lit only by the fire in the hearth. He took a quick survey of the space, admiring the thousands of books and ancient knick knacks lining the walls. His crimson gaze lingered on the old man in the padded chair beside the hearth.

The old Dákun Daju's gray-streaked, violet hair had been tied back in a messy ponytail that left his jet black eyes clear. He

83

held his head cocked to one side, relying on his sense of hearing more than sight.

No surprise, Dimitri mused, he went blind almost a decade ago. And I bet the old geezer can still put up one heck of a fight.

Dimitri grinned and finally stepped over the threshold. "How are you, Cousin?"

Nír'l snorted. "Old. You?"

"Still alive."

"What brings you to seek me out after so long, boy?"

"I came to you for advice."

"Oh?" Nír'l sat straighter in his padded chair. With a moment's hesitation, Dimitri knelt on the floor in front of the other Dákun Daju.

"How do I," Dimitri fought to suppress the embarrassing heat that rushed his face, "woo a female Dákun Daju?"

Nír'l smirked at the young man before him. "I never thought I'd live to see the day you became smitten with a real woman. Tell me about her."

Dimitri rolled his eyes, but complied with the request. "Her name is Godilai Locklyn. She's an assassin who is strong, intelligent, and absolutely breathtaking to behold. Her hair is the color of moonbeams and her eyes are like aquamarine jewels. I've lost myself in them countless times."

"Yeah! Yeah!" Nír'l snapped and sat forward. "Here's a hint, boy: poetry does nothing to win the heart of a Dákun Daju. Cut the mushy Hume crap!" Dimitri frowned and nodded. "Now, how well do you know this Godilai?"

"I've been traveling with her for almost a year now and feel like I've gotten to know her pretty well."

Nír'l nodded and closed his eyes. He sat in silent thought for several minutes, leaving Dimitri with growing anticipation.

"Listen here, boy," Nír'l said at last, "because my great grandmother's sister, your mother, Solahnj, bore you, the child of a Hume, you are seen as inferior in Dákun Daju eyes." Dimitri growled in annoyance. Nír'l raised a hand to silence him. "Therefore, you must go far out of your way to win the affections of a pure-blood.

"There is only one way you can pull off this feat, boy." Nír'l smirked when he heard Dimitri shift closer in eagerness. "You must put your life on the line to save her from a terrible threat. To her, that feat will mean you value her life more than your own. If you don't die in the process," he snickered, "she'll ask you why you saved her. Choose your words carefully when you answer, for the wrong thing will only push her further away."

"What if she still refuses to have me after I answer correctly?"

Nír'l guffawed. "Then it's time to start looking for another woman!"

Dimitri ignored the looks of the villagers as he strode through the muddy streets. He was fully aware of their unease; the people of Monrai didn't trust visitors. Lucky for them, he in no mood to start a scrimmage. The meeting with Nír'l earlier had him too lost in his own thoughts.

Just how am I supposed to save her life? Dimitri released a frustrated sigh. If only I wasn't half Hume.

With a snort, he shoved the tavern doors open and strode in. Ignoring the rowdy patrons and the summons of Vincent and Pox, he sat at a secluded table. A bar wench scurried over to take his order before disappearing to fill it. Dimitri propped his feet up on the chair across from him and let his eyes drift shut. Mere moments later, he felt someone approach.

"I figured you'd've been here 'fore me, not the other way around."

Dimitri scowled and opened his eyes. Kkorian stood before him, a strange emotion playing in the blonde's azure eyes. The Dákun Daju hybrid snorted and dropped his feet to the floor with a heavy thud.

"I've been in here every night for the last three days waiting for you." He growled. "What happened?"

Kkorian slipped into the seat across from Dimitri and sighed. "You have no bloody idea what I've just been through."

"Magnathor get the best of you?"

"Almost!" Kkorian paused only long enough for the bar wench to deliver Dimitri's order before spilling the details of his adventure in the Myst. After a lengthy explanation, he produced the scrap of parchment he had promised to get at their last meeting. Dimitri was quick to trade him a heavy pouch of coin for it. The pirate ran his fingers over the leather bag and exhaled slowly. "I don't know how much longer I can do this, Dimitri."

Dimitri's scowl deepened. He couldn't help wondering what exactly had truly transpired in the Myst. The story he had been told had to have more to it that the pirate wasn't willing to divulge. And if Kkorian was beginning to back out of their arrangement, things were going to get extremely tough. "Don't worry; your part in this is almost complete."

Torn between his feelings and his desperate need for money, the pirate merely sighed.

"Have they figured out where they need to go next?"

Kkorian looked up at Dimitri for a split second, then away. He quietly muttered the clue and the location it pointed to.

"All right." Dimitri sat back in his seat and watched the pirate for a long, silent minute. *Something changed him. He doesn't want to work for me anymore, no matter the pay.*

"Well, I should probably get back 'fore I'm missed." Kkorian moved to leave. Dimitri stopped him.

"Get me the next key and I'll let you leave my employment."

"Really?" The pirate sounded desperate and hopeful. Dimitri nodded and told the pirate of his plan to take the Dragon Diary from Xyleena when they next met in Vronan. "You're not going to kill them, are you?"

Dimitri was taken aback by the question. *Has he really grown that close to them?* The Dákun Daju cleared his throat, looked the pirate in the eye... and lied.

"The mind is more powerful than any spell or any weapon you can name. It is home to your greatest passions and your deepest fears. I was given the power to break the mind wide open and drown you in whatever I choose, be it dream or nightmare. And you won't even realize that it is all just an illusion."

– FROM "CONVERSATIONS WITH DRAGONS" BY
DJURDAK ZA'CAR

I bolted upright with a gasp. My gaze swept over the dark room. Nothing. With measured breaths, I calmed myself and sunk back into the pillow.

What woke me?

I heard a great snore in the back of my mind and suppressed a giggle. It wasn't the dragons; they were all still asleep. Pushing all thoughts from my mind, I let my eyes close and willed sleep to return.

Just as I stood on the border of awareness, a far-away scream yanked me back. I flung my blankets off and grabbed my tessens before bolting out the door. I paused in the street, listening for the scream again and hoping it would never come.

It did.

With an oath, I took off down a muddy side road as fast as I could. Another scream rang out. I turned left to follow it and prayed I wasn't too late to save to person at its source.

I skidded to a stop when the perpetual fog thinned. Five twisted beasts born of the Myst had a young woman surrounded. Before I could make a move, a flash of metal cut down two of the monsters. In another flash, only one remained.

I gawked as a white-cloaked figure stood to its full height in front of the woman and faced the remaining beast. The monster charged with a roar and was quickly dispatched. The cloaked figure sheathed its swords and helped the young woman to her feet. The woman thanked the cloaked figure profusely before running away.

After the woman disappeared into a house, I stepped out onto the street. The cloaked figure seemed to glance back at me over a shoulder. A heartbeat's hesitation and it was gone, sprinting down the street almost faster than I could see.

I took off after it, but only managed to follow a few blocks before all trace of it was gone. With a sigh, I finally gave up my chase. I stopped in the middle of the street and looked about.

Just who was that person?

Another great snore from the dragons was my only answer. I rolled my eyes and calmly made my way back to the Bird In Hand. At the inn's stone steps, I paused.

Those swords that killed the beasts... I gasped as realization sunk in. "They were dueling blades!"

"I am going to sit on you if you don't wake up. And if that doesn't work, I'll get the water bucket."

"Don't you dare, Kitfox." I mumbled and rolled over to look at him. A cocky smirk tugged at the corner of his lips and his amber eyes held a playful light. I knew that if I didn't get out of bed soon, he really would dump cold water on me. "Why are you always the one to wake me up?"

The Fox Demon shrugged. "Probably because the others already tried and gave up." He chuckled and moved to sit on the edge of the mattress. His hands slowly began to massage my back and shoulders as he smiled down at me. "Why are you so tense and tired?"

"Didn't you hear the screams last night?"

Kitfox shook his head negative.

"Several screams woke me in the middle of the night. So I went out in search of the source only to realize that a pack of Myst beasts were hunting a young woman. I was about to step in and save her when a white-cloaked figure dispatched all five monsters in seconds."

"Wow. Do you know who was under the cloak?"

"I have a guess." He quirked an eyebrow at me. "When I was still at the Temple of Five Souls, I enrolled in a dueling class. Don't ask me why." He chuckled and nodded his head in understanding. "Anyway, Lady Judge Zamora Argatör was invited to partake in a Demonstration duel against Freya.

"Last night, I saw the exact same dueling blades employed by Zamora during the duel cut down those Myst monsters. That says to me, the white-cloaked figure I saw was none other than Zamora herself!"

"Hang on a second; didn't you once tell me that Zamora is actually Amorez in disguise?"

"That is the conclusion I've come to." I said as I finally sat up in bed.

"So," Kitfox clasped his hands in his lap, "What did you two say to each other?"

I clicked my tongue. "Nothing; she just took off and disappeared before I could catch her."

"It has to make you wonder," he smiled and looked into my eyes, "what exactly was she here for?"

The Bird in Hand's attached tavern was bustling with noisy villagers. Rhekja and her hired hands were kept busy with heaps of breakfast orders, yet the Gazelle Demon made time to seat Kitfox and myself with our comrades in a quieter corner. Minutes later, she returned with a platter leaden with cereals, fruit, sweetener, and drinks. I promptly hopped up to help her distribute them.

"So," I sighed as I took a seat, "are we all set for Vronan?"

"We are awaiting a delivery of dried produce." Explained Shazza. "After it arrives, we will be completely stocked up for the trip."

I nodded and spooned some sweetener into my cereal. I knew I was going to miss eating like this in the next few days, but it was a pity that the meal before such a long jaunt was so plain. I really hungered for the breakfast platters I used to enjoy at the Temple. As much as I longed for the food there, I couldn't return.

I shoved those thoughts away and glanced at the faces of my comrades. Out of all of them, Kkorian was the one that held my attention the longest. His cerulean eyes seemed distant and sad as he pushed his cereal around the bowl. Just when I was going to ask if he was alright, he became aware of my gaze and smiled. I could tell in an instant it was forced, yet I would not call him on it just yet.

I will ask him in private.

Ask who what, Hatchling?

Nothing, Vortex. I smiled. So, are all of you ready for the long flight ahead?

Always! I rubbed my ear as all seven dragons answered in unison.

"The dragons are obviously ready to hit the road." Kitfox laughed. He winked at me and I smiled back.

"So am I." Thera grinned. "I have been eager to see Vronan since Kkorian first described it. Imagine one million people in only one city! How do you Humes put up with all that noise?"

Kitfox laughed. "You get used to it."

"Aye." Kkorian nodded. "After a while, you don't even notice how noisy or crowded it is."

"Do you think we'll have time to explore while we're there?"

Shazza stared the young Feykin down. "Who are you and what have you done with our Thera?"

"What do you mean?"

"You're usually not this..." I bit my bottom lip, trying to think of the word.

"Bubbly."

I pointed at Kitfox. "Yeah; what he said."

"Oh hush!" Thera blew a raspberry, earning laughs from the rest of us.

"I hate to interrupt the good times," Rhekja announced loudly and successfully captured our attention, "but Torrik just dropped off a delivery for all of you. It's behind the check-in counter when you're ready to pick it up."

"Thank you, Rhekja." Shazza tossed the Demon a pouch of coin. She deftly caught it and quirked an eyebrow as she jingled the bag. "Do with it what you will, but it is a thank you for your hospitality and assistance in our venture."

"It wasn't necessary, but it is much appreciated." Rhekja bowed her head. "And, as promised, I have sent word to my guild about the threat that we're faced with." She smiled at me. "The Schaakold-Vond'l will stand with you when the time comes, Dragon Keeper Xyleena."

It was late in the morning when the five of us collected our belongings and headed for the outskirts of Monrai. I released all seven of my dragons from the amulet at once, drawing attention of several villagers. They offered their help loading the packs of supplies on the dragons.

Once the preparations were complete, we thanked the villagers for their assistance and mounted the dragons. With a command from me, the flock took off in tight formation amidst cheers and applause. We circled the dreary town once before turning eastward towards Vronan and the awaiting Thedrún.

I saw firsthand just how hard it was for Artimista and Kadj. Almost every town we stopped in, the pair were ridiculed and attacked without provocation. I offered my help, but they had refused it. I can only hope that the feats they have accomplished during this quest are rewarded and remembered through the ages. Two brave Dākun Daju helped to save the Humes.

– FROM "THE DIARY OF AMOREZ" BY AMOREZ RENOAN

D imitri suppressed a shiver. A growing chill had been creeping along his spine since they first stepped foot in this strange cave, but he took it as a good sign that they were finally in the right location.

It had been almost a week ago when he had Pox warp the team to Vronan. They had quickly begun the search for the lair of the Thunderous Dragon of Light, only to come up with nothing again and again, day after day. The young Feykin had finally resorted to a special searching incantation, which had finally led them to the outskirts of Vronan but no further.

Dimitri took over from there, ordering his team to split up and find anything that looked suspicious. Almost an entire day had been wasted before Vincent stumbled upon a most intriguing opening in the side of a mountain. Had the fat, old Judge not tripped and fell through the rock mirage hiding the entrance, Dimitri doubted they would have ever found the cave.

Dimitri hadn't hesitated a moment and quickly ducked into the cavern. His team was obliged to follow, even though they had asked for a break. Looking back now, he should have granted their request. The inner workings of the cave were a jumbled mess resembling a labyrinth. Submerged off shoots and crystalline blockades had greeted them at every turn. Dimitri was sure they had been in the depths of the mountain for the entire night.

Finally exhausted, Dimitri stopped. Without a word, the Dákun Daju hybrid sat down with his back against a stalagmite. He closed his eyes and listened as his team happily settled in for their break. He really didn't want to waste their time on an interlude for he was sure Xy and her team were quickly on their way. But for his plan to succeed, he knew his team had to be ready and alert.

Mere minutes passed before Vincent's heavy snoring echoed off the rock walls. Dimitri scoffed and crossed his arms. He allowed his senses to extend further away from their make-shift camp. The salty-sweet scent of recently-formed stalagmites burned his nose. Water dripped somewhere to his left. A soft crackling erupted not too far beyond that.

"You hear that?" Dimitri opened his eyes to look at Godilai. She quirked an eyebrow at him before cocking her head to the side to listen. A moment later, she met his crimson gaze and frowned.

"Electricity?"

He smirked. "That's what I'm thinking." He got to his feet and started walking away. "Let's find the source."

Godilai was silent as she quickly followed him further into the labyrinth. Dimitri thanked the Gods for the time alone with her; how he had longed for it! Yet he could do nothing but enjoy her company. If Nír'l was correct - and Dimitri was sure the more experienced Dákun Daju was - any attempts to woo her now would only push her further away.

Dimitri paused mid-stride. The pathway he had followed emptied into a round expanse so large he couldn't see the ceiling. The far end crackled and popped as emerald green lightning jumped the void between walls. Seated just before the electric wall were two statues. One sculpture was the black marble dragon he sought; the other was an ugly beast that dwarfed everything in the room.

He couldn't even begin to name the creature it depicted. Great, cloven feet stood a distance apart and kept the colossal figure from tipping. Long tendrils of hair covered its legs but kept its sturdy torso bare. Two muscular arms grew from the right side of its body and one clutched a gigantic axe. A third, which formed into a strange sort of spiny shield, sprouted from the left. A flaring mane covered the beast's wide shoulders and neck, framing a bull-shaped head and long, twisted horns.

Godilai came to a stop right beside him and scoffed. "Don't tell me you are impressed by this."

Dimitri studied her for a long moment. He smirked. "Why not? You obviously are."

"Right." Godilai strode passed him and right up to the black dragon. Dimitri watched as she ran her hand over the dais beneath its claws to reveal the runes that served as the eighth key. He quickly removed his father's diary from the sack on his hip and scribed the runes on a page. He would get Pox to translate them later.

"Alright," he tucked the diary away, "I got what I needed. We can return to the others and begin preparations for—"

"Silence!"

Dimitri didn't need to be told twice. He had picked up the sound in the same instant Godilai had; a barely audible scraping of rock against rock. He met her gaze for a moment, before they both traced the sound upwards, to the head of the giant beast.

Dimitri gasped as the beast's head slowly shifted downwards. Its eyes flashed green with power and its weaponless right hand clenched into a fist. It released a deafening roar and slammed its fist on the spot where Godilai had stood a split second before. As the Dákun Daju rolled away and drew both of her swords, the giant monster snorted and growled as it lifted itself to its full height.

In a burst of unrivaled speed, Godilai launched herself towards the brute. It snorted as her blades bounced off its rock-hard body, leaving nary a scratch. She swore and back-flipped away just in time to avoid getting crushed as the beast slammed a hoof into the ground. Before the beast could move again, Godilai sprinted up its body to land a blow to its eye. Her sword shattered at the impact and the beast swatted her away with its shield-like arm.

94

"Levítum!" Dimitri's spell caught Godilai before she slammed into the wall. He granted her a moment to recover before cutting off the magic. She dropped to the ground silently, tossed her broken sword away with a frown, and drew a dagger from her boot. "Unless that can break rock, it won't do any good."

Godilai glared at Dimitri's back. "Then what do you suggest?"

"I'm not sure yet."

"You are useless!" She hissed and once again launched herself at the beast. Dimitri could only watch as she tried in vain to bring the monster down. She stabbed at its legs and torso, and only succeeded in shattering her other sword. Dimitri barely ducked in time to avoid the blade as it flew passed him.

Aggravated by her lack of success, Godilai hurled the remnants of her sword at the beast's head and resorted to pounding it with her fists. With each hit, sparks of electricity erupted from the point of impact.

The beast roared in agitation and swung its giant axe in a great sweep. Seeing the brute's intentions, Dimitri quickly cast a spell to block the blow and winced in pain as the magic drained him upon impact. Godilai looked back at him in shock before sprinting away from the monstrosity.

"Are you crazy?!"

"I couldn't bear the thought of you being killed by that thing." Dimitri muttered, ignoring her angry rant.

The ground shook violently as the beast took a step towards them, then another. Dimitri whispered a curse and wondered just how to damage a monster made of rock.

"You had better do something, Dimitri!"

Those sparks... That beast must be alive by the Thunder Dragon's power. The opposite element of electricity is... He snapped his fingers. "Godilai, distract that thing long enough for me to gather the energy for a spell."

Godilai frowned, but nodded in understanding. "Make it quick."

Dimitri retreated a little ways away as Godilai sprinted up to the colossus. Instead of landing pointless blows against the beast, she taunted it and dodged between its legs. Sending a prayer to the Gods to keep her safe, Dimitri closed his eyes and began charging the spell he hoped would work against the monster.

Unable to keep up with Godilai's rapid movements, the beast quickly grew irritated. Its eyes flashed and lightning crackled to life in its giant maw. Godilai swore venomously and dove out of the way as the beast unleashed a huge blast of electricity at her. The blast exploded just inches away from her and she screamed as the burning pain racked her body. She collapsed to the ground and remained very still.

The beast snorted in satisfaction and raised its giant axe. It brought it down in a huge arc and buried it deep in the floor of the cave, sending rubble flying in all directions. Realizing its prey was no longer there, it roared in fury and searched the cavern. It found what it sought moments later, slung over the back of Dimitri as he retreated into a smaller portion of the cave.

The beast's angry roar made Dimitri wince. Realizing he would never get away in time, he cast a spell to warp Godilai a ways away before turning to face the colossus alone.

"Come on!" Dimitri roared and the monster's eyes flashed green. An electric blast once again sparked to life in its giant maw. Dimitri sneered and brought his hands up in front of him. A blue aura engulfed his body as he summoned all of the energy he managed to gather. As he formed the aura into the largest water orb he could manage, he prayed it was enough to end the beast's terror.

The colossus launched the gathered electricity and Dimitri wasted no time in releasing his own spell. The giant orb of water shot out towards the beast, absorbing the blast of lighting and turning it upon the creature. The energy collided with the colossus, tearing a roar from its lips before forcing it to shatter.

I did it! Dimitri fell to his knees as huge chunks of rock rained down. He felt his body go limp and closed his eyes as he collapsed to the ground.

A warm sensation washed over him, relieving limbs weary from over exertion. He forced his eyes to open and stared into the depths of a concerned aquamarine gaze. He smiled; Godilai was unharmed.

"You are a fool, you know that?" Her tone wasn't reprimanding as he had expected. Instead, it sounded relieved and... happy?

"Yes you are." He finally tore his gaze away from Godilai to see Pox kneeling over him. Her brow was furrowed in concentration as she used her magic to restore his strength. Vincent peered over her, looking down on him in worry.

"About time you two showed up." Dimitri chuckled at their expressions. Pox immediately cut off her magic with a huff.

"If you two hadn't snuck away while Vincent and I were resting, you wouldn't be in this condition!"

"Silence, girl." Godilai muttered crossly. Pox glared daggers at her before getting up and storming away. "Vincent, go after her. We will follow in a moment."

The old Judge gawked at Godilai. He glanced at Dimitri to make sure everything was alright before doing as he was told. Finally alone again, Dimitri sat up and met Godilai's gaze. Her cyan eyes betrayed a curious emotion, but he knew better than to ask her what was on her mind; she wouldn't answer him anyway.

"You risked your life for me." Her voice was gentle and held a note of confusion. Dimitri blinked in surprise. He didn't even realize that he had saved her from the colossus; he had just been acting on impulse.

"Yes. Yes, I did." He forced himself to look away from her.

"Why?"

It was a simple question, but his heart skipped a beat at the very word. Still avoiding her gaze, he replied carefully, "Because I... I wanted to protect you."

A lengthy silence lapsed between them. Fearing his answer had ruined his chance to win her heart, he steeled himself and looked at her again. To his surprise, she was still staring at him; her expression betraying her emotions for the first time since he had known her. She was confused and angry, yet he could see happiness sparkling in her eyes.

"Am I really worth that much to you?"

He dared to grasp her hands in his own. "Godilai, you are worth so much more."

A tear escaped her. Without a second's hesitation, he moved to kiss it away. She smiled and he bravely and gently brushed his lips against hers. He pulled back slightly to gauge her reaction and was rewarded with a heated kiss from her.

Short of breath, they finally parted and gazed into each other's eyes. Dimitri knew then that Godilai would be his mate; his queen, forever. He smiled and caressed her cheek. Together they rose to their feet and walked in silence through the labyrinth to rejoin Pox and Vincent. They had much to do to prepare for Xyleena's arrival.

'Why twelve dragons?' That is the most common question I am asked. I usually shrug and answer with 'Why not?'. In truth, it was twelve because that is how many elements there are in the world. Earth, air, fire, water; everyone knows of those four. Chaos is another, as are: poison, life, death, time, light, dark, and void.

— FROM "CONVERSATIONS WITH AMOREZ" BY DJURDAK ZA'CAR

I gazed down through the gap between Helios' alabaster wing and neck, watching in awe as the jagged mountains gave way to the turquoise ocean. An enormous, wooden pier stretched the distance of the crescent-shaped coast, providing havens for the numerous ships at dock. Countless stone buildings, bleached white by sunlight, stood amidst the gold, orange, and red foliage of the foothills and cliffs. They climbed the height of the mountain in a tight spiral that ended just below the peak. And a great castle was nestled amongst heavenly fountains and exquisite gardens at the apex.

So this is Vronan. I smiled to myself as Helios dipped to lead the others in a lazy loop over the massive harbor town. I knew he was looking for a place to land, but the city was far too crowded to even consider an attempt. I thumped him on the neck and told him to land in the harbor instead. He obliged by diving for the open water.

Helios swooped low enough to graze his front claws across the surface of the water, using the friction to slow himself down significantly. Finally he plunged into the harbor with a great splash that sent a mist airborne. It turned into countless rainbows that seemed to hang there even as the mist sank back to the water. Mere moments later, the other six dragons splashed down in sync beside him.

After checking that my teammates were alright, I gave Helios the order to swim to shore. When we drew closer to the edge of the water, I noticed an ever-growing crowd swarming to the docks. Even the crewmen of the surrounding ships were glued to the railing, staring at us as if they didn't believe their eyes. I couldn't suppress the smile that etched its way across my face as they all started cheering at once.

"Yeesh!" Kitfox exclaimed and lay his ears flat against his head. "You'd think we were heroes or something!"

"Last I checked, we were heroes, Kitfox." Muttered Shazza. "After all, we are well on our way to preventing the Shadow Keeper from opening the Dragons' Gate and taking over the world."

The Fox Demon rolled his eyes. "You Dákun Daju really can't take a joke."

"I guess not."

"Speaking of the Shadow Keeper," Thera began, "I can't help wondering if Dimitri gave up." I glanced back at the Feykin in puzzlement. "We haven't seen hide nor hair of him and his ilk since we released Riptide and Wildfire almost three months ago."

"I am certain Dimitri is still out there; probably biding his time until an opportunity to steal Dragon Diary presents itself again." As I spoke I held the gaze of each of my teammates, lingering longest on Kkorian. With every word, the pirate seemed to grow more and more distressed and it worried me greatly.

He had been gravely ill during the two-week-long flight from Monrai; so much so that none of us thought he would survive. He only managed to pull through after Shazza forced him to drink some strange Dákun Daju concoction. Though Kkorian had been feeling better, I was concerned that whatever challenges we were about to face during our search for Thedrún would be the end of him.

That train of thought ceased when Helios announced our arrival at the dock. I sighed in an attempt to expel my fears and began to untie the leather straps that held me in the saddle. I was assisted up to the wharf by a pair of strapping, young men who couldn't seem to stop smiling. As I thanked them, Helios faded into sparkling orbs and wisps of white. His essence danced around me before entering the Dragon Eye Amulet.

Kitfox leapt from Kkaia's back while she was still a good distance out. He landed gracefully next to me with a cocky smirk and turned to help Kkorian out of the saddle astride Wildfire. Finally free of her burden, the Dragon of Fire huffed and took flight. Midair over the docks, she promptly burst into flames to dry the water off before vanishing into her own inferno. Searing hot fire swirled around me before disappearing into the Amulet. Riptide's cooling torrent and Kkaia's rocks and dust were soon to follow.

Villagers began firing questions at us in rapid succession. Kitfox did his best to accommodate them while Kkorian and I helped Thera and Shazza onto the wharf. The dragons they rode faded into their elements and vanished into the depths of the Amulet leaving Kúskú alone in the chilled water of the bay. The silver Dragon of Illusion seemed to study every person present before looking me in the eye.

"Stay safe." He whispered in his cryptic way of warning. Before I could inquire as to his meaning, he faded into mirrored shards and silver dust. As his element whirled around me, the mirrors reflected wild dreams and hellish nightmares before disappearing into the Eye.

I suppressed a shiver and finally turned my attention to the wonders of Vronan. White and grey standards atop several buildings fluttered to life on the sea-borne breeze. The Rising of Khatahn-Rhii had passed some time ago and autumn now had a firm grip on the world. Winter would soon be here. I wasn't looking forward to the season during my quest for the dragons.

The murmur of the crowd pulled me from my thoughts of changing seasons. Kitfox had done wonders for calming them and was in the midst of explaining the reason for our presence. As he spoke about the search for Thedrún, I scanned the faces of the crowd. Most of them seemed eager and shocked, while a scant few looked as though they didn't believe a word that was said regardless of the evidence that had just been swimming in their harbor.

Shazza quietly scoffed. "Can't win them all."

Just as I was glancing over my shoulder to say something to her, an apparition in white on the far left stole my attention. The white-cloaked figure seemed to feel my gaze upon it and froze. Keeping its face completely hidden, it slowly turned around to face me. The figure clapped thrice before turning and briskly continuing on its way again. I forced myself not to follow or call out.

What is Amorez doing here?

Amorez? Here in Vronan? Are you sure? Wildfire's excited voice echoed in my mind.

It was the same white cloak from that night in Monrai. It has to be her!

It is not. Came Kúskú's reply.

I frowned. How can you be sure it wasn't Amorez?

He provided no answer.

"You okay, Xy?" The concern in Kitfox's voice brought me back. I cleared my throat and looked at him with a smile and nod. I could tell he didn't buy it for second, but went along with my act anyway. "We've been invited by Raythur Gondin, the Magistrate of Vronan, to stay in the Anchorage Castle Hotel." As he spoke, the Fox Demon gestured to a lavishly-dressed, middle-aged man with a crooked grin. He instantly gave me the chills.

"That is very generous of you, Mr. Gondin," I nodded my head in respects to the Magistrate, "but I fear we are too pressed for time to stray from our mission at the moment. Perhaps we will stop in once we have acquired the dragon we seek."

The Magistrate's face seemed to fall for a moment, before he hid his disappointment with a rather large and unnerving grin. "That's quite all right, dear. I understand your haste." Without so much as another word, he turned and strode away.

Thera quirked an eyebrow at the Magistrate's retreating form. "Strange Hume. Just a moment ago he was bound and determined to all but drag us there himself."

"He wouldn't get very far." Muttered Shazza. "Besides, Xyleena-Sortim is right; our first concern should be finding the dragon."

102

"You sure you want to decline his offer, Xy?" Asked Kkorian. I looked at him, noticing the weary look in his azure eyes.

"I'm sorry, but I didn't think it was a good idea to go with him. He really gave me the creeps."

"I agree." Kitfox nodded and draped an arm around my shoulders before whispering in my ear. "You sure you're okay, Xy? You looked like you saw a ghost there for a bit."

"I promise, I'll tell you what I saw later." His brow furrowed at my words, but he nodded in understanding and let his arm drop.

"So, which way do we go to find Thedrún of Thunderous Crown?" Thera grinned as she looked at me. I clicked my tongue and closed my eyes to concentrate on the pulls of the five remaining dragons. Picking up on the closest one, I turned in the direction it lead and opened my eyes.

I was facing the same direction I had seen the white-cloaked figure disappear in. Maybe, with any luck, we would once again cross paths and I would finally be able to solve the mystery of who was really under the white cloak. I smiled and pointed. "We go that way."

I glanced back at Kkorian to check how well he was doing with the vigorous climb up the mountain. He was still weak from his fight against whatever had ailed him and I didn't want to push him too hard lest he never recover. Seeing how pale and sweaty the pirate was and how heavily he limped on his once-broken ankle, I decided to call a break to let him recover some.

I took a seat on a boulder next to Kitfox and watched as Kkorian slumped at the base of a tree. Shazza was at his side a moment later, providing water and that strange medicinal drink she had concocted. He took it gratefully and allowed himself to be gathered in her embrace.

"It's amazing to see how much Shazza has grown to care for Kkorian." Whispered Kitfox. I nodded in agreement. Those two had become so close after the fiasco within Kúskú's Illusion Castle that I couldn't help wondering if they would have a happy future together as husband and wife. Kitfox cleared his throat and looked at me. "So... are you going to tell me what you saw that made you go pale earlier, or are you going to keep it your secret a bit longer?"

I chuckled. "I knew you wouldn't forget about it." He made a face. "Remember that white-cloaked figure I told you about in Monrai?"

Kitfox said he did.

"The same one was here in Vronan."

"You're kidding!" I shook my head. "How did Amorez get here so fast? It's not like she has a dragon to ride."

"Kúskú said it wasn't her." I sighed. "And no, he didn't say who it really was."

"Damn." Kitfox's ears drooped in disappointment and I moved to rub his back affectionately. "I was so looking forward to actually meeting her."

"I was just going to yell at her for not telling me who she was sooner." Kitfox snickered at my remark.

"Kkorian has fallen asleep." Shazza announced softly. "I will carry him up the mountain so we are not caught out in the open upon nightfall."

"If you're comfortable with it, I don't see a problem with pushing on. He was the main reason why I decided on a break." I said as I watched the Dákun Daju Queen stand and gently scoop the sleeping Kkorian into her arms.

"Let's go."

The suns hung low in the sky at our backs when Kkorian roused from his slumber. He chuckled sheepishly when he realized he was being carried and by whom. Shazza flashed him a smile so quick he was sure he had imagined it.

"Feeling any better, Kkorian?"

He blushed at her question. "Aye."

"Good to hear."

"You've been asleep for several hours." Kitfox explained, slowing his stride enough to walk beside Shazza. "Instead of letting night creep up on us while you rested, we decided it was best to push on and find shelter at least."

"Well, thanks for not leaving me." Kitfox returned the pirate's grin and clapped him on the shoulder before rushing ahead to walk with me again. Kkorian returned his attention to Shazza. "Is there any way I could be put down?"

"I'm sure there is." Shazza replied softly. "The question is, why? With me carrying you, your strength is focused on getting better instead of being wasted on walking."

"Too right, but I really have to... uh," Kkorian's face flushed beet red, "hit the dunny."

I couldn't suppress the snicker that escaped me upon overhearing his embarrassing confession. As I pulled everyone to a stop, I caught Shazza giving Kkorian a quizzical look before letting him down. He thanked her and quickly vanished into the trees to relieve himself.

"What a strange man." Shazza muttered and crossed her arms.

"Yup." I laughed. "He's great fun to be around though, isn't he?"

Shazza didn't answer; not that I ever expected her to.

"Oi! Take a squizz at this, mates!"

Thera sighed and shook her head. "What in the name of the Five Souls is he talking about now?"

"Doesn't he ever say anything that makes sense?" Kitfox laughed and led the way through the trees after Kkorian. A scant few moments of brisk walking and we found him dancing in front of the side of a cliff. "What are you shouting about now, you nut job?"

"Watch this!" Kkorian made sure we were all watching before stepping up to the cliff face. With a huge grin plastered across his features, he reached out to touch the wall. His arm went straight through!

"No way!" Kitfox guffawed.

"How did you find that?" Asked Thera. A moment later, she cast a spell to cancel the mirage hiding the cave entrance.

The pirate scratched the back of his head and laughed. "I actually fell into it."

"You have issues." Thera deadpanned.

"Well if he hadn't fallen into it, we would have passed right by it and never even know." I replied, clapping the pirate on the shoulder. "Good work, klutz."

We wandered the labyrinth-like cavern for what felt like the entire night before I finally gave in to exhaustion. We divided the rest period into guarded shifts and quickly set up a rudimentary camp. The minute my head hit the pillow, I was lost to sleep.

I was awakened from my slumber what felt like only minutes later. Shazza apologized quietly and helped me set up for my shift on guard duty. I watched as she checked on Kkorian's condition before slipping into her own bedroll and letting sleep claim her.

Minutes passed in silence like hours. Bored, I decided to invent a game involving many pebbles and a few circles drawn into the stone floor with magic. Strangely, I kept losing. I snickered to myself as I collected the pebbles I had tossed.

"What's so funny?" I nearly jumped out of my skin at Kkorian's whisper. He flashed an apologetic smile and gathered his blankets to join me. "Boring night?"

"You have no idea." I muttered and tossed a pebble. It rolled passed the target and I tossed another.

"I'm sorry for slowing everything down."

I quirked an eyebrow at the pirate. "There's no reason to apologize, Kkorian. You have been sick."

"Yeah." He sighed and rested his chin in his palm. "I'm still sorry... for everything."

"Oh, quit acting so depressed." Came Kitfox's muttered reply. Kkorian looked the Fox Demon in the eye as he crept out of the darkness. "It's not like you."

The pirate slowly nodded.

"Did we wake you, Kitfox?"

"Huh? Oh. No." He yawned and stretched. "That annoying crackling and zapping sound did."

"'Crackling and zapping?'"

"You probably can't hear it." He pointed to his ears and swiveled them in the direction I assumed was where the sound originated. "It's a ways away, but it's loud enough to annoy me to death. I'm surprised it isn't irritating Shazza."

"Same here." Kkorian said, sending an affectionate look in the napping Dákun Daju's direction.

"Think you can track the sound to the source?"

"That would be easy. Why?"

I grinned. "I bet you that is where we will find Thedrún."

"I hadn't thought of that." He chuckled. "Should we wake Thera and Shazza and be on our way, or let them sleep a bit longer?"

"It's hard to sleep through all of your yapping." Thera grumbled.

"Sorry, Thera." The Feykin chuckled at my apology and spread her charcoal wings wide as she sat up. A moment later, she wrapped them around herself in a sort of cloak.

"I overheard something about a clue to the dragon?"

Kitfox gave her the run down on what had transpired while she had been dozing. He paused when Shazza suddenly sat up and looked around. The Dákun Daju frowned in annoyance and rubbed her ears before looking to Kitfox for an explanation.

After the entirety of the plan was explained and agreed upon, we packed up our belongings and fell in line behind the Fox Demon as he led the way through one twisted tunnel after another. He paused occasionally and sniffed the air; making a disgusted face at whatever his sensitive nose detected.

"I hope you're not picking up Dimitri's stench." Shazza muttered crossly.

107

"I can't smell a thing except salt water and the sickeningly sweet aroma of cave workings." Kitfox punched a stalagmite for emphasis as he walked passed it. "It's almost as bad as the stink of the warding incense used in Monrai."

"Are we getting close to the source of the sound you heard?"

His ears swiveled and he nodded. "It's only a few meters away now."

"You know what I don't get?" Thera interjected. "'Dear Thedrún of Thunderous crown; Sleeps beneath Lescan harbor town' is what the riddle said, yet we climbed half way up a mountain to get here! How is this beneath Vronan?"

"This labyrinth has been steadily descending in altitude." Replied Shazza. "From the distance we have traveled, I would guess that we are almost directly below the middle of the harbor now."

"I didn't even notice we were on a decline." I said, glancing upwards to observe the jagged and dripping ceiling of the cave. A flash of chartreuse light reflected off the surface of the stalactites and I gasped. "We must be very close to Thedrún now."

A rolling crackle of electricity charged the air around us. Kitfox pointed ahead with a laugh. "There's the source of all the noise."

"Wow!" I could only gawk at the spectacle beyond. The mouth of an immeasurably large cave loomed in the darkness before us. Emerald lighting sparked and danced over the space between its walls, creating a beautiful and deadly barrier. A black dragon statue stood just before the blockade; ever watchful. Large chunks of rock littered the ground all around. I could make out part of a face of an unknown beast carved into a portion of one boulder.

"Looks like there was another statue here." Remarked Thera. "It must have fallen over and broken."

"Too bad." Shazza smirked. "I would have loved to have seen a creature like this whole."

Kkorian shook his head. "No thanks. That thing is givin' me the creeps as it is."

I silently agreed with Kkorian as I stepped around him and the others. I stopped beside the black dragon statue and examined the electric barrier that blocked the way. The pull I felt from the Dragon of Thunder ended a short jaunt beyond. But how was I going to get passed the barrier?

"Something doesn't feel right about this place." Kitfox muttered quietly as he approached me from behind. I nodded in agreement, which seemed to surprise him.

"I remember seeing that second statue whole." I explained, watching as his expression contorted into a look of mixed worry and bewilderment. "It was modeled after a beast from ancient Earthic mythology; the Minotaur. It had been imbued with magic and Thedrún's own power. There was no way it could have simply fallen over."

"Then how...?"

"Any luck figuring out how to get through the barrier without getting cooked?" Thera asked as she bounded up to us. I slowly shook my head. The Feykin frowned and launched a spell at the barrier only to have the magic ricochet. "Figures that wouldn't work."

"What is this?" The three of us turned around at Shazza's voice. I discovered her standing a few paces away pointing to something on the floor. I moved towards her and grinned at the sight of the small and intricately carved depression in the stone. "You know what this is, don't you?"

"Yup." I chuckled. As I knelt beside the indentation, I removed the Dragon's Eye Amulet from its position around my neck. I inserted the Amulet in the carving with a long forgotten expertise and heard a soft click. A heartbeat later, the electric barrier vanished with a sizzle and I removed the Amulet.

"You're as cunning as a dunny rat to think that one up!" Kkorian laughed.

"Indeed she is."

I smiled as the new presence in the room stole the breath of my teammates. Thedrún was seated on his haunches as if he were the monarch of dragon kin. His ivory horns swept back and almost blended into his spiny mane. He kept his wings partially

109

folded and nearly locked the wing claws together just above his head.

His tail twitched slightly in amusement and lightning arced between the prongs of the trident-shaped blade at the tip. Occasionally, the perpetual lightning gathered there would crackle and shoot across the entirety of his hunter green and emerald scales.

The Dragon of Thunder seemed to smile as he rose to all fours. He strode forward, pausing ever so briefly to glance at the faces of my teammates before stopping at my side. His glowing, amber eyes studied me for a moment before he lowered his head to my level. "It is nice to see you again, Xyleena. You have changed since last we met."

"I'm not surprised to hear you say that, Thedrún." I returned the dragon's smile as I reached out to stroke his muzzle. "How have you been?"

"Locked in a perpetual prison of monotony." He answered as he sat. I felt a twinge of guilt at his words and nodded sadly. He snorted and bumped his muzzle against my hand. "Don't feel badly about it, Xyleena. I used the time to develop several new strategies."

"Still, I feel terrible about how long you've been locked away in here."

Thedrún chuckled and sat straight. "I guess you haven't changed as much as I first thought."

"You really think so?" The dragon nodded and cast a glance at each of my teammates. I smiled as I introduced him to each of them.

"Quite a team you have gathered." Thedrún looked back at me. "They almost match the team Amorez once led."

"I'll take that as a compliment." Thera smiled.

"Same here." Added Kitfox.

"As well you should. Amorez's team was nigh on impossible to match in battle once they actually worked together as a single unit instead of many." Said Thedrún. "I trust Kúskú has already tested your trust in each other?"

"You could definitely say that." Muttered Shazza. Thera mumbled something I couldn't hear.

The Dragon of Thunder nodded. "Then you are almost a match for Amorez's team. With a little more training, you will be able to fend off anything the Shadow Keeper will throw at you."

"I'm actually glad to hear that." Kitfox grinned.

"Well, I should let you all begin the journey back to the surface before you are too weary to." Thedrún made a sound like a laugh. "I shall be watching you all from within the Eye."

"Thank you, Thedrún." We chorused.

Thedrún bade his farewell and faded into his element. Emerald green lightning crackled and sparked as it danced around the room. Moments later, it shot into the Dragon's Eye Amulet and an eighth jewel shimmered to life amidst the filigree.

"Four left." I whispered, brushing my fingers over each gleaming jewel.

Kitfox massaged the small of my back and smiled when I looked at him. "Almost done."

A great wave of despair washed over me in that instant. I knew we would all have to say good-bye to each other one day and go on with our separate lives, but I had never imagined it would come so soon. I suddenly found myself wishing that the adventure would never end just so I could prolong my time with each of them; Kitfox especially.

I forced myself under control; now was not the time to think of such dispiriting things. We had much to celebrate. I clapped the Fox Demon on the shoulder and smiled.

"Let's get out of here."

He agreed.

The trek back through the labyrinth was agonizingly slow. It was as if each turn we took lead us down a path with a dead end or water trap. Weary and frustrated, Kitfox transformed into a fox and sniffed around until he found the original course we had taken. Once we were back on it, we covered a great distance before stopping for a few hours of rest.

As I laid down in my bedroll and waited for sleep to claim me, I observed my teammates. Shazza leaned against the stalagmite she was seated near; eyes closed and arms crossed. One orange eye cracked open as Thera passed in front of her. Upon discovering the Feykin was once again busy with deciphering portions of Dragon Diary, Shazza closed her eye again. I let my gaze shift to Kkorian. The pirate was seated a distance away from me, staring absent-mindedly into the light orb Thera had lit. I wondered what was going through his mind to cause such a dark look in his usually cheery, cerulean eyes.

My thoughts ceased when I felt a warm body snuggle up to me. Immediately knowing who it was, I grinned and rolled over, allowing myself the pleasure of snuggling into Kitfox's loving embrace. He chuckled and gingerly brushed some of my hair out of my face.

"Sweet dreams, Xy."

With his whispered words, I drifted off to the world of my dreams.

An unknown time later, I was jerked out of a sound sleep by Kitfox. His amber eyes glowed greenish in the near dark, silently warning me to remain still and quiet. A moment later I realized that every one of his muscles were taut and on full alert.

What's going on?

We are not sure, Hatchling. Quietly replied Vortex.

I kept my eyes glued to Kitfox, reading each little movement he made. His ear twitched. His grip around my waist tightened. He growled. My breath caught.

Faster than I could react, he shoved me away and attacked the would-be assassin. A split second later, a light exploded into existence behind me. Momentarily blinded by Thera's spell, I took the time to free my tessens from my belt and flare them. My vision cleared in time to see Kitfox roll away from the deadly blade of an angry Dakun Daju.

"Godilai!" Her attention jerked to me at my holler. Forgetting Kitfox, she snarled and lunged for me. I barely managed to block the feral swing of her swords before Kitfox slammed her into a stalagmite hard enough to shatter it. The two of them rolled to the ground amidst the rubble and dust. A moment of recovery and the two were back at each other's throats.

Shazza took a position in front of me and knocked two arrows. "How did she find us?"

"Don't know, but if she's here, Dimitri is sure to follow." Thera replied and quickly cast protective spells around us. She froze and met me with a worried look. "Where's Kkorian?"

My heart skipped a beat. "Oh no." I cast a quick glance around the cavern we were in, hoping Thera had just overlooked the pirate in her haste to protect us. Kkorian was nowhere to be found. Did Godilai get to him first?

In a paroxysm of hurt and rage, Shazza loosed her arrows with an anguished cry. Godilai yowled in pain before yanking the missiles from her shoulder and thigh. She hurled them back at Shazza, who deflected them with the arms of her bow. Before the Dákun Daju could heal herself, Shazza loosed more arrows.

Realizing she was fighting a losing battle, Godilai took off at a full sprint. Kitfox snarled and took off after her. Thera, Shazza, and I didn't hesitate to follow.

"We have to catch her before she's able to do anything to Kkorian!" Shazza proclaimed and bolted ahead of everyone. Kitfox wasted no time transforming into his fox form to keep pace with her. I sent a prayer to the Gods to keep everyone safe as the two of them disappeared from view.

A few seconds later, a yellowish glow appeared ahead. Metallic clangs rang out and a pained howl followed. Recognizing the howl in a heartbeat, I rushed towards the light.

Stay back!

Thedrún's warning came too late. Thera and I rounded a corner and slammed into the backs of several soldiers who were struggling to fend off Shazza's enraged attacks. We all toppled to the ground in a disheveled mess. I fought against the weight and chaos of limbs to right myself and collect my war fans.

"I wouldn't do that if I were you." I froze at the sound of the familiar voice. Taking a shaky breath, I looked to my left to see Dimitri standing at the edge of the pool of light. He held Kitfox pinned to a stalagmite and rested a dagger against his throat. Dimitri sneered. "If you move, I will kill him."

To make sure I got the message, Dimitri slammed his knee into Kitfox's ribs. A yelp of pain echoed in the cavern and tore tears from my eyes. "Please don't hurt him! Please!"

"Good girl." Dimitri scoffed. He ordered his minions to tie me, Shazza, and Thera up. Once they had completed that task, Dimitri tossed Kitfox at me. The Fox Demon helplessly slumped to the ground with a whimper and remained still. As I watched the soldiers bind Kitfox, Dimitri squatted in front of me. "Where's the Dragon Diary?"

"I don't have it." I muttered. Dimitri snarled and slapped me so hard spots danced before my eyes. The copper taste of blood filled my mouth.

Dimitri made a disgusted sound and stood to his full height. He moved to stand above Kitfox and met me with a sneer. "One more time; where is it?"

"It's true! Xyleena-sortim doesn't have the diary!" Shazza shouted. Dimitri made a face and slammed his foot down on Kitfox's ribcage, tearing another pained howl from the Demon.

"Stop it!" I begged through my tears.

"Then tell me where the diary is!"

I bit my bottom lip and looked to Thera. The Feykin nodded and faced Dimitri defiantly. "If you want it, you will have to untie me."

Dimitri guffawed. "Do you really think I'm that stupid, girl?"

"You don't understand!" Thera cried. "My bag has a warding spell on it. Only Xyleena and I can reach into it, so if you want Dragon Diary, you will have to untie one of us!"

"Fine." The Shadow Keeper humphed. "Raythur, untie Xyleena." I gawked as the Magistrate of Vronan lurked out of the shadows to do as ordered.

No wonder I got a bad feeling around him! And I'll bet every single one of the soldiers taking commands from Dimitri are his.

"Make any move to attack and I will end this pathetic Demon's excuse of a life!" Dimitri stepped on Kitfox's already broken ribs and sneered smugly at the pained whimpers. I nodded in understanding. The moment I felt the ropes go slack, I reached for Thera's pack. After a minute of digging, I freed the diary and faced Dimitri.

"Please don't hurt Kitfox anymore."

The Shadow Keeper scoffed and stepped away from the injured Fox Demon. He tore the diary from my hands and turned his back to me. As he paged through the book, he ordered Raythur to retie me. When I tried to fight the ropes, the Magistrate slapped me soundly. Kitfox growled and wheezed.

"You have what you were after, now let us go!" Demanded Shazza. Dimitri looked at her and laughed.

"As if I'd do such a stupid thing." With that, drew his dual sword from the sheath on his back. He seemed to hesitate, then looked over his shoulder. "Godilai, would you like the first kill?"

The Dákun Daju stepped into my line of sight and glared at me. "I will let you kill her lover first." Godilai sneered. "I want to hear her beg to join him in death as I slowly wring the life from her."

Dimitri chuckled and nodded. "Very well. Pox?" Thera's younger sister quietly answered the summons and he tossed her Dragon Diary. "Get to work on translating that."

"Yes, Dimitri."

"Now then." The Shadow Keeper looked at me and moved to stand over Kitfox. He held his dual sword poised for a killing stroke.

Tears spilled forth as the Fox Demon's amber eyes locked with my dragon green ones. "Kitfox..."

"Die!" Dimitri brought his sword down in a flurry.

I screamed.

"You have already left a mark on this world that will last throughout the ages," the dragon I had named Felwind said to me. He was, of course, referring to my unleashing Demona unto Arcadia and letting her poison annihilate all life in the surrounding forests. Yes, that scar would be remembered forever.

– *FROM "THE DIARY OF AGASEI" BY AGASEI DÉDOS*

A gunshot split the air. Dimitri's sword slammed into the stone floor, narrowly missing Kitfox's flesh. The blade sang an eerie moan, cracked, and finally shattered. The Shadow Keeper swore venomously and looked at the source of the gunshot.

"You gave me your word that you wouldn't kill them!" I gasped in recognition of the voice and forced myself to look away from Kitfox. Kkorian stood at the edge of the pool of light; a smoking pistol in one hand and rapier in the other.

Dimitri scoffed. "Fool! I had no intention of letting anyone live!"

"K-Kkorian?" Shazza's voice was a mix of confusion, hurt, and rage. "Kkorian, you're in league with Dimitri?"

The pirate's eyes met hers for the briefest of moments before he was forced to look away. I watched as shame and anger washed over his features as tried to explain his actions. "At first, I did it because I desperately needed the money. Then--"

"Traitor!" Shazza's scream echoed in the cavern.

Kkorian winced and forced himself to look her in the eye. "Then I fell in love with you, Shazza!"

"I can't believe I trusted you!" The Dákun Daju Queen openly cried.

"Please, Shazza, hear me out."

"No!"

"I--"

"Go away!"

"Shazza..."

117

"This is fun." Dimitri smirked.

"Shut-up!" Kkorian pulled the trigger.

Dmitri roared at the searing pain in his shoulder and bolted for Kkorian. Before the pirate had any chance to react, he was sprawled out on the ground with several broken bones. The Shadow Keeper stole the pistol away and aimed for Kkorian's head.

"Last words?"

Kkorian coughed blood and winced as he chanced a glance at Shazza. The Dákun Daju Queen only glared at him angrily. Deflated, Kkorian looked Dimitri in the eye. "I hope Shazza rips you to shreds!"

Dimitri scoffed and glanced at her. "She's next."

"Don't kill him." The Shadow Keeper faltered at Shazza's words and glared at her. She defiantly returned the look. "I invoke the rights of Et Sleikur ni Sango."

I grimaced at her words. Though I didn't know what she truly meant by invoking 'The Dance of Blood', I knew it wasn't a good thing for anyone involved. "Do you really want to do that?"

Shazza did not answer me.

Godilai chuckled and knelt in front of the Royal Dákun Daju. "Has that pathetic Hume really dishonored you so?"

"Yes."

Godilai was quiet for a long moment as she stared into the other Dákun Daju's eyes. Finally, she smirked. "Then you will have his blood."

"Godilai?"

"It is her right, Dimitri." The Dákun Daju looked at him over her shoulder. "Would you dishonor her, a pure Dákun Daju, by denying such an invocation?"

Dimitri scowled. With a frustrated sigh, he threw the pistol away and slammed his foot in Kkorian's face, rendering the pirate unconscious. That done, he stepped away. "Very well. Et Sleikur ni Sango will be her final right. Once the pathetic pirate has bled out, she will follow. As will the others who make up Xyleena's team."

"I demand to do it with the Hume in full health."

"What?!" Dimitri and Godilai roared in unison.

Shazza growled. "You have injured him too much. I demand to have him able to at least defend himself, else the Dance will end too quickly to allow for him to completely pay for my dishonor."

Dimitri glared at Godilai. "Now what do we do with them?"

"Sir?" Dimitri's gaze settled on Magistrate Raythur as he stepped around me. "If I may be so bold to propose an idea."

"Speak."

"Lock them in the Arctic Prison until the pirate is well enough for the Dákun Daju to kill."

"I like that idea." Godilai smirked.

"Really?" Dimitri quirked an eyebrow at her.

"Commit them to the frozen misery that is the Arctic Prison until the blood right is fulfilled. That way, they can all watch their comrades kill each other before we kill them."

"All of them?" The Shadow Keeper crossed his arms as he looked at me.

Godilai nodded and stood. "No one has escaped from the Arctic Prison alive in the last five hundred years, Dimitri. I seriously doubt this pathetic bunch could break out."

"If that truly is your wish, consider it a portion of my wedding gift to you." Dimitri smirked and took her arm. "Raythur, see to it that these five are imprisoned in the Arctic Prison under the highest security."

"Yes, sir." The lavishly-dressed creep promptly barked orders to his men. Shazza, Thera and I were forced to our feet and I was shocked to see that Shazza went along almost willingly with the forced escort. Thera apparently agreed with the tactic, but followed the Dákun Daju Queen grudgingly. I lingered long enough to watch a soldier grab Kitfox by the scruff of the neck and carry him at arm's length.

Enraged at the treatment towards the Fox Demon, I bolted forward and kicked the soldier soundly in the groin. Before I knew it, I was tackled to the ground and beaten. As I felt the world start to slip away and my vision faded to black, I locked eyes with Kitfox.

Dimitri chuckled as he watched a group of the Magistrate's soldiers pummel his arch nemesis for her defiance. He had to admit it was great fun to see her reduced to nothing more than a bloody punching bag for the revenge of a single man. His laugh died away when he caught the look she shared with the Fox Demon before losing consciousness; they really were in love.

With their wedding a few hours away, Dimitri hoped Godilai would look at him in the same way. He also knew better than to expect it; she was a pure-blooded Dákun Daju after all. If ever she betrayed her love for him with a look like that, it would be the end of her for an enemy might possibly see fit to use the knowledge of her weakness to their advantage.

Dimitri sighed. The life of a Dákun Daju is never easy.

Once the soldiers felt Xyleena had been thoroughly punished for her defiance, they picked her up and carried her off with the others. Dimitri scoffed and escorted his lovely wife-to-be out of the labyrinth.

The group barely spoke as the descended from the mountain. Pox would occasionally mutter something in Kinös Elda, but Dimitri could never catch what. Upon glancing at the young Feykin, he realized she was absorbed in the pages of Dragon Diary and her effort to translate its contents.

He couldn't suppress the exuberant grin that stretched across his lips. He finally had Amorez's diary! With it, he could gather the last few keys to unlocking the Dragons' Gate and, at long last, take his revenge on the people of Ithnez.

"You look ridiculous with that grin, Dimitri." Godilai said flatly. He looked at her with a frown only to realize a playful light flickered in her cyan eyes. He chuckled and brought her hand to his lips for a quick kiss.

"I am in a festive mood."

"Yes." Godilai's gaze shifted to the Feykin for a moment. "We have finally succeeded in obtaining the diary and defeating our enemies. It seems our impending nuptials are blessed."

"Just think," Dimitri dared to lean in and nibble her earlobe before whispering, "by the time the moons rise tonight, we will be united as mates forever. And in the weeks that follow, we will rise as the new High King and Queen of Ithnez."

Bonfires raged. Drums boomed. Voices sang. An old, bent woman in traditional Dákun Daju garb undulated to the night symphony and occasionally ululated to the tempo. She swayed this way and that as if she had no spine. With each step she rattled the ornate skull totems that she held in each hand.

The beat changed and the voices died away. The old woman danced in dizzying spirals around the couple standing in the midst of everything. The closer she got to them, the harder she shook the totems until the rattling was as constant as the stars above.

Dimitri paid little attention to the antics of the bent woman as she danced around him and Godilai. He was too captivated by the beauty of his soon-to-be-wife in her wedding trousseau to notice anything else. Gone was the armor-clad, heartless warrior that she portrayed. In her place was a woman in a knee-length, white dress that was embellished with colorful beads and eagle feathers. She was absolutely stunning. Though he was dressed similarly, he doubted he looked half as good as she did.

The drum beat ended with an exciting flare. Dimitri was forced to look at the bent woman as she stood between him and Godilai. The old woman took his arm and raised it parallel with the ground. Then, speaking only in Kinös Elda, she set a skull totem in his hand and ran a sharp fingernail over the flesh of his wrist. Once his blood was flowing freely, she repeated the process with Godilai.

Dimitri locked eyes with Godilai and suppressed the urge to smile as the old woman tied their bleeding wrists together with an ornate sash. The ceremony complete, the old woman ululated and the drums boomed with a renewed frenzy.

Without warning, Godilai leaned in and kissed him passionately on the lips. When they finally parted to catch their breath, Dimitri met her aquamarine gaze. Seeing the sheer lust for him swimming in her expression, he led her away from the noisy crowd.

Two apparitions in white watched from afar as the newlyweds snuck away to privacy. The two looked at each other for a moment. The shorter of the two slowly nodded. They turned away from the festivities and disappeared into the night.

It has been exactly one hundred years since the day a man named Agasei rose up in defiance against the entire world. The descendants of High King Aadrian I have declared today a day of reminiscence. Today we honor the many men and women who lost their lives in the fight against the Tyrant King.

– FROM "THE CHRONICLES OF ITHNEZ, VOL. X" BY CILLA TAEN,
COURT HISTORIAN

A heartbeat; gentle, tremulous... echoing.
A breath of cold, stale air.
Feeling slowly returned to numb limbs.
Dark eyelashes flittered.
Dragon green eyes slowly slid open.
The world came back into focus.

I groaned and forced myself to sit up even though every muscle in my body protested. A burst of pain exploded behind my eyes and made me cry out. Clutching my head and ignoring the throbbing pain as best as I could, I took a look around.

I was on a small cot that had been chained to one of the three complete walls. Prayers, hatch marks, and obscene things had long ago been carved into the ageless stones. Adjacent to the cot was a small latrine and a sink with a tiny mirror. They all looked like they hadn't been cleaned in eons. Opposite the rudimentary bathroom was a frosty, metal gate that spanned floor to ceiling.

I shivered from the sheer chill in the air and decided some exercise was in order. The instant my bare feet touched the stone floor, I hissed at the biting cold. I slipped into the thin footwear that had been set out for me and hobbled over to the barred portcullis. Looking through the frost-covered bars, I realized my cell was in the middle of a long and narrow corridor. Several other barred antechambers branched off from that main line.

123

I sighed and muttered a curse when I realized I could see my breath. "Don't they believe in heat here?"

"Apparently not." Came a muttered reply. My heartbeat quickened at the voice and I eagerly peered through the bars of the cell in front of mine. Kitfox was lying flat on the cot and staring up at the frosted ceiling. He looked unhurt except for the heavy bandages that covered his otherwise bare chest.

"Are you okay?"

Kitfox shifted his position so he could look at me. He smiled warmly and nodded. "I'll be fine. I just need a few days to heal."

"I thought Dimitri broke your ribs."

He winced as he chuckled. "He did. But I heal much faster than Humes, so broken bones are nothing to worry about."

"So you say, Demon." I smiled in relief as Shazza's voice came from the cell to my immediate right.

"If not for the anti-magic ward that surrounds this place, I could have healed you in seconds." Thera's voice called from the cell left of Kitfox's.

"How nice of them to put all of us in adjacent cells." I muttered.

"Not all of us." Shazza corrected sharply. I gulped at the barely contained rage in her voice. "That traitorous Hume was locked up in another wing."

"I can't believe he sold us out to Dimitri." Uttered Thera.

Kitfox sighed. "I told you that he couldn't be trusted."

I heard Shazza punch the wall in her fury. "The next time I see him, he's dead!"

I sighed and sank to the floor. Hugging my knees to my chest, I listened as the others bad mouthed Kkorian for what he did. I couldn't deny the fact that I was angry at him as well, but something told me that the pirate had been left with no other alternative. After all, Dimitri was a dangerous and conniving man who stopped at nothing to get what he wanted.

What if Kkorian tried desperately to pull out of whatever contract he had forged with Dimitri, but the Shadow Keeper wouldn't allow it? I expected at least one the dragons to provide an answer to my thoughts, but all I got was silence. I brought my hand up to brush against the Amulet in hopes of rousing them from slumber only to find the talisman gone. In a panic, I tore apart my cell looking for it.

"What's wrong?"

"The Dragon's Eye Amulet is gone!"

"Just like the diary and all our hopes of stopping Dimitri." Kitfox resigned himself to misery and stared at the ceiling again.

"We don't need the diary to stop Dimitri."

"Yeah right, Thera." The Demon muttered.

"In case you've forgotten, the Riddle of the Twelve was written in that diary." Said Shazza. "We kind of need that to find the rest of the dragons."

"The riddle, yes. The diary, no." I detected a smugness in the Feykin's voice and laughed.

"You made a copy of the riddle, didn't you, Thera?"

"Sure did!"

Kitfox wheezed in pain as he laughed at the good news. "You're brilliant!"

"So what?" Shazza's dark tone deflated the jubilant mood in an instant. "We're still locked up in this place."

"We'll find a way out."

Shazza scoffed. "I doubt that. This is the Arctic Prison, after all. It's not like we can just walk out of here whenever we please."

"You sound like you know all about this place." I replied.

The Dákun Daju muttered something I didn't catch. "I was one of the commanders here before I ran for Queen of Katalania."

"How about you give us the run down on it?"

"Fine." She sighed. "Several millennia before the Earthic Landings, the Arctic Prison was built by the Dákun Daju to house our hardest criminals. It is contained within a gargantuan, extinct volcano on an uninhabitable island north of the freezing wastelands of the Southern Stretch.

"The prison itself is fifteen hundred levels high and houses over one million inmates at any given time. The guards are mostly pure-blooded Dákun Daju warriors and a few Hume enforcers. They all reside in the lower twenty levels and are only able to leave via the monthly supply ship, which is permitted to be docked here for two hours at most.

"When the supply ship is here, the entire prison goes into full lock-down mode. Every individual level is sealed with stone and metal gates and powerful talismans designed to instantly kill anyone who tries to open the gates. Armed guards are stationed on each level while the supplies are unloaded. The ship isn't allowed to leave until it has been thoroughly searched for stowaways and every supply crate is accounted for. The lock-down is only lifted once the supplies are stored away.

"There have been escape attempts in the past and only one succeeded. A notorious Dákun Daju Assassin named Solahnj somehow managed to sneak out of her cell before the full lock-down went into effect. She snuck aboard the supply ship and stowed away to freedom, taking a Hume, who was later identified as Agasei, with her. All other attempted escapees were slaughtered before they could make it to a level below their assigned cell.

"Do you understand why we wouldn't stand a chance at escaping now?"

Kitfox cleared his throat in the uncomfortable silence that followed. "So what you're saying is, we're screwed."

"Exactly."

"Do they have a collection room for prisoners' effects?"

Shazza scoffed at my inquiry, but answered that there was usually one on each level.

"I'm betting that is where my Amulet is. If we can get there and summon the dragons, we can make it out of this place."

"Have you not heard a word I said?"

"I heard you plain and clear." I rolled my eyes at her venomous tone. "But not once in your story did you mention eight dragons tearing the place up in the prisoners' mad dash to freedom."

Kitfox guffawed despite his broken ribs.

"She's got a point, Shazza." Chided Thera. "If we could fight our way to the inmate storage room and summon the dragons, we could break out of here with ease. Then, using my

126

copy of the Riddle of the Twelve, we can finish the quest and kick Dimitri's sorry ass!"

Shazza was stunned into silence.

I told Symbilla that I could not think straight; that so many things were on my mind that I could not sleep. She seemed to smile at me as she said, "Perhaps you are thinking too much, Prince. Rest your mind a while with a distraction." It is difficult to find a distraction during a time of war.

– FROM "CONVERSATIONS WITH DRAGONS" BY DJURDAK ZA'CAR

Over two weeks had passed since our arrival at the prison. The four of us spent the long days often in silence or quiet conversation about nothing in particular. We were biding our time and allowing wounds to heal before facing the battle for our escape.

Late last night, while the guards weren't around, we discussed the best course to take in our breakout. Thera had suggested running outside and flying a-dragonback away from the prison. Kitfox quickly shot that idea down, stating that without the proper gear to fend off the frigid temperatures, we would freeze to death in no time.

Remembering that Shazza had told us that the prison had been built out of an old volcano, I suggested the idea of escaping through the lava tubes that were sure to still exist. It was a dangerous idea, and one that might ultimately lead to being stuck underground for an unknown amount of time, but we all agreed it was the best course to take.

On this particularly freezing afternoon, as I watched Kitfox run through some exercises with nary a sign of pain, a deafening buzz exploded in the air. Ignoring the cold, I threw off the blanket I had been provided and rushed to the door of my cell. Three heavily armed, Dákun Daju men, who I recognized as the guards stationed on this floor, strode passed just as the alarm died away.

"What's going on?" I dared to ask.

"Lock-down." One answered gruffly. I nodded in understanding and returned to my cot to huddle up in my blanket again. My gaze fell on Kitfox as he stepped away from his cell door while tucking something away in the folds of his bandages. Sensing my gaze upon him, he winked at me and put his index finger to his lips in the universal sign to keep quiet. I nodded and he smiled coyly while pointing to the locking mechanism on the door of his cell.

I suddenly realized what he had done. He just lifted the key! I fought the overwhelming urge to cheer, electing instead to flash him a thumbs up and a cheesy grin.

"I don't think the alarm was loud enough." Kitfox and I both chuckled at Thera's disgruntled remark.

"It's nowhere near as loud as the dragons when they roar upon reconstitution."

Kitfox nodded vigorously. "No kidding. Every time they do that, it makes me want to rip off my ears!"

"Quiet down over there!" Ordered one of the guards.

"Sorry."

"All right, Jailbirds! Meal time!" A guard's hoarse shout yanked me from my dreamless slumber. I groggily sat up in my cot to watch as the guard stopped the meal cart in the middle of the hall. He removed a tray and stepped up to the gate of my cell. Balancing the platter with long-practice expertise, he reached for the keys to unlock the food slot. Realizing that they weren't on his belt, he swore.

"Something wrong?" He glared at me and returned the tray to the food cart.

"Hey, Vakaron! Did I lend you my keys again?"

"No."

"Did you forget them in your quarters?" Kitfox offered. He raised his hands in surrender when the guard shot him a dirty look. "I do it all the time."

The guard cursed again and walked away. "Vakaron, come with me. Ioré, stay here and cover for us."

"Sure thing, Ru."

I listened as a pair of footsteps receded down the hall. Once they had completely faded from earshot, Kitfox walked up to the bars of his cell. The Demon glanced at me, then at Shazza, before looking down the hall.

"Hey! Hey, you're name is Ioré, right?" A quiet 'yes' was the only answer. "Can you come here a second? I want to ask you something."

The guard sighed in irritation and walked into my view. He paused at the food cart and glowered at Kitfox. "What is it?"

Kitfox waved him closer. "C'mere and look at this a second and tell me if you know what it is."

Ioré hesitated.

"Oh! I know what you're talking about!" The guard looked at me over his shoulder. "When it's light's out and everything is dark, there's a weird glow at the base of the bars on his cell. We were wondering what it was, but no one was around to ask."

Kitfox easily followed me in the lie. "Yeah, and now that you're here, maybe you can tell us what it is."

"What glow are you talking about?"

"You probably can't see it now due to all of the light." Shazza mixed her two-bits into the lie. Ioré sighed and stepped closer to the cell door. He scoffed and knelt down to take a close look at the bars.

"I still don't see anything."

"Really? Too bad." In a move so fast that I couldn't follow, Kitfox reached through the bars of his cell, grabbed Ioré by his head, and jerked. There was a sickening crunch as the guard's neck snapped then Ioré fell limp in the Demon's grasp. With a low growl, Kitfox shoved the lifeless guard away before removing the stolen keys from the folds of his bandages.

Shazza praised Kitfox for his swiftness and cunning as the Demon unlocked his cell door. He slipped through without a sound and quickly unlocked my door, then Shazza's, and finally Thera's. Together, the four of us slipped quietly to the opposite end of the corridor where the guards usually kept themselves.

"Isn't it weird that we're the only prisoners on this level?" I muttered as Kitfox took a moment to try to find the right key to unlock the door.

Thera shrugged. "We're high-profile criminals, apparently."

Kitfox snorted and finally managed to unbolt the door. He jerked it open and we all quickly filed into the room before sealing it again. Without a moment's hesitation, the four of us began to scour the crate-leaden shelves for our belongings.

"Here!" Shazza called out and pulled four crates down from the top-most shelf. I dug through the bin with my name on it and sighed in relief when my fingers brushed against the Dragon's Eye Amulet. I hastily removed it from the box and slung it around my neck. I smiled as the familiar buzzing burst into existence in the back of my mind.

Xyleena! All eight dragons chorused the instant they felt my mind meld with theirs.

Are you alright, Hatchling?

What happened?

Where have you been?

There's no time to explain, I told them, but when I summon you, come out fighting!

They eagerly chorused an agreement to do just that. I thanked them and dumped the contents of the bin on the floor.

Kitfox politely turned his back to us women to allow a modicum of privacy while we stripped from our prison jumpsuits and donned our armor and battle gear as quickly as possible. I snuck a peek at the Fox Demon while he dressed, and found myself admiring the way his toned muscles rolled with every move he made. His tail wagged slightly, granting me a nice view of his tight buttocks before his trousers covered it. Heat rushed to my face and I forced myself to look away.

I heard Riptide snort in amusement. What are you so worked up about all of a sudden?

N-Nothing. The Dragon of Water made a sound like a laugh.

"Is everyone ready to do this?" Shazza asked as she finished lacing up her bracers. I took a deep breath to calm myself and nodded once.

"We can't turn back now, so we might as well just get it over with." Thera said as she clicked the last piece of her wing armor into place.

"In case we don't make it out of this together," Kitfox looked back at us with the most serious expression I've ever seen, "I just want you all to know that it's been an honor to live and fight at your side."

"Indeed it has, Kitfox-fratim." Shazza offered him her arm and the Demon grasped it firmly.

"May the Five Souls guide us, protect us, and offer us their strength." I said as I clapped both of them on the shoulder.

Thera walked calmly up to us, embraced us with her wings, and bowed her head. "Meo sortime, meo fratim, illam durus."

We lingered in the embrace, quietly praying for the safety of the others. Finally we broke apart and made our way to the door. Kitfox took a moment to listen for any sounds from the other side. Deeming it safe, he pushed the door open and led the way out.

The minute we were all in the hall, Ru and Vakaron stepped off the ramp that led to the level below. Both guards froze in complete shock upon realizing we had tricked them to escape. Before either guard was given the time to raise an alarm, Kitfox and Shazza burst forth and silently dispatched them.

"That was close." Kitfox muttered as we dragged the bodies away from the ramp. I nodded in agreement and watched as he ran his claws over one of the several ring-hilted daggers strapped to Vakaron's belt. The Fox Demon promptly removed a pair of the blade rings before slipping them over his wrists.

"Let's go." Shazza whispered and knocked two arrows. She took the lead as we made our way down the ramp. The five guards stationed on the level were quickly slaughtered. Some of the inmates thanked us for the deed and asked to be let out of their cells.

The four of us ignored their pleading cries for freedom and started for the next level down. Having heard the commotion of the inmates from the floor above, three guards had come to investigate. While we were occupied with them, another managed to get away long enough to raise the alarm. Shazza ended his existence with an arrow between the eyes.

The earsplitting buzz that signified the start of lock-down mode blared a moment after his dying cry went out. A heartbeat later, the floor seemed to swarm with guards and reinforced, stone doors slammed shut over the ramps leading between floors.

Get ready! My fingers brushed the jewels of the Dragon Eye Amulet and the familiar tingling sensation flowed into my fingertips. I thrust my hand in the air and shouted, "Kúskú!"

Mirror shards and silver dust exploded from the Amulet. Instead of collecting into the form of the silver dragon right away as expected, the fragments gathered around me in a protective aura. They hovered midair for a moment, then shot out at the stunned guards. Every one of the Dákun Daju were mowed down with a flourish of blood and anguished cries.

"Yeah!" Thera cheered as Kúskú finally solidified with a fearsome roar that rendered the inmate population utterly silent.

Kitfox laughed. "Remind me not to get on his bad side."

"Kúskú, are you able to break down this barricade?" Shazza pointed her thumb at the reinforced stone wall that blocked our route. The Dragon of Illusion studied the blockade for a moment before shaking his head.

"Summon Wildfire." He looked at me. "Her powers of fire will reduce this wall to rubble with little effort."

I brushed my fingers over the crimson jewel that marked the presence of the Dragon of Fire. I called her name as I thrust my hand into the air. In an instant fire exploded from the Eye, turning the frigid air warm and balmy. With a great roar that got the prisoners cheering in excitement, Wildfire took shape.

Kúskú explained to her what needed to be done. Wildfire took a moment to look at the blockade. Finally she nodded and took position to break it down.

"Stand back." Shazza quickly ducked out of the way while Wildfire went to work. The dragon opened her jaws and a red light flickered to life. In a second, the light formed a ball of untold power and Wildfire released it with a growl. In a blink, a massive explosion shook the floor and searing hot rubble was sent flying in all directions. The ruby dragon snorted and preceded us down the ramp to the next level.

The inmates erupted in cheers upon seeing Wildfire and Kúskú. The guards, on the other hand, ran away in a panic when they realized they didn't stand a chance against the dragons. And so, Kitfox, Shazza, Thera, and I passed through level after level of the prison without as much as a scratch.

We had made our way through so many floors that I lost count of them all. Hardly a guard attacked us, though there had been a few overly-dedicated individuals who tried to end our escape. A few had even apologized for imprisoning the Dragon Keeper and let us go with wishes of good health and long life. I found the well-wishes to be rather odd considering they came from Dákun Daju.

Wildfire blasted away another reinforced door and we moved on. This time the ramp was much longer than the others and emptied out into a gigantic, round room instead of another straight corridor. I took it as a sign that we were nearing the end of our rush to freedom and pushed onwards as the ramp spiraled to the ground.

Our advance came to a halt the second we reached ground level. An army of Dákun Daju warriors had been amassed against us, bearing their arms in a ferocious display of might. I swallowed the lump in my throat and took a step back, subconsciously brushing my fingers across the jewels of the Amulet.

134

A huge Dákun Daju woman in heavy armor took a step towards us. "Surrender now or die in misery."

"You will be the ones to die in misery if you dare to stand against us!" Wildfire snarled defiantly. When the Dákun Daju did not back down, Kúskú stepped in front of her. The Dragon of Illusion sunk into an offensive crouch and glared; eyes flashing white for a split second. "I'm warning you; please let us go before you all die."

"We are not afraid of you, Dragon." The Dákun Daju spat. "Surrender or forfeit your lives!"

"Last warning; please make way."

The Dákun Daju woman scoffed, unsheathed her bladed tonfas, and took up a fighting stance. Taking that as a 'no,' Kúskú threw his head back and released an eerie cry. The army of Dákun Daju surged towards us. Kúskú took to the air and hovered on shimmering wings as he glowered down at the army.

"Mind!" Thera gasped at the dragon-uttered word. "Breaker!!" With a great flap of his wings, a silver mist rushed forth to surround the Dákun Daju. Their advance on us came to an immediate stop as the fog left them blind. Slowly, waves of terrified screams erupted from their lips as they crumbled under Kúskú's spell.

Out of the mist came visions of likes I had never seen. Twisted beasts, giant insects, dismembered apparitions, and countless others tore the army of Dákun Daju warriors apart. I cringed and looked to Thera for an answer. "What is 'Mind Breaker'?"

"Kúskú's power of illusion allows him to see into people's souls and discover their greatest fears." The Feykin's violet eyes never left the terrible scene before her as she spoke. "With Mind Breaker, he is able to turn those fears into a reality and trap people in a hellish nightmare that eventually kills them."

"I really don't want to end up on the receiving end of that attack." Kitfox shivered. I couldn't have agreed more.

When the last Dákun Daju crumbled to the ground and the tendrils of the mist diffused into oblivion, Kúskú fluttered to the ground. The dragon snorted and shook his head sadly. He muttered something about wasted lives before sauntering away.

Kitfox and Shazza followed a heartbeat later. Thera and Wildfire took to the air, probably to circle the room in search for an escape route. I lingered on the end of the ramp, staring at the ocean of bodies that had once been proud warriors. I couldn't fight the tears that spilled from my eyes. I didn't want for them to die, especially like that.

Kitfox was suddenly beside me, wrapping me in a tight hug. I leaned into his embrace and buried my face in his chest. He rubbed my back affectionately and I took comfort in his presence.

We must have stood like that for several minutes before I finally calmed down. He whispered in my ear, "Are you okay now, Xy?"

"I think so." I said. I pulled back just enough to look into his amber eyes. His brow furrowed in concern and he brought a hand up to wipe away the last of my tears.

"You are too soft, Xyleena-sortim." Shazza muttered bitterly. Kitfox sent her a dirty look. "Well, it's true."

"Like her mother, Xyleena has always valued life in all its forms." Kúskú said. "You frown upon such a virtue because you are Dákun Daju and do not understand the heart of Humes."

Shazza frowned. "You are right; I don't understand why tears are wasted on an enemy."

"For the same reason they are spent on friends and family." Kitfox interjected. The Dákun Daju Queen quirked an eyebrow at him in confusion. "They teach us something and we feel the need to honor them for that."

"How does an enemy teach you anything except how to kill?" Shazza crossed her arms.

The Demon smirked coyly. "If you really want to know, you'll figure it out."

"Hey, guys, I hate to interrupt your argument," Thera called to us from the opposite side of the room, "but I think Wildfire and I found a lava tube!"

"Agree to disagree." I said, glancing between Kitfox and Shazza. They both sighed, nodded, and let the subject drop. That resolved, I took both of them by the hand and led them what I hoped would be our way out of the Arctic Prison.

I do not know what I am doing. I only hope that in the years and ages to come, the actions my team and I take will resonate and inspire future generations to take a stand against the injustices in the world for without protesting the evil, one is merely accepting it.

— FROM "THE DIARY OF AMOREZ" BY AMOREZ RENOAN

Dimitri cursed himself for not learning Pox's teleport spell and drove the wyvern on. They young Feykin had approached him two days after he and Godilai were mated, telling him that she had learned of the locations to the last four keys. Dimitri had quickly split up his team to gather the keys. That was nearly two weeks ago, and now he was in a mad rush to return to his wife's side in Bakari-Tokai.

He desperately hoped his team was already at the tavern that once belonged to Luna, and eagerly awaiting his arrival with the piece he had sought in the Ancient City. With the last four keys in his grasp, Dimitri could finally unlock the route to the Dragons' Gate and release the Shadow Dragons.

He urged the wyvern faster.

The beast bayed in protest at being driven so hard and began to slow.

Dimitri growled and leapt out of the saddle. He landed with a grunt, rolled to his feet, and took off in a full sprint. A smile constructed its way across his lips; running was much faster than relying on that stupid beast.

It was nearly midnight when Luna's Tavern finally came into view. A single window was lit, letting Dimitri know that he was not the only one that had returned. He stopped on the doorstep and took a moment to catch his breath. He pulled the door open.

The attack came faster than he expected. He was barely able to unsheathe his knife in time to block Godilai's blade. Dimitri smirked and watched as the angry light in her cyan eyes turned playful and loving. A moment's hesitation and he captured her lips in a fierce kiss.

Godilai pulled him inside. "About time you got here." She grumbled before pinning him to the wall to kiss him again.

"How long have you been waiting?"

"Three days." She whispered, tugging his tunic out of his pants and pulling it over his head.

"Anyone else back?" He mumbled against her neck and unfastened her armor. It fell to the floor with a clang and her blouse was soon to follow.

"Pox was here before me." She briefly captured his mouth with hers and tugged on his belt buckle. "The fat Hume hasn't returned."

"Why am I not surprised?"

Godilai smirked and backed away from her husband. She sent him a sultry look over her shoulder as she ascended the stairs to the private rooms above. Dimitri watched as her nearly nude form walked away in the shadows of moonlight. He chuckled, thanked the Gods, and followed.

The keys could wait a little longer.

Dimitri was awakened by a finger gently tracing a pattern over his abs. He smiled and cracked an eye open. Godilai's stark white hair filled his vision. He brought his arms up to catch her in an embrace and kissed the top of her head.

"Did you sleep well?" She asked as she propped herself up on an elbow to look at him.

"Much better than the last few weeks." He said and stretched. "How about you?"

"The same." She flashed him a smirk before resting her head on his chest again. Dimitri sighed in complete satisfaction and let his eyes drift shut.

Dimitri was jolted from his nap as a loud bang vibrated the tavern walls. Godilai growled in annoyance and peeled herself off his chest to listen. Dimitri listened too, but all he could make out was mumbling voices from the floor below.

Godilai threw the blankets off and rolled out of bed. "The fat Hume has returned." She said as she tossed some clothes on the bed.

"About time!" The two of them dressed quickly and practically ran from the room. Godilai leaped over the banister and landed silently by Pox on the floor below. Dimitri chuckled and did likewise, landing right behind Vincent. The old Judge almost died of a heart attack as a result.

"Don't do that to me, Dimitri!" Vincent shouted. Godilai smacked the old man in the back of the head.

"Silence yourself, fool."

"Where's the key?" Demanded Dimitri. The old Judge held up a roll of parchment and it was promptly snatched from his grasp. Dimitri unfurled it, scanned over the runic writing, and handed it to Pox for translation. A moment later, the key he had collected was turned over as well.

The young Feykin mumbled something in Kinös Elda as she turned away. She walked to the bar and spread out both diaries and the four keys and promptly went to work. Dimitri fought the urge to bounce around in supreme happiness as he awaited the results.

Several minutes passed before Pox turned around to face her teammates. Dimitri held his breath as she began to read the twelve translated keys.

The Greatest Secret lies;
Just beyond human eyes;
On an isle moving by day;
Above a small world, dusted and gray;
Guarded by dragons from days of old;

140

Forever locked behind Immortal gold;
Twelve forgotten dragons share their Keeper's fate;
Awaiting their freedom from that dreaded Dragons' Gate.

Dimitri was stunned. "That's it?"

Pox nodded.

"Well, that was amazingly unhelpful." Godilai muttered and crossed her arms. "Now what?"

"There has to be something more to that poem." Vincent rushed to the counter to look everything over himself.

Pox sighed and pushed the hair from her eyes. "Let's think this over calmly." Dimitri and Godilai shot her a dirty look. "'The Greatest Secret' is obviously referring to the hiding spot of the Gate. 'Beyond human eyes' must mean that the Gate is out of sight of everyone. No surprises there. 'On an isle moving by day' is the first part that doesn't make sense. How does an island move?"

Godilai snapped her fingers. "Bedeb's rings!"

"What?"

"Think about it! The rings are made up of chunks of rock that look like small, grey islands."

"And they are in constant motion around Bedeb!" Dimitri laughed. "Godilai, you are brilliant!"

"Okay. So the Gate is on one of the millions of chunks of rock that make up Bedeb's rings." Vincent huffed and nodded. "I'm just wondering, how in the names of the Five Souls are we supposed to survive up there long enough to find out which one? Last I heard, there's no air to breathe up there."

"I have a spell that should take care of that." Replied Pox. "It creates a bubble of air that lasts about an hour. I used to employ it when I searched riverbeds around Thorna for oysters."

Vincent rolled his eyes. "Okay. Then how do you propose we find the exact location of the Gate? I can assure you, Dimitri doesn't want to spend a long time searching and neither do I!"

"The poem has to be referencing the exact location of the Dragons' Gate," Dimitri moved around the bar to take a look for himself, "otherwise Amorez wouldn't have written it."

Pox looked at her hand-written translation. "'Guarded by dragons from days of old' could be referring to the black marble statues."

"Or it could mean that Amorez's dragons are guarding the Gate." Dimitri muttered as he paged through Amorez's diary in tandem with his father's.

"Was 'Immortal gold' really written in majuscule like that before you translated it?" Godilai asked as she pointed to the words in Pox's translation. The Feykin took a moment to double check before nodding affirmative. "I wonder what that could be referring to."

"This, perhaps." Dimitri tapped a page in his father's diary and grinned. He flipped the diary around for his teammates to see and all three of them leaned in. There was only one thing written on the ancient parchment and it had been scribed in thick, gold letters that shimmered in the varying light.

Pox chuckled. "Immortal."

"Interesting." Godilai moved back and looked Dimitri in the eye. "How do we get behind this gold 'Immortal'?"

Pox promptly snatched the diary from the counter. Cradling the book in one hand, she tapped her finger over the gilded word. "Infé!"

Light exploded all around Dimitri and his team. A terrified scream ripped the air as an overpowering pull sucked them up. The blinding glow slowly retracted back to the depths of the ancient page from whence it came. The diary of Agasei seemed to hang in the air for a long moment before falling to the floor with a thump.

Dimitri's team was gone.

The four of them collapsed in a jumbled heap and the air was immediately stolen from their lungs. Pox held her breath and somehow managed to roll out from under everyone. With the little air she had left, she cast a spell. Semi-transparent, blue spheres instantaneously surrounded each of them. Pox took a few deep breaths before checking on the others.

Dimitri gasped and savored the air that Pox's spell had supplied. When he was finally able to breathe normally, he shoved the fat, old Judge off of him and got to his feet. He checked that Godilai was alright before taking a look around.

A gray and lifeless desert stretched out all around them. Rocks and craters dotted the surface, providing the most miniscule of landmarks with which to navigate. Overhead, a million stars shimmered in the perpetual blackness around the sapphire and emerald jewel that was Bedeb. The planet slowly turned in the void of space and its rings were obliged to follow.

"What a view!"

Dimitri silently agreed with Vincent; the view truly was magnificent. But he had not come here to admire the spectacle. The Dragons' Gate was nearby and they had to reach it before Pox's spell wore out.

"Let's go." Dimitri walked away. Godilai followed promptly. Pox drew an X on the ground with the toe of her shoe before going after the duo.

"Go where, exactly?" Vincent didn't receive an answer. Grumbling, the old Judge got to his feet and scuttled after Dimitri and the others.

The quartet trudged on in silence for a few minutes before the gray desert started to look familiar. Then Pox pointed out the X she had put in the regolith. Dimitri swore and looked around again.

"Pox, how much time do we have before the air runs out of these bubbles?"

The Feykin shrugged. "I can't say for sure because it varies depending on how quickly different people breathe. But, if I had to guess, there's maybe ten minutes more at most."

"Can they be recast if needed?" Godilai frowned.

"Yes, but," Pox took a moment to consider something, "I can maybe use the spell on all of us two more times before my strength is dangerously depleted."

"Let's hope that it doesn't take that long to find the Gate." Muttered Dimitri.

"I expected it to be close to this spot, where we were warped in, but I didn't see it."

"Me neither."

Vincent suddenly guffawed, earning everyone's attention. Godilai threatened him with a painful and slow death if he didn't explain himself. The Judge grinned stupidly and pointed a sausage-shaped finger straight up. "Look."

The Dákun Daju grumbled something and cast her gaze skywards. She promptly went silent, and then shot Vincent a death glare. Dimitri and Pox eagerly looked towards the heavens.

Floating in the void just overhead was an ageless archway craft in the old gothic style. A wrought iron gate filled the space between the cracking stones and a dragon skull lantern was fastened just under the keystone. It all sat atop a small, cobblestone platform and chunks of rock formed a simple stairway down to the surface of the desert.

Dimitri clapped Vincent on the back and sprinted towards the first step. Godilai and Pox were right on his heels as they leapt between the hovering rocks, steadily making their way up to the Gate. Vincent huffed and puffed as he tried to keep pace with the others.

The moment Dimitri landed on the cobblestone platform, the eyes of the dragon skull lantern burst to life with a red light. Dimitri took a deep breath to calm himself, reached out to grasp one of the handles, and gave a tug.

The portal did not budge.

He tried pushing.

The Dragons' Gate remained sealed.

Dimitri gave the handle another good yank. When that still didn't work, he looked back at his teammates. "Now what?"

"Infé!" Exclaimed Pox. Dimitri's heart skipped a beat when a loud clang followed. He turned back to the Gate and watched as the doors slowly folded inwards with noisy wails. A red light spilled forth from within, washing Dimitri in its aura.

The Shadow Keeper shoved the doors all the way open and took a few brave steps beyond the Gate. He gawked at the scene in front of him. A blood red sky cast an eerie light over black-sand that seemed to stretch onwards to eternity. Twelve huge dragons were curled up in the hot sand and Dimitri's gaze lingered on each one.

Dark scales, though as hard as diamond, betrayed scars from battles long since history. They glimmered in the unnatural light, giving Dimitri a glimpse at their true colors; blue, red, violet, green, black. Three of the dragons were strangely void of this armor; they were nothing more than mere skeletons. If not for their glowing, yellow eyes, Dimitri would have thought they had died and rotted.

The twelve magnificent beasts slowly awoke from their centuries of slumber. They rose to all fours, shook the sand from their frames, and stretched their long-unused limbs. Twelve pairs of piercing, yellow eyes settled on Dimitri as he took a few more steps onto the sands.

The largest of the Shadow Dragons snarled and smashed his bladed tail into the ground right in front of Dimitri. The Shadow Keeper reeled at the unexpected attack and landed hard in the sand. "Name yourself!"

Dimitri licked his dry lips and calmly took a breath. "I am Dimitri DéDos, son of your creator, Agasei."

The charcoal- and ruby-scaled Shadow Dragon looked at the tiny man before him with a hungry look in his eyes. Finally coming to a conclusion about something, the dragon snorted and retracted his tail. A moment later, a hunk of metal on a short chain dropped to the sands before Dimitri. "I am called Hyperion of the Apocalypse. That is the Amulet of Shadows. With it, you will be able to summon me and my kin."

"It is an honor to finally meet you, Hyperion." Dimitri couldn't stop grinning as he retrieved the Amulet from the sands. He got a better look at the ancient talisman as he dusted it off. It was an ellipse that teetered to a point at one end. In the middle, amidst many rare gems and gold, was a large, round jewel. Several colors seemed to swirl within its depths.

145

"Put it on, Dimitri." Godilai said softly as she finally ventured through the Gate to stand at his side. When her husband didn't oblige right away, she gently took it from him and did the honors herself. Dimitri shuddered at the overwhelming power that washed over him.

Hyperion snorted and turned to face the other eleven dragons as they gathered around. "Brothers, Sisters, meet our new Keeper!"

The Shadow Dragons roared.

Asking me 'why do you fight?' is like me asking you, 'why do you breathe?'. It is a necessity. I fight for my family, my friends, and my entire world because if I don't, who will?

– *FROM "CONVERSATIONS WITH AMOREZ" BY DJURDAK ZA'CAR*

Time had passed. How much, I really couldn't say for there were no glimpses of sunlight or moonlight in this never-ending tunnel. All I knew was the hunger pain in my stomach was slowly driving me insane. If I didn't get something to eat soon, I was going to take a bite out of dragon hide!

The dragons all snorted in amusement at that.

Of course you think it's funny! I pouted. Your hides are impenetrable by any weapon except the talons and teeth of other dragons.

And yet you wish to eat us! Helios laughed.

What do you expect? It feels like it's been days since I've eaten something. I'm starving!

You have only been in that lava tube for two days, Xyleena. Came Thedrún's bemused reply.

I grimaced. Two days?!

Kitfox's chuckle diverted my attention from the dragons. He faced me with that cocky smirk of his. "You're making funny faces again."

"Darn dragons are picking on me because I'm hungry and said I was going to eat them."

I could tell from his expression that Kitfox was trying his hardest not to laugh. Unfortunately, he lost the battle with himself and his roaring laughter echoed off the basalt and obsidian walls. Thera and Shazza both looked back at him like he had gone completely mad.

"I think this tunnel is getting to the both of them." Muttered Shazza. Thera nodded earnestly in agreement.

"Hunger is getting to me." I corrected and my stomach growled for emphasis.

Thera nodded solemnly. "I know how you feel."

"Too bad Kkorian isn't here; we could have eaten him." I watched Shazza stiffen at Kitfox's mention of the pirate. I felt bad for her. Just when she had grown to care deeply about Kkorian, maybe even love him, he broke her heart with his betrayal. I couldn't help but wonder how she would deal with her pain.

"I for one am glad we left that pathetic Hume to rot in the Arctic Prison." The Dákun Daju muttered and I shuddered at her dark tone. "Besides, with his injuries, he'd just slow us down."

"Xy, do any of the dragons know where we are?" Asked Thera. I could tell from her expression that she was desperately attempting to change the subject of conversation.

"I'll ask."

You are underground. Vortex answered flatly. I rolled my eyes in annoyance.

Underground where, exactly?

In a lava tube. I wanted nothing more than to smack him soundly for stating the obvious.

Don't worry. Kkaia spoke up just in time to soothe my frustration. You will find food, rest, and shelter shortly.

There's a town nearby?

The Dragon of Earth chuckled. You could say something like that.

I relayed her message.

"Why am I not surprised that the dragons didn't provide an actual answer?" Kitfox growled. "Just once I'd like to hear them say something like, 'The city of blah is three clicks ahead.'"

The city of blah is three clicks ahead. Atoka echoed smugly. I bit my tongue to keep from laughing and Kitfox eyed me suspiciously.

"What did they say?" I shook my head and tried desperately to quelch my laughter. I failed and Kitfox pouted as my laughter rang out. "Are they being smart-alecks again?" I nodded vigorously. He scoffed, but smiled anyway. "Figures."

148

"I would love to eavesdrop on some of the conversations you have with the dragons." Thera chuckled.

"I wish there was a way for you to hear them." I said once I could speak without laughing. "They say some of the funniest stuff."

Good to know we amuse you so much. Said Wildfire with a snort. Unfortunately, there is no way for your friends to hear us unless we are released from the Eye.

That is not entirely accurate. Thedrún interjected.

"What do you mean it's not accurate?" I ignored the concerned looks of my three teammates as I spoke aloud.

Should you ever take a mate, he will be able to take part in our conversations like this. Your father, Djurdak, surprised us one day when he joined in our teasing of Amorez.

I remember that now. The strangest thing about that conversation was the fact that Djurdak was on the opposite side of the planet at the time. Added Helios.

I chuckled and relayed everything Thedrún and Helios had said. Thera muttered something about how lucky my mate would be while elbowing Kitfox in the ribs. The Fox Demon quirked an eyebrow at her before looking at me. I tried to ignore his stare by focusing on the tunnel's path.

After a few minutes, Kitfox sighed and gave up trying to gain my attention. Smiling sweetly, I slipped my hand into his and gave it a reassuring squeeze. I saw him smile out of the corner of my eye as he squeezed back.

The four of us trudged on in a silence broken only by Thera summoning another light orb when her other one winked out of existence. A few meters ahead, the lava tube we traversed forked into three. Each of those tunnels was much smaller and far more jagged than the one we were now in. Navigating any of them would prove a challenge.

"Why does there always have to be a fork in the road?" Shazza grumbled. She looked to me.

Go left. Kkaia directed. I nodded and led everyone down the left fork.

Is this still leading us to the city of blah?

Atoka laughed. I have no idea.

That's reassuring.

Kitfox and Shazza froze midstride simultaneously. Thera and I watched them carefully. Kitfox's ears stood erect and flared as he swiveled them in the direction of whatever sound he had picked up. He released a low warning growl and all of us drew our weapons in a flash.

You need not fear them. Said Kkaia. They will not harm you.

Who are 'They' exactly?

The Wakari, an ancient and peaceful race of underground dwellers.

I smiled as the memory of my meeting with Verdelite in Sendai replayed in my head. I folded my war fans and returned them to my belt. "Relax, everyone, and speak softly. Thera, please kill your light orb."

"You know what's out there?" Thera asked as she extinguished the orb. After a moment for our eyes to adjust to the dark, we noticed a pale blue glow emanating from the opposite end of the tunnel. It was slowly making its way towards us.

"The Wakari are coming."

"Wakari?" Shazza spat the name angrily and knocked a pair of arrows. Kitfox moved to stand right in front of the angry Dákun Daju, grasping both missiles so they could not be loosed.

"Don't attack, Shazza."

"I will do as I feel necessary, Demon." She hissed.

"Shazza, if you attack them without just cause, I will bring you to your knees with a single spell." I warned. She gawked at me for a long moment and finally lowered her bow with an exasperated growl.

I can't believe you got away with threatening a Dákun Daju like that. Kúskú laughed.

I said nothing and turned my attention to the azure light, watching in silence as it drew ever closer. It seemed like forever before the pale blue glow reached the portion of the tunnel the four of us were in. Once the light washed over us, its advancement came to a stop. It was raised slightly higher, highlighting several extremely short, stocky bodies.

We couldn't help but gawk at them and nineteen pairs of huge, onyx eyes stared back at us. Unruly, thick hair covered almost every inch of their pale blue skin. Some of them sported what appeared to be rock armor while others wore clothing similar to what would be found on the surface. Each outfit was accented with shimmering grey or yellow stones.

Three of the most ornately dressed Wakari before us were astride creatures of likes I've never seen. Each of the three creatures stood on six well-padded feet. A thick coat of shaggy, dark fur covered the entirety of their bodies. A strangely colored and curved horn protruded from atop their elongated heads and gave the impression of multiple pairs of eyes.

Finally, the female Wakari astride the biggest creature moved forward. She said something in a guttural language I couldn't recognize and thumped her fur-covered chest proudly. Her large, onyx eyes stared at me as she awaited a response. When none came, she tried again; this time in broken Kinös Elda.

"Me Breccia, Corundum Shaman." She proudly thumped her chest again, causing a soft but resonating boom. "Who you?"

I took a slow step towards Breccia and bowed. "Greetings, Breccia. I am Xyleena, Dragon Keeper of Light. These are my friends; Thera, Shazza, and Kitfox." I kept my voice low enough to not hurt their sensitive ears as I introduced everyone. My actions seemed to surprise every one the Wakari gathered before us.

"You know Wakari?"

I smiled and nodded. "I met a friendly Wakari who lived under the lights in the big blue. Her name is Verdelite. Do you know her?"

"Verdelite?" Breccia rubbed her chin in thought.

A small male holding one of the strange, blue light crystals spoke up. Breccia nodded in agreement with whatever he said and looked at me again.

"Long time Breccia no see Verdelite. Thought Great Stone take her." Breccia was quiet for a moment, as if considering something. "You from surface?" I nodded. "Why here?"

"We were captured by the Shadow Keeper," Thera explained, keeping her voice barely above a whisper. "And locked in the Arctic Prison. Our only way of escape was through a lava tube that led us to you."

Breccia nodded. "You here long time. Hungry? Thirsty?"

"Yes, we are, but we don't wish to trouble you with our presence." I replied. My empty stomach loudly protested and I blushed in embarrassment.

"No trouble. You come Seramahli. Eat. Rest."

Shazza scoffed. "We are in a hurry to reach the surface, Wakari. We don't have time to waste on you."

I winced at the harshness and volume of her voice and hissed at her to shut-up in Standard.

Breccia snorted. She pointed a clawed finger at Shazza. "Dákun Daju starve." Her fellow Wakari yipped softly. "Xyleena, Demon, Feykin join eat with Breccia."

"We thank you for your hospitality, Breccia, and apologize for the manners of our Dákun Daju comrade." Thera bowed her head to the Wakari Shaman. Without so much as another word, the Wakari turned and led us further into the depths of their underground world.

It was a long and treacherous journey through the tunnels, but the Wakari made the whole thing look easy. It came as no surprise, seeing as how they have spent years climbing over the jagged rocks and creeping through narrow tunnels. Even the creatures they rode – tetrapexes as I learned upon inquiry - were experts at traversing the hazardous subterranean roads.

By the time the route we followed leveled out to a relatively easy path, I was sweaty, sore, and thoroughly exhausted. I could hear Kitfox and Thera panting lightly beside me and knew they felt the same. Shazza, on the other hand, had been completely silent the entire journey. I glanced back at the Dákun Daju Queen to see how well she was holding up. Her orange eyes were burning with a barely contained rage, making me wonder just what had transpired between the Dákun Daju and Wakari to cause such hatred.

Long before the Earthic Landings, both races were at war with each other. Explained Kúskú. Over what, no Hume, Demon, or Feykin is sure, but the war was never officially ended and much of the hostility between them remains.

I'm surprised Shazza hasn't attacked them or vice versa. Helios added.

You dragons sure know quite a lot about this world considering you weren't out in it that long.

Everything we know is the accumulation of knowledge from our creators: Amorez, Thernu, Moonwhisperer, Artimista, Freya, and Djurdak. Said Kúskú. For instance; he paused as if considering something, did you know that Demons aren't a result of crossbreeding between races?

No. Then again, I've been told all anyone knows of the Demon race are rumors.

Helios chuckled lightly. The Demons are the original inhabitants of Bedeb and much of the current population on Ithnez today are the descendants of those warped over by Thernu during Amorez's Dragon Quest. Before then, there weren't any Demons anywhere on whole of Ithnez.

Before I could reply to the dragons, our Wakari escorts yipped excitedly and burst forward with surprising speed. I stood with my teammates and watched as the Wakari stopped at the mouth of a jagged cave and pointed. Worried that something might have happened to the path beyond, I rushed towards them.

The jagged cave mouth revealed a narrow stone pathway that led down into the depths of an immeasurably large cavern that must have served as a lava chamber at one time. A vast city of stone glowed with a cerulean aura in the depths of the cave. Once my eyes adjusted to the lack of light in the area, I could make out intricate and winding passageways for walking as well as running water. Countless stone domes of various sizes were nestled between the paths and rock formations. Several unbelievably tall pillars disappeared into the never-ending darkness overhead.

"This Seramahli. Home of Corundum. Welcome." Without further explanation, Breccia led the way across the dangerous path to the city.

Once we stepped foot on more sturdy ground, we could actually gauge the subterranean city. Compared to Hume cities, Seramahli was very plain and simple. Bizarre, glowing crystals dotted the area, providing just enough light to see by, but nowhere near enough to harm Wakari vision. Every building was a rock dome resembling the ancient-style igloos still used in the barren fields of the Southern Stretch. Each edifice was about a quarter of the size of any Hume dwelling.

As we strode through the city to whatever destination Breccia had in mind, more and more Wakari took notice of us and followed. I was surprised to learn that they could move so quietly that nary a sound was heard.

After a long march, we found ourselves at one of the immeasurably high pillars that pierced the darkness overhead. Breccia dismounted her tetrapex and motioned to a doorway in the pillar.

"Breccia home."

It felt really weird being the center of so much attention. The Hume crowds of all the cities we've visited on the surface were nothing compared to the Wakari. It was as if the entirety of the subterranean city had shown up for the feast Breccia had had laid out for us in her vast dining hall.

And they all acted like toddlers! They climbed over each other for a closer look, then argued and cried about it. When they weren't doing that, they were trying to steal food from Breccia's table. She immediately put a halt to that. But her temper did nothing to sway the countless questions fired at us. The Wakari asked about the surface, the dragons, my quest, rocks and gemstones, and countless other topics. I tried my best to keep a cool temper and accommodate their almost endless curiosity, but it proved to be too much.

154

As if sensing my growing distress with the situation, Breccia banished every Wakari except her servants and guards from her dining hall. Once things had quieted down, I thanked her.

"Breccia sorry. They not like that. Curious. Overlanders no come Seramahli."

"So they've never seen people from the surface before?" Thera asked as she nibbled on one of the several tubers laid out before us.

"Only Rogue has. He under big blue long time."

I quirked an eyebrow at Breccia. "Rogue? Is that his name?"

"He Pyrex. Outcast Wakari." She waived her hand dismissively and ordered a servant to fill our cups.

"Pyrex?" Thera sounded as if she didn't believe what she had just heard. "Do you mean Pyrex Akregate?"

Breccia frowned. "You know?"

"My mother mentioned him a few times before."

"Who is he?" I inquired of Thera in Standard.

"Pyrex Akregate is the Alchemist who helped create the Shadow Dragons."

Kitfox almost choked on his food in surprise. "He's here? How can that be? It's been almost 500 years since the Shadow Dragons were created."

Thera asked Breccia of the out-casted Wakari's whereabouts. The Shaman snorted and muttered something to her servants in their guttural language. Thera pressed again for an answer.

"Outcast. No in city. Outside."

"How far?"

Breccia scratched her chin in thought. "Loud water." She pointed in the general direction.

"Is that the way to the surface?" asked Kitfox. "I don't know about you guys, but I'd kinda like to get out of here as soon as possible."

"No." I shook my head. "She said that's where Pyrex can be found."

"Why would we want to find him?"

"He might have information on the Shadow Dragons that we could use." Thera smirked.

"I never thought of that."

"Breccia, how do we get to the big blue?"

She met me with a bewildered look. "You no leave."

"Oh, no. We didn't mean this instant."

"No leave two waking."

Thera and I stared at her dumbfounded. "What?"

Breccia spoke to her servants again in her natural language and they meekly answered back. She sighed and tried to explain in Kinös Elda. "Next wake rest. Wake after you leave."

I looked sideways to Thera to see if she understood what the Wakari was trying to say. They Feykin shrugged.

Xyleena, Thedrún spoke up, The Wakari have a belief that every ninth day, called wakings due to the lack of a day-night cycle, is a day of rest and worship. Tomorrow must be their ninth day, so they are not going to let you leave until the day after.

I thanked Thedrún for the info and announced it to my teammates. Shazza swore loudly, earning a dirty look from Breccia and her guards.

"Breccia," my summons tore their attention away from the Dákun Daju. "will we be allowed to visit Pyrex next wake, or will we need to wait?"

She frowned. "Why visit Rogue?"

"He may have some information that we can use in our battle." Thera explained.

The Wakari was silent while she thought things over. Finally, she nodded. "Wakari no allowed. Overlander ok."

It was several hours after the feast before sleeping arrangements had been made for us. It came as no surprise that the Wakari didn't have any spare rooms for Overlander visitors, so they had amassed to sing a larger dome from rocks on the outskirts of Seramahli.

As I laid down on one of the many wool blankets provided, I couldn't help but think about what Dimitri was up to. Had he managed to find the Shadow Dragons while we were in the Arctic Prison? And, if so, what were we in for when we finally made it to the surface?

Rest, Hatchling. Do not trouble yourself with such dark thoughts. Came Vortex's gentle reply.

I sighed and snuggled into to Kitfox's warm embrace as he lay down beside me.

It had been a chance meeting; coming face-to-face with the Dákun Daju named Solahnj. She had been thrown into the cell directly across from mine. What she had done to end up in the Arctic Prison was beyond me, and she never spoke of it. But I was eternally grateful that, when she managed to break out, she took me with.

— FROM "THE DIARY OF AGASEI" BY AGASEI DÉDOS

D imitri stifled a yawn. It had been three long days since he had freed the Shadow Dragons from the Gate. When he told the dragons of his plans for revenge, Hyperion insisted on some training beforehand. So Dimitri and his team had snuck out of Bakari-Tokai, to the foothills of the Eyes of the Ages so he could train.

The days and nights that followed had been harsh. Each Shadow Dragon had drilled him over and over, making sure he memorized everything from summoning and basic flight maneuvers to complex spells and battle tactics. Finally, Hyperion had deemed the new Keeper ready for the battle ahead.

Now Dimitri stared across the grassland at Bakari-Tokai snuggled in the dark of night. Thanks to his Dákun Daju vision, he could see every one of the city guards as they made their rounds. But it was what he couldn't see of the city that made him hesitate; reliant on his dragons' previous experience.

Hyperion stood behind him, watching silently; ready to fly in and aid his sister should the need arise. He had sent Nightshade of Shadow out ahead of everyone to do a little reconnaissance on the Hume city. Now, over an hour later, he was quickly growing impatient for her arrival.

Hyperion's attention on the city was averted when a soft whistle on the wind passed overhead. A moment later, something big and heavy slammed into the ground a few meters away. Naturally, Dimitri's team reacted to the event quickly. They gathered their weapons and prepared to battle the unseen creature that had roused them from slumber.

"It is only me." As she spoke, a portion of darkness shimmered, revealing the plum- and navy-scaled dragon known as Nightshade.

Dimitri watched as the Dragon of Shadow settled on her haunches. "Well?"

"The Humes have modified the city since we razed it five centuries ago." Replied the dragon.

"Is that a problem?" Godilai asked as she took her place at Dimitri's side.

Nightshade snorted. "Even with their improved defenses, taking the Grand Capital will be easy."

Dimitri tried to suppress his growing excitement as he looked to Hyperion. "When do we attack?"

"Under the cover of absolute dark, when the last moon has set."

Dimitri's crimson gaze settled on the moons. Only two of the three were out at this time of night and the smaller of them was about to set. That only left the biggest of the three, the full-phase Noralani, with a few hours in the sky.

Dimitri sat and resigned himself to wait.

"It is time."

Dimitri's eyes slammed open. A quick glance towards the horizon verified Hyperion's words. A mere sliver of the moon remained above the horizon. By the time he and his team geared up and reached Bakari-Tokai, the dark would be absolute.

"It will be less than an hour before Rishai begins to break the horizon." Announced Nightshade. Dimitri frowned as he got to his feet.

"Will that be enough time to take the city?"

Hyperion chuckled darkly. "More than enough."

"I'll get Pox and the fat Hume ready." Godilai said as she strode away. Dimitri watched her for barely a moment before starting the task of affixing Hyperion with the riding saddle he had altered from wyvern use.

"While you meditated, we dragons developed an attack strategy." Dimitri nodded in understanding as he ducked under the dragon's chest to tighten the leather straps. Hyperion continued, "We will circle the city and attack from twelve points, culminating at the Grand Palace. Once there, we dragons will fend off any attackers while you find and kill the King. With his death, Bakari-Tokai will be yours."

Dimitri grinned as he thumped Hyperion's neck, signaling the saddle was in place. The Dragon of Apocalypse crouched low enough to allow his Keeper to climb up. Dimitri glanced over at his three teammates as he hauled himself onto the dragon's back. All of them were packed up and lashing themselves to the saddles astride Nightshade, Inferno, and Maelstrom.

The eight riderless dragons sauntered up to stand beside Hyperion in an arc. They stretched their limbs in preparation and waited. When Dimitri finished lashing the last strap around his legs, he looked back at his team, then at each dragon. Everyone was eager for his next command. He thumped Hyperion's neck and the dragon stretched his wings to their fullest.

Dimitri settled his gaze on the city ahead and exhaled slowly. He raised his right fist over his head. The dragons crouched low. He brought his fist down. The dragons sprang forward as if one body. All twelve dragons took to the air in an impressive formation. A moment later, they broke apart from each other to circle Bakari-Tokai. They would be upon the city in mere seconds.

Dimitri felt the presence of each dragon pulling on him in twelve different directions. They weren't quite in position yet, so he ordered Hyperion to hold back. The dragon obliged, hovering just far enough away from the city walls to remain unseen. One by one, the Shadow Dragons reached their positions and mentally sounded off.

Let's go! Hyperion's voice boomed in Dimitri's mind so loud he covered his ears by reflex. The great dragon surged forward at breakneck speed, flying low enough that when he

160

passed over the outer wall of the city, his wings cut the guards clean in half. Seconds later, Hyperion loosed a huge energy ball on the unsuspecting city.

Twelve explosions rocked Bakari-Tokai simultaneously.

Dimitri yanked his sword from the remains of the guard and shoved the ornate doors open. He passed over the threshold and paused as he met the King's cool, sepia gaze. The old man was still dressed in his sleeping robes, yet he looked impressive and proud as he sat on the throne.

Dimitri scoffed and finally approached him. "Well, if it isn't Djurdak Za'Car V. How nice of you to meet with me on such short notice."

The King did not move. "You must be Agasei."

"Not quite. I am his son, Dimitri."

"I wasn't aware he had an heir." Djurdak rose regally from the throne, causing Dimitri to flinch. The King smirked at the reaction before turning and taking a few strides to a table leaden with goblets and wine canisters. As he poured himself a drink, he looked Dimitri over. "I heard stories of a man resembling my son attacking the Temple of Five Souls and chasing a girl all over the world. That man also murdered my son and my mother." Djurdak eyed the Shadow Keeper over the lip of the goblet. "I take it you are he?"

Dimitri watched as the King took a long drink. "You are correct."

"Then I am the last of my bloodline." Djurdak gently set the goblet down. He sighed and looked away from Dimitri as three new warriors entered the throne room. "Ah, Vincent DuCayne. So you are the one who turned against my son and led him to his demise."

"What are you waiting for, Dimitri?" Vincent spat as he glared at the King. "Kill him and take control."

"There is nothing wrong with granting an old man one last pleasure before sending him to Havel."

Djurdak chuckled at Dimitri's words, stealing the attention of all in the room. "How civil of you." He took a moment to glance out the window. The first rays of morning had come at last, but it wouldn't be a cheery day. Thick, grey clouds had consumed the sky, threatening rain. Djurdak smiled gently as the first rumble of thunder echoed in the distance. "You may have your victory today, Dimitri," he met the Shadow Keeper's gaze and held it, "but it will not last. Surely as the suns set, so will your reign over this world. She will defeat you."

A scowl consumed Dimitri's features. With an enraged roar, he launched himself across the room. A flash of steel and Djurdak was no more. The Shadow Keeper faced his team as Godilai stopped the King's rolling head with her boot. Her cyan gaze looked up from the head to meet her mate's furious glare.

Dimitri sheathed his sword. "Go with Pox to the Arctic Prison. Make sure she is still there."

Godilai nodded. Pox quickly gripped the Dákun Daju's arm and uttered her teleportation spell. In a flash of light, the two girls were gone. Dimitri glanced at Vincent before striding out of the room. The old Judge looked down at the beheaded Djurdak. With a smirk, he turned and scuttled after his new King.

The twelve Shadow Dragons greeted their Keeper as he entered the palace courtyard. He glanced at each one to make sure there were no injuries. As expected, each dragon hide was flawless. Dimitri smirked and turned his attention to the guards and civilians that had been captured.

"Your beloved Djurdak is dead." He watched in delight as the faces of those present grew distraught or vengeful. "Those of you who oppose me as your new High King will join him in Havel."

Slowly, most of those gathered fell to their knees and wept. Only a few dozen stood defiant, glaring at the Shadow Keeper and muttering curses. Dimitri smirked and waved for his dragons to take care of the problem.

"Taimat." Hyperion gave room for the skeletal dragon as he jumped down from the wall around the courtyard. Dimitri watched in interest as Taimat looked at each one of the men and women still standing. With a snort, the undead dragon flicked his tail at them.

"Soul Collapse!" A red aura engulfed each person the dragon selected. En masse, the few dozen slumped to the ground and were no more. Those still kneeling cried even harder.

"That is what will happen to you should you defy the will of High King Dimitri!" Vincent bellowed over the wails.

"In a moment, they will not be able to." Said Hyperion. Dimitri looked up at the dragon in time to see his eyes flash red. A few moments later, the crying of those gathered died away.

"What did you do, Hyperion?"

The dragon looked down at his Keeper. "I simply made them your loyal servants."

"Mind control." Vincent nodded in approval. "Try it out, Dimitri."

"There you are!" Dimitri turned to the voice as Godilai and Pox jogged out of the palace. The look in their eyes told him something was amiss.

"What did you find out?"

"That wretch, Xyleena, and her entire team managed to break out of the Arctic Prison!" Godilai shouted. "They even slaughtered the army of Dákun Daju guards stationed there!"

"What?!" Vincent exploded. "I thought you said no one could escape from that prison!"

"Under normal circumstances, they can't." Pox said quietly. "But the prison doesn't have wards against dragon use and we didn't take that into account."

Godilai locked eyes with her husband. "What do you propose we do about this, Dimitri?"

"Simple." The Shadow Keeper smirked. "Vincent, Pox, you two take one hundred of our new soldiers to the Ancient City to await Xyleena and her team." He paused while they nodded in understanding. "While you're at it, take a pair of the dragons of your choice with you."

"I request Nightshade." Pox said with a smile.

"I'll take Wyrd."

"Alright." Dimitri glanced at the dragons named long enough to see them nod in understanding. Then he turned to the hordes of soldiers still kneeling before him. "I need one hundred volunteers to go with my commanders to defeat our enemies!"

Everyone stood.

I awoke with a pounding headache. Unwilling to face a long day under such circumstances, I promptly buried my face in Kitfox's chest. He chuckled softly and held me tighter. Content and comfortable in his arms, I felt sleep begin to take me over again. That was, until a growing hum had us all scrambling to see what was going on.

As the four of us rushed out of the rock dome serving as our temporary lodging, we were greeted by the Wakari. They all seemed surprised to see us up so soon, but were delighted none-the-less. When asked about the humming, the Wakari said it was a song to appease their god. Some of them even invited us to join them in paying respects to the Great Stone. We respectfully declined.

Once the throng of Wakari was out of earshot, Thera turned to me. "What do you say we look for Pyrex now?"

"Why waste our time doing that when we can just leave?" grumbled Shazza.

I rubbed my temples and sighed. "Seeing as how we aren't allowed to leave today, I think digging up as much info on the Shadow Dragons is a good way to spend our time."

"You okay, Xy?"

"Just a headache."

"Probably from sleeping on a rock." Shazza muttered and crossed her arms. I rolled my eyes, trying not to let her foul mood affect me.

We will do our best to help soothe your headache, Hatchling. I thanked Vortex and turned my attention back to Thera.

"Do you remember which way Breccia said the 'loud water' was, Thera?" I quirked an eyebrow when she frowned and looked around the dark chasm that housed Seramahli.

"I can hear some pretty loud water from here." Kitfox pointed to his ears. "Do you think that's what Breccia was talking about?"

"No way to know until we take a look." Thera replied. "Lead the way."

Kitfox took a moment to get his bearings before taking off in a direction. Thankfully, he led us away from the countless throngs of Wakari making their way to what I suspected to be the Great Stone. We paused at the city's outskirts to summon a dim orb by which to see in the never-ending dark. Cautiously, as to avoid slipping on the sharp basalt and obsidian terrain, we moved on.

It felt like half the day had passed before our path came to an abrupt end and a great wall of jagged rock loomed in the dark before us. Kitfox stopped for a minute to listen before leading us around to a portion of where the rock wall had cracked, leaving a gaping scar big enough for even a dragon to slip through. Just beyond the entrance, the sound of rapids echoed in the dark.

Thera dropped her nearly-expired orb on the ground and lit another. The instant the light burst into existence, a horrible screech went out. A moment later, a second screech joined the first, then a third. We drew our weapons and rushed through the crack. None of us were expecting to see what lie before us.

A small, dome house sat next to a fast-flowing stream. Everywhere we looked miniature dragons in several colors looked back at us. Some of them were screeching in alarm. Others were hovering overhead as if waiting for an order to attack. Most stood guard over the house.

"Silentium!" Everything went eerily quiet in an instant. I looked at the entrance of the house to see a well-dressed, Wakari male standing there. A golden, miniature dragon sat proudly on his shoulder. Surprisingly, the Wakari had his thick mane combed and tied back. His obsidian eyes stared at us as he took a few confidant strides towards us, hammer drawn.

"Pyrex Akregate?"

The Wakari froze in his tracks and looked at Thera. "You are familiar to me, Feykin. Who are you and why are you here?" Unlike the other Wakari who spoke just above a whisper, this Wakari's voice was loud and clear. Thera hesitated to answer. The Wakari glowered. "Speak quickly or I'll have my homunculi tear into you."

"I am Thera;" the Feykin shook herself from her stupor, "Daughter of Thernu Onyx, Creator of the Dragons of Light. This," she pointed to me, "is Xyleena, Daughter of Amorez Renoan."

It was the Wakari's turn to be surprised. After a moment of gawking at us, he smiled and ordered the miniature dragons to stand down. "I am surprised to learn they left heirs. Now that I know who you are I shall tell you. I am indeed Pyrex Akregate, Last Alchemist in the world and Creator of the Dragons of Shadow."

"I can't believe it's really you." Thera whispered.

"Your homunculi," I paused to point out a few, "I've seen one before. They're sentinels, right?"

"Aye, that's what Moonwhisperer called them." Pyrex looked at the gold homunculus on his shoulder. "They were his idea, and he was never fond of the term homunculus."

"You created all of them?"

"These ones, yes, but the ones on Katalania, no. Those were Moonwhisperer's doing." Pyrex smiled. "These guys protect me from intruders and Jormandr, among other things."

"Who is Jormandr?"

Pyrex met Shazza's gaze with a frown. "I'm not surprised the others didn't warn you. Jormandr is the name of the Wakari-eater; a giant snake made of rock and clay."

The Deimos Clay that forms Jormandr is what bore Kkaia of Rock. Thedrún added quickly. I relayed the info to my teammates.

"Makes sense." Pyrex chuckled and leaned on his hammer. "I used the clay myself to form Kula, the Shadow Dragon of Earth."

"Hold on a second!" Thera exclaimed. She dared to take a few steps towards Pyrex. The Wakari stroked the head of his gold homunculus when it hissed in warning. "Did you also use a Magnathor Fang to make the Shadow Dragon of Water?"

"No. I used Titan's Breath to make Maelstrom. That was a fun mess to collect, let me tell you. You should have seen how furious Solahnj and Tryn-Tryn got during that ordeal." Pyrex laughed, lost in the memory for a moment. He suddenly shook his head as if to clear it. "So Amorez used Magnathor's Fang, huh? I'm impressed she managed to obtain one."

"So you and Moonwhisperer used different items to make the dragons?"

"Obviously, Feykin."

"How exactly were the dragons created, anyway?" Pyrex took a long moment to consider Kitfox's question. The Demon crossed his arms as he awaited an answer.

"That is a really long story." Pyrex replied carefully. "The quick and simple answer is: combine an elemental catalyst with an Elixir of Life. Toss in a homunculus, add the secret ingredient, and voila! "

I was dumbstruck. In fact, my entire team was shocked into silence by Pyrex's revelation. It all sounded so easy that I was surprised there weren't more dragons in the world.

It wasn't as easy as he makes it sound, Xyleena. Kúskú muttered.

Shazza was the first of us to break out of the stupor and speak. "You mean the dragons were just sentinels once upon a time?"

Pyrex nodded. "More or less."

"Hang on a second!" Thera threw her hands up to pause further questions. "You mean to tell me you and Moonwhisperer both created an Elixir of Life?"

The Wakari snorted. "I can't speak for Moonwhisperer, but I successfully made sixteen Elixirs. I took one myself while the other fifteen went to making the Shadow Dragons."

"Fifteen? What do you mean fifteen? There are only twelve."

"Currently, there are thirteen Shadow and eleven Light." Pyrex laughed at our stunned expressions so loudly his gold sentinel protested. "You see," he cleared his throat and reached up to soothe the homunculus, "during the final battle, the Dragons of Light managed to kill two of the Shadow Dragons, Adoramus of Light and Felwind of Chaos. On the other hand, the Shadow Dragons killed one of the Dragons of Light. Abaddon of Ghost, the thirteenth Shadow Dragon I mentioned before, defected to replace the fallen Light leaving both sides with twelve."

"You're kidding." Muttered Shazza.

No, everything he said was true. Affirmed Vortex.

Our fallen brother, Taypax, was the original Dragon of Death for our side before Abaddon absorbed his powers and took his place. Added Helios.

"I can tell by the look in your eyes that the dragons are speaking to you." Pyrex spoke softly. I forced myself to meet his knowing gaze.

Kitfox touched my shoulder. "Is it true?"

I nodded slowly. "Taypax... Taypax was the twelfth Dragon of Light." I shook my head. "That doesn't make any sense! I clearly remember Amorez saying Agasei made twelve dragons and then she made twelve to counter balance the others."

"I can tell you for certain that every history book in existence miswrote the information. Then again, they never did get the story directly from anyone who actually lived and breathed the whole ordeal. Are you sure it was really Amorez who told you that both sides started with twelve?" Pyrex crossed his arms smugly.

Kitfox shrugged. "If we still had the Dragon Diary, we might have been able to look through Amorez's own writing to see if that was really the case."

Pyrex balked. "You lost the diary?!"

"Dimitri, Agasei's heir, stole it from us." I muttered.

"Ay! Ay! Ay!" The Wakari rubbed his temples as he paced in circles. "That explains a lot."

"What are you talking about?" Shazza deadpanned.

Pyrex stopped pacing and flashed us a gloomy smile. "When I created the Dragons of Shadow, I attached a fraction of myself to each one so I would know exactly where they were at all times. When Amorez locked them away some 490 years ago, I completely stopped feeling them. Then, a few days ago, I was nearly bowled over as their presence broke free of the Dragons' Gate."

"That's just great." Muttered Kitfox. "How are we supposed to finish collecting the last four dragons when we have all twelve of the dark ones roaming the land?"

"You don't have all twelve Lights?"

"Long story." I said darkly.

Pyrex frowned. Minutes passed as he quietly watched while we fretted about our next course of action. "Tell you what. I still have some high-ranking friends amongst my kin. I will talk to them to see if they can persuade others to join in the battle against Agasei's heir."

I thanked him profusely.

"While I do that, you four take one of my homunculi and find the last four Dragons of Light. Once I have gathered the Wakari to aid you, I will find you by sensing my homunculus. Hopefully we can gather our strengths in time to prevent history from repeating itself."

"We would love to be on our way now, but your dense kin won't let us." Shazza huffed.

Pyrex rolled his eyes. "Why am I not surprised? Look, regardless what those peons said, Overlanders like you aren't

170

bound by Wakari laws. You can leave whenever without fear of any persecution. In fact, if you follow the stream that way, it will take you to the surface faster than any other route." He pointed to the portion of the tunnel where I guessed the stream's source would be found.

"Thank you again, Pyrex. You have been a tremendous help." I said as I jogged passed him to keep up with my three friends.

"No problem." He smiled. "Just remember to be careful out there. And take Visler with you!"

Just as my team and I reached the river tunnel, a silver sentinel landed gently on my shoulder. I chuckled as it chirped and curled its tail around my neck. I briefly turned to wave good-bye to Pyrex, sending a prayer to the Gods that it wouldn't be the last time I saw him.

Ingredients:
Water — 12,282 liters
Carbon — 7018 Kg
Ammonia — 1404 liters
Lime — 526 Kg
Phosphorus — 281 Kg
Salt — 8...

– FROM "A PAGE TORN FROM A SCIENCE LOG" BY UNKNOWN

My legs felt like lead. My back ached. My head was pounding. Yet I pushed on. It was all for my teammates, I told myself. They were all in a hurry to see daylight again. I couldn't blame them; I was eager get out of this underground misery myself. It was what awaited us once we escaped Wakari lands that I wasn't ready to face. I couldn't stop thinking about all the additional challenges we'd face now that the Shadow Dragons were on the rampage.

If you are careful, you may be able to slip under the Shadow Dragons' radar and collect the last four of our brethren without a confrontation.

I frowned. How do you propose I pull that off, Thedrún?

Avoid cities as much as possible, especially the larger ones. Use your magic to cloak yourself and teammates as often as possible.

You're forgetting: Dimitri has the Dragon Diary. He'll know where the last four dragons are hidden.

He can't risk covering them all at the same time, Hatchling. He doesn't have the man power for that.

Maybe not the man power, Vortex, but he certainly has the dragon power for it.

I doubt he would spread his forces so thin given you have eight dragons currently in your possession.

I shuddered as Riptide's cool presence washed over my mind. Dimitri would be a fool to send only a few of his precious Shadows into a battle against all eight of us at once.

"You alright, Xy?"

"Yeah, Shazza." I nodded as I glanced at the Dákun Daju. "Just talking to the dragons."

"They have any suggestions for us regarding the Shadow Dragons and their Keeper?"

I sighed and finally came to a stop. As I took a seat on the ground to rest, my teammates gathered around. I looked at each in turn before telling them what my dragons had told me.

Kitfox nodded. "It does make sense for Dimitri not to separate his dragons to attack us. However, it doesn't mean he doesn't have a plan to stop us somewhere along the way to our other four. My question is: how long can we hope he doesn't notice our absence from the Arctic Prison?"

"I'll bet half the Katalanian Treasury that he's already learned of our escape and is amassing his forces in one place to face us." Shazza grumbled and punched the ground so hard the rock cracked. The sentinel on my shoulder squawked in response. I was quick to soothe its anger with a gentle scratching under the chin.

"Well, if he's anything like his father, Dimitri will be gathering his forces in the Grand Capitol." Replied Thera. "And that would leave us free to sneak around to find the remaining dragons."

I doubt he'd be that stupid. Muttered Wildfire. Then again...

"His Dákun Daju friend seems to be the brains of their little outfit," Kitfox added as he leaned against the wall with a thoughtful frown, "and I don't think she'd be dumb enough let him miss a golden opportunity to defeat us once and for all. I think he is indeed gathering an army, but he won't just stand by while we continue gathering dragons. He has the advantage, and Godilai will force him to put it into play."

I sighed. "You have a good point."

"So," Thera looked me in the eye, "What do we do?"

173

Unfortunately, you can't stay underground. Came Kkaia's quiet reply. Though the Wakari territories are vast and their routes stretch far, they do not run the entirety of the world.

It is also extremely hazardous to your health being underground for weeks or months on end. Added Helios.

I nodded in agreement. Not to mention we won't be able to fly over the long distances and that is a huge time-saver.

Agreed. The dragons chorused.

"We have no choice." I said at last. "We have to return to the surface and try our hardest to remain hidden from Dimitri's forces."

My team agreed.

After our break, we redoubled our efforts to reach the surface as soon as possible. Unfortunately, the stone path that had run the length of the river so far was quickly vanishing. I took the narrowing of the path with a grain of salt, hoping that it meant we were getting close to our destination. Finally, we were forced to step off the path completely and brave the knee-deep waters as they rapidly sped into the depths of the Wakari lands.

Thera and Shazza both lost their footing more than once, but managed to catch themselves. I slipped a number of times myself, causing the silver-scaled sentinel on my shoulder to chirp in alarm. Thankfully, Kitfox was always there to catch me and help ease the homunculus.

"Ya know," grumbled Shazza as she caught herself from slipping again, "this is making me wonder how that little Wakari was able to get to the surface all on his own."

"I was starting to think the same thing." Kitfox muttered. He reached out to soothe the sentinel again when it squealed. "What is he so nervous about? You didn't slip that time."

I felt Kúskú's mind suddenly meld with mine. The little one is trying to tell us something. I don't know what language he is speaking though.

You mean he can talk to you even if you're in the Eye? I spared a glance at the sentinel as he shrieked again.

It would appear so.

That little one is annoying! I'm going to eat him if he doesn't stop shrieking. Snarled Wildfire.

Please tell him to speak slower, Xyleena. I can't hear what he's trying to say.

I'll try, Kkaia. "Visler, please calm down. Kkaia can't catch what you're trying to say."

"The dragons can hear him?" All three of my teammates were as taken back by that as I was.

Jormandr!

I covered my ears at the dragons' united mental shout and echoed their warning. We all stopped dead in our tracks. I heard it then; a low rumble in the distance, barely detectable over the rushing water. I looked into the eyes of my teammates and knew that they had heard it too.

In an instant, the four of us were running as fast as we dared on the treacherous river stones. In the darkness behind us, the low rumble grew ever louder. Jormandr was gaining on us. I quickly measured the size of the tunnel we were trapped in, coming to the conclusion that there wasn't room to summon a dragon here.

If the need arises, summon me. Said Kkaia. I can meld with the ground and hold Jormandr at bay to allow you time to escape.

You and Jormandr are one in the same, Kkaia! You share his power to become one with the earth. Wildfire exclaimed. Xyleena, summon me. Fire opposes earth.

There isn't any room for you to fit!

Their shouted argument momentarily distracted me and I slipped on a smooth stone. Visler leapt from my shoulder with a disgruntled squawk as my panicked cry echoed and I splashed headfirst into the rampant river. A mere moment later, I was yanked from the depths with an audible gasp.

Shazza took a quick look at me, frowned, and – despite my protests - literally tossed me to Kitfox a few paces ahead. I was amazed that he somehow managed to maintain a dead run and arrange me in his arms at the same time. Visler was able to catch up and flew overhead, chittering up a storm as if lecturing me.

"Use heal." At Kitfox's gentle demand, I quickly looked myself over. I realized my ankle had been sliced wide open by the smooth obsidian that lined the riverbed. Without further delay, I uttered the spell and watched as the wound vanished without a trace. Kitfox flashed me a smile as he increased his pace to keep up with Shazza.

Instead of simply sitting back and enjoying the ride, I quickly started casting wards all along the tunnel. I even coated each one of us in multiple layers of magic. Hopefully, they would work to conceal our presence from Jormandr.

A blinding light exploded into existence in front of us. Instead of stopping, Kitfox and Shazza seemed to sprint even faster. Thera whooped and quickly took flight to lead the way. Within seconds, we were engulfed in light and the cold, dark tunnel finally gave way to a warm, sunny day.

Here, we have come to die;
As we have lived,
So shall we lie.

– CARVED INTO THE PILLARS IN THE TWINS' LAIR BY ARTEMISTA
AND KADJ-ARAMIL

I sighed and tried to enjoy the sunshine before it was gone for the day. Visler chirped groggily and tried to bury his head under my arm; his way of wishing my teammates would be quiet. The three of them had been quarreling for over an hour now about the desperate need for supplies. Though they had developed quite a list, they had yet to agree on how to obtain everything safely from the village just over a league up the beach.

After we had escaped the seemingly endless underground tunnels, we had found ourselves by the ocean. Shazza had taken one look at the small fishing village nestled between the ocean and the thick forest and instantly recognized the place. We were back on Katalania, several leagues due west of Nemlex. And the village before us was called Sauqe.

"That's the problem though!" Shazza was practically shouting. I cracked an eye open to look at her as she glared at Kitfox. "We need these supplies or we won't have a chance at finding the next dragon let alone finishing this quest."

"It is too risky for us to go into the village to get supplies." Kitfox replied sternly. "If Dimitri has any forces stationed there, we'll be spotted."

Thera dared to step between them. "I wish you two would just allow me to handle it."

"You are just as conspicuous as me or Kitfox; if not more so with those wings of yours. What makes you think you can safely get in and out of Sauqe with everything we need?"

177

Thera smiled despite the hostility in the Dákun Daju's demeanor. "We Feykin have been blending in to Hume society for centuries. All it takes is a little magic."

All three of them looked to me to settle the debate. Kitfox's amber eyes teemed with worry while Shazza's sunburst orange ones betrayed nothing but frustration. Thera, on the other hand, looked confidant in the ability she could sneak in undetected. I sighed and allowed my eyes to drift shut again. Focusing my thoughts inward, I reached out to the dragons, feeling their existence within the amulet.

Do you think Thera can get everything needed for our journey safely?

Why not? Was Thedrún's simple reply.

Atoka stifled a yawn. If you don't think Thera is capable of doing what is needed by herself, summon Kúskú.

That would be best. After all, my illusions would allow me to walk with her unseen. I can offer extra protection and a means of rapid escape in case she is recognized.

Good point, Kúskú.

"Well? What do you think, Xy?"

I opened my eyes and got to my feet. I faced Thera as I dusted myself off. "I'm sending Kúskú in with you as back-up in case something goes wrong."

Kitfox balked. "You're sending a dragon into the village with her? I thought we were trying to be inconspicuous here, not alert everyone to our presence."

"Relax. No one except Thera will be able to see him." I brushed my fingers over the silver jewel on my amulet and called for Kúskú. Within seconds, the silver Dragon of Illusion stood amongst us. Visler squawked in alarm and hopped up on my shoulder to hiss at Kúskú. The dragon snorted in amusement and sat on his haunches to wait for Thera.

"Thank you for trusting me, Xyleena-sortim." She smiled and handed me a roll of parchment. "It's the copy of the Riddle of Twelve I told you about. While I'm off shopping, why don't you see if you can figure out the next clue?"

I nodded. "I'll see what I can do."

"Best hurry, Thera." Kúskú said gently. "Night draws nigh; it won't be safe."

The Feykin wasted no time coating herself with her spell. We all watched in amazement as her onyx wings vanished without a trace and her silver hair turned brown. Her violet eyes shifted to green and her Feykin tunic and pants became a simple dress. Once the transformation was complete, she turned a smile on Shazza. The Dákun Daju grumbled as she held the list of necessary supplies out.

"Just," Shazza barked as Thera gripped the list, "promise you will be careful."

Thera nodded and Shazza slowly relinquished the list. The Feykin looked up to meet Kúskú's gaze. His eyes flashed white for the briefest of seconds and then he waited. After a moment, he nodded and the duo began their trek towards Sauqe.

I glanced at Shazza over the edge of the parchment as she passed in front of me again. If she didn't stop pacing soon, she would wear a permanent path into the beach. I shook my head and looked over my shoulder-perched homunculus at Kitfox. He had taken to sitting in a spot beside me, but I could tell he was too tense to relax. His amber eyes barely blinked as he stared at Sauqe, looking for any sign that Thera was returning.

Truth be told, I was just as worried about Thera as Shazza and Kitfox. Instead of letting my fears eat at me, I focused my energies into the puzzle before me. Without out its distraction, I would have summoned my dragons and stormed the village in a mad rush to find the Feykin back when the first lanterns were lit to fend off the night.

Ignoring the festering worry of my comrades and the light snores of Visler, I started writing again. Thanks to Thera's notes at the bottom of the page combined with my previous knowledge of the translation, I had been able to convert most of the riddle from the Ancient Runes. I had only twelve lines left now.

I chose to read the Kinös Elda aloud slowly in hopes of distracting Shazza and Kitfox. "Symbilla et Illa-Arnaxu sornipé; Ten Sutétim isila con strujaz ni ponet."

Shazza froze mid-stride.

Kitfox's gaze finally broke away from the village only to settle on me. "What did you just say?"

"'Symbilla the Life-Bringer dreams; On Southern isle with golden streams.'" I smiled.

"Uh... 'Southern isle?'" Kitfox quirked an eyebrow. "There are only about twenty or thirty of those."

"Are you counting the Southern Stretch or just islands in the south?" Shazza crossed her arms as she muttered.

"Okay. Forty, then."

"No." I said quietly as I read the poem over to myself again. "I think 'Southern isle' is referring to an island that is actually a part of the Southern Stretch. Look at the capitalization of the runes."

Kitfox shot me a peeved look. "I can't read Kinös Elda in any form, Xy."

Shazza snorted. "The entirety of the Southern Stretch is made up of freezing cold islands of ice that will be plagued by winter storms this time of year. How are we supposed to find a dragon in that?"

"I need a map." I muttered.

"It's a good thing I grabbed one then, isn't it?"

I smiled at Thera's voice and looked sidelong, over my shoulder, to see her walking up the beach. Her hair and eyes had been restored to their natural colors and her wings were once again visible. Several bags hung from her arms as she carried boxes of varying size. Several more floated in the air behind her, suspended by a spell. Kúskú was a step behind her, leaden with even more supplies. Kitfox was on his feet in a second, running to help relieve Thera of her burden. Once everything had been dropped on the beach, I told Thera the clue while I searched for the map she spoke of.

"Symbilla of Life is our ninth dragon, huh?" Thera said thoughtfully as she dug through a bag. A moment later, she produced the map she had procured. I thanked her as I unrolled it on the sand and pinned the corners with stones.

"I think you're forgetting that that map isn't the one from Dragon Diary. It won't be bewitched to show you the places that we can't see." Shazza said as she started sorting the supplies.

"I'm not looking for something you can't see." I muttered as I studied the Southern Stretch depicted on the map.

"Then what are you looking for?"

"A memory."

"Great idea." Kúskú laughed. "She is trying to invoke a memory by staring at the map."

I zoned the four of them out as Kúskú continued to explain. When I felt I had memorized every detail of the Southern Stretch depicted before me, I let my eyes close. I breathed slowly as I pictured the map in my mind. When I had the image firmly in my head, I ran my fingers over every line, tracing every inch of each island both mentally and physically.

A hand suddenly grasped mine, jarring me from the mental vision I had built. I opened my eyes to see Kitfox staring at me in complete surprise. He slowly lowered his gaze to my fingers. I looked down with him. He had pinned my hand over a blank spot on the map just south of Súkatam and my finger was still pointing to it.

"Unbelievable." Shazza chuckled.

"Nicely done." Thera quickly marked the spot with a circle of magic.

I looked at the faces of my teammates and smiled. "Symbilla, here we come!"

The next morning, we woke before the suns. Kitfox and Shazza packed the gear on Atoka and Wildfire while Thera and I disguised our presence with several layers of magic. I only hoped it was enough to keep us safe.

Once everything was packed up and ready to go, we mounted the two dragons in pairs and took off. We flew straight south from Sauqe for three days before we reached the southernmost tip of Katalania. There, we rested before setting out over the open ocean and facing the bitter cold that awaited us the moment we passed over the Southern Stretch.

As the small town of Hinaa flew by below us, it felt like we had entered another world. Everything was stark white and lifeless. The never-ending cold, made worse by flying into frost biting winds, seeped deep into bones. Despite the roaring fire and multiple cold wards, we shivered non-stop when we stopped to rest that night. Even the dragons and Visler were uncomfortable.

The temperature plummeted even lower the next day when we awoke to a dark gray sky. As we started the flight eastward, Atoka announced Atlidmé had risen into the world; winter was official. That left me feeling colder than I ever felt before. I sought solace and warmth in Kitfox's loving embrace as he rode behind me in Atoka's saddle.

Two more days passed in frigid misery before I spotted our destination. Symbilla's island was a vision of white engulfed in fog borne from the warmer ocean. As the dragons circled in for a landing, the air grew just warm enough to finally bring an end to our constant shivering and clattering teeth. Visler squealed in delight and freed himself from the hood of my coat to fly circles with the dragons.

Atoka and Wildfire managed to find a clearing between the heavy trees big enough to land in. Kitfox laughed as he jumped down from his spot astride the Dragon of Winter. As he helped me down, I asked him what he found so amusing. "It's Atoka's Glacial Island all over again."

Atoka snorted and dragged her claws over the ground. "Not quite."

Kitfox and I looked at each other before peering over the dragon's cerulean foot. Her scratch marks had peeled back several years of ice and snow, revealing a terrain never to seen anywhere else in the world; Pure gold.

"Oh!" Kitfox fell to his knees and kissed the aurulent ground before stuffing his pockets with every stone and leaf ingot he could find. Visler hovered over him, chittering excitedly.

"What is he up to?" Shazza called as she and Thera dismounted from Wildfire.

"Only what you would expect from a thief." Wildfire laughed before belching fire onto ground.

"Opportunist." Kitfox corrected. He flashed Shazza and Thera the gold nuggets he was now collecting from the spot cleared by Wildfire. They looked at me to as if telling me I should do something to stop them.

I shook my head in amusement. Deciding that taking some gold from the island wouldn't hurt anything, I watched Kitfox for a moment more. Finally, I closed my eyes and devoted my attention to locating Symbilla.

I focused everything towards the inner pull of the four remaining dragons hidden throughout the world. Finding the closest one nearby, I turned in the direction it was leading and opened my eyes. Visler landed on my shoulder as I began the trek towards the Dragon of Life. Thera and Shazza quietly followed suit with Wildfire hot on their heels. Ignoring his protests about needing a little more gold, Atoka picked Kitfox up with her tail and bounded over the snow after us.

We must have plodded through the snow for an hour before I called for a short break. While I rested weary limbs and dumped snow from my boots, Wildfire and Atoka kept Kitfox and Visler entertained. Both dragons removed huge piles of snow so the Fox Demon could gather more gold nuggets. Shazza and Thera watched them, occasionally poking fun.

Echoes of spectral laughter rang out through the forest like a bell. Our activities ceased in an instant and we all looked at each other in disbelief. Forgetting his desire for gold, Kitfox stood to his full height. His amber eyes observed our surroundings while his ears swiveled this way and that, trying to find the source of the laughter.

Visler hissed venomously before diving for my shoulder. I watched as his eyes danced over the surrounding forest as if he was following something.

Kitfox growled in frustration. "Whatever it is, it keeps moving. I can't pinpoint it."

"The echoes aren't helping." Muttered Shazza crossly.

"Is it Symbilla?"

My dragons and I all agreed that it was indeed not the Dragon of Life.

I stood and brushed the snow off before facing the surrounding woods. "Whoever you are, you are welcome to come and join us."

More spectral laughter was the only response.

"Please, show yourself. We promise no harm will come to you for appearing before us."

Frigid wind burst from the trees and whirled around us before culminating on a single point a few meters away. A beautiful woman materialized from the frosty air. Her skin was pale periwinkle and covered in skimpy lace formed from silver and ice. Beneath a silver crown, her ankle-length, white hair danced about her as if it had a life of its own. Fierce, crystal blue eyes stared at us.

"I don't believe it." Atoka was aghast. "She is a frost nymph."

"You have to be kidding." Thera whispered. "Why would a Daughter of Atlidmé be here?"

"Let's find out." I dared to take a few steps towards the nymph, watching closely for any signs of hostility while Visler coward in my coat hood. The nymph's crystalline gaze followed my every move. "My name is Xyleena. It is a pleasure to meet you."

The nymph did not move.

"Try Kinös Elda." Offered Shazza.

I repeated myself in the Ancient Language. The nymph continued to stare coldly at me. "Any other suggestions?"

"Yeah; how about we get away from her so we can find Symbilla?" The nymph's gaze settled on Kitfox as he spoke. She slowly raised her arm until it was parallel with the ground. Her clawed index finger uncurled from her fist as she pointed at him. He growled in response as his hands instinctively found their way to the blade rings on his belt.

The spectral laugh from before echoed around us and the nymph vanished in a whirlwind of snow and ice. Kitfox did not relax his guard until everything was silent once again.

"What was that about?" Everyone looked at me for an answer.

"I can't say for sure." I reached into my hood to soothe Visler while I considered a few things. "Some of the readings in the Temple say frost nymphs precede Atlidmé during his task of collecting souls to ferry to Havel." I caught the look of worry shared between Atoka and Wildfire. "The thing is, nymphs only appear over dying bodies and are supposed to be invisible to all who are still firmly in the living world. I have no idea why this one would appear before us and point at a perfectly healthy, living Demon."

"That's reassuring." Kitfox muttered.

Thera laid a gentle hand on his shoulder. "Are you sure you're feeling okay?"

"Why wouldn't I be?" He shrugged. "Aside from being a little cold, I feel fine."

"Maybe she was pointing at you because you're stealing from the island." Said Shazza. Kitfox pouted.

"We'll discuss it later." I said, shooting a look at my dragons. They nodded ever so slightly. "Right now, I want to find Symbilla and get out of here."

About half an hour after the frost nymph left us pondering over her random appearance and the fate of Kitfox, Wildfire announced that she had spotted a most peculiar stream. When asked about it, she merely smiled and said it would undoubtedly lead us to Symbilla. With her leading the way, we made it to the riverbank without trouble.

The stream Wildfire had described was a surprise indeed. Instead of finding flowing water as expected, liquid gold sloshed over the rocks as it made its way over the island. Everything it touched was instantly turned to solid gold. Kitfox dared to dip his belt in the flow. It turned to gold in a flash and hardened. He was thrilled to say the least and I had to pull him away before he dipped himself in.

After a few minutes to get over the initial shock of the stream, I moved my team on. Once again following the pull I felt from Symbilla, I lead everyone upriver about half a mile from the coast. A large hill with a nasty scar in its side loomed over us. The river of gold spewed forth from the scar-shaped cave and I knew we would find Symbilla within.

"Atoka, Wildfire, you two stay here and guard the entrance with Visler while we retrieve Symbilla." I said as I jostled the sentinel from his perch on my shoulder. He squawked indignantly and landed on Atoka's back where he promptly curled up and went to sleep.

"Be careful in there, everyone." Atoka said softly. "Dimitri could be lying in wait."

"And keep Kitfox from touching the liquid gold." Wildfire chuckled. Kitfox blew her a raspberry.

I was all smiles as I waved good-bye to my dragons and lead the team through the crack in the hillside.

A lagoon of shimmering gold filled the murky grotto and a small, rocky island was tucked in its midst. From our position by the cavern entrance, we could barely see the island in the dark. There was a rickety, wooden bridge spanning the distance between the shores. The longer I looked at it, the less I wanted to attempt to cross it to retrieve Symbilla.

The black dragon statue we had been seeking guarded over the bridge. Standing beside the statue, with her back to us, was a young girl with long, sable hair. I drew my war fans as a precaution less she be one of Dimitri's new minions and ordered the girl to turn around. With deliberately slow movements, she peered over her shoulder. A look of recognition crossed her features and she turned to face us completely.

Dragon green eyes burned beneath her jet black bangs as she stared at me. She was clad in silver armor and black leathers identical to what I had seen Amorez wearing. Two leather belts crisscrossed her midriff and two familiar, shimmering bars were affixed to each. I suddenly felt like I was looking at a 300-year-old mirror and I didn't want to believe what I was seeing.

"I don't believe it!" Cried Thera.

Kitfox gawked. "Is that Amorez?"

"No." I said as I stepped passed them. "That girl is me; or, more accurately, a look-alike of me from about three centuries ago."

"How in the names of the Five Souls is that possible?" Exclaimed Shazza. I could only shake my head in response. I had no memories to recall of the doppelganger's creation or her reason for existing.

"What do you suggest we do about her?" Thera asked.

"I don't remember why she's here, so we'll need to keep an eye on her while we retrieve Symbilla. The dragon will hopefully know what to do." With that, I lead the way to the hazardous bridge that spanned the golden lake. My three teammates fell in line behind me. All four of us eyed my double suspiciously as we approached. Surprisingly, she made nary a move as we passed within arm's length.

"You should let your hair grow out like that again." Kitfox said after a moment to stop and look at her up close.

I glanced back at my double. "I might consider it." I replied as I stepped foot on the first plank of the bridge.

My doppelganger shrieked in rage. In a burst of superhuman speed, she drew her own war fan and hurled it at me with deadly accuracy. I was frozen in place by fear and there was no way I could escape the deadly blades in time.

Kitfox was suddenly in front of me, pushing me back. He jerked and took a shaky step to steady himself. Every sense and sound fell away as I stared into his eyes. A look of agony crossed his features and he slowly looked down. I followed his gaze to find my doppelganger's tessen breaking through his chest from behind. Blood flowed down to stain his white tunic crimson. I returned my gaze to his face. He gasped before collapsing into me.

"Kitfox!" I fell to the ground with him in my arms. My senses slowly trickled back and the sounds of a battle echoed all around me. I figured it was Shazza and Thera retaliating the doppelganger's surprise attack and I chose to ignore it. Kitfox needed me now more than they did.

"S-Sorry." He tried to flash a cocky smirk, succeeding only in a grimace. He coughed and blood sprayed from his mouth. I wiped it away.

"Don't be sorry." I said as I looked over his wound for some way to remove the fan without killing him. Unfortunately, the blades were too close to his heart. He would bleed out before I had a chance to finish removing it and heal him. I forced myself to look into his eyes to tell him the truth, but the words just wouldn't come. He slowly nodded in understanding.

"I wanted... so badly... see you beat... Dimitri." He grimaced as he gasped for air. He slowly lifted his arm and cupped my cheek with his hand. I blinked through my tears and leaned into his caress.

"Don't leave me." I cried. "Kitfox... you can't... I need..."

His hoarse whisper reached my ears. "Stay strong."

Kitfox smiled one last time.

His eyes slowly drifted shut.

His hand fell away.

"Kitfox!" My anguished cry echoed over and over in the cavern. The next thing I knew, I was charging past Shazza and Thera, war fans drawn and thirsty for blood. I ignored the concerned cries of my two comrades as they tried to call me back to my senses. I would have none of it. My doppelganger needed to pay for what she did!

Momentarily thrown off by my enraged entrance into the battle, my double's guard faltered. I exploited this fault by slamming my tessen through it. I felt flesh and bone split before my fan stopped deep within her ribcage. I wasted no time in focusing a spell at the tip of my tessen. The magic exploded through my double's body, ripping her apart from the inside.

Her blood splattered everywhere and she released a horrid scream. I buried my other fan in her gut, twisting until I heard a sickening crunch. Another exploding spell rippled through her and the wretch fell to her knees. I roared and kicked her away just far enough to hurl another spell at her. Then another. And another. Again and again, over and over, my spells slammed into her.

Stop it, Hatchling!

Come back to your senses, Xyleena!

I finally stopped my barrage when I felt my energy dip dangerously low. It was over for good now and my doppelganger was no more. Just as I was turning around to return to Kitfox, a brilliant flash of light blinded me. It took a minute for my vision to clear, and when it had, I realized my double was back on her feet and glaring at me. There was no evidence that she had ever been injured let alone at death's door.

189

She snarled and launched herself at me. I deflected her attack with a quick spell and shuddered at the extensive drain it took on what little energy I had left. I countered the attack with a punch aimed at her jaw. She dodged it at the last possible moment and spun away with a laugh. I was quick to take up a pursuit, but something grasped my arm and yanked me back.

It was Visler. He must have darted into the cave when he heard the commotion. I turned my back to him and he released my arm from his jaws with a concerned chirp.

"You need to stop this, Xyleena!" Thera shouted. "You are going to kill yourself if you continue!"

I glared at the Feykin over my shoulder. "I don't care! I have to kill her!"

"Snap out of it!" Shouted Shazza. She promptly followed her outcry with a sound slap across my cheek. I saw stars dance before my eyes for a long moment before my vision cleared. When my sight came back to me, I glared up at Shazza before launching a spell at her to knock her away.

The next thing I knew, I was being yanked backwards and pinned against an armored body. A cold blade was held to my throat and hot breath spilled across my ear. It was my double; and she was ready to kill.

Visler screeched and dive bombed the doppelganger. She swatted him away with the hand that held the blade at my throat. Seizing the opportunity, I slammed my elbow into her ribs as hard as I could. Her grip on me broke and I bolted away.

She did not give chase. Instead, she took aim and hurled her tessen at me. It moved far too fast for me to dodge. A searing pain exploded through my shoulder as the blades of the fan sunk in.

I screamed.

A fierce roar answered.

Momentarily forgetting the pain, I looked around to see where the roar came from. The liquid gold of the lake rippled violently before surging upwards. A split second later, a dragon with shimmering, gold scales exploded from the depths. She slammed into my doppelganger, pinning her to the ground with a long, ivory claw. Symbilla growled at her prisoner before turning her sepia gaze to me.

"Xyleena, cancel the spell before this specter kills another innocent." I heard Shazza and Thera gasp at the dragon's words.

"It's too late…" I winced as I tried to get the blades out of my shoulder. Thera rushed over to help.

"Xyleena, you must--"

"I don't remember how to cancel the spell!" I bellowed.

The dragon snorted. "Listen, child, I can undo what was done, but only if you can get rid of the specter."

I gawked at the golden dragon, searching her eyes for any evidence of a deception. Finding only truth, I pushed myself away from Thera. As I slowly made my way towards the pinned doppelganger, a memory played in my mind.

Over three centuries ago, when I buried Symbilla here, I had set a trap before leaving. It was forever active, but wouldn't attack unless someone tried to cross the bridge it guarded. Because the magic would have been a constant drain on my energy, I had rigged an amulet to convert the energy of the dragon into a constant stream of magic. That amulet is what kept the specter alive. And it prevented Symbilla from using her real power.

I scowled at my double as I bent over her. I quickly freed the amulet from her breastplate and jerked hard enough to break the chain. Panic swept across her features as I stood to my full height. With one last look at my doppelganger, I let the amulet drop to the ground with a metallic ring. A moment later, I slammed my foot on it hard enough to render it into oblivion. The specter vanished with a scream.

I looked at Symbilla. "Revive him."

Her sepia gaze fell on Kitfox. "Are you sure?"

"Of course!"

"Calm down, my Keeper." Symbilla kept her voice soft, but stern. "I merely asked because my Soul Exhale has only been used once before and it forever linked that person with my life force."

"Meaning what, exactly?"

191

"If I were to use Soul Exhale on him, he will be as immortal as you and I are. However, he will feel my injuries as if they were his own. And if I were to die, then he would too. Do you truly wish that fate on this Demon?"

So many things ran through my mind in that instant I couldn't tell if they came from me or the dragons. I wondered if Kitfox would hate me for turning him immortal so that I could have him in my life. I closed my eyes and prayed to the Five Souls for an answer.

It was several minutes before I received an answer. A vision of a young, green-eyed girl with black hair and fox ears flashed in my mind so fast I barely caught it. Somehow, I just knew there was no way that Kitfox would be angry about the outcome of my choice.

"Xy?" Thera called softly.

I smiled as I opened my eyes. "Do it."

After a moment, Symbilla nodded. "Very well."

Shazza and Thera glanced at the golden dragon as she slowly approached Kitfox. They both retreated far enough to watch as Symbilla went to work. The dragon leaned in close enough to blow gently into Kitfox's face. As she did so, a tendril of gold smoke left her maw and seeped into the gaping wound in the Demon's chest. There was a flash of blinding light, then the wound vanished leaving only a faint scar as evidence it ever existed.

"It is done." Symbilla said as she backed away and sat on her haunches. I watched Kitfox closely, waiting with bated breath for him to move or say something. It felt like forever before he took a huge gulp of air and coughed. He bolted upright and felt his chest in disbelief.

I couldn't hold my excitement back any longer; I sprinted towards him. He looked up just in time as I threw myself into his arms and hugged him tightly. Thera was right beside me, glomming the Fox Demon in an equally tight embrace. His laugh rang out like a heavenly tune and he hugged us back.

"Good to have you back, fox-boy." Shazza's voice betrayed no emotion, but joy swam in her sunburst eyes.

"Someone mind telling me what happened? Last thing I remember is being in extreme pain while lying in Xy's arms and then everything went dark."

"My Keeper broke the doppelganger spell that drained my energy and kept me from using my full powers." Explained Symbilla. "Once I had been freed of that drain, I revived you."

Kitfox gawked at the dragon. "I... I don't know what to say. Thank you just doesn't seem good enough."

"There's a catch." I said as I withdrew from the hug. A look of dread crossed his features as he looked me in the eye. "In order to revive you, Symbilla had to give you part of her soul. That little bit of her also..." I paused and looked at Thera for help, "... how do I word this?"

"It's hard to explain." The Feykin interjected.

Kitfox pressed for an explanation.

Shazza was the one among us to find a comfortable explanation. "For every injury Symbilla receives, you will feel it as if it had been dealt directly to you and if she dies, so do you. On the other hand, you will live as long as the dragon does."

"So...?"

I smiled meekly. "You're immortal."

Kitfox stared blankly at me. A moment later, he fainted.

My brother surprised everyone when he stood before the court and announced that he did not want to be king. He said that I would make a much better ruler as I have already led our people wisely. The court asked him why he had changed his mind. Oh! How he smiled when he told us that the Dragon Keeper, Amorez, was to be his bride. I could not have been happier for both of them.

– FROM "A JOURNAL OF THE FIRST KING" BY AADRIAN ZA'CAR,
FIRST KING OF THE SECOND AGE

We chose to remain in the cave until Kitfox came to. Shazza had volunteered to go outside to tell Atoka and Wildfire what happened and to collect firewood. Thera stayed with me to heal my wounded shoulder and restore some of my energy. Once that was done, she lit a small orb and started to work on translating the next portion of the Riddle of the Twelve.

Shazza returned with an armful of wood. With a little help from Visler, a small fire was brought to life. The sentinel chattered happily and laid down on the heated stone mere inches from the blaze.

"Xy?" I laid a cold cloth against Kitfox's forehead before answering Shazza's summon. "Please explain to me why you hid the dragons in twelve different locations. Why not just one?"

I glanced at Thera, who was still bent over the rolled parchment containing Riddle of the Twelve. She looked up from her work to meet my gaze. "Because that would be too easy." I answered with a smile. I could practically feel the frustration flowing off of Shazza at my answer. She grumbled and sat opposite me to stare into the dancing flames.

"My Keeper is right, Dákun Daju." Replied Symbilla. Shazza looked up at the gold dragon. "Had the twelve of us been hidden in one location, it would have been much easier for the Shadow Keeper to obtain the Dragons of Shadow."

"No kidding! Dimitri almost kicked our butts the first time we faced him." Added Thera. "That was when it was just me, Xy, and Teka. And Xy didn't have nearly the amount of power or self confidence that she does now. If he had won and freed the Shadow Dragons back then, the world would have been destroyed for sure."

Shazza quietly agreed.

"Speaking of Teka," I muttered as I adjusted the cloth on Kitfox's forehead. "I wonder how she's doing. I hope she's safe wherever she is."

Thera chuckled. "Knowing that feisty sea wench, she's probably giving Dimitri more trouble than he can handle."

"That's what worries me." I sighed and looked away from the unconscious Demon at my side. "What if Teka, Zhealocera, Freya, and Amorez are all drawing too much attention during their mission to help us? Do they know the Shadow Dragons are loose? Are they even still alive?"

Thera and Shazza shared a look of concern before staring at me. I could tell they were both trying to say something to help ease my troubled mood. The words they were looking for eluded them, so they chose to remain silent.

Symbilla sighed. "You can't afford to think like that, Xyleena."

"Given recent events," I jerked my head in Kitfox's direction, "I think I have the right to worry about my friends."

Symbilla's gaze settled on Kitfox for a long moment. "Amorez and Freya have previous experience with all of this and I am confident that both of them are assisting your other friends in every way they can."

"They had better be." I grumbled and returned my attention to caring for Kitfox.

Silence descended over our rudimentary camp after that. The only sounds to be heard were the crackling of the fire and the scratching of Thera's quill over the parchment. I watched my friends closely in the hours that passed. They were sacrificing so much of themselves for me that I couldn't believe I had let them down.

A wave of regret washed over me as my gaze returned to Kitfox's face. He appeared so at peace in his sleep, but the scar on his chest glared up at me in the flickering firelight. It was as if the memory of the fatal wound was pointing at me; accusing me of allowing his death to happen.

"'Nexxa of Deadly Venom hides; far South twixt icy river slides.'" Thera spoke so suddenly that I jumped in surprise.

Shazza cracked an eye open to look at the Feykin. "Nexxa is the name of the next one, huh? I was hoping it was Abaddon."

"Why did you want to find him?" I asked.

"I just want to see what a Shadow Dragon looks like before going up against one in battle."

Symbilla lifted her great wedge of a head from the stone floor and chuckled. "They look like dragons. What more do you need to know? Besides, Abaddon is no longer a Shadow."

Shazza quirked an eyebrow.

"Well, after Nexxa, there are only two more. It shouldn't be long before we find Abaddon." Thera scrutinized the runes on the parchment. "And if I had to guess, I'd say Nexxa is also somewhere on the Southern Stretch."

"Good." The rough whisper had my heart fluttering. I slowly looked over my shoulder to see Kitfox finally awake. He smirked before sitting up and yawning. "How long have I been out of it?"

"Long enough." Muttered Shazza. "Feel better?"

The Demon slowly nodded. "Surprisingly, yeah. So, what was the clue?"

"Are you sure you don't want to take a few minutes to talk about what happened before rushing into the next puzzle?" Inquired Symbilla.

Kitfox glanced at the dragon before focusing on me. "There's really nothing to talk about. I know what happened and I'm okay with it."

Symbilla huffed. "Are you certain?"

"What's the next riddle?" Kitfox looked to Thera for the answer. The Feykin glimpsed at the dragon before reciting the clue to Nexxa.

"We think Nexxa is somewhere on the Southern Stretch." I added.

"I think you're right." He grinned. "Where's the map?"

Thera quickly cast a spell to summon it from where I left it in Atoka's saddle. She unrolled it on the ground as we all gathered around it. Kitfox leaned in for a close look.

"What are you looking for exactly?" Asked Shazza.

"There are six rivers in the whole of the Southern Stretch. Of those, only two actually intersect each other. I'm betting my gold belt that we'll find Nexxa in the middle of the intersecting rivers," He pointed to the spot on the map, "right there."

"What if you are wrong, Demon?" Symbilla called.

Kitfox rolled his eyes and looked up at her. "Then we'll have four other rivers to look at."

"He's not wrong." I muttered after a long look at the spot where Kitfox had pointed. "I can almost feel a presence there."

"Alright." Thera quickly rolled the map back up. "Let's get to the dragons outside and saddle up so we get out of here."

"No." I sighed. My comrades froze. After glancing at each other as if making sure they had heard correctly, they all looked at me in disbelief and concern. "No one else is going to die for me. I'm dropping you guys off in a town and doing the rest of this quest alone."

"The Souls you are!" Kitfox shouted. "There is no way in the seven circles of Havel that I'm letting you go out there alone to face Dimitri and his army no matter what you say. We chose to come with you and fight and not even Régon himself can stop us!"

Tears stung my eyes but I refused to let them fall. "B-but you... died."

"Saving you, Xy! And I will never regret my decision to do so." He said as he gently gripped my hands in his own and pulled me closer to him. "I gave up my life for you because I lo— I believe you are the hope this world needs to pull out of this darkness."

"Xyleena, you have to let them choose their own paths." Added Symbilla.

Shazza and Thera affirmed the dragon's statement.

"And if you try to sneak off without us, I will chain you to me!" Declared Kitfox.

I chuckled and rested my head against the Demon's chest. He promptly wrapped his arms around me and held me in a loving embrace. My heart skipped a beat when he gently laid a kiss on the top of my head.

"Please, Xy," Kitfox whispered so softly I barely heard him, "don't blame yourself for what happened to me. It wasn't your fault."

The tears finally slipped from my eyes. "Thank you."

Frigid winds raged over hill and valley. It kicked up newly fallen snow until the world outside had vanished in a thick wall of white. Thick rows of icicles clung to the windows and roofs. Gigantic snow drifts formed between buildings where the wind could not quite reach.

I sighed and watched as my breath crystallized on the window in seconds. I took it as a sign that the temperature outside had plummeted to dangerous lows. Suddenly, I was grateful that Atoka had warned us of the approaching storm well in advance. Despite the possibility of Dimitri's forces in the area, I decided it would be best to seek shelter at the inn of a small town called Cosín.

Luckily for us, there wasn't a soldier in sight when we strolled up the main road. We did get some strange looks from the locals that worried us, but – as it turned out – most of them were just concerned about us travelling by foot across the frozen wastelands. It was then that we learned the storm was expected to last at least a seven-day. That had been over three days ago and the storm had only gotten worse since.

I shivered and finally moved away from the window. The thick curtain fell back into place as I made my way to the fireplace. The ghosts of embers smoldered amidst the ashes. I prodded them before tossing some tinder and logs on. With a whispered spell, a fire crackled to life.

I stepped back to watch the blaze for a bit, thankful to be alone for once. The dragons had retreated from my mind, leaving a blissful silence. Thera had taken Visler with her in her room; for what, I could only guess. I found Shazza holed up in the tavern downstairs when I went for some lunch. She looked introspective and I couldn't help wondering if it had something to do with Kkorian. I had spotted Kitfox talking excitedly with another Demon at the bar before retreating to my room.

It was good to be able to relax like this; even if it was a fleeting moment. I sighed and sat in the chair that lingered on the edge of the warmth. A summons at the door forced me away from the comfort. I pulled the door open only to be greeted by a grinning Kitfox and two cups of tea. I chuckled and moved aside to grant him access.

"I hope I'm not disturbing you." He said as he placed the cups on a small table by the bed.

"Not at all." I smiled at him over my shoulder as I sealed the door. "Thanks for the tea, by the way."

Kitfox laughed. "It's not tea. It's a spice liqueur distilled here in the inn and served hot for days like this. A Demon I was talking to earlier suggested it."

"Oh?" I quirked an eyebrow at him as I got close enough to take the cup from the table. "Trying to get me drunk so you can take advantage of me?"

"No! No! That's not it! I swear!" He threw his hands up in front of him in defense as he turned an amusing shade of red. "I only brought it because I thought it would warm you up a-and...." I couldn't help laughing at his obvious embarrassment. He dropped his arms and frowned. "And you're picking on me again, aren't you?"

"Of course!"

"You're mean."

I grinned before picking up the cup and taking a sip. The mingle of spices left a delightful bite on my tongue as the heat of the liqueur left a traceable path down to my belly. "Ooh. That is good."

"Well, that's all you get." Kitfox said with a cocky grin as he stole the cup away.

"What are you talking about?"

"I shared with you, now it's time to go find someone who'll enjoy it without picking on me in the process." He paused to consider something. "Yeah, I think Shazza would enjoy this more."

"Oh no you don't." I snatched the cup back.

"Oh yes I do." He grabbed for the cup again.

"Mine!" I took off at a lazy run across the room. Kitfox laughed as he took up pursuit, chasing me all around the room. Both of us were breathless and laughing from the impromptu game in no time.

I heard a soft thud. Kitfox yelped and collided with me. We crashed onto the bed in a tangle of limbs. I was vaguely aware of the cup hitting the floor as I stared up into Kitfox's dazzling, amber eyes.

Kitfox slowly tilted his head towards mine. He kissed me, ever so softly - ever so shyly - on the lips. It left me dizzy and wanting more. He pulled away slightly and gazed into my eyes.

I felt no guilt; no rejection. Memories of Ríhan didn't haunt me. Not anymore. I loved him; loved Kitfox. I couldn't even remember when I fell for him. As if sensing this, Kitfox smiled. We kissed again, tenderly but urgently.

The next thing I knew, we were locked in a heated kiss. My hands moved of their own accord. Through his thick, lavender mane and over his muscled back. I pulled his tunic free of his trousers. I ran my hands across his hardened abs, slowly pulling the shirt up. We broke the kiss so I could completely remove the garment.

Kitfox cupped my chin tenderly and pulled me close. He kissed my lips, then my cheeks, my earlobes, my throat. I couldn't remember ever being kissed like this before. I loved it; loved the way he touched me as he undressed me. Tantalizingly slow caresses sent shivers down my spine.

A fleeting thought of 'Maybe we shouldn't do this' was quickly suppressed. I wanted this. I wanted him. And he wanted me. He was so aroused; so very hard. I loved that he wanted me.

I gasped as Kitfox entered. My fingers dug into the muscles of his back, pulling him closer; deeper. I captured his mouth with mine as we began to rock slowly, then faster, much more quickly. Our bodies flowed together in a rhythm that lasted well into the night.

I awoke feeling warm and fuzzy. Sensation slowly returned. I became aware that I was pressed against Kitfox, with one leg thrown over his waist. I smiled when I realized his handsome face was mere inches from my own. He was still asleep and holding me tightly as if afraid I would vanish like a dream.

I closed the distance between us and gently placed a kiss upon his lips. His hold on me loosened. He got my message; 'I am here, I am not leaving'. It felt so right, here in his arms, that I couldn't have even forced myself to leave.

I lay there, next to him, content with just watching him sleep. My gaze somehow found its way to the light scar on his chest. As I traced the jagged line with my fingertips, I recalled the image of the young girl that had flashed in my mind when I begged the Gods for advice. I had a feeling I knew who she was; or, more accurately, would be. I just wasn't sure if I should tell Kitfox about her.

I heard a key jostle in the lock and looked towards the door. The door swung open and a young chambermaid entered. She blushed furiously at the sight of me and Kitfox. She apologized earnestly, over and over, as she stumbled back out of the room. I couldn't help but laugh.

"What did I miss?" Kitfox mumbled as he stretched.

"Just someone who probably won't be a rush to clean any more rooms today."

He quirked an eyebrow. "Chambermaid?"

"Yup." I grinned as I lay my head on his chest.

He chuckled. "Well, it could have been worse."

"Yeah; she could have walked in on us in the middle of our little tryst."

His demeanor changed slightly. "You're not upset that we made love last night, are you?"

I lifted my head from his chest and looked into his eyes. "Kitfox," I placed a kiss on his lips and he relaxed, "I thoroughly enjoyed last night."

"I'm glad." He laughed lightly. "I thought you would be pissed and accuse me of actually getting you drunk." As if realizing something, he gawked at me. "You weren't drunk, were you?"

"No." I shook my head for emphasis. "And I'm not mad at you about anything either. I think... no. I just wanted it; wanted you." I smiled at how corny that sounded.

"Xy..." Kitfox took my chin tenderly between his fingers. He gazed into my eyes and licked his lips. He was nervous about whatever he wanted to say, that was obvious. I decided to ease it out of him with a sweat kiss. "Xy, I love you."

My heart fluttered. I felt... Gods! I couldn't describe what I felt. Every emotion that washed over me in that instant was indescribably good. It was the first time in over a year that I truly felt happy.

I rolled on top of Kitfox and claimed his mouth with mine. "I love you, too, Kitfox." I whispered before kissing him again.

Well, it's about time!

Kitfox froze, staring at me wide-eyed in surprise. He chuckled nervously and cleared his throat with a cough. "Did I just hear...?"

You can hear me?

I gawked at him. "You heard Riptide?"

Kitfox nodded numbly. "I think...."

Riptide exploded with cheerful hoots and hollers. Before we knew it, all nine dragons were chattering away excitedly, launching question after question at Kitfox. I had to yell at them to quiet down.

"Okay, can somebody please explain to my how I can suddenly hear you dragons when you're not in front of me?"

Simple! Riptide laughed.

You and Xyleena mated, and Dragon Keeper mates can hear us even from within the Eye. Explained Thedrún.

"Okay." Kitfox slowly nodded in understanding. "'Nuther question for you: since I am, as you guys put it, a Dragon Keeper's mate, does that mean I can summon you, too?"

The dragons went oddly silent. They were quiet for so long that Kitfox and I gave up on waiting for an answer. The two of us finally rolled out of bed and headed for the bath. Just as we sunk into the hot water together, the dragons returned with an answer.

We cannot say for sure whether or not you have the ability to summon us given the fact that it has never been attempted by anyone who is not a Dragon Keeper. Explained Helios.

The only way to tell if you can summon us, Kitfox, is to actually try it. I detected a note of excitement in Vortex's voice as he suggested the idea. And if it turns out that you do have the ability, it would give our side an extra advantage over Dimitri in the battles to come.

Yeah!

Try it now!

"No, he is not trying it now." I said sternly. Riptide and Wildfire groaned in disappointment. "We are at an inn in a village. If he actually manages to summon one of you, it would be pandemonium."

Kitfox chuckled and kissed my neck. "They certainly are an excitable bunch, aren't they?" He dipped a rag into the hot water. He let the run off drip down my chest before lightly running the rag over my skin.

"You have no idea." I sighed and leaned into his shoulder.

Xyleena, now would be a good time to tell Kitfox of the vision you had.

"Wildfire!" I seethed. "The next time I summon you, I'm kicking your butt clear into a snow bank!"

The dragons all laughed.

"What vision?"

I pulled myself off of Kitfox just enough to turn around in the tub. I wanted to look into his eyes while I divulged the secret. Taking a deep breath to calm myself, I spoke.

"After my doppelganger killed you, Symbilla gave me the option to revive you. She explained the pros and the cons of the feat and I couldn't decide on what to do. On one hand, I was afraid you would be furious that it turned you immortal. On the other, I didn't feel I could live without you."

He smiled at that.

"So I prayed to the Five Souls to give me an answer. They did."

Kitfox quirked an eyebrow. "Their answer was a vision?"

I nodded.

"Must have been one heck of a vision." He laughed. "What did you see?"

"A young girl with dragon green eyes and a beautiful mane of jet black hair." I smiled at the memory. "Best of all, she had lavender fox ears."

Kitfox looked thoroughly confused. "The Gods showed you a random Demon and that made you want to revive me? I feel special."

"You don't get it." I smiled. "That girl wasn't a random Demon." I watched him very closely, eager to see his reaction to what I was about to say. "The Gods showed me our daughter."

All emotion fled from his face and he stared at me. A few moments after allowing the info sunk in, he cheered. Water sloshed over the side of the tub as he glommed me in a hug. We laughed, we cried, we kissed.

It was bliss.

I discovered Helios sitting on the edge of the cliff, staring out into the night. His blue eyes glowed like starlight when he noticed my approach and turned his gaze upon me. I asked what he was doing and he answered in his usual, cryptic way, "It is during our darkest moments that we must focus longest in order to find the light."

– FROM "CONVERSATIONS WITH DRAGONS" BY DJURDAK ZA'CAR

Kitfox and I spent most of the following days alone together. Much of that time was spent talking over meals and getting to know each other better. I learned that I could talk to him about anything, no matter the significance. He was sweet, wonderfully chivalrous, and hopelessly romantic. I couldn't believe it took me so long to fall in love with him.

It was during one of our secluded dinners in the tavern that Thera approached us. I could tell from her expression that she suspected something was up between him and me. Though she was clearly curious, she didn't ask a word. Instead, she told us that the storm was expected to blow itself out some time before dawn; a whole day sooner than originally forecast.

We thanked her for the info and offered her to join us. She declined, saying we looked too cozy to interrupt. Kitfox and I watched her walk away in search of Shazza.

"So," Kitfox took a sip of wine, "we're leaving tomorrow morning for Nexxa?"

"Looks that way." I muttered. "It's too bad. I was hoping to spend a little more time alone with you."

Kitfox chuckled and took my hand; bringing it to his lips in a kiss. "At least we are still traveling together. I'd probably go insane if we weren't."

"You are already insane, Kitfox." I laughed when he beamed and completely agreed.

It was shortly after that that the two of us snuck away to my room. We spent the rest of the night lost in the throes of passion. Neither of us was looking forward to the marrow, when we would be forced to face the bitter cold once again.

I sighed and reluctantly passed over the threshold of the doorway. The biting cold of early morning quickly seeped through my multiple layers of clothing and I shivered. I wriggled my nose, trying to overcome the dry and frozen feeling that instantly overtook it.

The door slammed behind me. It was Thera. She said nothing as she adjusted her coat hood around Visler. I glanced at Shazza and Kitfox; they were ready to head out. I led the way down the main road, marveling at how loudly our footsteps crunched as we forged tracks through the pristine snow.

It felt like half the day had slipped by before the town of Cosín disappeared from sight. I brought my team to a stop in a relatively shallow portion of snow. I peeled a glove off and blew on it before digging into my coat. I found the Dragon's Eye Amulet and jostled it free of its confines of clothing. I looked at Kitfox as I put my glove back on.

"You sure, Xy?"

"We'll never know unless you try."

Kitfox slowly nodded. He removed his glove as he stepped closer to me. Ignoring Shazza's and Thera's inquiries about what was going on, he gently touched the jewel marking the Atoka's essence within the Amulet. He threw his hand forward and called for the dragon.

Nothing happened.

"Damn. I was hoping it would work for you."

Kitfox shrugged and put his glove back on. "I'm not surprised it didn't." I could tell he was putting up a front. His amber eyes betrayed such disappointment that I wanted to hug him in comfort.

"Would one of you two please explain what that was all about?" Shazza crossed her arms. I clicked my tongue and turned away to release Atoka and Wildfire from the Amulet. With the two dragons there to help explain everything, Shazza and Thera were let in on the secret.

"Let me get this straight," the Dákun Daju scoffed, "The two of you slept together."

We both blushed and nodded.

"And now he can hear the dragons while they're in the Amulet?"

Kitfox nodded.

"But he can't summon them?"

I shook my head.

"Nice try, Kitfox." Thera clapped him on the arm as she strode up to Wildfire. He quirked an eyebrow at me. I shrugged at his silent question; only Thera knew what she was thinking at that moment.

Shazza took off after Thera, mumbling something I didn't catch. Kitfox apparently heard it and glared daggers at the Dákun Daju's retreating back. With a low growl, he led me to Atoka and boosted me into the saddle. As he jumped up and situated himself behind me, I asked him what Shazza said to make him so mad.

"She thinks that I'm trying to steal your right as Dragon Keeper." He replied as he wrapped his arms around me.

I frowned. "You and I both know that that is not what is going on here."

"Do not fret over the words of the Dákun Daju, Xyleena and Kitfox." Said Atoka. "We must be on our way if we hope to get anywhere closer to Nexxa before nightfall."

I sighed. "You're right. We'll have to talk to her about it later." After checking to see if my teammates were all strapped into the saddles, I gave the command to fly. Wildfire and Atoka spread their wings and took a few bounding steps over the snow. They leapt into the air in tandem and were airborne. After reaching a safe altitude, they banked slightly left and flew off to the northwest; towards Nexxa.

Twice the suns set and thrice they rose again. Finally, the intersecting rivers Kitfox had spoke of nearly three weeks ago came into view. We had almost over flown them when Shazza pointed out a discolored speck in the perpetual white. I couldn't find the spot she had pointed out, so I let her direct the dragons where to land.

As the dragons back-winged to land, great clouds of snow were sent airborne. The tempest of ice and snow had cleared away a vast area, revealing a black dragon statue. I quickly realized that the statue was, in fact, the 'speck' Shazza had seen from the air. As I dismounted from Atoka's saddle, I thanked her. She merely shrugged.

"Well, we found the statue." Thera said happily. She put her hand over her eyes to block out the suns as she surveyed the perpetual white of the land around us. "Now the question is: where is Nexxa's nest?"

"It can't be too far from the statue." Kitfox started towards the black dragon. He stopped short as the ground beneath him cracked and rumbled.

"We're on recently frozen rivers, remember?" Shazza hissed. "One wrong step could send us all plummeting through the ice."

"That is easily remedied." Boasted Atoka. I smiled at the Dragon of Eternal Winter over my shoulder.

"Do it."

She nodded and punctured the ice with an ivory claw. Her eyes flashed as she lowered her head to the hole and blew. I could hear the river beneath us rumble and groan as it froze. Some of the ice erupted through the surface near where we stood, but the entire river remained solid. Kitfox took a few trial steps closer to the black statue. When nothing happened, he gave the okay and we all moved to join him.

"Are you able to sense Nexxa yet, Xy?" Thera asked. I watched for a moment while she studied the statue before closing my eyes. I found the three remaining tugs which led to the dragons and focused on the closest one. I frowned and opened my eyes.

"Straight down from where I'm standing." My teammates gawked at me in disbelief. "I'm serious. Nexxa is about a kilometer directly below."

"And just how do we get down there?" Grumbled Shazza.

Thera whistled to get our attention. She pointed to the black dragon. "Is it just me, or does this statue look different from the other ones?"

Kitfox walked slowly around the statue, scrutinizing over every inch of the marble. As he joined Thera on the left side of statue, he sighed and stepped back.

"I don't see any—" He paused, squinting. He quickly moved in for a closer look at the dragon's tail. "Oh."

"What is it?" Shazza and I asked in unison as we joined them.

"It looks like a lever." As she spoke, Thera reached out and gave the tail a good tug.

The tip shifted and locked into position with a loud click. A rumble sounded from beneath our feet, growing ever louder; ever closer. We drew our weapons in a flash, ready for anything. The statue slowly moved aside, revealing a marble slab as black as the statue itself. After the statue was clear, the slab fell away. Hot, putrid air exploded to the surface.

I gagged at the stench and moved further away, less I lose my breakfast in front of everyone.

"Good Gods, what is that stench?!" Cried Thera as she desperately tried to quiet Visler's upset careening.

"If I had to guess, I'd say it was the smell of a thousand rotting corpses." Kitfox said through the handful of snow he held to his nose. "It stinks worse than the Tomb of the Lost."

I groaned. "If this place has any of that undead-spawning, green fog, Nexxa can stay down there!"

My teammates wholeheartedly agreed.

Atoka and Wildfire looked at each other in concern, then at me. Wildfire was the first to speak her mind. "You can't leave our sister down there, Xyleena."

"Remember, you need all twelve of us dragons to reach your full power or the Shadow Keeper will win."

"I swear you dragons take things way too seriously sometimes." I muttered.

"Well, since we're forced into this stink hole, I suggest we get it over with as quickly as possible." Shazza knocked two arrows and stepped towards the passageway. She resisted the urge to gag and groaned in disgust as she descended into the darkness.

Thera took one last deep breath of fresh air before following Shazza. Kitfox and I waited together as Atoka and Wildfire faded into their elements and reentered the Eye. I summoned a light orb and took the first steps into the rancid darkness beneath the ice.

I really wished I hadn't come here. By the light of my orb, I could see it all too clearly. The floor and walls were all crafted of black marble. It seemed to stretch on for an eternity into the dark.

The entire place was coated in slime and gore. It made walking through the corridor a hazardous and smelly task. Half-decayed corpses of creatures I could no longer recognize were strewn everywhere. The air was so thick and putrid I could barely breathe.

Yet I pushed on, managing to somehow keep up with Shazza's determined pace. The further we pushed into the darkness, the more I remembered. These unknown creatures were once small trolls. They had been spawned from magic to serve as sentries in case the crypt was accidently discovered. What could have slaughtered all of them?

Nexxa?

Nexxa may be the second-most violent-natured out of the twelve of us, said Symbilla, but I doubt she would do something this terrible.

Wait, don't tell me, Kitfox interjected, Abaddon is the most violent?

Vortex chuckled. *You would be right on that count, Kitfox.*

Good to know that little bit of info in advance. *I'm still trying to figure out how I'm supposed to keep him in line if he's a Shadow Dragon.*

You'll figure it out, Love. Kitfox winked at me.

Thanks for the vote of confidence. I resisted the urge to throw up as I stepped over a dismembered head. *Gods, I wish I knew what happened down here!*

Do you have any memories of this place besides the existence of the trolls?

I tried to remember more about the place, but nothing seemed to surface. I sighed in frustration. *Nothing.*

Keep trying. Symbilla's gentle voice soothed me a little. *It'll come back to you.*

I thanked her and continued along the corridor after Shazza and Thera.

"Ugh!" Thera covered her mouth and turned away. I dared to lift the orb a little higher to see what caused her reaction. A grotesque and twisted corpse blocked the path ahead, its guts spilling across the marble. "Of all the places, why did you have to hide a dragon here, Xy?"

I flicked my wrist and sent the corpse flying with a spell. "It wasn't like this before."

"I wonder if Dimitri did something to it." Kitfox shuddered at the sound of the corpse smashing into something in the distance.

"Not likely." Shazza said as she drew to a stop at the brink of a much larger room. "Dimitri wouldn't have bothered coming down here since the runes he was always after are on the statue way above us."

Kitfox snapped his fingers. "Oh, right. I forgot about that."

"So, what caused all this?"

Shazza shrugged. "Ask the Dragon Keeper." With that, she took another step towards the room.

A ghost of a memory suddenly flashed in my mind. I screamed and yanked her back with a spell. "Don't!"

211

Shazza whirled around, furious. "What has gotten into you?"

Thera put herself between me and the enraged Dákun Daju. "Is it Nexxa?"

"No. Not her." I raised my hand to point at the shadows. On the opposite side of the room, six red eyes gleamed in the blackness. "Her!"

My teammates instantly geared up for a battle, but it would only be in vain. We didn't stand a chance; not against that thing. The creature that lurked in the shadows was a blood thirsty monster. It killed mercilessly and without hesitation. Nothing could defeat it; not even hordes of trolls.

Thera summoned a light orb and tossed it into the room before I could stop her. The beast hissed angrily as the orb rolled closer to her, scattering the shadows enough to reveal her true form. A tawny, feline face, framed by a thick mane of white stared straight ahead. Another head sprouted from her shoulder. This one resembled a shaggy goat with long, sharp horns. A third head was suspended in the air above the other two. This one was an enormous black-scaled snake, and its body became the creature's tail.

The lion head snarled as the beast stood to her full height, revealing front paws armed with huge claws and hindquarters which mirrored those of a goat's. She was much larger than any of us, but nowhere near as big as a dragon.

"Wha- What is that thing?!" Thera took an involuntary step back out of fear. Visler chirped meekly and buried himself even further into the hood of her coat.

"A chimera." I said softly. "She is the true guardian of this place. The trolls were supposed to be the first line of defense in case of a break-in, but she killed them all."

"We are so screwed."

Kitfox didn't know how right he actually was.

The snake head lingered overhead, tasting the air as the beast strode towards the light orb. Once it was within range, the snake struck so fast I couldn't follow. It sank its needle-like fangs into the orb and lifted it off the ground. It unhinged its jaws and swallowed the orb whole. Darkness flooded the room.

"What do we do, Xy?" Shazza hissed.

"Someone will have to distract the chimera long enough for Nexxa to be released."

"How about summoning a dragon?"

I quickly estimated the size of the room. "None of them would fit."

"Okay then," Thera sighed, "seeing as how you and Kitfox are the immortals among us, I vote you two keep the cursed thing busy."

"Gee! Thanks, Thera." Growled Kitfox.

"She's right." I said. They all gawked at me in disbelief. "Kitfox and I will distract it. Shazza, you find the key to freeing Nexxa. It should be on the wall behind where the chimera was resting. Thera, you back us all up."

Kitfox freed his blade rings from his belt while I flared my war fans. We looked at each other and nodded. I called for a light orb. It exploded into existence near the ceiling, enraging all three heads of the chimera.

With the beast momentarily distracted, Kitfox and I burst into the room. Thera was right behind us, coating us in multiple protective spells. Shazza lingered in the doorway, waiting the opportunity to race to the opposite side of the room.

The snake head was the first to realize the light had been a trick. It opened its jaws a stream of venom shot out. Kitfox narrowly avoided getting hit by the jet as he sprinted up to the chimera's hindquarters. In a flash of steel, he lopped off the entire tail. The dead limb wriggled helplessly on the ground.

The lion and goat heads roared in a mix of anger and pain and reeled around to catch Kitfox in a fiery blast of breath. The flame was deflected by one of Thera's spells and Kitfox flipped away unharmed. Stealing a move from my doppelganger, I hurled my tessen at the lion head. The blades sunk deep into her eye and threw her head back in an enraged roar. Kitfox and I raced up to the head while its throat was exposed and sliced clean through the flesh with our blades.

The lion head fell limp against the creature's body and now only the goat head remained. Kitfox and I were about to finish it when Thera called us off. As we ducked away from flailing limbs and sweeping horns, we asked what was wrong.

Thera pointed at the snake head. "It's playing you for fools!"

My gaze fell on the snake and I gasped in realization. It was still wriggling on the ground making a sickening squishy sound. Strange lumps were starting to grow from the spot where its head was removed from the rest of the beast. I had forgotten that the chimera could rapidly regenerate lost limbs or even a complete body as needed. If Nexxa wasn't released soon, we would be up against two chimeras instead of one.

"Shazza better hurry."

Shazza had sprinted across the room the moment the chimera's attention was completely focused on Kitfox and Xyleena. She crept along the wall, sticking to the shadows as much as possible, searching for some way to free Nexxa. Several minutes of frantically searching had awarded her with nary a sign of the dragon. She began to wonder if Xy had been mistaken.

She swore at the sound of the chimera's enraged roar and spared a moment's glance at the beast. Now, two heads had been rendered useless. She couldn't help wondering why, if it was apparently so easy to defeat, Xy made such a big deal out of the chimera.

Then she glimpsed the snake head. A feeling of dread overcame her as the dismembered thing wriggled on the ground as if it were planning something. Shazza muttered a curse unto the beast and returned her focus to finding the key to unlocking Nexxa.

She crept along the wall a little further and finally found what she had sought. Nesting in the wall in a four by three grid were eleven tiles, each depicting a portion of a whole image.

There was a blank space with which to move the other eleven around.

"A sliding puzzle." Shazza muttered to herself. She backed up a step to study the images on the tiles. After a minute, she smirked and began to move the pieces around.

I launched several spells at the chimera, knocking her off balance just enough to keep her from smashing Kitfox with her hooves. The Fox Demon quickly rolled out of the way, only to come face-to-face with the snake head. He yelped in surprise and jerked away before the snake could clamp its jaws over his head.

I heard Thera recharge our defensive spells and took a second to look for Shazza. I couldn't find her anywhere. I hurled another spell at the chimera and darted away as she brought her front paws smashing down.

"Look out!" Kitfox tackled me to the ground just in time. The chimera's regenerated snake head crashed into the ground exactly where I had been standing just seconds ago. Kitfox breathed a sigh in relief. "You okay?"

"Yeah." We both got to our feet before the chimera struck again. "Have you seen Shazza at all?"

"No."

"Where is she?!"

"We have bigger things to worry about." Kitfox pointed at the original snake head as we ran around the chimera. It now had four legs and was quickly growing in size. Soon, it would be as large and formidable as the creature that spawned it.

"What do you suggest we do?"

"I don't know. Everything we've tried has either backfired or been useless." We jumped apart as the new snake head crashed into the ground between us. "I don't even think Nexxa can help us at this point." Kitfox snarled as he took hold of the neck and jerked sharply. A sickening crunch later, and the snake head fell limp.

"That's not going to last long." I said before launching spells at both chimeras. The little one flew to the opposite wall and I finally caught a glimpse of Shazza.

"It's better than having to dodge it constantly."

"Come on." I grabbed his arm and pulled him after me. We dodged the chimera's sweeping horns as I led the way to Shazza. She glanced back at us as we stopped behind her. I hurled a spell at the chimera, knocking the beast away, and called for Thera. The Feykin was quick to fly to our position. With her help, a barrier was erected to shield us from the beasts. I told Shazza to hurry up with whatever was taking her so long.

"Two minutes."

"We might not have that long."

Thera cried out as the big chimera slammed into the barrier. I pulled energy from the Dragon's Eye Amulet and used it to reinforce the wall around us. I seriously doubted the magic boost would last the whole two minutes Shazza needed.

Thera struggled to remain standing as the chimera struck the barrier again. "Please hurry, Shazza!"

Shazza did not respond.

"Thera, use my energy." Kitfox demanded as he placed his hand on her shoulder. A combined strike from the chimeras left all three of us shaking from the power drain. One more combined strike drained Thera and Kitfox of everything they had left and they slumped to the ground.

I had to think of something, and fast! Another hit like that would finish me. The chimeras seemed to realize that they had the upper hand. They looked down on me smugly as they prepared to strike the barrier. As their combined mass collided with the wall of magic, I thought, So this is the end.

The barrier caved and so did I. The last thing I remembered before the world went black was a brilliant, green light.

Everything was black; never-ending, freezing. I was weightless; floating, numb. Seconds passed slowly. I let them. I wasn't in a hurry anymore. I was at peace.

A streak of sapphire flashed a ways ahead. A growing rumble echoed. I wasn't afraid; I no longer needed to feel. I was too numb. A crystalline sea serpent swam through the blackness, heading towards me. It was Atlidmé, I realized. He had come to collect me. I was willing to go with Him, but only if Kitfox was with me.

The God of Water and Death stopped just meters away. Beneath rainbow horns and turquoise fins, His green eyes studied me. He seemed sad.

Ja la mishi, nena.

Lost? I am lost? How could that be? I died.

Ja la nan mert. Iram ger.

Go back? Go back. Yes. Yes, I must go back! I was still needed. Atlidmé nodded and swam around me. He disappeared into the blackness. I smiled as I sent a thank you after him. I let my eyes drift shut. I had to go back.

Wake up!

Yes; I had to wake up.

Please, Xy! Open your eyes.

I felt something shaking me. I forced my eyes to open. The fuzzy visage cleared after a moment. It was Shazza. Relief washed over her features and she sighed.

"About time you came to. I was beginning to think I'd have to carry all three of you out of here."

I groaned as I sat up. "How long was I out of it?"

"About an hour or so." Shazza said as she retreated from me to check on Kitfox and Thera. I noticed Visler managed to free himself from the confines of Thera's coat. He was now lying beside her, licking her face as if trying to rouse her from slumber.

Kitfox groaned and rolled onto his side. He found me and smiled. "What happened? Last thing I remember was…"

"I solved the puzzle and unlocked the route to Nexxa just as the chimeras smashed through Xy's barrier." Shazza replied as she tried to rouse Thera. "The instant the path opened, a light shot out and the chimeras turned to dust."

"I shall thank the Gods for your good timing." Thera mumbled groggily. She reached up to soothe Visler as he chattered happily at her revival.

Almost another hour had passed before Thera, Kitfox and I had recovered enough to move on. Shazza cautiously led the way along the route she had unlocked. We found ourselves in an even larger room, surrounded by bronze chimera statues and marble pillars.

Sitting in the middle of the room, looking as smug as a thief on the Golden Isle, sat a sage green dragon. Her white wings were flared as if ready for a fight. And her bladed tail whipped to and fro impatiently. Nexxa nodded her head in respects as we approached.

"It's about time you returned for me."

I glared at Nexxa. "What do you mean 'it's about time'? Do you have any idea what we just went through to free your ungrateful ass?"

The dragon's jaw fell slack in surprise. Kitfox snickered and covered his mouth with a hand as he fought the urge to laugh. Thera and Shazza, on the other hand, stared at me in disbelief. Visler peeped and cocked his head to one side in confusion.

Nexxa shook her head and snorted. "Don't blame me because you made the mistake of triggering your own trap!"

"I didn't know there was one!"

"You set it!" Nexxa slammed her tail into the ground, easily cracking the black marble. "How could you not know?"

"Ladies, please!" Kitfox shouted as he put himself between me and the dragon. He turned to Nexxa after she and I calmed down a little. "Nexxa, Xy lost all her memories a few years ago. That is why she did not know of the trap until we had accidently triggered it." Kitfox turned to me. "Xy, please calm down. I know you are angry about what happened here and exhausted, but there's no need to take out your frustrations on your dragon."

I took a few steps towards him and caught him in a hug. He sighed in relief and rubbed my back. It helped me calm down even more. I kissed his cheek and whispered, "Thank you."

Nexxa sighed and yanked her tail out of the marble floor. "I apologize for my comments and temper, Keeper."

"And I apologize for mine, Nexxa."

"Well, now that that is settled," Shazza cleared her throat, "where do we go from here?"

"I suggest a long nap." Thera said after a yawn. "Xy and I spent so much energy on the chimeras that we could probably sleep for seven days straight!"

"I'm already sleeping." I murmured against Kitfox's chest. He chuckled.

"Might I suggest you leave this tomb before you sleep?" Said Nexxa. "Even without the chimera, it is still rather dangerous to be in here."

"Not only that, but the smell is enough to make me want to vomit." Shazza turned on her heel and took off for the chimera's chamber. Thera followed slowly, urged on by Visler and her own desire to get out of the tomb. I was barely awake when Nexxa faded into her element. Green globules of goo swam in the air before entering the Dragon's Eye. A pale green jewel flashed into existence amidst the filigree.

Nexxa was mine.

Bedeb's rings, though not nearly as grand as Saturn's, provide us with a spectacular treat. At night, when the moons are at just the right angles, their light reflects off of the rings, and breaks into countless rainbows. It is even more beautiful than aurorae.

– FROM "HISTORY OF BEDEB, VOL I" BY ACASIA FLEMENTH, MAGISTRATE ELECT

I didn't remember Kitfox carrying me out of Nexxa's tomb or that four dragons had been summoned to watch over us. All I remember was sleep; deep, blessed, uninterrupted sleep. I don't even remember dreaming.

What I do remember is waking up in Kitfox's arms in the dead of night. He was holding me close, providing extra warmth as he himself dozed. We were tucked between two thick sleeping furs and Wildfire was curled about us. Her wings and tail created an insulated tent to fend off the frigid temperatures.

A growing buzz in the back of my mind signaled to me that the other dragons were awake and concerned. I let their essences trickle into my mind.

It is good to see you awake, Hatchling.

Yeah, we were getting worried about you.

I smiled at their concern. How long have I been asleep?

Almost three days. Nexxa deadpanned.

Three days?! Is everyone else alright?

"Everyone is fine, Love." Kitfox murmured and kissed my forehead. I exhaled the breath I hadn't realized I was holding. "Shazza and I have been checking on you and Thera often to make sure of it."

"I'm glad." I said with a kiss.

"I should probably get you something to eat." Kitfox peeled away from me and rolled out from under the covers. I heard him shiver as he crawled over to the saddle bag still

220

hanging from Wildfire. He removed a few things and quickly returned to my side. He set them beside me before slipping back between the blankets. "Don't walk on snow barefoot."

I spent the next half hour or so warming him back up. When at last he stopped shivering, I propped myself up on my elbows to snack on the food he delivered. "I can't wait to get out of this frozen wasteland."

Kitfox wholeheartedly agreed.

"Abaddon and Zenith." I thought aloud.

"Hum?"

I looked Kitfox in the eye. "Just two dragons left."

"Yeah."

"Then it's off to face Dimitri and his Twelve." That very thought terrified me.

"He's nowhere near as powerful as that chimera."

He wasn't before he had the Shadow Dragons in his possession. Helios stated matter-of-factly. Who knows how powerful he's gotten since you last faced him.

Kitfox frowned. You are not helping.

I'm simply saying—

I know what you're saying, Helios. I do. But I'm trying not to think so darkly about our next confrontation with Dimitri.

Forewarned is forearmed.

Kitfox growled in annoyance.

We will be ready for anything Dimitri throws at us. I said firmly.

I certainly hope so. With that, Helios's presence vanished.

"Were they always such pessimistic pains in the a—"

"Yes."

"How in Havel are you able to put up with it?"

I finished my snack and smiled as I snuggled up to him. "I have you, Thera, and Shazza to keep me sane."

He laughed at that.

Kitfox and I spent the next few hours talking about nothing in particular. We finally drifted off to sleep shortly after dawn painted the eastern sky. This time I did dream. I dreamt of peace and of the man I loved. I dreamt of a beautiful girl with dragon green eyes and lavender fox ears.

I awoke with a start as a blast of cold air struck my face. Kitfox bolted upright with a fierce growl. We both relaxed when we realized it was Thera and Shazza who had slipped through Wildfire's wing, not an enemy.

Shazza quirked an eyebrow.

Thera acted like nothing had happened and summoned a chair from the snow. "I'm vexed." She said quietly.

I asked what was bothering her as I sat up and wrapped the furs around me and Kitfox.

"'Abaddon guards the Dead of old; Through Havel's Ancient gates of gold.'"

It took a minute for what the Feykin said to register in my still sleepy mind. "So Abaddon is our next dragon."

Shazza scoffed. "You apparently didn't listen to the riddle. 'Through Havel'?"

"Yeah. I caught that part."

"We have to go to Havel to get the next dragon?" Kitfox was definitely appalled at the very thought.

"According to the riddle, yes."

"And just how are we supposed to do that?"

The three of them argued rather loudly about options and the rules for entering and exiting Havel. Every single one of them involved someone dying and somehow coming back to life. While they argued, I repeated the riddle quietly to myself over and over.

Ancient. Ancient? Why does Ancient feel familiar? A vision of an ancient, stone ruin flashed through my mind. "That's it!"

My three teammates gawked at me in stunned silence. Thera was the first to speak. "Uh... What's 'it'?"

"The Forgotten City!" I beamed. "There is a path to Havel hidden within the ruins. I've seen it."

Shazza looked more skeptical than usual. "Are you sure you're not in some energy-deprived state of insanity?"

222

"Fine. You don't believe me, but Thera knows what I'm talking about."

The Feykin blinked in surprise. "I do?"

"Remember back when we first got Vortex? I told you and Teka that I had a dream about some old stone building that was overgrown and we talked about the forest of white trees."

"Oh yeah!" Thera laughed. "I remember that now."

"That building hides the path to Havel!"

"Wow. Imagine if Teka was here now." Thera chuckled. "She'd be dancing like a crazy woman and singing about how her theory of a dragon in the Ancient City was correct."

Shazza cleared her throat. "I hate to interrupt this trip down Memory Lane, but since we now know how to get where we need to go, maybe we should, I don't know, get moving?"

I blew a raspberry at her.

Kitfox tried not to laugh as he asked, "Which direction do we go from here?"

"North to Mekora Lesca, then west, to the island at the end of the Bangorian Mountains."

"Oh good!" He smiled. "Someplace warmer."

"Not good." Said Shazza. "Bakari-Tokai is on Mekora Lesca."

"I know that."

"Well, if I'm right about Dimitri, he'll be holed up in the Grand Capitol while his forces patrol the area. We've been lucky so far that we haven't run into any soldiers, but that luck won't do us any good if we fly right into the heart of that bastard's forces."

"First of all, we're not flying anywhere near Bakari-Tokai. Second, no matter what you say or feel, we need to get this dragon. And lastly," I paused, knowing what I was about to say would be a huge blow to Shazza's ego, "what kind of Dákun Daju is afraid of a fight?"

I was right. Her sunburst eyes burned with rage and her hands turned to fists. In an instant, she was in front of me. Kitfox was on his feet in that same heartbeat, holding her at bay and growling.

"Xyleena-sortim is right, Shazza." Said Thera. "You have been afraid since Kkorian betrayed us."

"Shut up!" Shazza screamed.

Thera didn't listen. "You are afraid because you loved Kkorian. I don't know, maybe you still love him."

Shazza roared her fury and fought against Kitfox even harder. The Demon held fast to the enraged Dákun Daju, not letting her escape.

"You also fear you may have grown to love the three of us like family. And that is why you are avoiding fights. You don't want to go through the pain of losing us too."

Shazza stopped struggling. She stared straight ahead as if in a trance. A tear slipped from her eye. Her lip quivered. Kitfox released her with a gasp. She collapsed to her knees, hiding her face with her hands. She swayed as she lamented. "I hate him! I hate him for doing this to me."

I choked back my own tears and dared to hug her. "You don't hate Kkorian."

"He left me weak!"

"No." Kitfox knelt in front of her. "Kkorian left you stronger."

Shazza looked up, into Kitfox's amber eyes. "Stronger?"

Kitfox smiled as he glanced at me. "Love has a strange way of making people stronger in the end."

I reached out to take Kitfox's hand in my own. "People in love will put themselves in danger to protect the person who holds their heart, even if it costs them their life."

"That makes you stronger?"

"Absolutely!" Thera affirmed. "I would die for my sister, but I wouldn't go down without putting up one heck of a fight in the process."

It was several minutes of silence before a small smile etched its way across Shazza's lips. "Thank you, everyone." She wiped her tears away and looked me in the eye. "Let's go get Abaddon."

It was on the Golden Isle of Symbilla that I realized Xyleena was no longer the weak and self-doubting girl she had been when this quest started. Somewhere along the way, she had changed; grown stronger both mentally and physically. Now she really was the Dragon Keeper I had been looking for. And I would gladly follow this her into battle.

– FROM "THE SECOND KEEPER" BY THERA ONYX

Jetep was a queer little town nestled between the spectacular Bangorian Mountains and the southern ocean. Unlike most of the towns on Ithnez, Jetep thrived on illegalities. Huge casinos and whore houses brought in many an unattractive visitor. It provided the perfect environment for hiring mercenaries and other shady dealings. Jetep was usually a lively place… Usually.

As I looked upon Jetep from our hiding spot in the surrounding trees, I quickly realized the reason for the town's bizarre calm. A battalion of well-armed soldiers had taken over, leaving Jetep a mere ghost of what it was. From what I could tell, only the inn and the general store remained open for business.

I heard Thera and Kúskú approach. "Well?"

"It's just as we feared, but we'll have to risk it." I said with a sigh. I finally tore my gaze away from the town to look at my friend. "We need those riding leathers or we can't fly anywhere."

"Agreed." Thera began to disguise herself with her magic. As she was doing so, Kúskú cast his illusion. I watched in amazement as the silver dragon turned into a beat-up, wyvern-drawn cart.

"You two watch yourselves in there, okay?"

Thera nodded. The fake wyvern grunted.

"Good luck."

Thera waved as she took off for the main road to Jetep. Kúskú fell in step right behind her. The minute Thera stepped on the cobblestones, she struck up a lively song. The false wyvern whistled along happily. Almost an hour later, the duo was upon the town.

Thera and the false wyvern were stopped by the soldiers on guard at the road. I watched them closely while Thera explained her reasons for coming into town. The soldiers took a few minutes to search the wagon, and finally bought her story. They allowed her to pass through the checkpoint. She struck up her tune again as she strode up the road. Minutes later, Thera hitched the false wyvern at a post and entered the general store.

I exhaled a fraction of my tension, but knew I wouldn't be able to completely relax until Thera and Kúskú made it back safely. Until then, I could only watch and wait.

"You're making me nervous." I jumped at Shazza's sudden appearance beside me. She scoffed and crossed her arms. "Relax."

"I won't be able to until Thera's back safely."

"I hear you." Her sunburst eyes scanned the town for a moment. "Something doesn't feel right about this."

I frowned and looked up at her. "What's bothering you?"

"Don't you think it's a bit strange that all of our riding straps broke on the same day?"

I shrugged. "They have been used extensively for the past year."

"True, but have you taken a close look at the breaking points?"

I shook my head negative.

"They all look like they've been cut."

"I think you're being paranoid, Shazza." I said with a sigh. "Which one of us four would suicidal enough to try to sabotage our quest by cutting through riding straps? Besides, the dragons' scales are sharp enough to cut through the leather. Why can't it just be wear and tear?"

"What about the homunculus?"

"Visler is off hunting with Kitfox."

"I know that." She growled in frustration. "Think about it for a minute. The homunculus was created by Pyrex, who, as we all know, was the creator of the Shadow Dragons. How do you know Visler isn't working in tandem with Pyrex to sabotage us just enough to give the Shadow Dragons the upper hand?"

"You certainly give Visler a lot of credit." Shazza threw her hands up in defeat and stormed away. I wasn't about to tell her that her suspicions of Visler might hold warrant. That very real possibility terrified me, and that was the last thing I needed right now.

I forced my ragged nerves under control. I could only deal with one pressing issue at a time, and Thera's safety was far more important at the moment than a suspicion. I took a deep breath and returned my gaze to the barren town.

I couldn't believe what I saw! A figure cloaked in white was walking up the main street. Unlike the others I had seen, this one had a severe, yet familiar, limp. The apparition in white paused right outside the general store and looked at the false wyvern that was Kúskú. The dragon's illusion flickered for just a second. The cloaked figure bowed at the waist, turned in the direction it was originally heading, and walked away.

I resisted the urge to run after the figure and instead, turned my focus inwards. Dragons, do you know who Kúskú just saw?

They were silent for a moment. Finally, Helios answered, He would only say it was someone you can trust.

What happened, Xy? Kitfox sounded very concerned. Did something go wrong?

I don't know.

Thera and Kúskú are fine. Symbilla said calmly. Xyleena was just worried about the figure in the white cloak.

She appeared again?

Yes. And Kúskú's illusion faltered for a second when she looked at him.

Whoa. Kitfox paused as if in thought. You dragons are absolutely sure the figure in white isn't Amorez?

We would not mistake the visage of our creator. Nexxa declared.

Then who in Havel is under the cloak?

Someone you can trust. The dragons all answered at once.

I hope you are right about that. I said softly. I cut the connection when I saw Thera leaving the general store. She pretended to tuck the package she carried in the cart before un-tethering the false wyvern. They left Jetep the same way they had entered, bidding a fond farewell to the soldiers on guard.

While the riding straps were replaced and Kitfox's kills cleaned and packed, I told Thera of the figure in white. In turn, she told us the mystery person was the least of our worries. Dimitri's power had indeed increased dramatically since he obtained the Shadow Dragons. He now had the power to turn every soldier that made up his new army into his faithful puppet. And, to make matters worse, he and Godilai - the new High Sovereigns of Ithnez - knew of our escape from the Arctic Prison.

Armed with this information, we redoubled our efforts to obtain the last two Dragons of Light. Within the hour of Thera's return with the new leather, we were packed and airborne. I could tell from their demeanor that the dragons, too, were even more eager to see the release of their siblings and the defeat of our enemies.

We raced through the sky; forgoing the need to stop for breaks or rest. Our personal comfort had taken a back seat to our need to get ahead. I only prayed that we still had time.

It is a strange thing to sit and talk a while with a dragon. They have a cryptic way of replying most of the time, or they say something that can be taken several different ways. They do offer some excellent advice, especially considering that they had not been out of their eggs for very long.

– FROM "CONVERSATIONS WITH DRAGONS" BY DJURDAK ZA'CAR

T he dawn was already old when the island home of the Ancient City broke the horizon. The white ruins and trees sparkled like diamonds in the late morning light. We followed the refracted rainbows like beacons to a dream. That dream quickly turned into a nightmare. Tucked between the ageless ruins and glowing trees, an army awaited our arrival.

I told Wildfire to circle the island slowly so we could estimate the size of force Dimitri had gathered against us, but stay out of range of any weapons. Just as we soared over the main body of the army, something huge exploded out of the trees. It made a bee line straight for Wildfire. She managed to barrel roll to the right just in time as a skeleton dragon zipped past. The undead dragon had been so close that I could see the pits in its stained bones and smell the decay of its little remaining flesh.

"Wyrd!" Roared Wildfire.

The skeleton made a sound like a raspy laugh as he twisted around in midair to glare at us.

"And Nightshade!" Atoka hollered as she back winged in midair to avoid colliding with a plum-scaled dragon I never even knew was there. Before I could do anything to help them, the undead one spoke.

"Time to die, little one. Fates Decide!" A huge, black disc exploded into existence in front of us. Light bent around the circumference as if it were being sucked in by the blackness only to be expelled outwards in a spiraling jet. Wildfire reeled, but it was too late. She, Kitfox, and I were swallowed up by the void.

Thera and Shazza watched helplessly as their friends were pulled into the black hole created by Wyrd. Even Visler chirped sadly from under Thera's hood. They didn't have the time to think of a way to free them from the undead one's grasp before Nightshade struck.

Atoka roared in pain as the Shadow Dragon's talons tore open her wings. As she fell out of the sky, Atoka spit in the direction of her attacker. The saliva struck Nightshade's wingtip and froze solid, causing the Shadow Dragon to plummet several meters before she could break the ice.

Thera and Shazza barely had enough time to heal the tears in Atoka's wings before she collided with ground. Her wings flared wide and slowed her just enough to break her fall. She kicked off the ground and sped like a bullet towards Nightshade. The Shadow Dragon did likewise, nose-diving at breakneck speeds. At the last minute, both dragons brought their hind legs out in front of them. The dragons smashed into each other hard enough to crush bones.

While talons and teeth competed for the upper hand, Shazza loosed arrows upon Nightshade and Thera launched one spell after another. Every attack rebounded off of her diamond-hard scales, leaving her unharmed. Wyrd dove out of the sky, colliding with Atoka hard enough to force her away from Nightshade. Unable to fend off both Shadow Dragons at once, Atoka had no choice but to try and escape.

Kitfox shivered as he looked about. By the light of a few flickering candles, he explored his surroundings. He stood alone at the apex of a citadel of ancient, grey stones. There was no way down from the tower that he could see, and he wasn't sure if he even wanted to. Everything was dark; never-ending black. Who knew what lurked in the void.

Kitfox sighed and turned away from the edge of the tower. A blazing fire burst into existence right in front of him causing him to yelp in surprise and almost lose his footing.

The wild blaze calmed, revealing three hags so old their skin was like leather. Their eyes had long since rotted away, leaving only empty sockets. The hags were garbed in dingy, white robes that betrayed nothing of origin. They stood in a triangle over a smoldering cauldron. An image of Kitfox appeared on the surface of the bubbling contents. The hags recited something in a language he did not know.

As they spoke, one of the hags passed a length of string to another. Together, they held it taught over the cauldron while the third raised a pair of shears to it. Kitfox felt fear grip him in that instant; indescribable, immeasurable fear.

"N-no! I can't die here. Not like this."

The string slipped between the blades of the sheers and rested at the pivot point.

"Stop!"

The hag pulled the shears away from the string ever so slightly and looked his way.

"I decide my own fate, not you!"

The hags cackled. "And what fate have you chosen for yourself, child?"

Kitfox swallowed the lump in his throat and forced his fears under control. "I choose to... to live out my life with the woman of my dreams; to be a loving husband and doting father, a best friend and a mentor."

The hags cackled again. The one with the shears promptly snapped the blades shut over the string. Kitfox flinched. He felt nothing. The hags' laughter slowly died away. One of them growled. He heard the shears snap shut again and again. Kitfox cracked an eye open to see what happened. The string was aglow with a golden light and the shears had melted at the points where the hag tried to cut through.

The hag scoffed as she tossed the shears away. She looked at Kitfox and waved her arm in a wide arc. Another black disc appeared, only this time, daylight could be seen from the other side.

"Go and live."

Kitfox smirked and leapt towards the disc.

Kitfox burst out of the black hole several kilometers above the ground. Without a dragon there to catch him, he plummeted towards land. He cried out for help until he slammed into something hard. The air was promptly knocked out of his lungs and he rolled along the solid surface, desperately trying to grab something to stop him.

A dragon roared in pain as Kitfox's claws finally managed to smash through the hard surface. Kitfox jarred to a stop. Only then was he able to realize the extent of his situation. He was still several kilometers in the air only now, he was attached to the undead dragon's hip bone.

Wyrd glared over his shoulder, at the Fox Demon on his back. "Stupid Demon! I'll kill you for that!" Keeping true to his threat, the dragon nosedived. Kitfox hollered at him to stop, begging the dragon for a moment, but it was to no avail; the Shadow Dragon simply wouldn't listen. Wyrd roared in rage as he crashed into the ocean.

Atoka was leagues away from the Ancient City, still trying desperately to escape from Nightshade's deadly pursuit. Thera and Shazza kept launching spell after spell in hopes of bringing the Shadow Dragon down. Even Visler sent barrages of tiny lightning bolts at her, but nothing had any effect. The Dragon of Eternal Winter was grateful that Wyrd had decided not to join the chase. If he had, the three of them didn't have a prayer of living through this.

Still, Atoka couldn't help but fret about their entire situation. Xyleena had been sucked into the Fates' Dimension along with the Amulet and the rest of the Dragons of Light. No one had ever escaped the Fates before and Atoka felt it unlikely anyone could. Without the full power of the Light, the future of this world was suddenly looking very bleak. They had failed.

"What's that?" Shazza exclaimed between spells. Thera's magic paused for a moment to find what the Dákun Daju spotted.

"Atoka, turn around!"

"What?"

"Go back to the Ancient City!"

The dragon didn't need to be told twice. In that instant, she felt the nine hearts of her missing brothers and sisters reenter the world. Xyleena had escaped the Fates!

The Light was back in the world!

Atoka roared in delight.

I popped out of the black disc the Fates had sent me through. Half a heartbeat later, an unconscious Wildfire burst out of a similar disc. We were both midair several kilometers above the ground and Atoka was nowhere to be found. As gravity took over and the two of us plunged through the sky, I somehow managed to stay calm enough to release the dragons from my amulet.

The eight of them coalesced in a spectacular display of lights and elements. They quickly realized what was going on and separated into teams. Nexxa and Riptide dove after me while Symbilla, Vortex, and Thedrún moved in to help Wildfire. Nexxa managed to catch up to me in no time. She swooped beneath me, flipped onto her back, and caught me in her forearms.

Riptide streaked by as Nexxa rolled over and fluttered to regain altitude. I watched as the Dragon of Water melded into the ocean without so much as a ripple. Just when I began to wonder what she was planning, Wyrd exploded from the watery depths with a shriek of rage. Kúskú and Kkaia spotted the undead dragon and dove for him. Seconds later, the ocean itself stretched skywards and coagulated in the form or Riptide. And she wasn't alone! She had Kitfox tucked safely between her front paws.

Riptide hurled several large globules of water after Wyrd. They struck and were frozen solid moments later as Atoka streaked by with an angry Nightshade on her tail. Riptide promptly turned tail to chase down Nightshade. A split second later, Helios whipped by to aid his siblings against the Dragon of Shadow.

Kkaia and Kúskú took advantage of Wyrd's frozen status and slammed into him. I watched the trio of dragons crashed onto the island, bowling over several of Dimitri's soldiers and leaving them crushed. Moments later, another pair of crashing dragons reduced the number of soldiers even further.

With the threat of the Shadow Dragons now hopefully neutralized, I told Nexxa to land on the island. I had an army of brainwashed thugs to defeat and a dragon to collect. I couldn't do that from the air.

Nexxa flew in ever tightening circles over the island, searching for a large enough clearing to land in. It was proving to be a difficult task as several soldiers would swarm the areas Nexxa chose. Before she could even get her hind legs on the ground, she would have to take off again to avoid skewering me on their weapons. We were both growing extremely frustrated by the failed attempts. Finally, I told Nexxa to find a clearing and get as close as she could to the ground and just drop me.

She was not fond of the idea.

As Nexxa passed over a part of the forest on the northern side of the island, I spotted Wyrd. He was trying, almost in vain, to free himself from the icy prison Riptide and Atoka made sure to keep him in. Several meters away, Helios, Kkaia, and Symbilla kept Nightshade detained in a prison of earth and light. Upon learning five of my dragons were land bound, I quickly searched the area for signs of my friends and the other dragons.

Several meters away from the imprisoned Wyrd and Nightshade, on the outskirts of the Forgotten City, the forest flashed with several colors. I knew right away that several spells had been cast in rapid succession. Thera must be there, but facing who – or what – remained a mystery. I could only pray that Kitfox and Shazza were nearby to help.

"Finally!" Nexxa hollered out. A moment later, she dipped so low her wings nearly grazed the treetops. I could see the faces of several soldiers as they looked up to see what flew overhead. Mere moments later, they took off in a hurry to swarm the spot Nexxa had picked. She told me to get ready and I did.

Half a heartbeat passed and I spotted a gap in the trees. Nexxa dared to dive even lower and her wings smashed through a few of the tree tops. She almost came to a complete stop in midair and loosened her grip on me. She beat her wings hard to regain altitude as I dropped several meters to the ground. I landed with a grunt and rolled twice, simultaneously freeing my tessens from my belt and flaring them with a flick of my wrists.

I paused for a moment, listening; observing. White trees loomed all around me. They cast shadows so long they almost plunged the area into a false night. A silver mist danced and swirled between the glowing trunks. It left the ground soggy and smelling of fresh rain. Everything was silent, unnerving.

A horse whinnied.

I spun around to find it. A large, black horse trotted away through the trees. It paused and looked over its shoulder, revealing a golden horn in the middle of its forehead. It was the Goddess, Nahstipulí, in Her ixys form. I blinked and she vanished without a trace. Had I imagined it? Before I could perceive an answer, Dimitri's soldiers began swarming the area. I uttered a spell to distract them and took off through the trees in hopes of locating my missing teammates.

Thera spun away to avoid the plasma ball Pox had hurled at her. The sphere struck a tree and exploded with great fury, knocking several soldiers off their feet. The tree was rendered into nothing and countless splinters rained down on the area.

Thera growled in frustration as she coated herself with more wards. Her mind raced, desperately trying to devise a plan to free her sister from Dimitri's control without getting herself or Pox killed in the process. She dared to peak out from behind the tree she cowered behind to glance at Pox. The younger Feykin wasted no time hurling another spell at Thera's head.

"Heile esso!" A ball of violet fire shot out from Thera's hand just in the nick of time. Both spells struck each other and erupted in an explosion that leveled several surrounding area. Soldiers caught in the blast disintegrated into nothingness while others were thrown meters away from where they were standing.

Thera's knees shook and threatened to give out as her wards sucked away the energy needed to deflect the blast. She placed her palm flat against the tree, drawing in energy from its life force as she peered around its girth again. She located Pox a few meters from where she had been, blown away by the force of the blast. She was shakily crawling to her feet and trying in vain to reapply her own wards. An idea suddenly occurred to Thera and she quickly moved towards her sister.

Pox was too drained at that point to stop her sister from whatever she schemed. She fell back on her backside and hugged herself with her ebony wings as she trembled, both in fear and from the immense drain of energy. Thera stopped in front of her and cast a sphere around them for protection lest the soldiers try to interfere. Pox resisted the urge to cry as she looked into Thera's violet eyes. A look of pity crossed the older Feykin's features and she sighed.

"Pox," Thera's voice was as gentle as a kiss, "Piper, please tell me, did Dimitri give you anything when you met?"

Pox slowly nodded.

Thera knelt. "What did he give you?"

"This." Pox gingerly touched the ancient necklace draped around her neck.

"Take it off."

Pox refused. "The Shadow Keeper will brainwash me if I do."

"He already has, Piper." Thera whispered. Slowly, she reached out to grasp the necklace. She uttered a spell, gave a good yank, and the necklace fell to pieces. Pox gasped and looked about confused.

"Wh-where am I? How did I get here?"

Thera smiled in relief and hugged her sister tightly. Pox fought the embrace and begged for answers. "Your mind has been under the control of the Shadow Keeper for the last year and a half, but I finally managed to free you from him."

"Year and a half?" Pox was aghast. Before the sisters could exchange any more words, another presence burst into the clearing. Thera peered over her shoulder as soldiers rushed in. Shazza quirked an eyebrow at the Feykin and loosed arrows into the soldiers. She slapped several more away with the arms of her bow as she knocked and loosed more missiles.

"Kitfox needs help."

Thera glanced at Pox. "You ready?"

The younger Feykin nodded.

Together the three of them raced through the forest as fast as they could, taking out several soldiers along the way.

I dodged several low branches as I sprinted through the perpetual white forest. A horde of soldiers followed in my wake, making quite a ruckus in their haste. I could almost laugh at their clumsiness. Almost.

A vision in lavender and black flashed between the trees to my right. Recognizing who it was, I whooped in joy and promptly changed directions. As if sensing something was about to go terribly wrong for them, the soldiers redoubled their efforts to catch me.

An arrow whispered past my cheek and dug into a tree trunk with a loud thunk. I chose to ignore it, for retaliating the attack could prove a problem should the soldiers manage to surround me in the time it took to kill the archer.

The trees thinned at last, but the soldiers did not. I sped through the blockade with a frenzy of flashing steel and blood. Kitfox gaped at me as I came to a stop directly in front of him. Visler chirped happily as he landed on my shoulder and nudged his small head against my cheek. I stroked his body to calm him while I looked Kitfox over. The Demon was a mess of bloodied cuts and mud and his clothes had been torn, yet the disheveled look somehow flattered him. I whispered a few healing and warding spells and he sighed in relief.

"Thank you." He said and darted around behind me to block a blow from a soldier. Visler hissed and took flight to spit lightning at a few soldiers. Kitfox and I stood together, our backs facing each other as we sunk into fighting stances, ready to defend ourselves against the swarms of soldiers closing in around us.

"Have you seen Shazza or Thera?" I asked over my shoulder.

"We got separated."

Before anything else could be said between us, the soldiers surged forward. I charged the first wave of soldiers in a short encounter, killing or incapacitating at least four in the first few seconds. Still more rushed forward, and more again. Every one of them met a similar fate as those who had come before. Soon, a few dozen men were slumped and lifeless around me and still more were moving in.

Gods! How many are there?

A flare of violet light exploded from the trees and a huge fireball tore through the ranks of soldiers. The inferno burned itself out in seconds and a black ash fluttered to the ground like snowflakes. The stench of untold numbers of burnt corpses stung my eyes and burned my nose. Most of the few remaining soldiers haphazardly retreated further into the woods. I took a moment to rest and check on Kitfox. He was a few meters away, desperately batting at the purple flames clinging to his tail. It was several seconds before they were finally extinguished.

"Thera!" He shouted at the trees. "You burned my tail!"

"You'll survive." She laughed. Visler dove for her as she entered the clearing with Shazza and Pox in tow. Upon seeing the younger Feykin, Kitfox sunk into a defensive stance and glanced at me as if asking for help.

"You need not fear me, Demon." Pox said quietly. "Thera broke the spell which held my mind hostage."

"Dimitri used an ancient necklace as a catalyst," explained Thera, "and when I broke it, Piper was freed from its influence."

Kitfox slowly relaxed his guard.

"Do you know how many soldiers Dimitri sent against us?" I asked.

Pox shook her head. "I'm sorry. The last thing I remember is being in the Elders' Chamber in Thorna. Everything after that is a complete blank."

"I know how you feel."

"So," Shazza coughed and waved her hand in front of her face to clear the smoke, "what is the plan now?"

I let my eyes close. Focusing on the remnants of my dreams from so long ago, I pieced together a memory. "We have to get to the Temple." My brow furrowed as I recalled the building. "It's secluded from the rest, surrounded by trees..." I opened my eyes, "... on the western edge of the city."

"Let's get going before those soldiers decide to come back." Shazza said as she knocked a pair of arrows.

A deep baritone guffawed in the darkness. "Too late."

The five of us flourished our weapons in a flash. The shadows of the forest closed in all around us and with them came countless soldiers. The grotesque Judge, Vincent, strode confidently from the trees, passing between lines of soldiers until he was just meters away from me. He stabbed the handle of his giant axe into the ground and smirked as he leaned against it.

"Well, well, well." Vincent chuckled. "What are you going to do now, little girl."

"Oh, I can think of a few things." I grinned. "For starters," I pointed a folded tessen at him, "I think I'll take a few kilos off your backside. Kinda lighten the load for you."

His smugness evaporated with a snarl. "Kill them!"

In an instant the countless hordes of soldiers surged forward; shields up, swords drawn, bloodthirsty. I bellowed as they engaged me and lashed out right and left with my war fans. I felt the flesh of their necks shred as the many blades sliced through. They fell away, clutching their throats and gurgling for only a second before their lives were snuffed out. More soldiers moved in and the dance was repeated.

Blood soaked the earth and the glowing, white trees turned an eerie crimson. The hordes of soldiers continued to throw themselves upon our blades. There were no painful hollers. No cries of anguish. No pleas for mercy. Just silence. Death. Massacre. Slaughter.

Dimitri, what have you done to these men?

I wept. For every blow I landed, a tear was shed.

Baféjo ni Heile.

I gasped at the familiar, spectral whisper. I kicked the corpse of yet another soldier away and dared a glance deep into the white forest. A red light danced between the glowing trunks as if beaconing to me. Memories of the nearly forgotten dream that started this whole quest suddenly came flooding back.

"Come on!" I shouted. I launched a spell to clear a path between the soldiers and took off after the red light. Kitfox called out to me, asking what was happening as he, Shazza, Thera, and Pox took off after me. I didn't answer; there wasn't time to.

Behind us Vincent bellowed, "After them!"

The soldiers, of course, obeyed without question.

We raced through the forest for about thirty meters when, out of the corner of my eye, a crimson and gold bird launched off a branch. The phoenix burst into flames with a screech and streaked through the trees. A wall of crimson fire roared to life in Her wake and promptly took up chase.

She screeched again as She passed in front of me and I smiled. She sped off with the fire close on Her tail, disappearing into the thicket. I kept running, onwards, towards the wall of fire. My friends hollered for me to stop, and I yelled back, "Keep up with me!"

I sped through the crimson flames without hesitation and without injury. As I had anticipated, the inferno was nothing but an illusion meant to throw off the soldiers. I finally slowed to a stop just as my teammates crossed over the roiling barrier. I could tell from the look in their eyes, they had no idea what had just happened. Before they could utter a word, the first wave of soldiers came face to face with the inferno. For them, the fire was as real as the ground they walked on and they ignited in an instant.

I turned my back on the massacre. With a whispered prayer for the dead, I calmly lead the way towards the Forgotten City.

The white cloaks were getting to me – actually to all of us. Xyleena had mentioned one of them helping a maiden in Monrai, another was spotted in Vronan, and yet a third was recently observed in Jetep. Who was under those cloaks? Were they helping us or…?

More riddles. Just when I had had my fill of them.

– FROM "THE SECOND KEEPER" BY THERA ONYX

The silver mist roiled as I lead my teammates through the forest. The shadows of the trees had grown even longer, stretching eastward as if trying to touch the horizon. The darkness gave the impression of midnight, and I had to summon a light by which to see.

Over an hour had passed since we left the soldiers to burn. The damp, uneven ground we strode on had finally taken to a steep incline. I knew then, our destination was drawing nearer. Another hour had passed with the six of us plodding along through the muck and branches. The muscles in my legs burned from the exercise and begged me for rest.

I pushed on.

The soggy earth soon gave way to ancient stones, and the city loomed out of the trees before us. I paused beneath a half-standing archway to admire the ghost of a memory.

The Forgotten City had been built in multiple tiers, carved into the sides of the surrounding hills. Everything was centered around a trio of huge, rectangular yards which stepped gradually down until the lowest one nearly touched the rolling sea. The first level of the city above the yards was vast and overgrown with foliage that, at one time, was part of a luscious garden. Many walkways and stairs that once led to the upper levels had been reduced to nothing more than gravel. The second tier contained the majority of the buildings, most of which were nothing but piles of rubble now. The third and fourth tiers were similar to the second, but with more room for gardens. A fifth and even a sixth tier had been carved into the hills in a few places. Both of those levels were barren save for foliage and a few large chunks of stone.

The city had had a proper name once; I remembered speaking it. But like so many things in the distant past, it, too, had been forgotten. Only ghosts and legends remained.

"Why was this place abandoned again?" I jumped at Thera's sudden and loud inquiry.

"I heard a plague wiped out the entire population." Kitfox replied.

"Not quite." Shazza and I chorused. We exchanged a look while the others looked on in a mix of confusion and awe.

I took several steps into the city and turned to face my friends. I raised my arms as if to catch rain and smiled. "Behold the first Hume city of Ithnez."

"We Dákun Daju called it S'vil-Tokai, City of Intruders, but the Humes named it Arcadia."

I snapped my fingers and pointed at Shazza. "That's it! That was the name! I couldn't remember."

"Ironic." Mumbled Kitfox. I blew a raspberry at him, turned quickly on my heel, and started off through the city. He and the others were quick to follow.

"The Humes were forced to leave S'vil-Tokai because of Agasei." Shazza explained. "During the time of his ascension to Dragon Keeper, his newborn Dragon of Venom attacked the island. When she was done having her way, the trees had turned stark white and the mist rolled in; proof that the area was no longer able to sustain life."

"But the Humes stayed anyway." I added, hopping over a thick root that wove its way across the stone walkway. "They stayed until famine and sickness claimed most of the population."

"After that, the Humes fled to Mekora Lesca, and settled in the area which would later become Bakari-Tokai, City of Survivors."

"Yeah," I sighed, "then Agasei up and attacked again, claimed an easy victory, and declared himself King of all Ithnez."

"I confess a curiosity," said Pox. "You said the cities' names, Bakari- and S'vil-Tokai, meant City of Survivors and Intruders. I thought those were Earther words. What language is it?"

Shazza smirked at the young Feykin. "It is the real Ancient Tongue of Ithnez, Daihindi, Holy Language of my people. It was combined with the Earthers' Standard dialect and transformed into Kinös Elda."

"Thanks for that interesting history lesson." Kitfox said cheerfully. "I am a bit surprised that you knew so much about it though, Shazza. Pay attention in school?"

She scoffed, and ducked under a mess of dangling tree roots as we passed through an arch. She paused to look around. "Are we leaving S'vil-Tokai?"

"I told you," I said, casting a glance at her over my shoulder, "the Temple is on the western edge of the city."

"Are we close to it?" Asked Pox.

I nodded.

"What's so special about this Temple anyway?"

I smiled. "You'll see."

I led the way around a bend in the path and the trees thinned. I smiled as I came to a stop and my teammates gathered around. The Temple of Arcadia towered over us.

The Temple was made of white quartzite blocks, polished as smooth as glass. The forest had overtaken much the building in the centuries since the city's abandonment. Thick vines and roots crept along the walls, competing for room and cracking the pristine shell like an egg. Great portions of the rock had crumbled away; the ground was littered with evidence of the decay.

A gate of golden lattice marked the entrance. Perched just above the gate was a black dragon statue. Unlike the others, this one had its wings outstretched as it stood on all fours. Its head was bowed as if in respect to the holy area it had been placed in.

Between the doorway and my team, a narrow bridge spanned a tranquil stream.

"Follow me." I softly said. I took the first steps onto the bridge. When the ancient stones didn't crumble away as I had expected, I moved a little more confidently over the bridge. My teammates walked single-file behind me.

I pulled the gold gate open, surprised that the hinges did not protest the movement after centuries of disuse. My teammates filed into the Temple. Kitfox lingered beside me, taking hold of the gate as he ushered me over the threshold. The gate slipped shut with a resounding clang. Birds roosting in the remains of the Temple rafters squawked and took flight on a thunder of wings. They rushed through the gaps in the Temple roof in hopes of escaping whatever disturbed them. Finally everything fell silent.

I took a breath and moved past my teammates. I stepped down the five stairs, into the body of the Temple. I stopped in the middle and looked about while the others joined me.

The main room was circular and large enough to fit at least three dragons abreast. A raised platform ran the circumference of the room. Upon the platform stood five statues, placed at specific intervals to create a pentagram. The statues each measured about five meters high and depicted the Hume-forms of the Gods or Goddesses for which the Temple had been built.

They were the Five Souls of Creation. I bowed my head in respects to each of them, pausing longest in Zahadu-Kitai's direction to quietly thank her for her help escaping the hordes of soldiers.

Directly opposite the entrance, behind the formless statue of Régon and between two crumbling staircases that once led to the priest quarters above, a door was hidden.

Anyone else who would set their eyes on the door would think it nothing more than decoration, but I knew better. The door was craft from the same stone as the Temple making it appear as nothing was there, but inlayed into the bricks, in a pentagram pattern, were gold plates; five in all. Each plate was about the size of my hand and had an elemental seal embossed upon it. And every so often, a light representing the element on the plate would radiate outwards before fading away.

"It's locked."

My teammates shot me a quizzical look.

"The Path of the Gods is locked." I pointed at the five radiating seals.

"What exactly is the 'Path of the Gods'?" Asked Kitfox as he peered around the statue of Régon to look at the door.

"The Path is the only way for a living person to reach Havel." I watched, bemused, as my teammates seemed to grow evermore impressed by the doorway.

"Can it be unlocked?"

"Of course." I smiled as I moved towards the door. "It just takes a Priestess and some patience."

I knelt before the door and clasped my hands before me in prayer. I forced every thought and worry from my mind, focusing only on invoking the attention of the Five Souls. "Daughters and Sons, Creators of All, Appear now, Your Priestess calls." I quietly repeated the chant over and over.

Time slipped away. I let it. There was no rush. I knew the Gods would hear me and come. I repeated the chant again. As the last word fell from my lips, a horse snorted. I heard my teammates gasp in surprise and shuffle around for a better view. A smile spread across my lips and I slowly opened my eyes.

Before me was the ebony ixys I had seen vanishing into the depths of the white woods. Her form was transparent as She stood half in front of me, half behind the door. She shimmered as if a great heat rolled off Her and Her body morphed. Seconds later, the ixys was replaced with a nude woman. She had long, flowing brown hair and dazzling emerald eyes. A golden horn protruded from the middle of Her forehead, the only sign She had ever been an ixys. In a flash of emerald light, Nahstipulí was clad in a flowing, black dress adorned with flowers and vines.

I thanked Her for coming in Kinös Elda.

"I know why you have called, Child." She replied back as She stepped further beyond the door. Her transparent form solidified until I felt like I was face-to-face with a normal person.

"Then you know the importance of our passage into Havel."

Nahstipulí's gaze swept across the faces of each of my teammates before settling on me again. "They cannot come."

"May I ask why?"

"We cannot protect their souls in the Realm of the Dead. Should they attempt to pass into Havel as they are, they will die. You alone are protected as you follow a holy path."

"But..." I looked at Kitfox over my shoulder. His brow furrowed in concern. His ears drooped as Thera quietly translated the conversation for him. He thanked Thera and strode forward. Nahstipulí watched him in interest as he drew closer. He finally stopped less than a meter away from me and slowly bowed to the Goddess.

"Please forgive my interruption," he said in Standard, "but I would like to say something to Xy."

Nahstipulí nodded and stepped away.

Kitfox turned to me and took my hand in his. "Xy, I know you're scared to do this alone; I can read it in your face. But you have to remember: you are strong and I have all the confidence that you are going to succeed."

"But..." I caught him in a tight hug and fought the urge to cry. "I don't know what I would do if I run into him."

"Him?"

"Ríhan." Kitfox flinched slightly at the name and I knew he hadn't thought of that. "What if he's still in Havel? What will I do if I run into him?"

Kitfox sighed, kissed my cheek, and held me tighter. "Xy, I love you. Just remember that and," his voice grew to a whisper, "remember our daughter," he smiled lovingly. "Everything will be fine."

"Thank you." I said before claiming his lips in a tender kiss.

"Oh, and I'll tell the dragons where you went when they show up."

I nodded.

After a moment more of lingering in each other's embrace, we broke apart.

Nahstipulí looked at me over Her shoulder as I stepped towards Her.

"I am ready."

The Goddess said nothing as She walked up to the door blocking the Path of the Gods. She tapped each golden plate and the radiating lights vanished with a puff. The sound of stone scraping stone echoed in the Temple as the heavy door slowly crept aside. I took my place at Nahstipulí's side and peered over the threshold.

The Path of the Gods was a golden staircase that seemed to stretch onwards, to eternity. It was surrounded with cosmic colors that swirled like smoke in the wake of a passer-by.

"Take my hand."

I did as She told me.

Together we passed over the threshold. I glanced back at my teammates as the door began to slide back into place behind us, lingering longest on Kitfox. I caught his reassuring smile just before the door finally shut with a resounding thud. I breathed slowly to calm my nerves and turned my attention to the path ahead.

Hand in hand, I walked with Nahstipulí.

I had no idea how long Nahstipulí and I climbed the golden stairs. It could have been minutes or days. Either way, my legs did not burn from the trek. And an end to the climb was nowhere in sight. I began to worry that the Path would not end before a lifetime passed in the world outside.

The Goddess did not seem to notice my growing fears. She just kept Her emerald gaze fixed on the winding stairs ahead, almost as if looking for something.

More time passed and we climbed on. I sighed to expel my frustration and developed a way to keep myself distracted on the trek. I began to imagine things in the colors that swirled and warped around us like one would look for shapes in the clouds. I managed to find several animal shapes before a soft chuckle caught my attention.

I looked at Nahstipulí. Only then did I realize we had stopped walking.

"You certainly have quite an imagination, Child."

I blushed as I murmured a thank you.

I was about to ask why we stopped when Nahstipulí waved her hand in a wide arc. The cosmic colors danced away, revealing an archway of gold lattice. Within the archway, a strange, turquoise liquid swirled and spun into a funnel. Standing guard, on either side of the portal, were two almost identical ice nymphs. Each bared a trident and shield formed of ice and silver armor. They stared coldly at me.

"It is Atlidmé's time." Nahstipulí said. "Because of this, you must go on alone."

"You can't enter Havel during another Soul's time?"

Nahstipulí shook her head. "Only the Angel of Chaos may interrupt our individual reigns."

"I did not know that."

"Go now, Child." Nahstipulí pulled me forward slightly and released my hand. "Do not fear becoming lost, for help awaits you on the other end of the bridge."

Before I could ask Her what She meant, She vanished in a flash of emerald light. I stood there a moment, staring at the swirling liquid in contemplation. I took a deep breath and, slowly, moved towards the golden archway. The nymphs' chilling gazes followed my every move. I paused a step away from the portal and looked at the nymph on my right.

"I don't suppose you can give me a head's up on what lies beyond?"

The nymph merely stared back.

I sighed and let my eyes close. Finally, I moved past the golden archway. The turquoise liquid made a slurping sound as I pushed my way through it. Suddenly a great rush of wind ripped past me and stole my breath away. I threw my hands up in front of me to spare me from the onslaught. I had to fight to remain upright as the violent gale threatened to bowl me over. The windstorm ended almost as quickly as it began, leaving a light breeze brushing against me.

I hesitated for a moment, then, slowly, lowered my arms to my sides. My eyes flittered open. My vision cleared. I gasped.

Built upon an island was a city of crystal and gold. It was so vast that I could not even begin to fathom how many souls resided there. Hundreds of towering spires pierced the clear blue sky and refracted the light into countless rainbows. Smaller buildings and even plants of likes I had never seen spread across the island.

The island itself was suspended in a void, surrounded by thundering waterfalls that threw great plumes of mist airborne. The mist gave the impression that the island was floating in the clouds. Jutting out from the island, at five separate points, were long, crystalline bridges adorned with gold filigree. They floated just above the surface of the rushing turquoise water. At the end of each bridge was a circular platform large enough to hold a dragon comfortably.

I stood on one of those five platforms, gawking at the spectacle that was Havel. After several minutes of observing, I shook my head and forced myself under control. I did not come here for sightseeing. I told myself. I need to find Abaddon.

With that, I strode forward.

I had only just reached the half-way point over the bridge when disembodied warble caused me to pause. Seconds later, a large shadow flew by overhead. I looked up in time to catch sight of Atlidmé as He slithered through the sky towards the city. Several orbs of sparkling light swirled around Him as he flew. As I watched Him, I realize it was He who was the source of the song, and the lights were souls of the departed. He was using the song to comfort and guide the souls to Havel.

A soft smile found its way to my lips as I watched Him. When at last He and the souls vanished from sight, I strode forward once again.

At the end of the bridge, I stopped to look around for the help Nahstipulí told me would be waiting. When I didn't see anyone, I decided on taking a short rest. As I sat cross-legged on the crystalline walkway, I cast my gaze skyward. Atlidmé slithered passed overhead, heading away from Havel. This time, He was alone in His journey and silent.

"Magnificent, isn't He?"

My heart was in my throat the instant the voice spoke. I knew immediately who it was. I did not want to face him. Not now. Not after the scars left after his murder had finally healed. I wasn't sure I could handle reopening those old wounds.

"How have you been, Xy?" He said, drawing nearer.

I clenched my fist and fought back tears. I silently begged for his presence to just be a nightmare; that I would wake up any second now.

"Xy?"

I flinched as he touched my shoulder. The first tears finally slipped from my eyes. They traced a cool trail down my cheeks before the breeze kissed them away.

He retreated slightly. "It's alright, Xy," he whispered softly, "you don't need to mourn for me anymore."

"Ríhan," I said quietly, surprised at how even my voice was despite what I was feeling, "I thought I had stopped mourning your death months ago."

"Then why do you cry upon hearing my voice and fear looking at me?"

"Because..." I swallowed a sob, "Because I don't want to betray Kitfox."

I could hear Ríhan smile. "You won't betray him."

"How do you know?" I forced myself to finally face my old friend. He looked the same as he did the day he died; almost as if his murder never happened. His blue eyes sparkled beneath his blonde bangs as his smile widened.

"I know because you love him."

My brow creased as I looked at him in confusion.

He sat down facing me. "Ever since you woke up in the Healer's in Sindai, I've been watching out for you. I know how much pain you've gone through since I died as well as all the joys you've experienced. I know all about your quest for the dragons, your friends and how important they are to you, and your relationship with Kitfox."

"You—" I gaped. "How?"

Ríhan chuckled. "The Souls let me remain in Havel for a specific reason; the same reason for which you have come."

"Abaddon?"

He nodded. "I was charged with the task of guiding you to your dragon once you arrived. Until that time, I was allowed to keep watch over you through what They called the Oracle Mirror."

"So… Once I have Abaddon, you have to leave?"

"That, I am not sure on." Ríhan shrugged. "I've proven myself to be quite reliable and helpful in…" he coughed, "situations. I think the Gods may keep me on a little longer."

"I see." I looked down to pick invisible lint off my armor. "So, you know all about me and Kitfox?"

"Well, not everything." Ríhan smiled. "I do know he's a nice guy and would do anything for you, even die."

I jerked my head up to meet his eyes. "You know about that?"

"Of course I do. I'm the one who sent the ice nymph to try to warn you in advance."

"That was you?"

He burst out laughing. "Yeah. I'm sorry it didn't work the way I planned. Though, it did have some very interesting consequences for both of you."

"I— I don't know what to say." I looked down at my armor again.

"You don't have to say anything." He said softly.

We lapsed into a comfortable silence after that. I knew Ríhan wanted to tell me all about his time here. He was the sort to blurt about his adventures to anyone who would lend an ear. In the past I had always that ear, but for reasons unknown, he said nothing. I, on the other hand, simply basked in his presence, realizing just how much I had missed him after so long.

Finally he stirred, getting to his feet and stretching. Then he looked down at me. With a smile, he extended his hand.

"Come. Someone wants to meet you."

"Who?"

"You'll see."

I slowly reached out to take his hand and he helped me to my feet. He took the lead through the city, winding our way from street to crystalline street and over bridges of solid gold that crossed over pristine streams of turquoise water. I was impressed that he did not get lost in the vast labyrinth that was Havel.

Occasionally I would linger behind Ríhan to observe things. Things like orbs of dancing lights loitering around a gold fountain or more lights chasing each other down one of the many streets. Ríhan would let me watch for a minute before calling me away. As we walked on, he explained that the dancing lights were the souls of the dead. Most of the dead were not allowed to retain the shapes of their bodies because they weren't in Havel for very long. A select few, like himself, were allowed to keep their bodies in order to perform important tasks on the Gods' behalves.

Ríhan hasn't changed one bit. I mused. He is still a plethora of information.

After what felt like hours of walking, Ríhan stopped beside a solid, golden door. It was set upon the opaque walls of a round building. Though the building wasn't nearly as tall as those around it, it still towered over the two of us. And it could easily fit two dragons abreast within.

Ríhan turned to me and smiled. "You ready?"

"Boy, I hope so."

His smile widened as he pulled the door open.

I preceded Ríhan into the building. The room just over the threshold was as small as my quarters at the Temple. There were no decorations; just opaque walls of crystal and a door I would have almost overlooked if not for the golden handle. Figuring our destination was on the other side of this bland vestibule, I moved to open the door. Ríhan stopped me.

"Trust me," he chuckled nervously and slipped passed me, "it's safer if I do it." He rested his hand on the handle of the door. There, he hesitated. "You might want to back up a bit."

I quirked an eyebrow and took a couple steps back.

Ríhan took a deep breath. In a single movement, he jerked the door open and ducked for cover. A split second later the tail blade of a dragon smashed into both door and wall, sending large chunks of crystal hurling everywhere.

"Calm down you blundering lizard!" Ríhan roared from the floor.

The dragon yanked his tail blade from the wall with a ferocious snarl and I got my first clear look at him. Abaddon was unlike any of the other dragons. His scales were as black as darkest night; a sharp contrast to his ivory horns and talons. As diamond hard as I knew they were, several scales had been ripped away on his right ribcage. The scar left behind glimmered the same shade of violet as his eyes when he moved. But the most amazing feature was the dragon's near-transparency. I felt as though if I were to reach out to touch him, my hand would pass right through.

"You are fortunate to be dead already, Boy, else I would eat you alive piece by piece!" His voice was deep and seemed to echo, almost as if there were two of him.

Ríhan stood to his full height while dusting crystal shards off his shoulders. He looked sidelong at me and, with a sigh, said, "I swear he gets crankier every time I visit."

I couldn't help but chuckle as I followed him into the room.

"And who is that tasty-looking morsel?"

"She…" a melodic baritone stated loudly from behind the black dragon. A chair squeaked as it slid across the floor and a tall man strode out from where he had been hidden. His hair was black with graying streaks along his temples and tied back in a low tail. He was clad in a regal blue tunic adorned with gold embroidery and gray trousers. A jewel pummeled sword hung from his thick, leather belt. He smiled warmly as his sepia gaze settled on me. "… is your Dragon Keeper."

"That puny little thing?" Abaddon snorted. "Don't make me laugh."

Keeping my eyes locked on the unknown – yet somehow familiar – man, I raised my left hand towards the dragon. With a simple flick of my wrist, Abaddon skittered across the floor several meters. His talons left several long gouges in the floor as he screeched to a stop.

I finally looked away from the man to stare the ghostly dragon down. "If you are still laughing, I can show you more."

Abaddon snorted again and moved towards me. For a long moment, the only sound in the room was his claws clicking against the floor with each step. A mere meter away, he finally stopped. He stared at me in silence. I stared back. At long last, he sat on his haunches and relaxed. His tail wagged behind him like that of a happy feline. "You have not lost your fierce spirit, small one. I am glad to learn this, given the extent of your memory loss."

With the dragon finally calmed, I turned my attention to the man in blue. "Who are you?"

The question seemed to catch him off guard.

"Xy," Ríhan placed a hand on my shoulder, "that is Djurdak, your..."

"Father." The dragon interrupted. The moment the word was spoken, a thousand memories rushed back to me. Several special ones replayed as if I were there to watch them all over again.

I was six. He was teaching me how to ride a wyvern for the first time. He panicked when the creature bolted and I nearly fell off. Later, he treated me to some sweats at our favorite stand in a long-forgotten town.

I was fifteen. He and I were on a hill top close to our home, nestled comfortably in the long grass. We watched the stars on a rare moonless night. He had carried me to my bed that night.

I was nineteen. He was showing me the mysterious silver rod from Earth for the first time. It was then that he revealed to me he was once the High Prince of Ithnez. He had given up all claims to the throne for mom and me.

I was twenty-three. He sat at the dinner table, trying not to laugh as I paced before him. I was ranting about how mom drilled me on the day's battle lessons over and over. That night, he took me out to dinner and treated me to my first pint of ale.

I was twenty-nine. His hair was just starting to gray at the temples. He sat with mom across the room from me, a grim look in his eyes. A Healer passed between us. Her words echoed over and over, "Your heart is failing."

I was thirty-one. I gazed upon his peaceful face one last time. I cried as the lid of the ornate casket slowly closed.

The memories faded away like tendrils of smoke on a breeze. I blinked through tears, a bit shocked that I had not noticed I was crying. I wiped away the cooling trails they left behind and tried in vain to force myself under control.

A wry smile touched Djurdak's lips. "She remembers now."

I stifled a sob and ran for him. He threw his arms wide and caught me in a loving embrace. He kissed my forehead as I wept on his shoulder. I held him firmly, never wanting to let him go.

"I missed you, Daddy."

His breath hitched and he held me tighter, whispering gently in my ear, "I missed you too, my princess."

We lingered together in that embrace for a long while; neither of us wanting to end it. It was Abaddon who finally tore us apart with a snide remark on how pathetic we were being. I sent the ghostly dragon skittering across the floor with a silent spell for a second time. He snorted in amusement and laid down where he stood.

I glared at the dragon, angry that he interrupted the first moment I had with my father in centuries. I was about to say something about it when I spotted a strange, red light over the crest of spines on his back. The dragon noticed this, and situated himself to follow my gaze. The movement revealed to me the source of the light.

Between two chairs, a deformed quartz-like crystal sat atop a gold pedestal. It was as red as a cherry and seemed to glow from an inner source. I made a quick comparison on sizes, realizing that the crystal was only a hand's breath taller than I. Within the depths of the quartz, I could I make out the shape of a twisted shadow. The shadow seemed to be the source of the light that I had spotted.

"Ah. That." Abaddon grunted. I detected notes of sadness and disdain in his echoing tones. "That is Agasei."

My jaw fell slack.

"More appropriately, it is what was left of him after your mother kicked his sorry ass." Djurdak laughed.

"What is he doing here? I thought he would be locked up in a deeper area of Havel, where the rest of the evil souls are sent for punishment."

Ríhan clicked his tongue as he strode towards the twisted crystal. He stopped several meters away, as if he were afraid to draw closer. "The evil souls get sent to the bottom of the falls, to a misery beneath the island housing Havel. They spend centuries being purged of their crimes. But those are all mortal men and women."

"Agasei is immortal and kept alive by dragon power; the same as you and Amorez." Djurdak said. "The Gods were unsure what to do with him, so they locked him up where someone could keep a constant vigil over him. I was the first of many to be chosen for the task."

"Then you buried me here three centuries ago," Abaddon sounded bitter about that decision, "and the Gods charged me with guarding him. I have yet to see Their wisdom in the decision."

Djurdak snorted. "Same here."

The dragon growled.

"Don't get me wrong, Abaddon, we are glad to have you with us." I could tell Djurdak was speaking honestly. "It is just confusing to have a former Shadow Dragon guard his former Keeper."

"Why did you switch sides anyway?" I asked. Out of the corner of my eye, I saw my father wince. Ríhan shook his head, closing his eyes as the dragon furiously snarled.

"Am I not good enough for you, little girl?" Abaddon's voice grew rough and his violet eyes flashed red as he shouted at me. "Would you rather have only eleven? I am sure it would make your quest so much easier on you!"

"That is not what I meant, Abaddon." I kept my voice even, as to not infuriate him further. "I was simply wondering what influenced you to leave the Shadow Dragons."

A sound like rolling thunder escaped the dragon's throat. "Look at me closely, child. Tell me what you see."

I blinked in surprise at the friendliness in his tone. Did his voice just change? I thought to myself as I did as he directed. As before, I saw a near-transparent, jet black dragon with a terrible scar on his right side. I shrugged. "I see you."

"Look again." He growled.

This time, I walked straight up to him and slowly studied every nook, every cranny, every scale, talon, fang, and spike. As my inspection traced the edges of his scar, the dragon took a breath. That is when I saw something was amiss. The violet flesh moved as he drew in air, but his transparent exterior remained the same. A moment later, the transparent portion of him took a shorter breath while the violet flesh remained still. I shot him a perplexed look and he seemed to smile.

"What exactly was that?"

He craned his neck until his enormous head was a mere hand's breath above the floor. His violet eyes stared straight at me. "Were you told of Taypax?"

I said I had been told a brief history of his fate.

Abaddon nodded. "During the final battle between Shadow and Light, both he and I were mortally wounded. As we lay next to each other dying, we made a pact. Because I was ghost element, I could possess him and, with what little remained of what would be our combined strength, heal our wounds just enough to allow us both survive. In short, it guaranteed that we would both live on instead of fading into memory like my brothers, Felwind and Adoramus."

His voice took on that strange, friendlier tone again as he continued. "The plan had been to stay in our combined body just long enough for our wounds to heal and then go our separate ways. We didn't realize that, as our wounds healed, we became forever fused together as a single dragon. Well, almost a single dragon." He made a sound like a laugh. "There are times when I am in control instead of Abaddon and vice versa."

My jaw dropped. "You are both Taypax and Abaddon?"

"Yes." The dragon's voice echoed as if two had spoken at once.

His voice took on a deep, gruff tone as he continued the story. "When Taypax and I discovered we could not separate as planned, we approached Amorez. We told her of our plight, but neither she nor Thernu could do anything to help restore us to our original bodies."

The friendlier voice, which I realized was actually Taypax, spoke now. "When Amorez revealed her plans for the Shadow Dragons, she gave Abaddon the option to join the Light. It made sense to me as I knew she did not want to punish one of her own for something we had not been a part of."

They finished their story as one echoing voice. "The decision was an easy one to make, for neither of us wanted to be sealed beyond the Dragons' Gate."

"That is just amazing!" I exclaimed. "I can just imagine how crazy my teammates are going to react when they meet you two."

"Their story is unique amongst the dragons." Said my father as he walked up to me. "And I believe that they have the advantage over all the others."

I nodded in agreement. "With their two minds occupying one body, they would have a better awareness on their surroundings. It would be very difficult for an enemy to get the drop on them."

"I've always wanted to know, Abaddon," Ríhan pricked the dragon's attention, "how did the other dragons react when they learned of your fused body?"

"The Shadow were furious, especially after they learned I had decided to become Light." He snorted as if dismissing their disapproval. "Light, on the other hand, were wary about a hidden motive. I had none, of course; I simply wanted to survive. Still, it took over a century for me to gain their trust. With Zenith, it took even longer."

"Makes sense." Djurdak nodded. "Zenith has always been very protective of his Keeper and kin."

"Zenith is the last dragon I have to find, and then it's off to face Dimitri."

"Best not to dawdle then." Said the voice of Taypax. "I know for a fact Zenith despises being kept waiting, so Abaddon and I can rush you back to the living world."

"But…" I looked longingly at my father.

He smiled sadly. "I know, kiddo, but you can't stay here forever."

"Yeah, Xy," Ríhan was suddenly next to me, draping an arm over my shoulders and smiling like a fool, "you still have to kick the bad guys' butts, get married, have kids. You know, all the good things in life."

"Do you think I can visit again sometime?"

"I can't say for sure, but anything is possible." My father said as he leaned in to kiss my forehead. I captured him in a hug and fought the urge to break down crying again.

"We'll still be watching over you, Xy, just so you know." Ríhan said as I drew him into a hug. Not trusting my voice, I merely nodded. I finally broke away from them and moved closer to Abaddon. I paused to look at them over my shoulder.

"I'll miss you." I choked out.

"We both will miss you, Xy."

"I love you, my princess. And give your mother my love when you see her."

I nodded.

With the final farewells behind us, I knew I could linger no more. I slowly reached out to touch Abaddon. My fingers passed through his transparent scales until they touched the fleshy surface beneath. I gave him the all clear. He uttered three words in Kinös Elda. In a heartbeat the world fell away and everything went black.

261

Kitfox stood leaning against the Temple's golden gate, staring outwards into the receding night. The suns were just starting to rise. Their warming rays painted the sky a medley of colors and the white ruins of Arcadia reflected the iridescence almost like a mirror. Even the perpetual, rolling mist turned to rainbows in the light. As beautiful as the scene was, he found no comfort in it. For his mind was elsewhere occupied.

Over a day had passed since Xy ventured into Havel, guided along the Path of the Gods by Nahstipulí Herself. In her absence, the tight-knit team separated, almost until the three had resigned to their own comfortable state of solitude. He had tried – in vain, as it turned out – to keep them together and keep spirits up. Shazza sought no friendship or conversation as she sat in a constant vigil before the doorway Xy had disappeared through. Thera was slightly more open to his company, but most of her time was spent talking gibberish with her younger sister.

So Kitfox had vanished from the Temple for a while.

During his solo escapade, he explored the ruins and walked around the island. As he did so, he located the ten Dragons of Light. They were all together on a beach, sunning themselves or dozing. Even little Visler had made a nest for himself in the hot sands. They had all greeted him warmly, asking how he and the others were. He had sat in the sand and lounged against Kkaia's foreleg as he told them what was happening between him, Shazza, and Thera. The dragons had told him not to let the incident bother him, for everyone needed some time alone once in a while.

Still, the situation did not sit well with the Fox Demon. He feared that this 'alone time' might prove to be the team's downfall. Especially if Vincent and what remained of his battalion were to mount a counterstrike against them. The dragons had only then told him that all of Dimitri's forces – Wyrd and Nightshade included – had retreated from the island. They suspected they were planning on regrouping with the main army back in Bakari-Tokai. Kitfox had suddenly wished to be a fly on the wall when Vincent reported his failure to Dimitri.

The dragons did not want to be flies.

The remainder of that day had been spent on the beach with the dragons. He had talked and dozed with them until the day was old. Hungry, but not eager to return to the dreariness of the Temple for a meal of dry bread and jerky, Kitfox had decided to fish. He had completely disrobed and dove into the sea. That had turned out to be a huge mistake. Not minutes after he surfaced with his first two fish, Shazza strode from the trees. When she realized he was naked, she froze and went wide-eyed. After an embarrassing few moments of awkwardness, she turned around long enough for him to don his trousers. After that, she refused to look at him as she told him about something in regards to guard duty that night. He hadn't paid attention.

As she spoke, Kitfox could have sworn he saw the ghost of a blush on her cheeks. The dragons could not figure out what had gotten into her to make her behave so strangely. Kitfox had not been in the mood to explain it to them. He had finished fishing – this time with his trousers still on – and hauled his catch back to the Temple to share with the others.

Kitfox sighed and folded his arms across his chest. He was in such a somber mood he barely notice his clawed fingers tracing the glyphs that formed the tattoos circling his biceps. Xy had asked him once what the scrolling letters meant. He couldn't read the language himself, but knew what each word stood for: Protect, Guide, Honor, Love; the four virtues he vowed to live by when he joined Tahda'varett. And each of those virtues had come into play several times since starting this quest. He had guided those who had quickly become his closest friends, proven himself to be an honorable ally, and sacrificed himself to protect the one he loved. He wouldn't be surprised if his guild promoted him to Alpha upon his return home to Zadún... If he ever returned home.

He sighed again and dropped his arms to his sides. He shook his head to clear it of the dark thoughts and once again wished for Xy to return. He longed for her company and her touch, her smile, even her laugh. He knew that she had no choice but to complete the task of acquiring Abaddon alone, but he worried about her. The thought of her in danger was eating away at him and nothing anyone said to the contrary cheered him up.

Something rustled behind him. His ear twitched at the sound. Light footsteps approached.

"Yes, Thera?" He said without looking behind him. The footsteps faltered for the briefest of moments.

"How did you know it was me?" Thera whispered.

He chuckled and swiveled his ears back and forth. "You have the second-softest footsteps out of the group. And the rustling of wings was a dead giveaway."

"Ah." She stopped beside him.

The two of them stood side by side, silently watching the painted sky lighten to a pale blue. Kitfox kept his ears swiveling, catching the sounds of waking creatures. A mouse skittered around the rocks, probably looking for food. A few of the heartier insects who did not suffer from the winter chill buzzed about. Several types of birds chirped as they bobbed along the branches of the alabaster trees. It was a strange melody, but one that managed to relax Kitfox's nerves some. He yawned.

"You should get some rest." Thera said quietly. "You haven't slept since Xy left."

"Yeah." He muttered. "I'm just so worried about her that I don't know if I can get my mind to be quiet long enough to sleep any."

"I could use a spell to help you."

"No, thanks." He flashed a smirk as he turned into the Temple. "I'd hate to sleep through her return, too."

Thera smiled knowingly as she watched the Demon retreat further into the Temple. He padded silently to the opposite wall and sat beside the doorway. He crossed his arms as he reclined against the wall. He let his eyes close, and a moment later, he was still.

Kitfox cracked an eye open after he was certain Thera was no longer looking at him. He sighed and looked sidelong at the doorway to Havel. "Come back soon, Xy."

The final days of the quest were the hardest. Each one of us knew that, pretty soon, we would be facing an enemy that had so far proven to be unbeatable. Trying to keep our spirits up with that fact bearing down on us proved to be the toughest challenge of the Dragon Quest.

— FROM "THE DIARY OF AMOREZ" BY AMOREZ RENOAN

My stomach lurched as I twisted in the black void Abaddon had pulled me into. I felt like a leaf that had been thrown into white water rapids; spinning, twisting, tumbling, turning. I could not distinguish up from down or left from right. Everything was numb, backwards; alien. Only one thing was certain: the blackness.

A split second later everything went solid again and the dizzying spiral finally stopped. If not for a steadying hand on Abaddon, I probably would have fallen over.

"We have arrived in the Realm of the Living, young one." The echoing voice of Abaddon declared. "You can open your eyes now."

I waited a bit for the sick feeling in my stomach to recede. Only then did I dare to open my eyes. Abaddon was beside me, staring off into the distance as if something was calling him. We were standing in an overgrown, rectangular field. The sea crashed against the rocks behind us, spraying us with icy water that made me shiver. As I looked at the white ruins all around us, I realized then that we were about an hour's walk away from the Temple.

"How did you get us all the way over here?"

The dragon snorted. "I used a warp spell."

"I wasn't aware dragons could use magic like that."

"I believe Abaddon and I are the only ones who are able to use magic of likes which you witnessed." Said the voice of Taypax. "I am not sure how this came to be, or if any of the other dragons now have the ability."

266

"I doubt it." Abaddon growled.

"You two get all the more amazing the longer I am in your presence."

The dragon released an echoing laugh.

Eager to return to my friends, and without a word to the ghostly dragon, I took off through the tangled vegetation. Abaddon said nothing as he walked behind me. Whenever the overgrowth grew too thick for him to pass through, he would take a bounding leap. And the ground would shake with the impact of his landing. I sort of wished that the miniature earthquakes would alert my teammates and they would all come running to investigate.

Sadly, they never did.

I couldn't suppress the sudden, overwhelming fear that Vincent had rallied the remaining troops and the two Shadow Dragons and managed to capture – or kill – my teammates. Plagued by that very real possibility, I freed my tessens and bolted ahead. Abaddon was quick to speed up his pace.

"Why so hasty?"

"I have a bad feeling." I said. I hurtled over the thick root that crossed the path, nearly tripping in the process. A moment later, I passed under the exit arch. The ground shook and the paving stones cracked as Abaddon leapt over the structure. His tail hit a portion of the remaining wall, causing several large chunks of mortar to crumble. The two of us ignored the rumbling debris in our rush to the Temple.

I rounded the bend in the path as quickly as I could, but someone was blocking the route and I couldn't stop in time. We collided so hard we knocked each other off our feet. I landed heavily and gasped as the wind was knocked out of me. My lungs burned as I tried to breathe again.

"Xy!" Thera's face loomed over me. She looked torn between absolute joy and guilt. "Xy, I'm so sorry."

I could only nod as I coughed and gasped for air. Before I had fully recovered, a streak of lavender and white scooped me up in a tight hug. I smiled in spite of myself and returned the embrace with equal enthusiasm.

"You have no idea how worried I've been about you." Kitfox kissed me over and over.

"I would wager she does." Abaddon replied, his voice echoing.

Kitfox froze. Slowly, his amber gaze moved away from me, only to settle on the dragon. He blinked in surprise and his jaw dropped slightly.

Thera muttered an oath in Kinös Elda. "That's Abaddon?"

"Not entirely." Said the voice of Taypax.

To which Abaddon added, "But that is a long story."

Kitfox and Thera gaped at the dragon. Their surprised gazes slowly shifted to me, silently begging for an explanation.

"Where are Shazza and Pox? If I am to relate the story, I would like all of you to hear at once so as I won't have to repeat myself."

"They're in the Temple." Thera managed to answer.

"Who's in the Temple?" called Shazza. I peered around Kitfox to see her and Pox strolling over the narrow bridge towards us. I smiled and waved in greeting. Pox happily returned the wave while Shazza merely quirked an eyebrow.

"I'm glad to see you are all in one piece." I said once Shazza and Pox joined the rest of us. "I was worried that Vincent had rallied Dimitri's troops for another attack."

"Nah." Kitfox grinned roguishly. "The dragons told me that what remained of the soldiers had retreated from the island, Shadow Dragons included."

"Good." I breathed a sigh of relief.

"Agreed." Muttered the Dákun Daju as she scanned Abaddon up and down.

"Okay, so spill," Thera demanded, "how does Abaddon have two voices and that strange, ghostly exterior?"

"I'm surprised your mother didn't tell you that story." I smirked. A mix of confusion and curiosity swept through the Feykin's expression. I glanced up at the dragon as I began to retell the story he told me.

It took me just over an hour to tell my teammates about the story behind the black dragon's ghostly appearance. They were as shocked to learn about Taypax's and Abaddon's fusion as I had been. Of course they had asked a few questions of the dragon, mostly regarding how they both managed to get along so well. Abaddon's voice was a constant echo, so I knew both dragons were in agreement with the answer.

Finally bored with the questions and loitering, Abaddon excused himself.

I asked him where he was going.

"I shall bathe in the sun on the beach with my brethren."

With that, he took a few bounding leaps and was off, gliding just over the tops of the white trees.

Once the dragon vanished from sight, Shazza spoke. "Care to tell us what took you so long to get back?"

I turned to face her. "What do you mean?"

"Xy," She sounded rather perturbed, "You have been gone for almost three days."

I gawked at her in disbelief.

"We've been so worried about you." Kitfox emphasized his point with a gentle kiss to my forehead.

"It's been three days?" My friends all nodded. "It felt like maybe a few hours."

"So what happened that took so long?"

With a sigh, I began to regale them with the story of my time in Havel. I watched their faces as I described the crystalline and gold city, the thundering falls, and even Atlidmé Himself. Their eyes lit up almost as if they were small children being told a tale of the greatest heroes doing amazing deeds. I told them of my time with my father and Ríhan. A soft smile touched Kitfox's lips as I spoke of my old friend. The Demon was extremely surprised to learn that it was Ríhan who had sent the ice nymph to warn us of his impending death.

"If I had known that, I would have sent him a 'thank you' message."

I patted his arm as I said, "Ríhan already knows how grateful we all are that you are still here with us."

"He sounds like a really nice guy." Said Pox. "I wish we had gotten the chance to meet him."

"Yeah." I choked out.

"Oh! That reminds me." Thera exclaimed before she dug through the small sack on her hip. She muttered incoherently as she fished for whatever she was after. I could tell it was her way to change the subject of conversation and I was grateful.

Finally, she pulled out the rolled up parchment that contained the copy of the Riddle of the Twelve. As she unrolled it she said, "Pox and I spent most of the last three days translating the riddle, but we can't figure out what it means."

"What does it say?"

"This is the clue to the dragon: 'Dorman rests Zenith of the skies; Beneath Mirror's surface he lies.' But it goes on to say: 'When the hearts of twelve beat as one; Evil far and wide shall be done. These sacred dragons now are yours; This diary you need no more.'"

"'Beneath Mirror's surface?'" Kitfox muttered. He cupped his chin between his fingers to think.

"How exactly does one fit a dragon in a mirror?" Demanded Shazza. She crossed her arms and shifted her weight to one leg as she awaited an answer.

I slowly shook my head. "It feels familiar, but I can't remember why."

"Well, I know of a scrying mirror in Thuraben, but I doubt that is the mirror the riddle referenced." Said Pox.

"What is a scrying mirror?" Kitfox asked.

"Thuraben's scrying mirror is basically a large bowl of obsidian polished so smooth it reflects anything that stands over it. To scry, we pour water into the bowl and wait for it to settle, then we–."

"That's it!" I shouted. Everyone looked at me, wide eyed and confused. "The mirror in the riddle isn't an actual mirror. It is a body of water so smooth it looks like a mirror!"

Shazza snapped her fingers. "I've heard rumor of a lake in a mountain range that is so calm it is almost unseen."

"It is not just a rumor." I smiled. "It is actually called Mirror Lake and it rests in the middle of the Eyes of the Ages almost due north of..." Dread suddenly took hold as I recalled the location. I swallowed the lump in my throat and forced the words, "It lies due north of Bakari-Tokai."

The expressions of my teammates immediately turned sour. I could tell they were thinking the same thing as I; do we dare to venture so close to the center of Dimitri's forces?

Kitfox was the first to break the dreary silence. "We have no choice." He sighed. "We'll have to risk it."

Thera slowly nodded in agreement.

Shazza unfolded her arms with a sigh. "Very well."

"We'll rest here for the night." I said. "During that time, I suggest we come up with a plan to outsmart Dimitri and remain unseen."

With that, the five of us retreated into the Temple of Arcadia. There was little talk that night around the fire as each of us dwelled on our own dark thoughts, devising some way to make it through the challenges that lie ahead.

As I rested my head on the pillow that was Kitfox's arm, I looked at the statues of the Five Souls looming over us. With a prayer for their help, I drifted off to sleep.

I could only watch for a few moments as Dragon Keeper faced off against Dragon Keeper. This to the death battle would decide the fate of our entire world, and I prayed that Amorez would win. I heard their weapons meet with a resounding ring, even over the holler of the soldiers attacking me.

— FROM "AN ONLOOKER'S JOURNAL" BY THERNU ONYX

Godilai strode quickly through the marble halls, her footsteps nothing more than the ghosts of whispers. Her long, white hair flowed behind her like a silk scarf on a breeze. She kept her features emotionless, but her cyan eyes burned with a mix of worry and barely contained rage. She did not look forward to breaking the news to her husband.

Less than an hour ago, she had been summoned from the royal suite she shared with Dimitri by a page reporting Vincent had returned. Godilai had rushed to meet the ugly and rotund Hume, eager to see if he and Pox met with success. Alas, when she had entered the main lobby of the palace, the old Judge stood alone, looking and reeking of fear.

She had inquired about Pox.

"The wretch's Sorcerer freed her from Dimitri's control." He had answered.

She struggled not to reveal any emotion at his words as she asked about the rest of the campaign.

Vincent did not dare to look at her as he regaled her with the story. It had started out great, with the brat, Xyleena, getting swallowed up by Wyrd's attack. After that, things went terribly wrong. The brat had somehow freed herself from wherever the dragon had sent her and went on to destroy all but thirty-two of the force Dimitri had sent against her. Godilai had resisted the urge to strike Vincent for his failure… barely. Without a word, she had turned away from him and strode from the room. Behind her, she heard the old Judge roaring at the servants in a mix of anger and fear. She silently hoped Dimitri would let her remove the useless bastard from their lives; Permanently.

Godilai paused outside the double doors of her husband's study. Two guards stood to either side, their halberds crossed over the doorway. She knew her husband was working on details to fortify the city against attackers and had asked not to be disturbed, but he had to know of Vincent's failure. She only hoped the surprise she had in store for him helped soothe his anger.

She growled, "Move."

Slowly, as if unsure if they should do as they were told, the guards uncrossed their halberds. Godilai wasted no time in shoving the double doors open and striding through. The oaken doors slammed against the marble walls of the book-lined study so loudly the sound echoed and they nearly closed themselves behind her. Dimitri sat at a long table with a map of the city spread out before him. The room was lit by a summoned orb that hovered over the table.

Dimitri's crimson gaze looked up from the map before him to settle on her. He knew something was wrong in an instant. "What happened?"

Though she did not show it, Godilai was surprised by his friendly tone despite the interruption. After a moment to think of what she was going to say, she stepped closer to him. "Vincent –"

"I know all about that." He sighed and reclined back in the seat. "Wyrd and Nightshade reported the failure to me while they were still leagues away from the city."

"I was not aware they could do that."

"It's not like I ever expected the fat bastard to win. What I didn't count on was losing Pox in the process. Bah!" He waved his hand dismissively. "There was something else you wanted to tell me." He noticed a quick flash of awkwardness cross her face before it was erased. Whatever she had been hiding from him for the past few weeks must be something that absolutely terrified her. Why else would she act this way?

His dragons did not bother to answer.

It took Godilai a few minutes to work up the nerve to finally tell him. Once she made up her mind, she slowly exhaled a deep breath. "Dimitri," they locked gazes, "I am carrying your child."

For a long moment everything was silent, awkward; uncomfortable. Then Dimitri surprised her with a loud and joyous laugh. The chair he sat in fell backwards with a thump as he rushed towards her and hugged her tightly before pulling her down to his level to place a tender kiss on her lips. The guards outside rushed in to see what was wrong and Dimitri excused them with a wave of his hands and a threat.

Finally he calmed down, but a big smile was plastered to his face. His expression changed in an instant when he noticed Godilai's worried frown. "What's wrong, Love?"

"I fear for our child." She said slowly. "I fear that when Xyleena and her dragons come – and I know they will – a battle will rage that will cost me dearly. I do not want to lose you or the child."

Her soft confession unnerved Dimitri. His once elated mood had suddenly turned somber, almost as if he were attending a funeral. Had this been the reason she was afraid to talk to me about it sooner?

Dimitri shuddered as the bulk of Hyperion's mind invaded his. Send her away, the dragon growled.

How can you say that?

Do you not wish to protect her and the child growing in her womb?

Of course I do! Dimitri silently shouted at the dragon.

Then send her away. With that, Hyperion's presence vanished. Dimitri scowled and sat heavily on the edge of the table.

"What did the dragon say?"

Dimitri's gaze slowly shifted to his wife's face. He sighed and told her what Hyperion had suggested.

"I would prefer not to leave." Godilai said, honestly.

"I know." He muttered sadly. After a long moment, he stood up and embraced her. "All I want is for you and the baby to be safe."

274

She slowly and reluctantly agreed. "I know of a place where no Hume will ever find me. It is a small city inhabited only by Dákun Daju and hidden in the western Arctica Mountains. I will be safe there."

Dimitri nodded. After a moment's consideration, he moved a hand to touch the Shadow Amulet resting above his heart. With a sigh, he removed it and placed it in her hand. "Take this with you so I will know where to find you when this is over."

Godilai donned the amulet and nodded once. "I shall leave at first light tomorrow."

"Come then, my love. We will bed together tonight, for tomorrow shall be a bitter sweet parting."

The duo strode from the room arm in arm. A long moment later, the orb of light that lingered over the table winked out of existence.

The next morning, Dimitri escorted Godilai slowly through the palace. They did not speak; there was no need to. Everything they felt for each other was shared the night before. All that remained to be spoken was a farewell.

As they neared the gates leading to the courtyard, they drew to a stop. Dimitri embraced Godilai and, for once, she hugged him back. After a moment, she turned to leave.

He stopped her. "Godilai," She slowly turned to look at him. He smiled at her as he said, "name our child something bold and fierce."

Her brow creased and confusion flashed in her cyan eyes. "Why are you saying this?"

"Just in case..." A wry smile touched his lips.

She understood. "I promise to give our child a name that will make even the Gods quiver in fear."

He smiled at that, reassured.

"Promise me something?" Her voice was soft, almost like that of a scared child.

"Anything."

"Promise that you will come back to me."

He agreed and she claimed his lips with a passionate kiss. They released each other after a long moment, and she turned away. With one last look at him over her shoulder, Godilai walked away.

It was weird to hear our beloved Taypax's voice coming from the body of the Shadow Dragon. Together, the two of them explained how they had merged to save each other's life. It was difficult for Amorez, who had become something of a mother to the dragons, to decide on the fate of the two.

— FROM "CONVERSATIONS WITH DRAGONS" BY DJURDAK ZA'CAR

"I still say we fly straight there!" Shouted Shazza.

"Yeah, and pass within a league of Bakari-Tokai. Are you out of your mind?!" Kitfox shouted back, a fierce snarl lacing his words. "No way. We should skirt around the capitol as much as possible."

"And take even longer getting to this Mirror Lake? We don't have the supplies for it! Much less the time!"

"Enough, you two!" Thera tried to separate them, but the fight only continued, growing in volume. She sighed in defeat and plopped down between me and Pox to sulk.

I paid little attention to the argument as I was in a silent conference with all eleven of my dragons. *Kúskú, do you think your illusions can hide us all effectively enough to deceive Dimitri?*

I have done something similar in the past, his liquid voice echoed in my mind, *but that was when I was accompanied by several hundred Feykin to feed me energy. By myself, I cannot cloak all eleven of us plus five riders at once. It would require more energy than I am capable of.*

How many do you think you can cloak?

Kúskú was silent for a moment; calculating. Finally, he answered, *I believe I can cloak all five riders and three of us at most.*

I think you are forgetting to take into account Hyperion. Spoke the double voice of Abaddon. *The last time you tried one of your mirror tricks on him, it didn't work. That same possibility* might still apply now, and if he should spot whoever is flying, they will be doomed.

The other dragons mumbled an affirmation of the fact.

How bad is Hyperion?

It was Abaddon alone who answered, Hyperion of Apocalypse took over the role of leader of the Shadow when Felwind of Chaos died in battle. Though the two of them were very similar in temper and elemental control, Felwind was still stronger; and ruthless. He used to delight in raiding villages and torturing the inhabitants with his power over chaos. I cannot say for certain just how powerful or bloodthirsty Hyperion has become in the last four centuries. His power now might dwarf Felwind's or it might not. Either way, he alone will be the biggest threat you will face when you battle the Dragons of Shadow and their Keeper.

I sighed and reclined back slightly. What do you guys suggest we do?

Vortex spoke first. I think you should get to Zenith as soon as you can, for he is the strongest of all of us.

I agree with Vortex. Chorused Kkaia, Atoka, and Kúskú.

You do realize that the fastest route for them takes them right by the Hume capitol and all twelve Shadow, right? Nexxa chastised.

Yes, I am aware of that. Vortex huffed.

It will be suicidal to fly that way. Stated Helios. I suggest you take a safer route, away from the city.

Nexxa and Thedrún agreed with him.

Okay, let's take a vote. I said, sitting straight up. All of you in favor of a direct path, speak your names.

Vortex, Kkaia, Riptide, Atoka, Wildfire Kúskú, Symbilla, and Abaddon all said their names. And I counted each of them off on my fingers. That means it is eight in favor of a direct route and three against.

Nexxa growled in frustration, but remained silent.

I heard Helios sigh. Just be careful, alright?

Yeah, we don't want anything to happen to you or your friends. Added Thedrún.

Thanks for your concern. I smiled though they couldn't see, and I closed the connection. Shazza's and Kitfox's argument had grown very loud, so much so that I doubted they would hear me if I tried to shout over them. So I stood up and cast a spell to summon a spark of lightning between them. They both shut up in an instant and looked at me. "The five of us are taking three dragons and flying straight there, no diversions."

Kitfox gaped at me in disbelief while Shazza grinned victoriously.

"Are you sure?" It was Thera who spoke. I looked at her over my shoulder.

"With Kúskú's illusions and the power of three spell casters, we should be able to skirt the capitol unseen."

"I sure hope you're right about that." Kitfox sighed.

Mere minutes later, the five of us had our gear packed up and ready to go. I led the way out of the Temple of Arcadia. I paused on the other side of the narrow bridge and turned to face the Temple. I bowed my head and whispered a prayer of thanks and asked again for their help in the challenges to come. Once I felt satisfied with the prayer, I shouldered my pack and led everyone out of Arcadia, towards the sandy beach where my dragons awaited.

The first day aloft was spent in suppressed apprehension as we left behind the relative safety of Arcadia, only to draw closer to our biggest threat: Bakari-Tokai. My three dragons flew on at breakneck speeds and I feared their wings would snap from the strain.

I was seated in the saddle astride Kúskú at the head of a small v formation. Kitfox was situated behind me, holding me tightly as if worried I might slip from his grasp. To my left was Thera, alone – save Visler, who was safely tucked under the hood of her wool cloak – in the saddle on Abaddon. She appeared at ease, despite the worry I knew was consuming her mind. On my right was Pox and Shazza astride Nexxa. Both of them mirrored Thera's state.

This is going to be a long ride. I had thought.

I had been right.

On the second day, I was scared out of my mind when all my dragons suddenly shouted a warning and dove for the trees. The moment the dragons touched the ground Kúskú, Thera, Pox, and I went to work hiding our location. And not a second too soon! An enormous red and black Shadow Dragon flew by just inches off the tops of the trees, looking down as if scanning for a meal. I gawked at his bulk for he was much larger than any of my dragons, and more muscular. He could easily fit the head of any one of my dragons – save Abaddon and possibly Nexxa – between his jaws.

Abaddon introduced us to the leader of the Shadow Dragons, Hyperion.

As the giant dragon flew by over head for a second time, I had to plug my ears at the volume of his wings flapping. Now I know why you guys are so afraid of him.

Bah! Vortex scoffed. Bigger isn't always better. That big bulk of his slows him down too much to catch us. That is how we got the upper hand on Felwind.

Ha! You have not been on the receiving end of his Tetra Vortex technique like I have. Growled Taypax.

That is the main thing you need to be wary of when facing him. Abaddon and Taypax said in their unified voice.

Once we have Zenith back with us, there won't be any need to fear that ugly old vulture! Riptide laughed.

It was nearly two hours later before the dragons deemed it safe to return to the air. We flew for hours without interruption and at last I could see the Grand Capitol on the horizon. Granted, it was merely a black spec against the blue water and green fields, but I could still see it. I just hoped that Dimitri and his dragons weren't watching from the towers.

It wasn't until Rishai began to set in the east that we were forced to land in a panicked frenzy again. This time two Shadow Dragons, both ones I had never seen before, circled overhead.

Abaddon recognized them as Talisman of Ice and Maelstrom of Water. Though neither of them was nearly as large as Hyperion, they still had several meters on my dragons.

It wasn't until after the last rays of sunlight had faded into memory that we were able to fly on again. And fly we did. We did not dare to stop that night for food or rest; we were too close to the capitol for that.

It wasn't until Aruvan nearly broke the horizon on the third day that I could finally see the Eyes of the Ages. They loomed so high above the lush forest at their feet that their caps vanished into the clouds. There were a few shorter mountains in the range, and each of those was capped in fresh, white snow. The snow gave me the impression that the entire range was like the jaws of an enormous monster hidden in the ground, waiting patiently for a meal to wander too close.

"Those mountains are too tall for us to fly over." Announced Kúskú. "We will do our best to get you as far into their midst as possible."

"Alright." I replied.

And so the day passed, watching as the mountains drew ever closer and Bakari-Tokai grew further and further away. By midday, even more of the range of mountains grew visible, revealing jagged peaks, mountains so narrow they looked like giant needles, and dots of vegetation hearty enough to survive in the frigid heights. I even spotted the old volcano, Mount Vurapoyan, with its cap and half the cone blown clean off from its last eruption.

By sunset, we had just flown over the first of the foothills that guarded the Eyes of the Ages. I peered earthward just in time to see a pair of bligens rush into the thicket. Within seconds, the cats' black and white fur had them thoroughly camouflaged. I smiled, for seeing bligens was a very rare occurrence, and returned my attention to the looming mountains ahead. It would be long passed nightfall before we managed to breech the outermost wall of them. So I reclined slightly against Kitfox and napped.

I was jostled awake some time later and nearly screamed when Kúskú dipped his right wing without warning. I breathed a sigh of relief when I realized we weren't under attack. He was only circling around a mountain. At long last he leveled out. But another mountain blocked his path. This time he dipped his left wing and we circled that mountain.

Back and forth, we zigged and we zagged through the mountains. Once or twice, the dragons had to climb in altitude to pass over a mountain they could not circle. During those climbs, the winds grew so cold and the air so thin I had to resort to magic to keep warm and provide air.

At midnight I squinted through the dark to see an immeasurably wide and tall mountain blocking our way. It was then that the dragons' progress finally ground to a halt. They landed on the side of the mountain and apologized through wheezing breaths.

"We can fly you no further." Kúskú panted. "The air is growing too thin to hold our weight, much less keep us breathing."

Kitfox and I dismounted, taking our saddle bags with us. I patted the silver dragon on the foreleg and thanked him for his help. "You, Abaddon, and Nexxa should get some rest within the Eye. You've earned it."

The trio of dragons did just that. As soon as the jewels marking their places in the amulet faded, I summoned forth Wildfire. With her there to watch over us, we could spend several hours sleeping without worry. We could also use her wings for insulation against the cold and the perpetual flame on the tip of her tail for warmth and light.

"Sleep well," I said to my friends as I snuggled up to Kitfox, "Tomorrow at dawn, we're hiking."

The morning light of Aruvan painted the sky and mountain snow. Thick, grey clouds turned to rainbows as the light brushed against them only to vanish a moment later as they warmed. A slight breeze moved in from the east as if telling the world the sun had risen at last. All was calm and peaceful.

I stood atop the snow, staring out at the jagged peaks of the Eyes of the Ages. For a moment, I was just a girl standing at the top of the world. I was not a Dragon Keeper on a mission to save the world. I did not need to fear for my life or those of my friends'. I had no enemies. For a moment, I was free. Free of all worries, obligations, and doubts. I was just me; on the mountain top.

I wanted to stay like this forever.

But as Rishai began to break over the horizon, I forced myself to turn away. I had wasted enough time. Now we had to get moving.

The snow crunched loudly as I walked up to the cocoon of Wildfire's wings. I gently parted her wings and slipped between the gap. The short blast of cold air instantly roused Shazza and she pulled a dagger as she bolted to her feet. When she realized it was just me entreating entrance, she relaxed.

I asked her to wake up Thera and Pox. She nodded once and started on the task. I set about doing the same for Kitfox and Wildfire. A look of confusion clouded Kitfox's gaze for a moment, then he recalled what was happening. He yawned widely, revealing his fangs, as he peeled the fur blankets off. I clapped him on the shoulder and left him to begin the chore of packing up.

I glanced over at Shazza as she moved away from Thera to rouse Pox. Thera was quick to rub the sleep from her eyes and begin packing. Visler complained about the early rise, and firmly attached himself to Thera's shoulder, where he dozed. The younger Feykin was a bit more stubborn to wake so early. Finally Shazza resorted to ripping the blankets off the sleeping girl.

It wasn't long after that that the five of us and Wildfire were packed up and trekking along through the snow atop the mountain. The dragon complained of the cold and wet and asked to trade places with another dragon. So I summoned Atoka. The ice dragon, of course, had no problems with the cold. In fact, Atoka acted more like a child with a new toy. She bounded here and there, rolled, and kicked up great clouds of snow. She even took a running start and slid over the snow on her stomach! We all had a good laugh at her antics. I couldn't help but wonder if she did it on purpose just to cheer us up.

We trudged on for several hours, pausing only once to let Kitfox hunt the wooly goats that thrived in this region of the mountains. It wasn't long before he caught a sizable nanny, and one that would feed us for quite a few meals. We lashed the carcass to Atoka without bothering to clean it. The cold temperatures coupled with Atoka's ice powers were sure to freeze it in no time anyway.

We started off again. After a while, the sky overhead turned as black as night despite both suns clearly being visible. It was also getting harder and harder for us to breathe. So Pox took a minute to weave a spell that covered each of us in special bubbles that supplied air. Then she taught the spell to me and Shazza. Thera already knew it and cast a larger bubble around Atoka.

It was late afternoon when my empty stomach begged for a break. So I found a rather level spot in the snow and called everyone over. Atoka formed a cocoon with her wings and sealed it with a blast of icy air. As I cast a fire spell to warm us, Shazza and Thera dug the dried jerky and bread out of the pack. Kitfox went to work on stripping the wool from the nanny, a task that interested Pox. The young Feykin sat a bit away to watch him.

After several minutes spent bent over the carcass, Kitfox noticed her gaze. He smiled. "Want to learn?"

Pox smiled and moved closer.

I watched the lesson as I ate, amazed that Kitfox had the patience to teach one as young as Pox. I couldn't help wondering if he would be the same way with our daughter.

"This is always the least glamorous part of hunting." Kitfox said with a laugh. "Now, I've already cleared a good portion of the wool away from where I'm going to be cutting, so I'll have to teach you that some other time.

"Because this is a female, what you do is take your knife," and he showed her his, "and insert it here," he sunk his blade into the carcass at some point between the hind legs that I couldn't see, "and make an incision along the belly, all the way to the throat. Be careful you don't cut too deeply. Doing so might nick the intestines and contaminate the meat. Now, Atoka and the weather partially froze this, so it is a bit tough to cut, but it should look something like this when you're done." Pox took a minute to look at the cut and nodded.

"What you do now is break the rib cage so you can remove the heart and lungs. Most hunters have a hammer or axe to do this part. Me? I just do this." He punched the area of the chest where sternum was, and there was a sickening crack as the bones gave. "It is also recommended that the pelvis be broken to make it easier to remove intestines and reproductive organs. I don't like doing that because I always end up with a nasty mess and bunch of very sharp bone shards in the meat, so I'll fish all of that gunk out the hard way.

"So now that the ribs are broke, we open her up and remove all the organs. Watch yourself on the ribs though because they tend to be quite sharp." He leaned in and started plucking out the organs as he had described. "And that is pretty much how you clean a kill."

"And the dragon watching gets to eat all the good parts." Atoka said, eyeing the organs sprawled out on the snow. Kitfox chuckled and began tossing her the bits and pieces. She caught them with a great snap of her jaws and licked her lips. Visler complained with a squawk, so Kitfox tossed the homunculus the goat's heart. He chirped happily and dug in, eating greedily until the last morsel was gone.

"Thank you for the lesson." Said Pox.

Kitfox grinned as he scooped snow from the ground to wash the blood off his arms. "No problem."

"Who taught you how to clean kills?" Shazza asked.

Kitfox continued scrubbing off the blood as he looked at her. "Freya did. Why?"

The Dákun Daju shrugged. "Just curious. You do good work." She uttered a short string of Kinös Elda and the blood on Kitfox's arms slipped to the ground.

"Thanks."

Shazza dipped her head in a nod.

Kitfox caught my stare as he turned to pack the carcass. He winked at me and smiled. I couldn't help but smile back.

After a few more minutes of resting and digesting, I called the team back into action. By nightfall – actual nightfall, not the fake one caused by the height of the mountain – we were already on the descending side of the mountain slope. Clouds began to form, and the mountain top was shrouded in fog. Our clothes quickly grew damp and uncomfortable. I asked if anyone wanted a break, but they all voted to keep going. So Thera and I lit orbs of light and we pushed on.

Several long hours passed before we broke through the bottom of the thick cloud barrier. Once the wet fog of the clouds receded, we could see what lay before us. And my high hopes suddenly came crashing down. Even more mountains stood before us, stretching on into the din of night and vanishing like ghosts. Mirror Lake was nowhere to be found.

I sighed in defeat and called for a rest.

"You can rest when we're closer to the lake." Said Shazza.

I gaped at her. "There's no way I can scale who knows how many mountains in sear—"

"Xy, the lake is right there!" She growled, pointing into the distance. I followed the invisible line drawn by her finger to the dark valley below. It took me several minutes of watching before I realized there were actually little pinpoints of light amidst the jagged teeth in the valley. As I studied them, I realized they twinkled.

I smiled in spite of myself. "Stars."

"Well it's about time." Kitfox muttered as if just noticing it. "I thought we were never going to find the darn thing."

"Come on." Shazza said and walked away. "I want to get off of this mountain."

"Same here." Thera called as she followed in the Dákun Daju's footprints. Though I was eager to reach the lake, I just didn't have the energy to climb all the way down the mountain slopes.

Atoka yawned widely and snapped her jaws shut with a strange click. "We dragons are not made for walking long distances like this. Flying requires less energy."

An idea suddenly occurred to me and I called for everyone to stop a moment. I touched the jewels of the Dragon's Eye and summoned forth Kúskú, Nexxa, and Abaddon. With the trio of saddled dragons to ride, we reached the valley home of Mirror Lake in only a few minutes.

The temperature was quite warm compared to the slopes of the mountain, so much so that it lulled me even deeper into exhaustion. Before I ran completely out of energy, I changed into some drier clothes. Too tired and wore out to endure eating or talking, I unrolled my sleeping skins and laid out on them. Before I knew it, I was adrift in dreams.

My eyes flittered open. The fog of sleep slowly diffused. I began to recall where I was. I had no idea how long I had been sleeping, but it did not feel like it had been long. The sky overhead was a deep sapphire with wisps of white clouds, meaning at least one sun had already risen. It was impossible to tell the time, for the jagged mountains blocked the light and left the valley locked in perpetual twilight.

I groaned as I sat up and looked about. Kitfox was already up, and bent over a small fire. I could hear meat sizzling and guessed he was cooking the goat he killed yesterday. A light breeze carried the scent of the meal towards me, making my mouth water in anticipation.

Just as I was about to throw the blankets off and join him, I heard him mumble something. Curious, I leaned to one side to look around him. Pox sat on the opposite side of the fire, affectionately stroking Visler's small wedge-shaped head. She was saying something, but I couldn't hear. Whatever it was, it made Kitfox chuckled.

"What's so funny?" I called as I tossed the blankets aside and got up. Kitfox promptly turned around to face me, and I could see the humor burning in his amber eyes.

"Pox, here, was picking on Visler."

The Sentinel croaked, as if in disgruntled agreement.

I smirked. "That's one reason to have him here."

As I strode forwards to join them by the fire, I took a look around the valley. Mirror Lake was only meters away from our camp. The surface was as smooth as glass. Not even the breeze sweeping the valley woke a ripple on the surface. Mountains appeared across the face of the water, reflected perfectly as if they were there instead of the lake.

My gaze moved further away from the lake, sweeping across the valley. I spotted Nexxa, Atoka, and Kúskú, lounging in the long grass not too far away from our camp. Though the entire valley was green with life, it was only grass and moss; flowers and trees held no sway here.

"Where are Abaddon, Thera, and Shazza?" I asked as I sat next to Kitfox.

"They are searching for the dragon statue." He said, kissing my cheek. "I was going to wake you once I had breakfast ready, but you beat me to it."

"I have never had goat..." admitted Pox, "... at least not that I can remember, anyway. It smells good, so I am eager to try it."

"Well, good, because it is done." Kitfox smiled. He quickly grabbed a few plates from the pack beside him and piled the meat on them before handing them to me and Pox.

I thanked him as I dug in. While I ate, I watched Pox to gauge her reaction to the new meal. I couldn't help but wonder if I had acted the same way when I first woke up in the Temple after losing my memory. After a close look at the meat, Pox put a small bite in her mouth. Her eyes lit up as she chewed. She quickly took another bite, bigger this time.

"So you like it, huh?" Kitfox laughed.

Pox nodded.

Visler complained loudly; he wanted meat too.

"Fine, you greedy little thing." Kitfox growled and dropped some pieces on the ground. Visler practically attacked them. Kitfox snorted and said, "What are we going to do with the little turd?"

"You can eat him." Said Abaddon as he strode up. Shazza and Thera were with him and both looked excited to tell us something. Upon seeing Thera, Visler chirped happily and bolted towards her. In a flutter, the little homunculus landed on her shoulder, wrapped his tail tightly around her neck, and rubbed his head against the bottom of her chin.

"Where did you guys go off to?" I asked as I popped a bit of meat in my mouth.

"We found the dragon statue. It is over on the other side of the lake." Thera pointed in the general direction. "And you will never guess what is growing around it." She grinned ear to ear as she spoke.

"You're right, I will never guess." I said as I took another bite of the goat meat.

"Midnight Nautili!"

Pox, Kitfox and I all gaped at Thera. "No way!"

She nodded vigorously.

"That is the rarest flower in the world and you found more than one in the same spot?" Kitfox sounded skeptical.

"It is the truth." Shazza said sternly. "There were three of them around the statue."

That's odd, I thought to myself. Every rumor I had ever heard of Midnight Nautili speaks of them on the open water, blooming under the light of a full moon. Then a thought occurred to me. "Is the statue on the lake?"

Shazza nodded. "It sits upon a black dais, which is set a bit of a swim out from shore."

"'Beneath Mirror's surface he lies.'" I muttered to myself. Kitfox's ear twitched, catching the sound, and he sighed.

"We have to swim to get to Zenith?" Pox sounded nervous and I couldn't help wondering whether or not she could swim.

Shazza and Thera both shrugged, but it was Thera who said, "We didn't check that because all we were doing is looking for the statue."

"I do not think swimming is the key to reaching my brother." Said the voice of Taypax. I looked at the ghostly dragon as he continued. "There must be a way to unlock a hidden route that leads under the lake."

"Given our experience with the other dragons," Kitfox said, pointing to Abaddon, "his guess makes more sense."

Shazza and Thera agreed.

"Well then, how about we get going?" I popped the last morsel of meat in my mouth and got to my feet.

Aruvan had just crested over the jagged mountain peaks by the time we reached the opposite side of the lake. The sun's light did nothing to chase away the twilight engulfing the valley. The air, however, grew noticeably warmer, almost tropical. And a thin veil fog swept over the area.

Thera and Shazza led us around a peculiar bend in the lake. Then, at the water's edge, they stopped. Kitfox, Pox, and I crossed the short distance to stand beside them. The four dragons hung back, watching.

Thera pointed out across the lake. "There."

I looked out across the mirror and found the dragon statue. It was just as Thera and Shazza had described. It appeared a bit bigger than the other ones we found. And the dragon depicted in this one stood on its back legs with its wings spread wide. Its neck arched downward, almost becoming one with its chest while its tail arched upward. It was set upon a black dais almost a dragon-length from shore.

And floating in a small v around the dais were the orchid-looking Midnight Nautili. All three flowers were in full bloom, revealing pearly, dark blue and royal purple petals. Veins of magenta and cyan and even silver accentuated each petal. It was the most beautiful thing I had ever seen. Yet I couldn't help believing they were bewitched and set there for a reason. After all, those flowers were only supposed to bloom under the light of the full moon while on the open waters of the oceans.

Pox sighed. "Are we going to have to swim?"

Thera and Kitfox tried their best to tell her otherwise. She didn't believe them. Their conversation turned into a mumble as I focused all of my attention on the three flowers. They did not belong here; of that, I was certain. Yet they had a specific reason for being there. Something about them was screaming at me from a distant memory.

Why the flowers? Why here? I asked myself in an attempt to force the memory to the surface. What are they pointing to? Realization struck me in an instant. The triangle formation they sat in was indeed pointing to something. I followed the invisible line they drew, only to stop at the exact spot where Shazza stood.

"Move." I said as I crossed the meter between us in a few quick strides. She looked at me as if confused, then backed up. I ignored her questions as I fell to my knees and rubbed the moss away from where she had been standing.

A round, stone slab as large as a step and as ancient as the mountains themselves began to appear. As I scraped the moss off, I saw runic lettering carved into the stone. I couldn't make out the words just yet, so I kept working. Slowly, the letters on the stone became a whole phrase.

Ligam ni Skura bó inferom.

By now, I had everyone's attention, and they waited eagerly for me to reveal what I had discovered. I stood up and faced them.

"'Speak of Twelve and enter.'"

Kitfox's ears drooped and a frown replaced the excited smile on his lips. "Why couldn't you make the dragons' lairs easy to get into?"

I shrugged.

"That defeats the purpose of hiding them." Shazza muttered. "'Speak of Twelve...'"

"Try our names." Offered Kúskú.

I nodded and turned around to face the black statue. Slowly and clearly, I named all twelve dragons in the order that I had found them.

Nothing happened.

"Any other ideas?" I asked over my shoulder.

"How about the Riddle of the Twelve?" Thera shrugged.

"Okay." I nodded. Once again, I faced the black dragon statue and spoke slowly and clearly.

In this mystery must you delve,
To find my sacred dragons twelve,
And vanquish evil from this land;
Now listen close the clues at hand:
Vortex the Wind on water borne,
And west of magic castle lore;
Great Kkaia of Rock I took,
And hid away on isle that shook;
Deep in ice, Atoka I bound,
Just north of Arctic castle found;
Helios sings to free his light,
'Past the dead long Lost must you fight;'
Riptide the Torrent points the way,
To fire beneath Dragon Bay;
Wildfire the Blaze will come back,
When water falls upon attack;
Kúskú of Illusion now sleeps,
On isle hidden in Mysty deep;
Dear Thedrún of Thunderous crown,
Sleeps beneath Lescan harbor town;
Symbilla the Life-Bringer dreams,

On Southern isle with golden streams;
Nexxa of Deadly Venom hides,
Far south twixt icy river slides;
Abaddon guards the Dead of old;
Through Havel's Ancient gates of gold;
Dormant rests Zenith of the Skies,
Beneath Mirror's surface he lies;
When the hearts of Twelve beat as one,
Evil far and wide shall be done;
These sacred dragons now are yours,
This diary you need no more.

Still nothing happened.

Thera sighed and stepped forward. She pulled the roll of parchment containing the Riddle from her pack. She wet her lips and slowly read the words aloud, this time in Kinös Elda.

As the last line of the poem died away, a rumble sounded from under the water. Thera and I sprang back from the edge as the ground suddenly gave way. It sloped down, under the water, yet left the lake's surface intact by about a half meter. Though the ground shook with the formation of the ramp, the lake remained as calm as ever. The rumble ended with a resounding boom and everything fell silent once again.

Kitfox broke the silence with a laugh. After a moment, he faced Pox and said, "Toldja we didn't have to swim."

Pox rolled her eyes and playfully punched him in the arm.

"Come on. It'll close soon." I said, taking the lead towards the ramp. Just before I stepped onto the slope, I glanced over my shoulder, at the four dragons.

"We come." Abaddon said in his double voice. He and the other three dragons faded into their elements and entered the Dragon's Eye. I looked down at the amulet and smiled.

One jewel left.

With a deep breath to calm my nervousness and excitement, I started down the ramp. Thera was right behind me followed by Kitfox and Pox. Shazza brought up the rear, grumbling as she stooped almost in half to fit in the tunnel.

The walk to the end of the ramp was short, ending in a magnificent archway of black marble. Between the ebony columns, a strange, dark blue liquid that reminded me of mercury swirled and rippled. The whole thing sat just beneath the dragon statue and I figured the two must be one and the same. At the archway, I paused for only a moment to make sure my team was ready. When I felt confident that they were, I closed my eyes and passed through the strange liquid that formed the doorway.

The ice cold and tingly sensation quickly faded, leaving me feeling warm and strangely weightless. I cracked an eye open, and then blinked in utter astonishment. The hall I found myself in was dark, but that did not matter, for the walls and ceiling were the real beauty of this place.

It was as if someone had taken the entire cosmos and placed it on the walls for all to see. Countless stars and planets sparkled like diamonds as they drifted in the velvety blackness of space. Giant, swirling clouds of dust in colors and shapes of likes I had never imagined filled several of the gaps between the pinpricks of light. It was mysterious and vast, flowing seamlessly over every millimeter of wall and ceiling.

Only the floor remained untouched by the stunning beauty, but it was hardly plain. No; the floor was a strange, dark blue liquid, much like the doorway I had just walked through. It moved in gentle ripples and reflected the images off the walls and ceiling like a twisted mirror, but that only made the room all the more dynamic. Looking down, I could see I stood on top of the unknown liquid as if it was solid. I took a step to test it and smiled as the ripples ran away from the displacement.

Each one of my teammates had a similar reaction to the room. Pox even wished that she could stay here several lifetimes to just watch the infinity moving in the vacuum. Sadly, we did not have time to linger. So, with one last long look at the cosmos, I started forward. I hadn't even gone two steps when a familiar voice called out.

"Well, it's about time you got here."

I could just imagine everyone on board gathered at the port holes to watch as the Haven made her final approach to the sister planets; our new homes. We had been waiting 71 years for this moment. Relief and good cheer had swept through the ship the closer we got.

I looked at my mother as I helped her move closer to the window. She was tearing up, and I could not help but wonder if she was thinking of her father; wishing that he could have been here to witness the fruition of his work. I wished he was here, too.

— *FROM "PERSONAL LOG: HAVEN" BY AADRIAN ITHNEZ II*

I stopped where I stood, and frowned. My teammates instantly forgot about the spectacle on the walls and surged towards my location, weapons drawn. Before us, in a semi-circle, stood six figures of varying height, all clad in similar white cloaks. Cloaks that matched the ones I had seen on the apparitions in Monrai, Vronan, and Jetep. Their hoods were up, obscuring their faces so I couldn't tell who they were...

... Or so they thought.

"Finally decided to quit lurking in the shadows, hey, mom?" I said rather crossly, in the direction of the figure at the far left of the semi-circle. The figure seemed unaffected at my hostility, but my friends all gaped at me. I ignored them for a moment and continued, "I suspect I know three of the people with you," and I pointed at the ones, "but who are the other two?"

After several awkward moments of silence, the figure I had been speaking to reached up and slowly pushed the hood down. Amorez was finally revealed. Her red hair was a bit longer than the last time I had faced her, but still styled in the same strange spiky mess. Gone were her black framed glasses, and I could clearly see her dragon green eyes burning with a mix of anger and hurt. Yet, her face was blank of emotion. It was like facing a Dákun Daju.

296

"I have not been lurking in the shadows, Xyleena." She said finally, her voice soft, yet laced with her hidden anger.

I crossed my arms and shifted my weight onto one foot. "Sure you haven't. You've only spent the last who knows how many decades hiding from the rest of the world and scheming. Tell me something," I held her fierce gaze with my own, "did you even know that I had fallen from the Gate and lost my memories? Did you care?"

"That is enough, Xyleena." She hissed.

"Ah! So you didn't know."

A second cloaked figure suddenly stepped forward. "No, we didn't know where you were or what happened to you!" She tore off the hood as she spoke and I was not surprised to see it was Freya. Kitfox, on the other hand, was. The Wolf Demon ignored her adopted son for a moment to continue yelling at me. "We had told you that going to the Dragons' Gate to try to convert the Shadow Dragons was a dumb idea, but – as usual – you didn't listen! And now you blame your own mother for what happened to you?"

"I didn't say that." I said, my tone even but laced in fury.

"You implied it!"

"Freya." Amorez said in a firm tone. The Wolf Demon snarled, then was still. Amorez sighed and faced me. "Look, it happened and there is nothing any of us can do about it, so how about we move on from the subject?"

"Fine." I shrugged. "Then you can tell me who they are."

Amorez looked sidelong at the four remaining figures in white. She nodded her head once and all but one slowly reached up to push their hoods down.

I had already known one of them was Zhealocera, so I was not surprised to see her present; happy, but not surprised. Though the new scar over her left eye had me wondering what she had gone through in the past year. Everything else about her was pretty much the same, except her violet hair was shorter and she had beads woven into her long braids.

Teka was one of the people I had not expected to see here at all, but her presence put to rest several worries I had regarding her. They half-Feykin sea wench hadn't changed much in the last year. Her gray hair was still styled in her messy mohawk and bound by her bandana. She looked tired and wore out, but otherwise healthy.

A very familiar Feykin was also present. She looked almost exactly like Thera and Pox, but her violet eyes were wiser and her silver hair was much longer. The moment her hood came off, Thera and Pox had ran to her and glommed onto her in a fierce hug, crying and calling her 'mother'. Visler peeped in curiosity and concern, but remained firmly attached to Thera's shoulder.

"Thernu Onyx." I smiled as the Feykin looked up from her daughters to meet my gaze. "I am glad to see you are still alive and well."

She loosed a laugh that sounded like a song. "I might not have been had you actually caught up to me that night in Monrai."

"That was you?"

She grinned as she nodded. "I had to use a quickening spell to get away from you."

"But you had Amorez's dueling blades."

"No, I had mine." She smiled. "They work wonderfully when you have to fight, but cannot use magic less you give yourself away to an enemy."

Kitfox finally stepped forward to join the conversation. "Were you in Vronan, too?"

"No. I was." Said Zhealocera. "There's a rather large but secret Dákun Daju community there and I figured I'd stop in to do some recruiting. Amorez did join me a bit later on though."

"And which one of you broke Kkorian out of the Arctic Prison?" I asked and I grinned smugly at their surprised expressions, especially Shazza's.

"How do you know he's free?" Demanded the Dákun Daju queen.

"He was the white-cloaked figure I saw in Jetep." I said. I peered around her, to the only figure in white with the hood still up. "The limp you got after breaking your ankle in Kúskú's illusion was a slight give-away. I'm curious though; did you sneak into our camp at night and cut our riding straps for a purpose other than forcing us into Jetep to learn of Dimitri's success?"

All eyes were on the hooded figure then. Slowly, nervously, he reached up and pulled the hood down. Kkorian flashed a wry smile as he pushed his long, blonde bangs out of his eyes. Shazza roared in rage and was upon him in a heartbeat, slamming him into the wall and pinning him there with an arm of her bow. He winced in pain, but did not fight against the angry Dákun Daju. Kitfox, Zhealocera, and Freya all rushed over to try to pull her off of him, but it was useless. She was too angry.

"How dare you show your face to me now?!" Shazza shouted, pushing the bow even harder into Kkorian's chest. I feared she would take this too far, so I summoned energy for a spell just in case. Out of the corner of my eye, I caught Amorez and Thernu preparing to do the same.

"Shazza, please," Kkorian coughed, "let me explain."

"And give you another opportunity to lie?"

"I swear I will never lie to you again."

"You're right." She suddenly pulled away from him. In the time it took for Kkorian to slump to the ground, she shoved off her cousin and the two Demons, knocked two arrows, and aimed at him. I could see tears chasing a trail down her cheeks as she looked down the arrows at Kkorian. I knew then that I did not need to use the spell.

"Don't do this, Shazza." Kkorian pleaded. "Please. Just give me a chance."

Shazza pulled at the string of her bow even harder and she stifled a sob. "Do you have any idea what you've done to me, you bastard?"

Kkorian hung his head in shame. "I'm so sorry. I only entered Dimitri's service because I was so desperate for money that I would do anything at the time. And the work he gave me sounded easy... boy was I wrong.

"Then I met you, Shazza," and he looked her in the eye to emphasis his truth, "I don't remember how or when, but I fell in love with you. I didn't mean to, but I did. That's why I tried desperately to get out of Dimitri's service. He told me I could leave after the mission in Vronan and gave me his word he wouldn't hurt anyone. Then he pulled that nasty trick..." Kkorian shook his head and sighed. "I want to kill him. Kill him for all the pain and misery he's put each and every one of us through."

Shazza was still unconvinced and she kept her arrows trained on him. However, there was a slight weakening in her strength on the string; almost as if she had hope.

"Shazza," Zhealocera gripped her cousin firmly on the shoulder, "Kkorian has been with me almost exclusively since we broke him out of the Arctic Prison. I can tell you from experience, he is a good man and one to trust."

"Aye, he is." Teka said with a smile. "Good sailor, too."

Shazza's strength on the bow string loosed even more. After several long moments, she finally let the string relax. Zhealocera released her grip on her cousin and moved away. Shazza put her arrows back in her quiver, never once breaking eye contact with Kkorian. Cautiously, he reached out to her as if to shake her hand in a truce. She ignored his hand. In a split second, she gripped the collar of his shirt and yanked him off the floor to her height, where she locked her lips on his. He was stunned for a moment, then wrapped his arms around her and deepened the kiss.

Kitfox looked at me, a knowing smile on his features. I smiled back and closed the distance between us. At his side, I took his hand in mine and he kissed my cheek.

"I'm glad to see that that is finally resolved." Amorez said. She noticed my closeness to Kitfox. I could see the dislike in her eyes, but, thankfully, she chose not to say anything. Finally, she called for everyone's attention and they gave it. "Not to put a rush on anyone, but there is a specific reason why we have all come here."

"Yeah," I nodded, "and he's further in this cave of wonders, probably eavesdropping on everything like he always does."

That earned a few smiles.

"Well, that," Amorez nodded, "and we need to discuss a few things that lie in our future."

"Let's get the dragon first." I said. "He can help sort out this whole mess and maybe provide some answers."

It was maybe one hundred meters from the entrance of the cosmic cave to the dragon's nest; a quick walk, by most standards. However, it took much longer than needed. Everyone would frequently pause to ogle at some of the wonders moving amidst the darkness on the walls. Even I took a long moment to watch a large and colorful, spiraling dust cloud spin.

When at last we reached the giant room that served as Zenith's nest, everyone stopped. Only Amorez and I moved deeper in. This room was exactly like the rest of the cave, but an enormous shadow occupied the room. The dancing lights reflecting off of the liquid floor made it hard to see, but I could swear the shadow was moving.

I resisted the urge to summon a light orb. Instead, I called out, "Zenith?"

The shadow moved. A wave of the strange liquid forming the floor jostled me, and I nearly fell over. Finally, a single glowing, white eye appeared in the dark. Then another. Recognition flashed in the large orbs, and the giant shadow moved closer.

"Welcome back, Xyleena Renoan." Zenith's voice rolled off his tongue in a deep baritone as if he were singing a song. "It is good to see you again, though you do not recall our last meeting."

I felt heat rush to my face in embarrassment, and I was glad for the lack of light. "I am glad I get to see you again, Zenith. How have you been?"

A rumble like thunder echoed from his chest, almost as if he was purring. "Nothing has changed, yet everything is different."

While I pondered his cryptic response, Amorez spoke, "You already are aware of the problems in the world today, are you not?"

301

"Indeed I am." He answered, his tone solemn and full of sorrow. "I had truly hoped that there would never be a repeat of the events that plagued this planet nearly five centuries ago."

"History, it seems, is doomed to repeat itself." I muttered.

The great dragon agreed.

"We are a bit better prepared this time though." Said Amorez.

"Oh?" I faced her. "And just how are we better prepared?"

I could see the whites of her teeth as she smiled. "This time we have an army ready in advance."

"Really?" It was Pox who spoke.

"Demons, Feykin, Dákun Daju, and Hume have flocked to our side since Dimitri razed Bakari-Tokai." Freya replied. "Right now, as we speak, they should be taking up position in the thickest woods around the capitol. By the time we get there, they should be ready to start the offensive."

"Hopefully they won't kill each other before the battle actually begins." Muttered Shazza.

"They won't." Kkorian said with a grin. "We ensured all the races would get along by selecting three generals to represent each. Those generals are in charge of keeping their blokes and sheilas in line and resolving disputes until we arrive and sort out the lot."

"Is that what you guys were doing when you were going around to random towns in your white cloaks? Building an army?" Asked Kitfox.

"Like I said, we were recruiting." Said Zhealocera. "And boy did we get quite a response from the Dákun Daju when I told them that their queen was fighting alongside the Dragon Keeper."

"The Feykin were a little more reluctant." Admitted Thernu. "It is our nature to avoid the world outside our homeland. In the end, Amorez, Teka, and I managed to persuade a large number to join our fight."

"It is the same story with the Demons." Added Freya. "That was until the Schaakold-Vond'l and Zön-Rígaia Guilds vowed to help the Tahda'varett. After that, it was almost easy to gather Demons."

"Wow. All the races of Ithnez will be fighting together." I could hear the smile in Pox's voice.

I frowned. "Not every race." I said with a sigh. "The Wakari are still undecided, but I seriously doubt they would come to our aid."

Amorez was stunned to say the least. "You actually asked them to help?"

I shrugged. "Why not? This is as much their world as it is ours. Why shouldn't they fight for it?"

"Xyleena makes a good argument, Amorez." Said Zenith.

"Don't get me wrong," Amorez looked from the dragon to me as she spoke. "I am glad to hear you asked for their help. A bit surprised, maybe, given the fact that they haven't bothered to help us before. But you are right, my daughter."

Everyone was quite for a long moment after that. Then Teka sighed and took a few steps forward. "Not to rush everyone, but shouldn't we move this along? We do have an army to return to, and preferably before Dimitri takes notice of it and decides to attack."

I nodded in agreement, then turned to the dragon. "Before we leave, you'll have to enter the Dragon's Eye, right?"

"That is correct."

"Then, do you mind if I summon a light to see you? I would like to remember what you look like. Plus, I'm sure my friends would like to see you for the first time."

Zenith seemed amused by the request. "Of course you and your friends may see me, Xyleena."

I held my breath as I summoned an orb of light in my hand. I forced it upwards, almost to the ceiling of the room and the Dragon of the Heavens was revealed to all. His scales were a pearled, royal blue and deep purple. Magenta and silver highlighted the tips of each, almost as if a painter had brushed the colors on. The scales along his chest and stomach were a lighter blue, matching the long, flowing spines on his back. The membranes of his great, bat-like wings were a purple so dark it looked black. Silver veins ran through them, giving the impression of marbling.

And he was enormous! Standing at about thirty meters high at the shoulder, Zenith dwarfed the other Dragons of Light, maybe even Hyperion. Everyone – save Amorez, Freya, and Thernu – gawked at the sheer size and beauty of the regal dragon, and he seemed to smile at our adoration.

"I will see you again soon, young ones." He said.

With that, he faded into wisps of countless colors and sparkling stars. His essence circled the room before gathering around me in a tight spiral. As he did so, the celestial scenes on the walls and ceiling faded away, leaving only cold, black stone. At long last, the wisps converged and Zenith was within the Amulet. The last empty jewel flashed with life, and a great warming sensation ran the length of my spine. I heard a single, resonating heartbeat in the back of my mind as all the dragons welcomed Zenith into their midst.

The Twelve were whole once again.

It was a strange feeling; having all twelve dragons together after so many centuries. Their joy at being reunited bubbled in the back of my mind. It was overwhelming and contagious, and I couldn't fight the smile their good mood wrought. I don't know how long I stood there, unable to focus on anything except the dragons' jubilance. When at last my attention returned to the room, I realized Amorez had been talking.

"... and when we get to the camp, we'll have a meeting with the generals so we can develop a plan to take back Bakari-Tokai."

Several heads nodded in agreement.

"I'm confused." Admitted Kitfox. "How are we going to get to the camp if the Feykin there are hiding its location? Not to mention, we don't have enough saddles to ride a-dragonback all the way there."

"There is a simple solution to that." Said Thernu. "I can warp us there."

"Warp?"

"It is quite a bit like teleporting," Thera explained, "but instead of moving just the caster to a different location a few leagues away, warp can move several people over far greater distances. The main problem with warp spells is the fact that they drain copious amounts of energy and have been known to kill the caster."

"Not to mention: the more people you warp, the less likely it is to succeed. With eleven of us needing to warp, it would require three or four trips to do it safely." Pox finished.

"I am glad to see you two have kept up on your studies." Thernu said, taking a few steps forward until she was between me and Amorez. "However, the Masters you have been studying under have not properly taught you about energy catalysts."

"Energy catalysts?" I spoke up at last. "Like the ones needed to create the dragons?"

"Not quite." Thernu said, reaching into a petite pouch on her belt. A moment later, she pulled a small, purple bead out and showed it to everyone. "This is my own energy and the energy of life forms all around me. I compressed into a glass bead to store it for use when needed. They are easy to make, though there is an art to it."

"So… with that," Shazza pointed to the bead in Thernu's hand as she spoke, "you can cast spells more powerful than you traditionally could on your own?"

"Correct." Thernu smiled.

"Thernu has some of those beads so loaded up with energy that she can level the entire range of the Eyes of the Ages with a single spell." Freya said with a laugh. The rest of us – save Amorez – gawked at the older Feykin in complete shock.

Thernu merely shrugged it all off. "Just one of the benefits of being a well-learned Necromancer."

"How does it work?" asked Thera.

"Like this." Thernu uttered something in Kinös Elda that I didn't catch and threw the bead on the ground. The bead shattered with a resounding crack and a brilliant, blue light exploded into existence. The light swirled around and formed a pillar that extended several meters into the air. At the spot where the bead shattered, a strange glyph appeared on the floor.

"See you on the other side." Amorez grinned and waved as she stepped onto the glyph. A split-second later she was engulfed in light and was no more. Freya did not hesitate to follow behind the former Keeper, but the rest of us were more than hesitant.

"How did you create a single point of warping?" Thera sounded completely at awe.

Pox, too, was astounded. "I was always told that it was impossible to warp people without physical contact with the caster."

"It is quite a lengthy explanation that I do not have time to speak of at the moment." Thernu replied. "The warp portal only lasts a few minutes, so please hurry and step on the glyph."

My teammates were still hesitant about the portal. As a result, I decided to go first in hopes that they would follow me. With a calming breath, I crossed the short distance to the glowing portal. Just before stepping on the glyph, I looked at each of my teammates and smiled. Finally, I touched the glyph with my toe.

The cave fell away like a dream.

The Path of Gods was a mystery to us. We knew that only priests and monks could walk the Path to the world beyond. Many who made the trip vanished forever, while the scant few who returned spoke of heaven in the form of a crystalline city.

Where had the Path come from? Why had it been hidden on the isle of Arcadia? Did the Dákun Daju know about it? So many questions, and only a handful of answers.

— FROM "A PRIVATE LOG" BY AN UNKNOWN PRIEST

I barely managed a count to three when the world suddenly burst back into existence. After a moment to regain my balance from the dizzying ride, I took a few steps forward and looked around.

Several conifer trees loomed all around me. They grew so close together that I could not even see the sky through their thick foliage. The forest floor was littered with pine needles, old leaves, and several boulders. Countless tents in various colors filled in what little space was left between the trees. Several paths had been cleared for easy walking.

Amorez and Freya were nearby, talking to a group of Feykin who looked like they had been guarding the area from intruders. When they realized I had arrived, they turned their attention to me and welcomed me to the camp. Within minutes, my entire team plus Zhealocera, Teka, and Thernu were once again in our midst.

"Come; let me introduce you all to one of the generals of the Feykin forces." Amorez draped an arm around my shoulders as she led all of us closer to a trio within the group. My gaze immediately fell on the regal woman who stood between two gruff, male Feykin. She was young and tall with dark skin and a fierce, willow green gaze. Her swan-like wings were spread wide, making her look larger and fiercer than those around her. The golden armor protecting the edges of her wings matched the

307

ornate breastplate and bracers she wore with long, pale green skirts. A fancy spear on a golden and green staff that was longer than I was tall was draped over one shoulder.

"Everyone, this is Aidana Wovril. She is a powerful Sorceress and the youngest Feykin to ever grace Thuraben's Council of Elders." Amorez said in Standard. Then she switched to Kinös Elda without missing a beat and introduced the Feykin to us.

"We have long been awaiting your arrival, Dragon Keeper." Aidana said in strangely accented Kinös Elda. "With you now here, we can begin preparations for the retaking of Bakari-Tokai."

"That is the exact reason we warped straight here." Thernu said when I did not respond to Aidana right away. "If you know where Zhücka and Míjin are, we can gather them and the other generals, and begin the planning process in the privacy of the big pavilion."

Aidana's gaze finally broke away from me to look at Thernu. "I know where they are, but not where the other generals can be found."

"Then we will just have to split up to find them." Amorez said with a friendly smile.

Aidana agreed.

"I will take Xy in search of the Demon generals." Freya announced in Standard. "I have a pretty good feeling I know where they can be found."

"Alright." Amorez nodded. It wasn't long before we all split into separate teams to find the generals of each race. Kitfox and I went with Freya further into the woods while Thera, Pox, and Thernu joined Amorez and Aidana in their search. Kkorian and Teka went in search of the Hume generals. Zhealocera and Shazza left to find the Dákun Daju leaders.

~~~~ * ~~~~

Even from a distance, I could tell the Demon Freya and Kitfox were leading me to was more animal that Hume. He was tall - standing head and shoulders over everyone around him -

308

and did not wear a shirt of any kind. A thick tuft of black fur that stood on end ran the length of his spine and converged to form a tail. A wide, beaded belt circled his waist. Animal fur and strips of leather dangled from it. Like Kitfox and Freya, he wore no shoes, but fur wrappings were tied around his shins with thin strips of leather. Black, spiraling tattoos and scars covered great portions of his muscular body where his rust-colored hair did not.

Freya and Kitfox came to a stop just behind him and I behind them. Freya cleared her throat before speaking and the Demon's ear twitched. "I beg a moment of your time, Honorable Alpha."

The Demon slowly looked over his shoulder at her. Upon recognition, he turned to face her completely, but his gaze fell on me. I noticed then that his eyes were mismatched, with the left being yellow and the other being solid white with a jagged scar over it. I took a moment to study him further, learning that he was nothing like Kitfox or Freya. His thick mane of rust-colored and black hair fell to his shoulders and several feathers and beads were woven into the locks. More hair covered a great portion of his face, chest, and arms. His nose was broad and flat, his cheekbones chiseled and prominent, and his ears long, pointed, and covered in more reddish hair. Long fangs protruded from between his lips. He looked wild and untamable, powerful and intimidating. I rather liked him.

"I would like to introduce you to the new Dragon Keeper, Xyleena Renoan." Freya's voice stole his attention away from me for the briefest of moments. "Xy, this is Blood Fang, Alpha Elite of the Tahda'varett Demon Guild."

"It is an honor to meet you, Blood Fang." Unsure of how to properly greet a Demon as high-ranked as he, I resorted to bowing slightly at the waist.

Blood Fang remained quiet for a long while and I feared that I had paid him disrespect. Finally, he flashed a smile. "You hold quite an honorable position for such a young pup, Xyleena Renoan." His voice was deep and surprisingly gentle; a sharp contrast to his appearance.

"She is no pup, D'go-Pahngíl. I thought you would have known that." Spoke a woman's voice from behind Blood Fang. A look of annoyance crossed his features and he glanced over his furry shoulder at the one who spoke.

I looked around him and gawked at the woman. She was about my height with flowing, bright crimson hair that fell to the middle of her back. Orange ears with tufts of black hair protruded from the top of her head. Her eyes were green and the pupils within were nothing but narrow slits. Her skin was as orange as Shazza's eyes and covered in countless irregular, black stripes. A long, thin tail tipped with an inky spot swayed back and forth behind her. She was clad only in a black fur band over her breasts and a matching short skirt. A necklace of leather and talons was draped around her neck and a similar band ran the width of her thigh, where a knife was sheathed.

Upon realizing she had my attention, she smiled, revealing needle-like fangs. "Good day to you, Dragon Keeper."

"Hello." I replied, feeling extremely awkward.

"She is Aralyn, leader of the Zön-Rígaia Feline Demon Guild and another one of the three generals placed in command by Freya and Amorez." Blood Fang kept his eyes on her as he spoke.

The Cat Demon pouted. "Don't sound so drawl, D'go-Pahngíl. You are so boring when you do that."

"Um… Don't take this the wrong way, but what does D'go-Pahngíl mean?"

Blood Fang looked at me as he answered. "D'go-Pahngíl means 'Blood Fang' in the tongue of our forefathers' forefathers."

I nodded and thanked him for explaining that to me.

"Such a polite little thing, aren't you?" Aralyn chuckled. Kitfox and Blood Fang both shot her dirty looks.

Before anything could be said or done about the comment, I decided to cut in. "Perhaps we should get moving? We still have a few generals to gather for the meeting Amorez is calling."

"Yes, that would be wise." Said Freya.

With a snort of annoyance, Blood Fang looked away from Aralyn. "Cloud Strider should be over by the other horses of his guild." He pointed to the trees in the direction we were to go to find the meeting pavilion.

"Alright." I said and waved for him to lead the way. He quirked an eyebrow in curiosity and proceeded to lead the way through the throngs of Demons.

Word of my arrival had spread quickly through the camp. As a result, it had not taken long to gather all twelve of the generals. Most of them had already been waiting in the large pavilion when I arrived with Kitfox, Freya, and the two Demon generals, Blood Fang and Aralyn. The Horse Demon known as Cloud Strider had met up with us just minutes ago. I couldn't help but stare at him and the other generals I hadn't yet met as we awaited Kkorian and Teka's arrival with the Humes.

Cloud Strider was similar to the Gazelle Demon, Rhekja, who I had met long ago in Monrai. He was Hume from the waist up, and very handsomely built. His face was broad with high cheekbones and his eyes were a rich almond color. His chestnut hair was long and tied in several tight braids. The rest of him was a tan horse with black and white freckles. I later learned that he was the leader of the Schaakold-Vond'l Equine Guild.

The Dákun Daju generals were the most bizarre beings in the room by far. True, they were not half animal like the Demons, but their extreme height, odd hair and eye colors, and their meager, spiked armor made them look absolutely ridiculous in my eyes. The shortest one, a female by the name of Vitaani Utoahrína, stood over three meters high. I found it remarkable that she was actually quite attractive, despite her orchid pink eyes and spiky mohawk of neon blue hair. One of the male Dákun Daju generals, V'Nyath, would not stop his attempt to woo her. Irritated by his obvious lust, she had jabbed him in the ribs with her elbow and punched him in the face hard enough to knock out a couple teeth. When I asked if everything was okay, V'Nyath merely laughed and called it a 'love tap'. Zhealocera, Shazza, and the other Dákun Daju male, Zalx, had to step in before Vitaani murdered him.

Then there were the Feykin generals, who all stood a bit of a distance away from everyone. None of them spoke a word, and they watched everything with an air of indifference. Yet I could detect a deep-seated curiosity in them, almost as if they were bursting to ask a thousand questions about those before them. Aidana seemed to have more control of herself than her younger, male comrades, Zhúcka and Míjin, who kept their gazes moving from one new person or thing to another. And they kept ruffling their wings as if nervous about something. Amorez had asked them if they were alright, to which the blue-eyed Míjin refused to answer.

Finally, after what felt like hours of waiting, Kkorian and Teka pushed their way through the flaps that served as the pavilion's door. Kkorian apologized for taking so long and stepped aside to introduce everyone to the three Hume generals.

First to step into the tent was a young woman with skin the color of chocolate. Her jet black hair was curly and – for the most part – hidden beneath a bright green and yellow bandana. A great, billowing hat adorned with long, flowing feathers from exotic birds sat atop her head. It lilted to one side as if to hide her face from everyone. She wore a long, leather coat over a loosely tied, white tunic and green bustier. Heeled, thigh-high leather boots covered her skin-tight leather pants. And the whole look was topped off with several leather belts and sashes that held multiple rapiers and pistols.

"This, mates, is Katchina 'Black Kat' Hayes." Kkorian said with a roguish grin. "She was the first sheila to ever cap'n a pirate crew into the Myst to and come out alive. Learned a lot from her, I did."

Katchina did not say a word as she strode further into the room. She did, however, pause by Amorez to nod her head in respects. Amorez did not return the gesture, which bugged me. I did not have time to dwell on the issue as Kkorian and Teka introduced the other two Hume generals who were just now entering the pavilion. The first of which was a lavishly dressed,

312

middle-aged man with a military hair cut and a jewel-pummeled saber at his hip. His brown hair was graying at the temples, but it gave him a rather distinguished look.

"This here is Sir Nyx Killinger, Commander of the Dragonsworn Brigade and former Military Advisor to the High King." Teka smiled as the Lord Knight paused to kiss both her cheeks before moving on.

Kkorian rolled his eyes and introduced us to the third and final general, who was waiting patiently at the doorway. He was surprisingly young, with short, dark hair and a trimmed goatee. He wore an immaculate, white tunic and dark blue pants. The pouch on his belt was emblazoned with a green crescent moon, meaning he was probably in the medical field. He carried no weapons that I could see, a fact that worried me slightly considering the company he was in. "This is Jaxith Carter-Reed and I don't know anything about the bloke."

Both Jaxith and Kkorian chuckled at that. After a moment, Jaxith took the initiative to introduce himself. "I am a fourth generation Healer, specializing in triage surgery. I used to own the free clinic in Aadrian, but it was practically destroyed when Dimitri decided to sack the city. On the plus side, I have actually been trained in hand-to-hand combat by a Dákun Daju Assassin, who recently became my wife."

"Good on ya, mate!" Kkorian slapped Jaxith's back. Though the Healer winced, he returned the slap with equal enthusiasm. I could only shake my head in amusement at the two.

"Right!" Amorez clapped her hands to get everyone's attention. "Now that we are all here, we can begin planning for the retaking of Bakari-Tokai, and believe me, folks, it won't be easy."

As the former Dragon Keeper spoke, Thernu went around the circumference of the room, muttering a spell so quickly I only caught a few words. When at last she had returned to her starting position, she flashed a thumbs-up to Amorez, who nodded. Then the older Feykin cast another spell. This time, the center of the room was filled with an intricate and – as far as I could tell – accurate model of the Grand Capitol.

Amorez continued as if nothing had happened. "First, let me tell you all the latest numbers of our forces. The Feykin remain strong at 350 spell-casters. Another small guild of Demons has joined us, bringing their counts up to 983. The Dákun Daju remain unchanged at 1337. And the number of Humes has grown to just over 8000."

I couldn't believe that our army was so small! Especially when compared to the Grand Army of Ithnez, which we would most likely be facing the vast majority of in the days ahead.

Amorez continued. "Now, one of our spies has recently returned with some info. With this knowledge, let us review the new additions Dimitri has made to the city's defenses, the numbers of his soldiers, and details of the Shadow Dragons. I suggest you all take notes."

I sent a letter to the nearby Dákun Daju clan, inviting them to join us at the newly completed Temple. They returned it drenched in what I imagine to be blood. Try as I might, I cannot seem to find a way to peacefully resolve the Hume-Dákun Daju conflict. Perhaps I should listen to the advice of my Archbishops, and just let the quarreling continue until each side realizes how foolish they are being. How does one merely stand aside while two peoples try to annihilate each other?

— FROM "MAKING PEACE IN A HOSTILE LAND" BY PALAVANT MIRANDA

We must have talked for hours upon hours in that pavilion. First we discussed everything we knew about the Shadow Keeper, his dragons, and the upgrades to Bakari-Tokai's defenses. Then we began plotting ways to sack the city. Each idea was shot down one after another.

Tempers were beginning to flare.

Not to mention, the room was quickly growing uncomfortably hot and the air was beginning to reek. The sweat on my forehead dared to trickle into my eyes, and I couldn't help but wonder if this is what those little fish felt like when they were stuffed into the old cans.

Finally, with no end in sight to the planning, Amorez called for a meal break. Thernu promptly canceled her spells and the door flaps were opened. We all filed out of the pavilion, eager to cool off in the fresh, night air and fill our bellies. What we least expected was to hear panicked shouting from the opposite side of the camp. Without a moment's hesitation, the lot of us rushed towards the commotion. Even Visler, who had been fast asleep on Thera's shoulder through the entire meeting, squealed and raced ahead of us.

315

We arrived in the clearing where the commotion was within minutes, weapons drawn and fearing the worst. We had severely over-reacted. In front of us, holding aloft a white flag of truce, were a dozen Wakari. They wore armor that looked like hollowed out mountain rocks. At their waists were a menagerie of awkward-looking hammers and axes, all of which were crafted of more rock. All twelve sat proudly astride their wooly, six-legged mounts. And Visler was perched on the shoulder of the Wakari holding the flag aloft. I could not help but feel a bit relieved at the visage. Pyrex had kept his word and managed to gather allies amongst his kind.

I called for everyone to calm down as I took the lead in approaching the mounted Wakari. An awkward hush fell over the four races that made up the Army of Light. They observed my interaction with a race long forgotten.

I graciously welcomed the Wakari in Kinös Elda and apologized for the reaction of the soldiers.

After a moment, the Wakari immediately left of the one holding the flag ushered the Tetrapex forward. As the six-legged mount crossed the short spans towards me, the Wakari removed the hollowed rock of a helmet. I instantly recognized her as Breccia, the Shaman of the Corundum Tribe.

She flashed a yellowed, toothy grin and spoke, "Breccia come. Bring army. Ready for big fight under blue."

"It is good to see you, Breccia, and thank you so much for coming to our aid." I couldn't suppress the huge smile the little Wakari had brought out in me.

"Just how many soldiers did you bring, Honorable Shaman?" Thera asked as she, Kitfox, and Shazza all joined me in front of Breccia.

"Breccia bring many from all tribes. Hard to convince fight worth it."

"I understand." I replied with a nod. I couldn't help but wonder if she had only managed to convince these eleven to come with her. As I swept my gaze over them, the Wakari holding the flag removed his helm.

It was Pyrex himself. And he was smiling very smugly.

"We somehow convinced some one hundred and fifty..." he paused to gauge my reaction. I couldn't hide my disappointment.

Only one hundred and fifty? I sighed inwardly. Well it was better than none.

Pyrex's smug smile widened, "... thousand Wakari to join the fight."

I gaped at him in total surprise.

Shazza broke the surprised silence with a loud inquiry in Standard, "Did he just say one hundred and fifty thousand Wakari are here to fight with us?"

The news spread through the Army of Light like wildfire unchecked. Several thousand more warriors had arrived. Morale was at an all time high despite the fact that the new arrivals were only a meter tall at best. They were able warriors. They were here when we needed them. That was all that mattered.

As we broke bread with the Wakari, some details about the battle to come were exchanged. Amorez admitted to not having a plan worked out yet, but now that the Wakari were with us, there was a better chance at forging a successful campaign.

Breccia only made one demand. "When battle of big city won, Wakari want mountain home under big blue."

Amorez looked sidelong at me to see if I knew what the little Shaman was talking about.

"You want to build a new Wakari city on the surface?"

Breccia nodded once.

I leaned back on the bench as I considered her request. It had been several centuries since the Wakari were last on the surface of Ithnez. I couldn't help but wonder what sort of things would occur between them and the Dákun Daju, who they once warred with. Especially considering the war was never officially ended; just put on hold when the Humes arrived to colonize the planet.

While Amorez inquired about details on the Wakari's plans for a new city, I snuck away to speak with the Dákun Daju generals about the idea. The three of them plus Zhealocera, Shazza, and – oddly enough – Kkorian were seated with them. Vitaani and Zalx greeted me as I walked up to their table. V'Nyath merely waved.

"I don't mean to interrupt your meal and conversation, but I have a rather touchy question to put to you."

"It seems Humes are in abundance of questions as of late." Zalx replied, eyeing Kkorian over the lip of his goblet. The pirate smirked wolfishly and raised his glass to Zalx. They both waved for me to take the seat between as they killed their drinks and poured each other another.

"And what is your question, Xyleena-sortim?" Asked Vitaani.

I slowly sank into the chair between Kkorian and Zalx as I thought of how to word everything without sounding like a nut. Finally I said, "How well do Dákun Daju and Wakari get along these days?"

V'Nyath's face flushed as he fought the urge to either laugh or holler. Zalx loosed a loud guffaw. Zhealocera cracked a wry smile. Only Vitaani and Shazza retained their stoic masks.

"The old war has been forgotten by most Dákun Daju." Admitted Vitaani. "The Wakari have cowered underground for so long it is no longer our desire to destroy them for past wrongs. However, there are some among us who still vow to claim their blood."

I nodded in understanding.

"Why do you want to know this?" Asked Shazza.

"Well," I leaned forward slightly and rested my elbows on the table. "The Wakari have a price for coming to the surface to help us in the battle ahead."

"No surprise there." Muttered V'Nyath.

"What is the demand that they are making?"

"They want to build a new city in the mountains. Exactly where, I can't say for sure, but they do want it above ground."

Vitaani quirked an eyebrow. "Is there a particular reason this should concern us?"

"I was just worried that the Dákun Daju would," I paused to consider my words carefully, "continue the war."

Zalx snorted. "Those greasy little rats are no longer worth our time or blood."

V'Nyath, Vitaani, and Zhealocera agreed with him.

We spent a few more minutes talking about the issue. Then Amorez called for the generals to reconvene in the pavilion. I heard a few muttered oaths, but they all got up and left their tables. They marched in rows towards the tent. I lingered behind, watching.

Breccia had apparently named two Wakari to be generals along with her. One was Pyrex, and the other was a male I had never seen before. All three of them were at the front of the line, speaking excitedly with Amorez.

The Demons walked past me then, blocking my line of sight to the Wakari. Kitfox stayed at my side while Freya, Blood Fang, Aralyn, and Cloud Strider moved on. I smiled up at Kitfox as he snaked an arm around my waist.

"Come on," he said and kissed my forehead, "let's see if those guys can finally agree on something."

Several more hours were spent holed up in the pavilion. With the Wakari now a huge part of our army, the plan to retake Bakari-Tokai was forged anew. I found myself amazed at how quickly ideas and suggestions were accepted. We were like a family coming together to decide on what to eat for dinner.

At long last, the plan was complete and agreed upon. We broke our meeting with orders from Amorez to tell the individual battalions of their tasks. With that done, we could retire for the rest of the night and prepare to break camp early in the morn.

The march on Bakari-Tokai was about to begin.

Angel Breath. That is what Symbilla had called her ability. It granted life to whoever received it. Immortal life. But there was a catch; That person would live so long as the dragon lived and would hurt when the dragon hurt. Still... the child, an innocent caught in the crossfire of Agasei's fury, deserved to live.

Was it worth it?

— FROM "THE DIARY OF AMOREZ" BY AMOREZ RENOAN

I woke to the ghost of a kiss upon my brow. I could not even remember ever falling asleep the night before. Yet there I was, laid out atop a pile of sleeping furs within the confines of a small tent. Kitfox was beside me, holding me to his bare chest in a sweet embrace. His amber eyes still looked drowsy, as if he had just woken up as well.

"The call to wake up went out a minute ago." He mumbled.

I stifled a yawn and said, "Are the suns even up yet?"

Kitfox shrugged. "Too dark around here to really tell." His ear twitched, catching a sound. He frowned and his body turned tense. "We are about to be disturbed."

I quickly tried to recall where I had set my war fans. Slipping a hand beneath my pillow, I found one and held it firmly. A moment later, I heard faint footsteps stop just beside the flaps that formed the tent's door. Whoever it was hesitated then. My grip on the fan tightened. Something was uttered in a whispered tone and the footsteps quickly retreated. Still Kitfox remained tense and uneasy.

Then a familiar voice spoke. "Xyleena, are you going to sleep all day? We need to get moving, you lazy girl."

I sighed in relief. It was just Amorez. "Yeah, we're coming. Just trying to wake up a little before the mad rush."

"'We?'" I detected a hint of disapproval in her voice. "Is that Fox Demon… uh…? Kitfox? Is Kitfox with you?"

"Yes." He growled.

"Freya was wondering where you went. Please find her before we set out today to let her know you're okay."

Kitfox quirked an eyebrow, like he did not believe what he had heard. "Alright."

Amorez thanked him and finally walked away.

"I get the distinct feeling she does not like the fact that I am courting you." Kitfox muttered after the old Keeper had left ear shot.

"I got that impression, too, Love." I kissed him on the lips. "But I am not about to let her opinions of us ruin our relationship."

He kissed me back. "Me neither."

After a long minute of lingering in each other's embrace, we forced ourselves out of our bed of furs. While he pulled on his tunic, I started packing up our belongings. With that done, we stepped outside to take down the tent. Countless others were already up and in various stages of preparing to head out. Those who had already completed their tasks were helping others. Even the Wakari were darting around the camp grounds, assisting with whatever they could. I was totally amazed at the change in the people of Ithnez. The old issue or racism had at last been buried.

I smiled.

By midday, the Army of Light had managed to traverse almost a quarter of a league through the thick forest. We ate a light lunch while we walked. And we never stopped in one place for very long. Along the way, we enjoyed the merry songs of Feykin and Hume alike. The Dákun Daju surprised us all with a fast paced melody of their own.

And thus, the first day passed without incident. That was, until nightfall came. As we settled into camping space at dusk, a chorus of war cries exploded from the direction of the chuck wagons. Several warriors, myself and Amorez included, rushed to see what was going on. When we arrived on the scene, we saw Breccia – atop a small mountain of crates – and Vitaani standing face to face. Their arms were tied together with a long, white cloth and a string of jewels.

Amorez was the first to ask what had happened.

"The old war is settled at last." Replied Vitaani. The gathered Dákun Daju released another chorus of war cries. Even the Wakari cheered, though not as loudly as their new, official allies.

The second day passed in a very similar pattern as the first; with songs and merry making. It wasn't until late afternoon that we encountered our first problem.

It started as a curious thumping in the distance. Amorez and I had the Feykin spread out through the marching battalions as a precaution. But the sound never grew louder. Then the trees thinned just enough to see the sky overhead. And that was when a huge shadow flew past. A warning cry went out and the Feykin immediately cast their spell.

We had been spotted by a Shadow Dragon.

Abaddon, who was that dragon? I replayed the image of the huge shadow in my mind for him to see.

He was quiet for a moment as he concentrated on the image. Given the small size of this dragon, and the visible fluctuations of air under the wings, I would have to say it must be Ether the Wind.

Is Ether a threat?

She is more than likely spying on us and relaying the info to her Keeper.

Wonderful. Muttered Kitfox. Now that bastard can prepare for us even more.

I doubt she had a good look at the exact size of our forces. Replied Kúskú. The forest you are in is very hard to see through from above.

If being spotted by that little dragon bothers you so, how about having the spell casters cloak as many warriors as they can?

It is a good idea, Taypax, but I wouldn't want them to waste all of their energy before the battle, which is when we will need them the most.

So we continued on, ever more wary of the skies overhead. That night, we left nearly triple the number of guards on duty as before. We were too close to Bakari-Tokai now to take any chances, especially with the Shadow Dragons looming overhead.

The third day saw fit to rain on us. At first, several warriors believed it was the work of the Shadow Dragons. They had been adamant about mounting an attack against them. But their paranoia was proven false when we left the relative safety of the forest behind. Not a dragon was in sight; only open fields of tall grass and a menacing sky overhead. That revelation had calmed them slightly.

However, more worries grew apparent. Out in the open as we were now, we had no shelter should Dimitri actually send forth his dragons. Before widespread fear swept the hearts of the Army of Light, I released all twelve of my dragons from the amulet. Sparkling lights and elements bedazzled the sky in a marvelous display and all twelve coalesced midair with just meters between them. As one, they roared; a great, deafening chorus that shook even the heavens and drowned out the storm growing overhead.

The army cheered and the dragons floated to the ground like feathers. The moment they landed, they were swarmed by soldiers, each wanting to get a closer look at the legendary creatures. The dragons, of course, did their best to accommodate everyone's curiosity and eagerness. The twelve of them spread out to different sections of the army so that they could walk beside the warriors.

Feeling much safer under the protection of the twelve dragons, the army eagerly pushed onwards. We trudged through miles of overgrown grasslands and sloppy mud. We were quickly growing too weary for travel, yet we forced ourselves onwards.

When the last of our horses died, we resorted to one of the local reptiles to use as replacements. We called them wyverns after an old, Earthic myth because they looked like dragons. They were about the

323

D imitri scowled. He had had his dragons scouting the area around Bakari-Tokai for days; searching for the small group Hyperion had spotted during his patrols nearly two weeks ago. The dragons had reported nothing. That was until a few hours ago, when Ether reported movement in the forest almost due north of the city. Dimitri had immediately ordered her to observe and report back to him everything, but do not engage in a battle.

So the smallest Shadow Dragon had done just that. Only moments ago, she had contacted him again. This time, she spoke of several hundred two-leggers marching through the trees. Just how many there were, she couldn't be sure; the trees kept them hidden well. Dimitri promptly ordered all of his dragons to return to the city. Then he called a meeting with the commanders of his army.

Dimitri sat in the court yard, nestled safely on a padded throne between Hyperion's massive forepaws. The enormous dragon, as always, watched over the goings on of the Humes and his Keeper. Especially when it came to the fat, useless one, Vincent. For some reason Dimitri had yet to discover, the dragon did not trust Vincent at all.

Since they had a few minutes before the commanders arrived for the meeting, Dimitri decided to ask. "Tell me, Hyperion, what bugs you about Vincent? Is it his near-uselessness or something else?"

The enormous dragon snorted. "The fat Hume and his continuing failures are merely irritating. Nothing more."

"Yet I sense something about him troubles you; particularly when he is around me. What is it?" Dimitri dared to press the subject.

Hyperion growled, but did not speak.

"Do you think he will try to kill me?"

"As if the rotund fool could actually pull off that feat." Hyperion made a sound like a laugh. "No, Keeper, he cannot kill you."

Dimitri thought on it some more. A shadow of a doubt revealed itself in the back of his mind. He had been ignoring it for some time, but he was aware of the very real possibility. Finally, he voiced his concerns to the dragon. "He will betray me, won't he?"

"There is a very good chance of it." Replied the dragon. "That can be changed, however, if you desire it."

Dimitri smirked. "Yes, please do turn the fat bastard into one of the mindless drones who loyally serve me."

The first of the commanders had finally arrived. The two of them greeted their king with salutes before standing at attention. Moments later, a third soldier did the same. Then a fourth and fifth. A sixth, then a seventh arrived minutes later. They all greeted Dimitri with salutes before standing at attention. At long last Vincent appeared, wheezing and sweaty as usual.

"It shall be done." Hyperion muttered, watching as the fat Judge scuttled into his place between the soldiers.

Dimitri waited a few moments for Vincent's labored breathing to quiet down. Then he spoke, "I have received word that our enemies are closing in upon us from the northern woods. The exact size of their army is currently unknown. What we do know is that they number in the hundreds and consist of Hume, Feykin, Dákun Daju, and Demon warriors. And let's not forget that the other Dragon Keeper and her dragons are with them. So I ask you, gentlemen," he sneered at the word, "what do you suggest we do about this?"

"Sir!" The soldier at the far left called out.

Dimitri granted permission for him to speak.

"Sir, I suggest we recall the forces we left in Aadrian and the surrounding cities. With those extra eighteen hundred or so, we should be able to successfully deter the Dragon Keeper's attack."

"You forgot about the wretch's dragons, fool!" Vincent huffed. "What do you propose we do about them?"

Hyperion snorted. "You puny two-leggers need not worry yourselves over them. We of the dark will take on our counterparts."

"Since you suggested the idea of pulling the forces from Aadrian," Dimitri pointed to the soldier as he spoke, "I will leave you in charge of seeing the task is complete. I want them here in a day. No excuses."

"Sir! Yes, Sir!"

Dimitri rolled his eyes in annoyance and waved for the soldier to leave. The soldier bowed stiffly and sprinted away. "Any other ideas from you lot?"

"Sir!" Cried the soldier next to Vincent.

"Speak."

"I suggest we move the main bulk of our defenses to the fore of the city. Since we know they will be attacking by land and by dragon, we can afford to sacrifice some of the guards and equipment on the eastern water front."

Dimitri said he would think about that one. Then he asked for more ideas. One by one, the soldiers gathered before him spoke their suggestions. Dimitri suddenly wished Godilai was here. Her input on the strategies provided would have been quite beneficial to the defense of the city. It would have also been beneficial to his campaign if he had a small battalion of Feykin under his command. Their magical abilities would guarantee his victory for certain. As it was, he could only listen to the suggestions and hope to come up with a winning plan.

After several hours of listening to the soldiers and discussing the odd thing or two with Hyperion, Dimitri had his strategy formulated. He felt it was absolutely perfect and was certain that the little wretch would not be able to overthrow the defenses. He explained the plan to his soldiers at great length. At long last, he sent them out to see to their tasks' completion.

The soldiers scurried away. By request of his king, only Vincent remained. He stared at Dimitri. Dimitri stared right back. Finally, the old Judge spoke.

"What did you want to see me for, Majesty?"

Dimitri flashed a crooked smile, and pointed upwards with a single index finger. Naturally, Vincent followed the invisible line drawn by the finger. His gaze lingered on Hyperion's wedge-shaped head, and then moved higher.

"What am I looking for, exactly?"

Dimitri sighed in frustration. "That was just to prove how useless you are to me."

Vincent growled in absolute fury and returned his gaze to his king. But Dimitri had vanished through the open door of the palace. So he was alone with the enormous dragon, who was staring down at him with hunger in his blood red eyes.

"You are lucky to get to live." Hyperion growled. His eyes flashed red for a split second. Vincent's mind fell away, swallowed by the blackness of the dragon's mind controlling power. "Now, go and make yourself useful to your king."

Without a word, Vincent obediently turned and scuttled out of the court yard.

Dark clouds grew ever thicker. A dark night had settled in. I stood at the apex of a hill. Zenith sat silently at my side. Together we watched the building storm. Blue lightning flashed. Thunder ripped the atmosphere. I could see the towering spires of Bakari-Tokai piercing the sky like daggers. They were illuminated for a blink by the arcing electricity before vanishing into the darkness like ghosts.

Each time the lightning crackled, I could see different parts of the Grand Capitol. As the intelligence reports said, the outer wall had sustained massive damage from Dimitri's attack. The once black marble stone had been replaced with another material that looked like dull grey mud. Six of the twelve Shadow Dragons sat perched on the battlements. Beneath them, soldiers scurried to complete whatever tasks they had. I could not help but wonder where the other six dragons were lurking.

Just outside the wall, the fields were in shambles. Several farmers' buildings lay in ruins and great portions of the streets had been reduced to gaping craters. I could barely see the shadows of soldier and citizen alike hunkering down for the night in whatever shelter they could find. It was a miserable existence.

In the heart of the city, the black palace stood proudly amidst the rubble. It, too, had sustained damage during Dimitri's takeover. A large portion of the southern wing lay in rubble amidst the gardens. The palace was surrounded by a wall of black marble as well. Unlike the outer wall, this one appeared undamaged, save a gap in the top stones where a portion of the damaged wing had fallen.

Less than a quarter league separated the Army of Light and the outer most wall of the city. It was all flat land ahead; easily traversed even if soaked by the approaching storm. According to plan agreed upon by the generals, we would be upon the city before the suns rose. The soldiers were advised to rest well this night, but I could almost drink their unease. They, like me, would find little rest tonight.

"You should say something to everyone before the final trek into battle." Zenith spoke so suddenly that I startled.

After a moment to recover, I replied, "What am I supposed to say to them?"

"Something moving to motivate them."

"Have you ever tried to 'move' a Dákun Daju?" I laughed. "Not exactly an easy thing to do."

"If there is one person alive today who can manage the feat," the dragon snaked his head about to look me in the eye, "it is you."

"Thanks for the vote of confidence, Zenith, but I don't have a clue what I would say."

The dragon chuckled. "I am certain you will think of something, little one."

"Eavesdropping on the future again?" I teased. Zenith merely hummed as he returned to his full height. I watched him stare off into the distance for some time. As I did so, I could not help but wonder what was going through his mind at that moment. Was the dragon as worried about the future of the world as I was? I found that unlikely. Zenith was the seer of seers after all. He knew everything about the past, the present, and the future. If something terrible was going to happen in the battle ahead, he would have said something.

At least, I think he would have said something.

"You should focus more on what you are going to say to the troops in the morning," Muttered Zenith, "and less on what I am thinking."

I gaped at him.

"And no, I did not hear your thoughts. I merely listened to what you said, just moments before you put your thoughts to words."

"I am not surprised." I said with a roll of my eyes. "You have always spied on the future, but you never really speak of the things you witness."

The dragon chuckled and lay down. "I do not wish to alter the course of history by revealing the events I witness, whether they good or bad."

I walked over to Zenith and sat on one of his giant forepaws. I marveled at the silver-brushed, sapphire scales as I took a moment to order my thoughts. Finally, I said to the dragon, "What do you see when you look into tomorrow?"

"You wish for me to reveal to you the results of the war? You know I cannot do that."

"That's not what I meant, Zenith." I said, shaking my head. "I just want to know if you see any happiness."

"Why do you want to know such a silly thing, young one?"

"Because I…" my voice hitched as I fought the urge to cry, "I'm terrified. If I am to go into battle, I at least want to know that whatever happens, there will be happiness in the future. That alone will give me hope."

Zenith was quiet for a long moment. Slowly, he lowered his head so that I could see his beautiful eyes. I could see a sadness in them, as if he was upset that I was so scared. His ruby tongue snaked out to kiss away the tears that had rolled down my cheek. At long last, he spoke. "There will be much happiness, little one."

I reached out to hug his snout, whispering 'thank you's as I took comfort in his words.

The eastern sky had just begun to lighten. Dawn would soon be here. The call to arms had come at last.

With a sigh, I forced myself to stand up from Zenith's forepaw. As I stretched and loosened muscles, I listened to the sounds behind me. The generals were rousing their individual battalions and calling them into formation. It would not be long before the entire army was assembled and ready to head out.

I decided it was time to face the inevitable and gather my friends. With a farewell pat on the dragon's foreleg, I made my way into the camp. As I wove my way through the people and tents, I made sure to keep my head up and smile at passer-bys. I wanted to relay confidence to those who gazed upon me and let them know that, even though I was scared, I believed we could do this. We could win.

I found Kitfox in conference with Freya and Amorez. Upon seeing me, they uttered good mornings. I took Kitfox's hand in mine as I returned the greetings.

"Are you ready?" Asked Amorez.

"As ready as I'll ever be."

She merely nodded in response.

"Be careful today, okay?" Freya said as she captured me in a tight embrace. I returned it with equal enthusiasm.

"You, too."

With that, we parted ways; the older warriors going off to gather their team while Kitfox and I went in search of ours.

Kitfox and I found Thera standing at the edge of a group of Feykin with her mother and sister. They exchanged a fond farewell. Then Thera joined us in the search for Shazza and Kkorian. We found the duo ready and waiting in the heart of the camp. The pair of them calmly made their way over to us. With my entire team finally back together, I felt more confident than I had the night before.

Without a word, I moved to the absolute center of the campgrounds. Once there, I uttered a string of Kinös Elda and a mound of dirt rose at my command. When I deemed the height of the mound descent enough for what I was about to do, I canceled the spell. With a deep breath, I cast a spell to amplify my voice. Then I spoke, loudly and clearly for all to hear.

"I call upon you; all of you! Hume. Feykin. Dákun Daju. Demon. Wakari. Grant me a few moments." Countless soldiers paused in their tasks to heed my words. Some of them even moved to gather around the mound I had created. I made sure to look each one in the eye. When a giant crowd had gathered before me, I continued. "We all face a difficult time now, but we have cause to be joyous. For the first time in nearly five centuries, the entire world is united in friendship. The racism that had been plaguing our planet longer than anyone here can remember has finally been put to rest. Today, and in the days to come, we are all one race. We are Ithnezians. Let us pray that the battle to come will forever fuse the friendships we have made. For right now, in our darkest hour, we have found the light."

Cheers erupted from the crowd.

I smiled and hopped down from the mound of earth. Many of the warriors clapped me on the arms as I made my way to my friends. Kitfox, Thera, Shazza, Kkorian, and I gathered in a circle. The rush of soldiers around us was forgotten for a moment.

"You guys ready to do this?" I asked as I met each of their gazes. Though their faces remained stoic masks as they answered, I could read the uncertainty and fear in their eyes and the tension in their bodies. They were as apprehensive about the battle as I was. I forced myself to smile, hoping it would ease their worries. "We can do it. Together."

Shazza called my name and I looked to her. She took a deep breath and crossed her right hand over her chest. A moment later she exposed her throat. It was a gesture of the highest honor, and one that I had never expected from the Dákun Daju. Slowly, she lowered her gaze to me. "It has been an honor to live and fight at your side. May we meet again in the face of victory."

"We will meet again, my friend," I affirmed with a smile, "and victory will be ours."

Kitfox extended his hand outwards, to the center of our circle. "To peace." He said.

Thera quickly put her hand over his and smiled. "To family."

Kkorian mirrored them, resting his hand firmly on Thera's. "To friends."

Shazza followed suit, surprising us all with her words, "To love."

I smiled as I rested my hand at the top of theirs. "To a world united."

I fiddled with the riding straps for probably the hundredth time. From my place astride Zenith, I watched as the Army of Light made their way across the fields. They moved silently in the predawn light, trying not to draw attention from the tower guards or the Shadow Dragons stationed on the battlements. They had made sure to pad their weapons and armor with cloth very well to reduce the noise. So far, it appeared to be working in our favor. In mere moments, everyone would be in position and the battle to decide the fate of the world would begin.

I adjusted the straps again and quickly ran through the plan in my head. Once the battalions were in place, my team, my dragons, and I would take flight and lead the charge through the wall and into the heart of Bakari-Tokai. After that, it was our duty to keep the Shadow Dragons occupied until the city was ours.

Sure, it sounded simple enough.

But I knew better. Nothing ever goes according to plan. And Bakari-Tokai would not be easy to take. So I mentally prepared myself for the worst and prayed that it did not come to be.

"Get ready, little ones." Zenith announced.

I drew in a deep breath and gripped the saddle harder, preparing for the rapid take off that was sure to happen. I looked left, to Kitfox and Thera, then right, to Shazza and Kkorian. They were as tense as hardened steel; any more pressure and they might snap.

I felt Zenith tense.

His talons dug into the earth.

A low rumble of a growl escaped him.

I exhaled slowly.

This is it. Please, Gods, let us get through this.

"Now!" Zenith lurched forward, roughly jarring me in the saddle despite my readiness. The other dragons were right behind him, heads and tails low; streamlined. They bound over the land like a flock of birds as they spread their wings wide. Within seconds all of them were airborne in tight formation just meters off the ground.

The dragons divided into four wings of three and two of the wings pulled ahead of the others, then around to attack from the west. They streaked silently through the sky towards the sleeping Bakari-Tokai. Within seconds they passed over the waiting army and a few soldiers ducked in response to the dragons' low flight path.

Meters away from the western side of the outermost wall of the city, Zenith reared. I felt as if I was going to slip out of the saddle as he pulled a vertical barrel roll. As he did so, I caught a glimpse of Nightshade before she vanished into the shadows. She looked both amazed and furious that we were able to sneak our way up to the city without their notice.

Well over the western gate of the city, Zenith flared his massive wings and seemed to hang in the air. Nexxa was at his side a heartbeat later. He loosed a magnificent bellow, which was echoed by the other dragons, and flapped his wings once. Nexxa was his mirror image. In an instant a mass of crackling blue energy and another of green shot out and slammed into the wall. Two massive explosions ripped through the wall and huge chunks of rubble rained down. Two more explosions rocked the northern portion of the wall a moment later.

The alarm bells of Bakari-Tokai rang out.

With a chorus of war cries and hollers, the Army of Light surged forward, towards the gaping holes in the wall. They met with little resistance as they streamed through the gaps and over the rubble-strewn streets.

My attention on the battle below was stolen away when a dark mass slammed into Zenith. The resulting tumble through the sky nearly threw me from the saddle. I resorted to using a spell to keep myself in place while I searched the near-dawn sky for our attacker. Zenith managed to pull out of the tumble a few meters above the ground and struggled to regain altitude. Our attacker turned out to be none other than Nightshade, but she was not alone. A smaller, splotchy dragon and one of the skeletal dragons were with her.

Zenith snorted in fury and annoyance. "I hope you are ready, little one. This is about to get rough."

I gripped the saddle tighter as I shouted. "Let's bring these Shadow Dragons down!"

Zenith roared, long and loud.

The other Dragons of Light echoed the call.

Nightshade seemed to hesitate for a moment before she issued her own challenge. She dove for Zenith as he raced skywards. The two dragons crashed together head-on with a resounding thunder. More crashes filled the air as the other dragons collided. They grappled, kicking each other with their hind legs while struggling to grasp the other's neck between their jaws. Ivory talons loosed horrible screeches as they scraped across jewel-scaled underbellies. Fierce snarls and growls mixed in to make a cacophony of a chorus.

Nightshade was meters smaller than Zenith and her legs and shoulders were not as muscular. Yet her fierceness and flexibility in the fight more than made up for her slight disadvantages. Zenith was forced to break away from the smaller dragon and change tactics.

The Dragon of the Heavens bolted skywards, leaving behind the battle. Nightshade hissed and dared to take up pursuit. They climbed and climbed in dizzying spirals, bursting through the thick cloud layer and beyond.

"Cast the bubble spell to give you air." Zenith growled. I quickly did as he said and a soft blue bubble formed around me. His rapid ascent quickened even more. The sky plunged into blackness and stars flickered to life in the vast emptiness. I couldn't help but stare at the twinkling display in awe as Zenith continued to climb. I could recognize the constellations I had been taught long ago, but nestled among them were even more stars. It was like looking upon sparkling silver dust strewn upon black velvet. Magnificent.

At last Zenith pulled out of the deep ascent and flared his enormous wings. He came to a complete stop and hovered, weightless. I felt myself start to float out of the saddle astride him and held onto the straps tighter. The heavenly dragon looked down on the planet below and huffed.

I forced myself to look away from the dazzling stars. Peering between Zenith's wing and neck I marveled at the beauty spread out below. The ocean was a deep aquamarine blue of likes I had never imagined. And the tops of the clouds that would otherwise warn of storms were painted a medley of colors. The spectrum of colors made the menacing clouds look almost harmless, perhaps even friendly.

The junction where the vast heavens touched the planet was hazy and curved just enough to betray the planet's spherical shape. A brilliant, yellow light had just been born on a section of the eastern horizon. The suns would soon make an appearance on the battlefield far, far below.

Only one thing worried me: Nightshade was nowhere to be seen. That troubling fact did not seem to bother Zenith in the slightest. In fact, he seemed rather amused.

I frowned. "What's so funny?"

"She believes her shadow will protect her, but she could not be more wrong." He said. After a moment more of admiring the view, Zenith brought his forepaws forward, as if clutching a large ball. A glowing, blue glyph I could not read suddenly materialized in the space just below his paws. "Galactic Tsunami!"

The glyph pulsed with white light and a low hum reached my ears. A split second later, a mass of blue energy exploded downwards heading straight towards the surface of the planet. It started out as a mere ripple in space, but grew rapidly as it descended. As it sped away, the girth of the energy grew wider and wider, taller and taller until it was several kilometers across and high. Then it warped and took on the appearance of the strange, silvery liquid that formed the floor of Zenith's lair. Within the bizarre water, I could see stars and planets, huge clouds of cosmic dust, and so many other heavenly things.

The moment the wave of energy solidified, Zenith tucked his wings close to his body, tipped forward, and fell through the sky. As he and I hurtled downward, I caught sight of Nightshade, trying in vain to outrun the torrent of cosmic water heading right towards her. A heartbeat before the massive attack struck, she loosed a horrid and furious scream. Then she was no more.

Dimitri stood at the balcony railing, a glass of wine in hand and a placid look upon his face. He watched the battle in front of him with unblinking, crimson eyes.

The dead and dying littered the streets and the gutters ran red with torrents of blood. Howls of agony echoed off the rubble, adding an eerie tone to the chorus of clashing steel and angry shouts. Though his soldiers had suffered many losses, they were really nothing. To his enemies' eyes, they appeared to be winning.

But he knew otherwise.

A smirk touched his lips as he glanced downwards. Nestled in the palace gardens, some two hundred thousand soldiers stood at attention. They waited as if on the edge of a blade for the perfect moment to strike. But that was still a while in the future.

A quick succession of thunderous booms from the northeast stole his attention. He frowned and quickly strode to the far right of the balcony to find the source. Just beyond the lattice steel gate protecting Bakari-Tokai's harbor, eight ships sat. He scoffed and cast a spell to enhance his vision.

Three of the ships flew pirate flags atop their masts. Another was the very recognizable stone ship, Shadow Dance. The other four were once part of the Royal Navy before he took over the city. Every one of them had their cannons aimed at the city and a continuous barrage of lead balls smashed through the buildings. Soldiers screamed in pain and fear as the structures collapsed around them. A well-aimed shot managed to strike the palace and burry itself deep within the wall just beneath his feet.

He swore an oath and canceled his spell.

Do not fear those pathetic insects, my Keeper. Hyperion's voice boomed in Dimitri's head. The Keeper looked upwards –

towards the tallest of the palace towers – where the massive Dragon of Apocalypse stood watch.

Dimitri scowled. Do not mistake my anger for fear, Hyperion.

The dragon did not respond.

With a growl of annoyance, Dimitri turned to make his way back to the middle of the balcony. He hadn't even taken two steps before the breath was knocked out of him and he stumbled, almost falling to his hands and knees. It took him several moments to recover. When he did, he shot a look of inquiry to Hyperion.

The ruby and black dragon was looking skywards over his shoulder and a feeling of slight concern trickled through their mental attachment. Feeling both bewildered and worried, Dimitri looked upwards in hopes of seeing what had bothered Hyperion. He gasped in shock at the giant wave of silver water cascading down from the heavens.

He watched the tsunami grow larger and larger as it sped towards the ground. Upon seeing just how large the wave was, a cold feeling of dread overcame him. For it was headed straight for the palace and there was not time for escape.

Dimitri heard Hyperion growl and mutter something. In an instant, a sphere of shimmering red energy engulfed the entirety of the palace and its gardens and extended several meters beyond. Just seconds after the sphere went up, the massive wave struck. The ground rumbled and shook; the ocean parted as the silver wave sliced into it. A blast of thunder erupted and a massive wind tore at the city. A cloud of dust and debris was hurled into the air, blocking out the early morning sun.

Yet none of the explosion penetrated the red sphere of energy Hyperion had erected. Dimitri breathed a sigh of relief as he cast his gaze over the city. The air was gray with dust so thick he could not see anything beyond the borders of the red sphere.

What in the Gods' names was that? He mentally shouted at Hyperion. And why was I nearly bowled over?

The dragon lowered his gaze to look at his Keeper. The attack was Zenith's Galactic Tsunami. Had he been just a bit

338

higher in the borders of space, my force field would not have held up to the force of the wave. Hyperion growled. As for what you felt; it was Nightshade. She was caught in the blast.

Dimitri felt his heart skip a beat.

She will be alright. Hyperion said after a moment. I have already ordered Anima to tend to her wounds.

Dimitri silently thanked the Gods for his dragon's survival. After a moment to calm his raked nerves, he returned to the center of the balcony. There, he calmly waited for the choking dust to settle so he could observe the battle once again.

When the power cells of our guns and cannons – supplied to us long ago by the ARIES Group – began to fail, we had to resort to a different means of defending ourselves. We took a cue from the Dákun Daju as well as our own history and began forging weapons from the variety of metals we had available. It worked, but it took quite a bit of training to master such primitive devices.

– FROM "THE CHRONICLES OF ITHNEZ, VOL. II" BY ADJIRSÉ DÉDOS

"Hold on!" roared Vortex.

Kitfox did not need to be told twice; his Demon hearing had already picked up the sound of the massive wave rumbling through the sky. He gripped the riding straps as hard as he could and hunkered down against Vortex's back. The wave struck and a blast of noise erupted with the impact. Kitfox covered his ears and screamed in agony, but he could not hear it.

A rush of violent wind slammed into them, jolting them and nearly sending Vortex tumbling before his powers over wind adapted to the sheer onslaught. A dust cloud promptly followed and Kitfox was forced to squeeze his eyes shut and hold his breath. He clung to the dragon even tighter and prayed the upheaval would soon subside.

Minutes passed like hours. His lungs burned, yet he dared not breathe the heated and dusty air. At long last the raging windstorm calmed and Vortex returned to a steady flight path. Kitfox slowly opened his eyes, fearful of what he might see.

The air was choked with dust so thick he could not discern ground from sky. Vortex huffed and flapped his wings hard, jarring Kitfox in the saddle. The Demon only hoped they were gaining altitude; not crashing. After several solid pumps of his wings, Vortex broke free of the choking cloud. Kitfox coughed and swallowed huge gulps of air. When his lungs no longer burned, he looked down on the city and frowned.

He was somewhere over the northeastern quadrant of Bakari-Tokai. Of that, he was certain. But it was what he couldn't see that had him worried beyond words. Was the Army of Light still fighting after the massive wave, or had they been leveled along with the city? He would not be able to tell until the thick cloud of dust settled.

Can you not hear me? Vortex asked, but his voice seemed far away and muted.

Kitfox blinked in surprise as he looked at the back of the cerulean dragon's head. Then he opened and closed his mouth several times, trying to clear his ears. When that did not work, he touched his ears and felt a thick gel pooling there. Pulling his fingers away, he realized his fingertips were covered in blood.

He swore loudly, but he could not hear it. That damn wave destroyed my hearing.

Symbilla comes. Vortex replied after a silence. Thera is with her. They will heal you.

Thank the Gods. Kitfox sighed in relief. While they waited, they set about trying to clear away some of the dust cloud with gusts of wind.

As Vortex back winged in preparation to launch a third Storm Assault on the dispersing cloud, a movement at the edge of vision caught Kitfox's attention. The regal blue dragon dove out of the sky at breakneck speed and vanished in the cloud close to the red force field.

Kitfox couldn't help but wonder, What is Zenith up to?

A groan escaped Amorez as she shoved aside wooden beams, gravel, and other debris. She pushed herself off the ground with a wince. She was bloodied and bruised, and her eyes and throat stung from the presence of the dust. Her ears rang loudly from the explosion, but she quickly cured that with a spell.

With one quick look at her surroundings, she grew absolutely livid.

Zenith, you fool! Are you trying to kill us all? She barely managed to keep her anger in check as she recalled the battalion under her command to her. Several of the soldiers were clearly shaken by the devastation of Zenith's Galactic Tsunami, but they did not appear to have any major injuries. Once the lot of them were finally on their feet and ready to move out, Amorez led the way.

Navigating the streets within the choking dust reminded her of the few extremely foggy nights she had spent in Pletíxa so many lifetimes ago. She quickly pushed those thoughts aside; now was not the time to get lost in memories. There was still a battle to be won.

A shadow suddenly loomed before her. Amorez quickly sunk into a fighting stance and hollered. Behind her, she heard her battalion ready themselves for an attack.

"Relax, old friend. It is only me."

Amorez sighed in relief as Freya's voice carried over the din. After a moment, the Wolf Demon and what remained of her battalion stepped forward to reveal themselves. Freya was a mess of tangled hair, several bruises and bloodied cuts, and debris. Her angled face and amber eyes betrayed a mix of relief and anger.

"What was Zenith thinking launching his Tsunami towards the city?"

Amorez scoffed. "I've been wondering the same thing."

"Do we continue on with the plan to take the palace despite the inability to see?"

"The issue of sight is being resolved as we speak." Amorez cast a look skywards. Though she could not see through the lingering dust, she felt Vortex prepare to launch his windstorm. She only hoped that the attack would blow the dust away and not result in more damage to the city.

"Then we continue as we planned." Freya nodded once.

Amorez returned her attention to her old friend and smiled. "We continue."

The two leaders issued the commands to their battalions, and then they were off. As they navigated their way through the rubble-strewn streets, they did not encounter anyone save members of their own militia. It wasn't until they reached the center of the city that a feeling of dread clutched Amorez's heart. As she gazed across the long stretch of bridge that led to the palace still half concealed in dust, she shivered.

Something's wrong.

Hyperion's intense gaze passed over the curtained city. He knew his counterparts and companions were hidden within the dust storm, dueling for the upper hand in a fierce aerial battle. With the billowing cloud of dust and debris, he could not keep tabs on either. He released a growl of annoyance.

Focusing on his link with his brothers and sisters, Hyperion sought out the smallest of the twelve. Ether!

The Shadow Dragon of Wind responded to his summons immediately.

Get that cursed dust out of the way!

I'm on it, Hyperion.

The link was severed.

Hyperion continued to watch as two dragons exploded outwards from the cloud. The one closest to him, he recognized as Ether. The other one, he realized a moment later, was Vortex. Apparently both wind dragons had the same idea for dispersing the dust. With both of them working on it together, the city would be cleared in no time. So Hyperion ordered his companions not to attack Vortex.

As the two wind dragons set about clearing the area, Hyperion glanced at his Keeper. The man leaned against the balcony railing as if he were undisturbed by the events around him. Hyperion was no fool; he could see just how nervous and unsure his new Keeper was. Perhaps it had not been a good idea to send his mate and unborn hatchling away. Had she been here, she would have brought out the strength in him as she had before. Right now, he was merely a shell of himself; uncertain.

Hyperion snorted, coming to a conclusion. It was up to him – no one else – to make sure his Keeper did not fall.

With renewed determination, Hyperion returned his gaze to the city. A flicker of movement just above the force field caught his attention. In a heartbeat, Zenith himself burst through the billowing cloud of dust and back winged to stop midair. There, he floated; held aloft by his own power to distort space.

The pearly blue dragon gazed through the force field and snorted. Hyperion hissed in fury and spread his wings wide in an attempt to intimidate the other dragon. His tactic failed; the proof lying in Zenith's glowing, white eyes and refusal to fly away.

Without a word, the Dragon of the Heavens brought his forepaws together as if clutching a ball. Immediately recognizing the gesture as the beginning of the Galactic Tsunami, Hyperion summoned the energy for his own attack.

The air around him suddenly grew charged and flashed red and black. In an instant his body was wreathed in a hellacious inferno. With a silent warning to his companions of what was to come, the Dragon of the Apocalypse released the onslaught of power with two words:

"Tetra Vortex!"

The raging inferno surged forward in a roaring wave. It passed through the red force field without hindrance, causing Zenith to abandon his attack and dart away. Out of the sky, four pillars of twisting red and black fire fell like comets. Each struck in sequence with the rolling inferno and sent jets of flames and destruction thousands of meters into the air. The jets arced and fell back to the planet, where they exploded with tremendous force and kicked up even more arcing flames.

The horrendous wave of destruction continued unabated until over half of the city had been consumed. Then, like the apocalyptic nightmare it was, it faded into memory.

In its wake, the Grand Capitol of Ithnez burned.

A morez kept her senses on high alert. Every little abnormal noise or movement was scrutinized before it was dismissed as paranoia. Something was wrong; Bakari-Tokai was far too quiet. Dark and dreadful thoughts plagued her mind continuously. What happened to the hordes of soldiers said to make up Dimitri's massive defense? Had the intelligence reports been wrong the whole time? She wisely kept her worries to herself as she and Freya led their battalions over the bridge. There was no sense in starting a full-on panic amongst the soldiers; they were on edge enough as it was.

The tremendous dust cloud that had been kicked up by Zenith's Tsunami was slowly beginning to fall away. Gaps in the cloud provided a scant few seconds with which to see ahead. Amorez felt safer in those moments that she could see, but her fears were not completely put to rest.

After a long while of trekking over debris, the battalions finally reached the mid-way point across the bridge. There, they met up with several others from their army, including Blood Fang, Aidana, and Pyrex. Amorez was glad to see them and learn that most of their battalions had managed to reach this point. Together they at least stood a chance at victory, no matter what lie in waiting.

The five squadrons formed up and moved out, marching over the remainder of the bridge at a faster pace. The outline of the palace loomed before them some minutes later. Just before it, a mass of soldiers was gathered and waiting. The five squadrons quickened their pace and they prepared to meet their enemies in battle once again. As they drew nearer, they realized the soldiers gathered before them were their own allies.

Amorez forced herself to relax a little as she greeted Thernu and Vitaani. It was then that she learned of the plight they all faced.

"Hyperion has erected a barrier of energy around the palace." Thernu said with a frown. Amorez looked beyond the Necromancer, to the wall of pulsing red energy that had forced their army to a stop. "We've been trying to break through the field, but nothing has worked so far."

Amorez sighed and looked her old friend in the eye. "Give me the run down on it."

Thernu spent several minutes describing the barrier's size and composition, as well as the spells she used in trying to disarm it. During her entire explanation, Pyrex's grin grew wider and wider. Finally, Amorez asked him what the little Wakari found so entertaining about the field.

Pyrex chuckled and crossed his arms smugly. "If you cannot go over or through, go under."

The other generals stared at him in awe.

Thernu was the first to snap out of it. "Though it is unlikely that Hyperion's barrier descends all the way to the bedrock, how do you intend to go under the field and what will you do when you have reached the other side?"

"You forget, Feykin," Pyrex nodded his head slightly, "I was there to offer my services when this great city was built. I can still recall several of the tunnels leading to the structures used to keep it from sinking."

"Just what do you intend to do once you have reached these tunnels?" Growled Vitaani. "It is not like you little Wakari can dislodge a dragon from his perch. And I doubt you built them large enough for any race other than your own to fit."

"You are right about the girth of the tunnels, Vitaani, but wrong about what we Wakari are capable of doing." Pyrex laughed. "All we have to do is knock out the structures holding the castle above the water. Once it starts sinking, that ugly lizard will have to take flight or go down with the palace."

Vitaani thought a moment, then nodded in agreement. "It is a sound plan."

All eyes were instantly on Amorez, awaiting the final decision of their plan. The former Dragon Keeper sighed and cast her gaze to the looming shadow beyond the barrier. The black palace had always reminded her of the only man she had ever loved, her husband, Djurdak. There were so many artifacts in there that had once belonged to him, it would be a shame to lose them. But those were merely material things. Their only daughter was a much greater treasure.

After several minutes of silent brooding, she came to a decision. A feeling of guilt washed over her and she closed her eyes. Slowly she said, "We sink the palace."

Pyrex wasted no time calling the Wakari to him. In their guttural language, he explained the new plan. Within minutes, every one of the little warriors was ready and moving out, Pyrex at the lead. Amorez stood, transfixed on the palace; burning the memory of it into her mind.

"This will not be easy to deal with." Thernu whispered.

Amorez merely nodded.

"It is a noble sacrifice." Freya murmured. "Djurdak would be proud of your strength." Then, with a slight nod, she and Thernu moved away. They took the other generals with them to give their friend a moment to herself.

A tear slipped from Amorez's eye, and she wore it proudly before the wind kissed it away. For a moment, she imagined it had been Djurdak himself whisking it away, whispering in her ear that everything was alright. She touched her cheek as the ghost of its presence faded, and a soft smile touched her lips.

"Tetra Vortex!"

Amorez's heart skipped a beat as the abrasive voice echoed and she screamed, "Into the water!"

She watched for only a second as everyone sprinted towards the edges of the bridge. They dove off in great masses, but Amorez knew not all of them would make it in time. Cursing the Shadow Dragon, she rushed to the edge and jumped. In the instant she was airborne, a great inferno exploded out of the barrier. She splashed into the cold water just as the heated wave rushed by overhead.

From my place astride Zenith, I could only watch helplessly as the inferno tore through Bakari-Tokai, bathing the city in flames and destruction. The Dragon of the Heavens released a sound like a growling whine as he, too, watched the annihilation unfold. We were both powerless to stop it.

I lost track of the time, for it felt like forever as the hellfire raged uncontrollably. At long last the attack faded into nothingness, but fires still smoldered over much of the city and smoke choked the air. Glowing motes were strewn into the air; becoming black ash that drifted downwards like rain fit for a funeral.

"Land." I said through distraught sobs. Zenith must not have heard me for he made no movement. I repeated the command louder, harsher.

He looked at me over his shoulder, concern all too evident in his white eyes. "Are you certain?"

"Just do it."

Zenith lingered in the air a moment, and then slowly began to drift towards the ground. *Brothers, Sisters, to me. Our Keeper needs us now.*

In one voice the other eleven replied, *We come.*

Zenith dared not land on the charred bridge that connected the palace to the city. Through the smoke-filled air, I could see the stone beneath us glowing; pulsing from the heat it had withstood. Though it was beginning to grow dull and gray, it would probably be days or even weeks before the stone cooled naturally. As I widened my gaze to take in the city from this new perspective, I began to wonder if anyone was even alive to continue this campaign. Save for the sound of countless crackling fires, the city was as silent as a graveyard.

Wildfire was the first of my dragons to arrive. She sauntered along the hot stones completely unaffected by the heat. She nodded her great wedge of a head in respects as she folded her wings and lay down on the bridge to wait.

"Freezing Wave!"

I recognized the voice as Atoka's and sighed in relief as her ice storm blanketed the area in cold. Huge clouds of steam erupted from the ice as it struck the searing hot stone and evaporated instantly. It took the Dragon of Eternal Winter a few more tries to cool the stone enough that the ice could linger. Only then did she and the others land and the riders dismounted.

I promptly ran to Kitfox and he gathered me in a tight embrace. He whispered soothing words in my ear as I buried my face in his tunic and cried.

"What do we do now?" Thera asked, her voice a mere ghost of its former self.

"What can we do?" Shazza snarled. "Everyone was wiped out in that inferno! Now there is no way of taking the palace and forcing this all to end. That bastard, Dimitri, has won, and we are left with nothing!"

A mourning silence descended upon all of us. Even the dragons grew quiet. We all stood together on the bridge, lost in our own thoughts and misery. I looked into every one of their faces, and could see the mix of hatred and despair swimming in their eyes. I knew they were desperately looking for a path; anything that would take this day away from Dimitri.

I sighed. Placing a gentle kiss on Kitfox's cheek, I peeled away from him. I felt like I was in a daze as I slowly made my way to the edge of the bridge. I gazed upon the sapphire water for a long moment, marveling at the simple beauty of it. Then I closed my eyes and began to whisper prayers for the dead. Grief took me over. Hot tears fell like rain. My throat constricted. And still, I prayed for them. For every warrior who was felled here today, I prayed.

I was vaguely aware of the water sloshing, then dripping onto stone. Somebody softly called my name. I chose to ignore the summons and focused more on the prayers. Someone suddenly grasped me by the arm, causing me to jump and open my eyes. To my supreme shock, it was Amorez; drenched, dirty, slightly bruised, but otherwise in one piece.

I looked around in awe, learning that several more people – including Blood Fang, Aidana, and Vitaani – were being helped out of the water by my friends and dragons. Most of them appeared unharmed, but handfuls more had been severely burned in the blast. The surviving spell casters quickly went to work healing the wounded. My attention slowly returned to Amorez.

She flashed a wry smile. "You are an honorable priestess, my daughter. I am sure the dead are grateful for your prayers."

I could only nod.

Amorez turned away to behold what little remained of the Army of Light. She sighed in a mix of frustration and sadness. She muttered, "Curse you, Hyperion."

"Freya?" Kitfox's call rang out over the din. When he got no answer, he called again. "Where's Freya? Has anyone seen her?"

Grim faced, Blood Fang approached the younger Demon. He mumbled something to Kitfox. I watched, heartbroken, as his face contorted with misery before he hid it with his arms. He fell to his knees and howled his lament.

Freya was no more.

That fact brought forth new tears from my eyes. I quickly made my way to Kitfox and knelt beside him. I put my arms around him and held him close. I whispered a special prayer for Freya, asking the Gods to guide her safely to her next life. The words seemed to ease some of Kitfox's pain, but I could tell it would be a long time before he would be okay.

"What are we going to do now?" Asked a voice in the crowd.

"There's nothing we can do." Replied another. "Not with so few of us left."

Murmurs of surrender swept through the crowd.

"Aren't you all forgetting something?!" Zenith growled. An awkward hush fell over the army as they gazed upon the heavenly dragon. "Nearly five centuries ago, during the final battle against Agasei, Amorez did not have even two hundred soldiers with her. Not counting the dragons, they were outnumbered nearly sixteen to one. Still, they dared to take on the Shadow Keeper and his dragons. It was a long and difficult battle to be sure, and many were lost. But everyone worked together that day to bring down the darkness! You are many more and I firmly believe that this day can still be won."

"Zenith is right!" Exclaimed Amorez. She quickly moved to Zenith and hopped up on his front paw so she could be seen by everyone. "Right now, as we speak, the Wakari are hard at work on a plan to dislodge the Shadow Dragon, Hyperion, from his perch atop the palace." She pointed to a spot on the opposite side of the pulsing red barrier. Excited murmurs escaped the lips of many in the crowd. "With that ugly lizard dislodged, his field will drop. Our goal of storming the palace and ending Dimitri's reign are well within sight. We can do this! We can win!"

It had been three days since the Rising of Khatahn-Rhii; three days since King Proteus Za'Car II passed into Havel from the illness he had long fought. The world still mourns for him, yet celebrates the upcoming coronation of his eldest daughter, Princess Tenna. She will make a grand High Queen.

– *FROM "THE CHRONICLES OF ITHNEZ, VOL. VII" BY BRAM MOORE,*
COURT HISTORIAN

With some of the army's morale restored, the few remaining generals gathered at Zenith's feet to discuss new plans. It was then that Amorez and Thernu told us of the exact details of the Wakari's work. I could not help but take a moment to wonder what the palace would look like when it was sunk.

"The main problem is, we have no idea how long it will take Pyrex and his crew to knock out the supports holding the palace aloft." Thernu said. "I doubt Dimitri will let us sit here and wait for that to happen."

"Agreed." Growled Blood Fang. "If we were wise, we would try to get a small force beyond the barrier to keep his gaze focused elsewhere."

I had to agree with him.

"That would not be a very safe task." Said Aidana, with a flutter of her ivory wings. "Because we do not know precisely when the palace will begin to sink, an escape for the team that goes in is very unlikely."

"And good luck finding volunteers for a suicide mission." Vitaani added with a snort.

"I'll do it." I said. Everyone gaped at me in utter disbelief. I repeated my words, this time much more firmly.

After a moment, Kitfox took a step forward and said, "Me, too."

"Sign me up." Kkorian smirked.

Shazza nodded. "Same here."

"And me." Thera added without hesitation.

If the five of us took Amorez by surprise, she was good at hiding it. "You are all very brave to volunteer for such a daring mission, but I'm afraid it will not work. Thernu and several other Feykin have already tried to drop the barrier, and they have met with no success."

"Then we do not drop it." I said, looking up at Zenith with a smirk. "We simply bend space around it."

The Dragon of the Heavens made a sound like a laugh. "You are still a spitfire by heart, little one!"

Thernu frowned as she looked up at the dragon. "Can you manage it, Zenith?"

"Of course." He nodded. "The only problem would be Hyperion's sensitivity. There is a very real possibility of alerting him to the rouse the moment I distort his shield. Then again, he might not feel anything at all."

"Alright." Amorez nodded. After a moment of thinking, she faced me with a serious expression. "What is your plan once you are in there? Do you have one?"

"I am going to find Dimitri and I am going to kill him."

She frowned. "That's it? That is your plan?"

"Look, no one – not even you – knows exactly what Dimitri has hidden away in there. For all we know, he could have an army hidden in the courtyard. Therefore, the best plan is to simply find him and kill him."

"She has a point, Amorez." Replied Vitaani.

The former Keeper looked to her oldest ally for advice. When Thernu said nothing to contradict what had been said, Amorez looked at me. I looked back at her with fierce determination. Finally, she gave in. "Alright." She said with a sigh. "Just promise me one thing, Xy."

"What?"

She captured me in a fierce hug. Slowly, awkwardly, I wrapped my arms around her and returned the embrace. "End this." She whispered. "One way or another."

I nodded. "I will."

After a moment, we released each other. Then, without a word, she took the lead in the short jaunt to the pulsing barrier. Zenith followed in our wake, his ivory talons clicking against the charred stones. This movement caught the attention of several, and they all stood up to form a semi-circle around us. When they realized what was about to happen, they started applauding.

I glanced at my teammates; they were ready. I gave Zenith the command to begin. The heavenly dragon brought his left paw forward until it was a breath away from Hyperion's force field. A strange, amethyst glyph appeared on the pulsing surface. A second later, the glyph turned black and grew into a gaping, black hole.

"Hurry, little ones, and be safe."

I took the lead in the rush to the portal. Kitfox and Thera were right on my heels and Shazza and Kkorian were a pace behind them. We entered the portal with just seconds between us, then everything went numb. A chilling blackness surrounded me, and in that blackness, complete silence. I felt weightless. Burning hot and yet freezing cold.

The queasiness from the spacial distortion lasted for only a moment, then everything turned back to normal. I found myself standing on the bridge less than a meter from where I had passed through the portal. My four teammates were with me, gawking as if they could not believe what had just happened.

I took a good look at this side of the force field. Unlike the other side, everything here was still in pristine condition. It was like going back in time, to before the war and the dragons' attacks had ever happened.

At long last, I returned to my senses. I freed my tessens from my belt and flared them. Without bothering to look back at my team, I started jogging forward, over the bridge and to the palace.

"Did you have to destroy the entire city?" Dimitri grumbled, glancing sideways at the red and black dragon atop the spire.

Hyperion merely snorted.

"You have no idea how long it is going to take to rebuild Bakari-Tokai after this."

"Would you have preferred to have been wiped out by that wretched Zenith and his Galactic Tsunami?"

"No, but –"

"Then stop complaining about my tactics!"

"Hey!" Dimitri roared as he stormed towards the end of the balcony closest to Hyperion's perch. "I am the Keeper here," he jabbed himself with his index finger, "not you! You take orders from me! See that you remember that, Dragon!"

Hyperion's eyes flashed with rage. "What you have failed to realize, my Keeper," he laced the word with venom, "is that I only unleashed Tetra Vortex as a means to save your life. Ignoring the fact that I leveled the city as a result, you have to understand that I have done nothing but follow your orders to protect you at all costs."

Dimitri took a few deep breaths to calm his temper. Then he spoke, making sure to keep his voice level. "I understand what you did, Hyperion. I really do. And I am grateful. But I was seriously hoping to have most of Bakari-Tokai still standing after today to celebrate our victory."

"The only victory that would have been celebrated today would belong to them." The dragon jerked his head to an area beyond his force field.

Dimitri admitted the dragon was correct in that matter.

"So what are your orders now?"

The Shadow Keeper's gaze fell upon the ocean of troops still at attention in the gardens. "Sweep the city for survivors." He said and looked up at Hyperion. "If any are found who are not willing to surrender and swear fealty to me as their king, execute them."

"What about the other dragons and their Keeper?"

"Same thing."

356

"They will not be easily turned."

"Then they will be destroyed."

"Very well." Hyperion nodded his head once. Then he retreated inwards, focusing on his connection to his siblings. Taimat?

Yes, Hyperion? The raspy, wraith-like voice of the Dragon of Death echoed in the back of Dimitri's mind, and the Keeper shivered.

Rouse the dead into battle and gather the Shadow near the barrier. Hyperion growled like a bloodthirsty animal. It is time to end this campaign once and for all.

It shall be done. Their mental connection was severed.

Hyperion glanced at Dimitri. The Keeper smirked and nodded. The dragon nodded back, then directed his attention to the waiting army below. "Follow your king's orders. Search the city for survivors. Kill any who do not surrender."

The army pounded their weapons against their shields and hollered wordlessly. Then a horn sounded from among them, blaring in a low, ominous tone that lasted nearly a minute. As one, the army marched briskly forward to the tune of many feet. At their head, in gleaming black armor, rode the fat Judge, Vincent, upon a black wyvern. He carried his enormous, golden axe in his right hand and a tower shield in the other.

A devilish sneer constructed its way across Dimitri's face as he watched the army move out, across the bridge.

Amorez stared at the pulsing barrier, worry eating away at her. Had Xyleena and the others gotten through safely? Did Hyperion sense the disturbance in his field? What sort of horrors lay in the area beyond? These questions and more filled her mind.

"If you keep chewing on your bottom lip like that, soon you will not have one." Blood Fang quipped.

Amorez smiled in spite of herself and looked over her shoulder at the Demon. He sat cross-legged on the ledge of the bridge a short distance away. He watched her with his one good

357

eye, and grinned like the wolf he was. Amorez clicked her tongue and made her way to him.

"Mind if I join you?"

"Feel free." He nodded. "It's not very comfortable though; stone rarely is."

That tore a chuckle from her as she sat beside him. "Do you mind if I ask you something?"

He shrugged. "Depends on what it is you ask."

"Do you have any children?"

"Mmh." Blood Fang shook his head. "Not really. Freya did adopt Kitfox as her pup, so I guess – in a way – he is mine as well, but he shares none of my blood."

"I'm sorry. I did not know you and Freya were mates."

"She was never one to brag about herself." A sad smile touched his lips. He sighed and scratched his ear. "And being the Tahda'varett Alpha's mate is as boastful as one can get."

"Have you spent much time with her and Kitfox?"

"Freya, yes. The boy, no. He and I never really got along." Blood Fang chuckled and pointed to his scarred eye. "He did give me this though, so he should be proud." His ear flinched and he shook his head as if bitten by an insect. "What is that awful noise?"

Amorez's brow furrowed. "What do you hear?"

"A shrill and eerie cry that could wake the dead." He growled.

Amorez's gaze quickly swept over the army, realizing that many of the Demons present were experiencing the same thing. Her search turned skywards, drawn by a growing shadow on the horizon.

"Everybody arm up!" Zenith bellowed.

Amorez hollered over the sudden rush of activity. "What is it?"

"The Shadow Dragons are on approach and Taimat is using Corpse Song!"

Panic seized her heart in an instant. If Taimat was using his technique to raise the dead, they were in for a very miserable battle. She bolted to her feat, shouting. "You heard the dragon, arm up!" It took them longer to gather their weapons and form up than she liked. Frustrated, she continued shouting, trying to get them to move faster. "Quickly, you fools! Quickly!"

"Spell casters with me at the rear!" Thernu shouted, her voice amplified by a spell.

"Those at the front, form a wall with your shields!" Shouted Amorez as she made her way to Zenith. "Middlemen, make sure nothing gets past you, and whatever you do, protect our spell casters!" Then Amorez turned to Zenith. "Take the Light airborne and keep the Shadow from wreaking havoc on us."

"We will tear them asunder if we have to!" The heavenly dragon unfolded his wings and leapt skywards with a roar. His wings made a sound like thunder as he flapped them hard to gain altitude. Once clear of the ground, the other dragons began to spring into the air after him.

Amorez took a deep breath and pushed her way into the front of the ranks. With Hyperion's barrier pulsing behind them and deep water flanking either side, their battlefield would be narrow and close-knit. She wouldn't be surprised if several warriors received wounds from their own side.

"Amorez!" A panicked cry at the back of the formation stole her attention. She looked over her shoulder just in time to see the red barrier vanish, only to reappear seconds later several hundred meters back. And in the distance the barrier had shrunk, several hundred thousand soldiers appeared. The rows and rows of soldiers marched towards them fearlessly, lead by a man astride a black wyvern.

Amorez swore. "Casters to the middle! Another defensive line to the rear! Go! Go! Go!"

"Take out the bridge." Blood Fang growled, suddenly beside her.

"But what about Xy and the others?" She gaped at him. "If we destroy the bridge, they won't be able to escape when the Wakari sink the palace."

"You can't worry about them now." He shook his head. "Trust them to find their own way back."

Slowly, she nodded. Though she hated the idea, she ordered the bridge's destruction. "Casters, destroy the eastern bridge!" When they hesitated, she repeated herself, this time more fiercely. "Destroy it!"

A chorus of spells rang out. A twisted menagerie of elemental attacks lashed out at the stone. Several explosions rocked the bridge, sending dust and debris skyward. Still it stood. Again, a chorus of spells went out and again the bridge remained. Before the casters could try for a third time, Wildfire dove at the damaged section and released her attack at very close range.

"Spiral Blaze!" There was a flash of red light, then an enormous pillar of fire exploded upwards. It twisted in the air, becoming a tornado that danced across the surface of the bridge. It lasted only seconds, but the attack had the desire effect. A large section of the bridge was now melted away, leaving a gap large enough that not even a Dákun Daju could leap across.

With the bridge destroyed, and their biggest threat hopefully delayed by several hours, Amorez felt a little more confident about the battle ahead. She turned her attention to the growing threat to the west.

I swore as the dismal sound of a low horn echoed upon the palace walls. The rumbling thunder of thousands of footsteps followed moments later. Despite being less than a hundred meters to the palace, we were still trapped on the bridge. And on the bridge, there was nowhere to hide... Nowhere, except the water.

"Bubble spell." I uttered to Thera. She nodded and began casting. To the others, I said, "Into the water."

They did not hesitate. We slipped into the water as quietly as possible, floating a few meters from the surface. And there we waited. I could not tell how long we were submerged. It could have been minutes. Or it could have been hours. Either way, it felt like forever before the first row of soldiers passed before us.

My heart hammered in my chest, so hard I feared it would give out. Calm down. I told myself. Just calm down. They won't find you.

I certainly hope not. Kitfox grumbled. By the way, you called it.

I looked at him over my shoulder. What?

He laughed. When you argued with Amorez about what Dimitri was hiding in the palace, you said an army. You called it.

You're funny. I stuck my tongue out at him. He grinned back.

Do you think the dragons will tell Amorez about this?

I'm not sure if they can still communicate with her telepathically like this. But I told Zenith of the army anyway.

That is not the only threat they are currently faced with, Little Ones. We dragons will try our best to prevent a two front battle.

My brow furrowed in concern. What do you mean?

Taimat has begun using his Corpse Song, a technique which raises the dead and forces them to fight under his command. Soon, all those that died this day will be under his spell and ready for battle.

Wonderful! Kitfox snarled. Should we turn back and help?

What good would the five of us do in a battle against thousands?

She is right, Kitfox. Stay on your current mission and leave the armies to us.

Be careful. I said, then I closed the connection to the dragon's mind.

The sooner this is over, the better.

I could not have agreed more.

Thera had to recharge our bubbles for nearly a second time before the mass of soldiers finally passed by us. Cautiously, I floated to the surface, ever-watchful for lagging soldiers. Seeing none, I reached out to grip the side of the bridge, then I hauled myself over the edge. Shazza was the next one to surface, then Thera. Kitfox chose to linger behind to help shove Kkorian onto the bridge, then he, too, climbed out of the water.

I took up the lead again, dashing over the remaining hundred and some meters to the palace grounds. The fools had left the ornate gates wide open when they left, making our entry all the more easier.

Or so I had thought.

The moment I slipped beyond the gates and into the luscious gardens, I spotted movement out of the corner of my eye. I shrunk back to hug the protective wall that circled the palace grounds, taking my teammates with me. We lingered where the shadows were longest for they provided cover. I searched for the source of the movement.

Trees of all kinds stood amid the black marble structures and walkways. Their multi-colored leaves shook in answer to a directionless breeze. Long beards of moss and ivy hung heavy from several branches. Exotic flowers from all over the world blossomed, and their sweet aroma filled the air. The grass had been trimmed recently; some of the blades escaped collection to linger on the walkways. Tracing the winding paths with my gaze alone, I discerned a way to enter the palace, hopefully without notice. I did not find anyone or anything that would have moved to alarm me.

Kitfox jabbed my shoulder with his fingers, winning my attention. He pointed at his ears, then towards a point the sky. Dimitri's talking to someone in that direction. I followed the invisible line drawn by his finger. There, standing at the banister of a balcony, stood Dimitri. He was looking sidelong, over his shoulder as if speaking to someone behind him.

I silently told Kitfox to eavesdrop on the conversation.

He's saying something about a section of the bridge being destro– He suddenly grew pale, and his eyes bulged. Oh, Gods! He's talking to Hyperion!

A cold wave of fear stole my breath away. There was no way we could take Dimitri on with Hyperion standing watch over him. The dragon would no doubt kill us the second he laid eyes on us.

As I gazed towards the distant point where I figured Hyperion must be standing, only one thought ran through my mind: How can we ever hope to win?

Amorez jerked her blade free with a sickening slurp and kicked the nearly-headless corpse away before finishing her stroke to sever the head completely. Her eyes followed the rolling appendage for a moment before another undead soldier tore her attention away. That one, like all the others before it, was quickly beheaded.

She pivoted on her heel to engage another, but found none. She shook her head in disbelief and cast her gaze wider. Only a few of her warriors were still facing the soulless, walking dead that had once been friends, allies, or enemies. They would be dispatched quickly, which meant that she a few moments to rest and observe the battlefield.

Countless beheaded corpses and ribbons of blood were strewn everywhere upon the bridge, even the water. Her army had lost few to the undead horde, but those few had been quickly revived by the eerie sound of Taimat's Corpse Song. They were dispatched right away for the second time; often with tears in the eyes of their killers. Amorez cursed the Shadow Dragon for forcing this despair upon them.

A frown touched her lips as an angry roar echoed overhead, and she looked skywards. The dragons were still locked in a fierce aerial battle. She watched as they darted and somersaulted, barrel rolled and dove, grappled and bit. Despite having the strength of greater numbers, the Dragons of Light appeared to be losing to their evil counterparts.

A voice in the crowd screamed her name.

She lowered her gaze to find a Demon pointing to something to the aft of their army. She followed his direction to the area beyond the melted section of the bridge, where Dimitri's main army stood in wait. They had not made a move to gather materials in order to cross the gap. That fact worried her, for it meant they had another plan, and one that would probably mean the end of her rebellion.

A flicker of movement to the left stole her attention from the ocean of soldiers. Just as she averted her eyes, Talisman of Ice flashed by, skimming the surface of the water with a forepaw. In her wake, the water froze and turned as solid as stone, effortlessly filling the gap between the bridge sections by which Dimitri's soldiers could cross. And cross they did. In great waves, the bloodthirsty soldiers surged forward.

"Line up!" Amorez bellowed, rushing forward to face the oncoming wave. "Line up, now!"

The exhausted remnants of the Army of Light were not quick enough to respond. In the time it took for them to realize what had happened, over a thousand of Dimitri's soldiers were among them. At that point, it was no longer a battle; it was a horrible and bloody slaughter. Every one of those that were killed were reanimated and brought back through Taimat's never-ending song.

Blood soaked the bridge and seeped into the water, staining it with crimson. The cries of the dying rang out, a miserable crescendo to the eerie tone of the Corpse Song.

Amorez found herself hard-pressed to defend herself against the onslaught. Somehow, in the midst of the bloodshed and misery, she managed to call for a dragon.

Thedrún answered with a fierce roar. He dove out of the sky, heading straight for the bridge at breakneck speeds, nearly slamming into the icy segment as he shouted, "Magnetic Charge!"

Several enormous bolts of chartreuse lightning exploded from the sky at his command. They struck the icy segment in rapid succession, hurling huge chunks of ice and several unlucky soldiers into the air. They collided with the electrified water and kicked up great clouds of mist and crackling energy. A deafening rumble of angry thunder followed.

Amorez had been waiting for that exact moment. While Dimitri's soldiers recoiled from the explosion of noise, she rushed forward with a furious howl. She was aware of nothing but the weight of the dueling blades in her hands, the men in front of her, the spray of hot blood across her face. She twisted and ducked, parried and thrust, disarmed and beheaded.

When at last the soldiers recovered from the sound wave, she once again found herself hard pressed to fend them off. Finally, Thernu appeared at her side. Together, the two began blasting the soldiers into oblivion with their most powerful spells. Even then, some of them remained intact enough for Taimat's song to reanimate their bodies.

A cry from the north went out. Amorez quickly slew her attackers and dared a moment to look. The black stone ship, Shadow Dance, had managed to break through the harbor walls and sail right up to the docks. The top deck was crowded with Hume Pirates and Naval Officers, Dákun Daju Assassins, and Feykin. As soon as they were within leaping distance, those that could, bolted from the deck, rushing to aid their companions. Amorez sighed in relief. Help was soon to arrive.

Having finally decided on how we were going to deal with Dimitri's draconic protection, I led my team around to the side of the palace, and away from the Shadow Keeper. We made sure to stick to the shadows so as not to be seen. Luckily for us – albeit slightly unnerving – there was no one about the palace grounds.

Once around to the southern side of the palace, I began to look for the servant's entrance. Sure enough, a door with ornate, silver filigree stood less than fifty meters away. It was propped open with a wooden bucket as if to allow the cooling breeze in. With a quick glance around to make sure the grounds were still empty, I bolted for the door. The others were right on my heels.

We squeezed against the wall and listened for a moment. A soft noise came from within and I silently swore an oath. Kkorian pulled two pistols from their holsters. Cocking them, he looked at me. I nodded. He kicked the door open and burst in, pistols drawn, and the rest of us were right behind him.

It took a moment for my eyes to adjust to the dimness within. When at last I could see, a kitchen was revealed to me. A few servants were present, going about their chores, but none of them seemed to even notice that we were there. My gaze fell upon a young, blonde girl in the way back. She smiled warmly and pointed towards an ornate pair of doors on the northernmost wall. With a nod of thanks, I led the way across the kitchen, but kept an eye on the servants just in case.

At the doors, I paused and flared my war fans. I leaned against one of the doors, pushing it open just enough to peer beyond. The room on the other side was barely lit and smelled of bouquets. After a moment to listen to the silence, I pushed the door open the rest of the way and strode forward.

It is the dining room. I realized as I looked about. An elaborate table with matching chairs filled most of the space. On the wall to my right, flanked by suits of armor, was a hearth with glowing embers. The wall to the left was decorated with a several portraits of the ruling families before Dimitri's ascent. My father, his brother, and their parents were featured in the middle of the wall. I could not help but smile sadly as I took the image in. With the Wakari about to sink the palace, it would probably be the last time I would ever see that painting. As much as I wished I could take it with me, I knew I could not afford to be bogged down by it; not with a battle looming right before me.

So, with a bitter sigh and a heavy heart, I forced myself to look away.

The wall opposite the kitchen's entrance had another set of ornate doors, and they were the only other exit out of this room. With one last look around the room to make sure it was clear, I rushed ahead, leaping over the table and chairs as opposed to going all the way around.

At the second set of doors, I once again paused to ensure the route was clear. Seeing and hearing no movement, I pushed my way into the room beyond. I was met with an extravagant hallway of black marble walls, silver and gold filigree columns alit with delicate candelabras, and a thick and immaculate, white carpet. The wall space was filled with expensive looking nick-knacks, portraits, and even weapons stored in cases lined with silk. Amazingly, as I led the way down the hall, I could recall the histories of most of the artifacts I set my gaze upon, but I could not remember when or how I had learned of them.

I pushed those thoughts away as the hall drew to an intersection. Another memory replayed in my head. Going right would lead us to the throne room. Straight ahead was a drawing room, where an ancient artifact from Earth was placed: a grand piano once owned by Noralani Ithnez. The path to the left would take us to the main lobby, which was often used as a ballroom due to the sheer size of it. The balcony where we would find Dimitri was on the second level, up a curving flight of stairs and through huge glass doors.

I led the way down the hall to the left without bothering to check for guards. I had a feeling Dimitri had either sent them forth with the rest of the army he had been hiding, or –and this thought scared me – he pulled them to serve as his personal guard while he watched the battle from the balcony. If the latter was indeed the case, then we had more to worry about than just the looming Hyperion.

Sure enough as soon as the end of the hall was in sight, I spotted several soldiers on guard. I quickly ducked behind one of the ornate columns and signaled to my team. We separated into three groups as we huddled beside the columns to develop a plan that would get us passed the soldiers.

Want to try that spell Thera used to create mirror images of us to trick Dimitri's team in the twins' lair?

My head jerked to Kitfox, who stood with Thera on the opposite side of the hall from me. He flashed a coy smirk as I gaped at him. With a glance towards the soldiers, I nodded; it was worth a shot. He turned to whisper to Thera. After a moment, she flashed a thumbs-up and began to weave her spell. The air shimmered and condensed, and before my very eyes, all five of us appeared in a small group in the middle of the hall.

Tell Thera that there are three ways to leave the lobby ahead. As I spoke to Kitfox telepathically, he relayed the info verbatim to Thera. The obvious one is the main entrance, which would probably be the hardest one to get to. Then there are two halls going in opposite directions. They are situated atop the stairs. The third exit is where we are now.

I watched as Thera nodded. Then Kitfox replied, She is going to go for the main exit so we can lock the soldiers outside. Hopefully that will buy us enough time to do what we need to do.

With my approval, Thera began to work her conjures as she needed. I watched as our reflections confidently strode by. As they stepped foot into the lobby beyond, I whispered a prayer, begging for this ploy to work.

"**A**aaggghhh!"

Amorez screamed and bit her tongue hard enough to draw blood. In a pain-filled fury she swung her blade at her attacker, beheading the man who rode the black wyvern with practiced ease. She collapsed to her knees amidst corpses and her severed left arm. She gaped at the mangled and crystallized limb, knowing full well that even with magic, it could never be reattached. Sacrificing a portion of what little precious energy she had left, she uttered a spell. In a flash of immense heat that tore another scream from her throat, the stump that was her left of arm was cauterized.

Amorez fought the urge to cry as her exhausted body succumbed to the agony that she was powerless to heal. She sheathed the sword she carried and picked the other from the ground. It took great effort, but she somehow managed to return to her feet. A wave of dizziness nearly knocked her down again, but she widened her stance and forced her body back under her control.

Her attention was stolen as a pair of dueling dragons crashed into the water less than twenty meters away from where she stood. Seconds passed before the Shadow Dragon, Kula, roared of victory and took flight.

She swore and cast a quick, but furious glance skyward. Looking beyond the fighting dragons, to the heavens where the

Gods were sure to be watching, Amorez yelled, "Why won't you help us?"

She returned to herself and not a moment too soon, for a mangled corpse sought to claim her life while she was distracted. With an enraged roar, she lopped off its head. Instead of letting her rage spend the last of her energy, she used it and ran headlong into a large group of undead and living soldiers. In a flash of steel and blood, seven were felled never to rise again. She kept her momentum going and, like a juggernaut, sought out the next group, then the next.

In the back of her mind, one a single thought burned: If I am to die today, then I'll be damned if I go down without a fight!

Enormous, arching columns of granite loomed in the darkness far, far overhead. The very sight of them filling the cavernous void brought a smile to Pyrex's face. Without a moment to even admire the ancient construction, he ordered the Wakari stone workers to quickly begin demolishing the pillars.

They split into teams of six and surrounded nearly thirty of the granite columns. With a quick prayer unto their god to guide their hammers and chisels well, the Wakari struck up a song to soften the stone. As they sang, the pounding of hammers and chisels echoed in the cavern.

I watched awe as Thera skillfully maneuvered our reflections through the crowded lobby. The instant the soldiers had spotted them, they took up pursuit in attempt to kill. Thera always managed to stay one step ahead of them. Whenever a spell was needed to clear the soldiers away, the talented Feykin somehow managed to make it look like her reflection had cast it.

After a few intense moments of fighting, our reflections managed to make it through mass of soldiers. They exited through the main entrance and scattered. The soldiers were obliged to follow, clearing out of the lobby in great swarms until only about thirty remained.

Thera slammed the main door shut and sealed it with magic. In the precise moment the door closed, I burst from my hiding spot behind the pillar and my teammates were right behind me. We made quick work of the few soldiers that remained in the room. Then Thera set about sealing all other exits with magic enchantments that no one could cross.

Now it was just the five of us against Dimitri and Hyperion.

I took a deep breath and let it out slowly. I let my gaze trace a route up the curving staircase to my right, then to the glass doors behind which Dimitri stood. After a moment or two to gather my nerves, I moved to the stairs. I glanced back at my teammates, making sure they were all ready. When they all nodded, I took the first steps onto the flight. It was a deliberately slow and quiet ascension, for we prayed that Dimitri was still unawares of our presence.

I stepped off the final stair and paused to wipe the sweat from my hands and brow. The grip on my tessens tightened as I crossed the distance between the stairs and the doors. Glimpsing through the sheer curtain, I could see Dimitri. He was still at the banister with his back towards me. This restored some of my lost hope, for it meant that we had actually managed to get the drop on him.

I took a few steps away from the door and readied myself for a rapid sprint. Glaring daggers at Dimitri's back, I told Thera to shatter the glass. The second she started casting, I burst forward and passed through the doors just as the glass exploded outwards.

Dimitri did not even have the time to turn before I was upon him. With a holler, I swung my tessens at his neck hard enough to smash through his spine. My war fans passed through him like a hot knife through butter, and I backed away to wait for his head to fall off.

Even after several seconds, nothing happened; not even the appearance of blood. Dread seized my heart as I dared to step up to Dimitri. I jabbed him in the back with my fan, but the weapon went right through as if he was nothing more than air. I muttered a curse and reeled about as a chorus of dark laughs erupted from behind me.

Between me and my dismayed teammates, Dimitri – the real Dimitri – stood beside the shattered doors, a smug look upon his face. He waved his hand in dismissal, and a slight 'poof' from my left signaled that his reflection spell had been canceled. I glowered at him, which made him smirk all the more.

"Don't look so upset." He sneered. "I merely played the same trick on you as you did on me." He pulled his weapon from its sheath and took a few confident strides forward. I dared a glance at Thera, silently begging her to cast something – anything – so long as it killed this bastard. Dimitri caught the hidden message in my look, and peered over his shoulder at my teammates. "I wouldn't do anything stupid if I were you."

A dark laugh from above echoed like rolling thunder. I knew without even looking that it was Hyperion. I swallowed my fear and forced myself to look up at the enormous Shadow Dragon. He sat perched atop a guard tower, looking amazingly like a smoky gem accented by blazing rubies. Had it not been for the evil aura he gave off, I would have complimented him for his grandeur. I held my tongue and chose to glare at him instead.

He snorted in amusement. "Do not think that by simply glaring at me, you can scare me off, two-legs. I am not like one of those pathetic lizards you call the Dragons of Light."

"Just you wait." I growled. "My dragons and I will take you, your siblings, and your puny Keeper down."

Both Dimitri and Hyperion scoffed, but it was the dragon who spoke. "From where I sit, your dragons can't even defend themselves against my brothers and sisters. What makes you think they stand a chance against me?"

"We will find a way." I said, my voice thick with furious determination. I finally looked away from Hyperion, to look Dimitri in the eye. "You'll see. Light always breaks through the darkness."

"I doubt that you could break through my darkness, girl. After all, you are holding only a match against a never-ending sea of black that I and my dragons bring about." Dimitri gloated. "Look for yourself." He used his dual sword to point towards the bridge behind me. I did not dare to turn my back on him to look. "The army you raised in hopes of defeating me is dwindling down to nothing. Soon, there won't be anyone left, not even Amorez or your dragons. Everything you have worked so hard for... everything you have done to get this far was pointless. Face it, you cannot win."

I silently prayed that what he said was not true. But the tone of his voice told me that it was. The Army of Light was dissolving into nothing but a memory. I glanced at my teammates, noting the mournful looks in their eyes. Everyone's except Kitfox's.

He's wrong. A slight smirk touched the Demon's lips. We still have a good chance of winning this. The Wakari are working on it now, remember?

I felt my despair ease slightly as I recalled the brave little Wakari and their mission. I squared my shoulders and looked Dimitri in the eye again. "You forget; I still have that match. I'm sure I can find some way to use it to my advantage."

Dimitri's cocky grin faltered slightly. Then, without warning, he struck.

Zenith loosed a furious roar as the skeletal dragons, Wyrd and Anima, forced him out of the sky. The ground quivered upon their impact, and a great plume of dust and debris was sent skyward. After a moment to recover, the undead duo took to the air with horrid shrieks claiming victory. Zenith remained planted to the ground, struggling to take back the breath that was knocked from him.

While he lay in the crater of his impact, he stared up at the sky. He could recall a few times when Amorez had looked to the heavens and pleaded for help. Though he never could understand why she did that, right now he felt that anything might be worth a try if it meant rescuing them from this dismal situation.

So Zenith allowed his eyes to close. His breathing slowed. His mind cleared. He relaxed into a meditation. Then he focused on a distant point in the heavens. It was nowhere in particular, but he hoped his voice would carry to whoever was out there. Whoever was waiting.

Finally, with both mind and tongue, he spoke. "Forgive me, for I do not know your name. I was only made aware of your presence out here, amidst the heavens, through my friend and Keeper, Amorez." A gentle lick of wind kicked up. Zenith snorted to clear his nose of the dust, less he sneeze and lose his concentration. "I come to you in a time of great need and on behalf of my Keeper, my friends, and my family. We are all facing our doom against a darkness that has taken over our lands." The breeze stirred. "I ask you for help in lighting up the darkness and banishing the evil it bore. Any amount of assistance, in any form you can give, would ease an enormous burden placed upon our shoulders." Zenith sighed and allowed his eyes to drift open. Keeping his gaze locked on that distant point in space, he whispered, "I can only hope that my message reaches you in time to save Amorez and those who fight with her."

A long minute passed with Zenith eagerly awaiting some kind of miracle to fall out of the sky. With the exception of the wind picking up even more, nothing happened. He growled his disappointment. Coming to the conclusion no miracle would ever happen with wishes upon the stars, he decided it was time to rejoin the battle. He would make his own miracle if needed.

Just as he managed to roll to his feet, a violent gale nearly bowled him over again. He grunted and hunkered down against the sudden windstorm, growling even as it stole his breath away. The wind roared like a tornado as it spun faster and faster, picking up dust and debris and hurling it several kilometers into the air. Even corpses and soldiers from the battle upon the bridge were thrown skywards.

As suddenly as it had appeared, it was gone. Zenith allowed himself to relax a moment and look around. The

374

windstorm had spun over most of Bakari-Tokai, clearing it of much of the debris and death. But what bothered him about the tornado was its sudden appearance on a cloudless day. He knew it was not Vortex who summoned it, for the Wind Dragon was too wounded and exhausted to muster the strength. And it was not Ether, for she was locked in a furious brawl with Riptide.

Zenith looked to the sky in wonder, watching as the swirling vortex of wind moved higher and higher. It seemed to reach a certain height, and then linger there. A brilliant white light exploded out of nowhere, and the battlefields immediately fell silent as every head turned to see what was happening. The windstorm and the light came together, coalescing in a shape all too familiar to Zenith: a dragon.

This unknown dragon was unlike anything anyone had ever seen before. He was armored in pearly white scales that shimmered like mother of pearl. His sweeping horns and razor-like talons were golden like a setting sun, and his eyes were as blue as the mid-day sky. He was held aloft by six paper thin wings which bent the light like prisms and threw rainbows in every direction. He was massive, easily about thrice the size of both Zenith and Hyperion combined. Yet he was lean and muscular, majestic and deadly. Perfect.

Zenith felt his heart begin to race. He knew that dragon; Amorez had spoken of him many times before. The white dragon was none other than the God of Wind and Autumn, Khatahn-Rhii.

And He was their miracle; their light in the dark.

Zenith roared in delight, and his brethren echoed it. Khatahn-Rhii seemed pleased by their welcoming chorus, for He looked down at them with pride. Then He, too, released a roar. It was long and loud and seemed to shake even the heavens. Echoes of the sound went on for minutes long after He closed His jaws with a snap. The Shadow Dragons mewed like frightened kittens and darted for the relative safety of the ground. Khatahn-Rhii paid the cowards no mind. Instead, He folded his six wings tight against His body and dove towards the bridge and the stunned soldiers which stood upon it. Feather-like clouds and swirls of wind arose in His wake.

Less than a hundred meters from the ground, He pulled out of the dive. Spreading His wings wide, He flapped once and the air shook with the sound of thunder. His flight leveled out and He glided gently over the bridge. As He did so, His eyes began to glow and white powder fell from His wings like snow. The powder touched the soldiers under Dimitri's mind control spell, and they looked around as if waking from a dream. When the powder touched the undead, they burst into ash and were no more. The wounded soldiers that made up what little remained of the Army of Light found their wounds healed and their strength restored.

Once completely over the bridge, Khatahn-Rhii flapped His wings again, this time to gain altitude. Several kilometers into the sky, He flared His wings to stop again. He looked down on the world below and released another magnificent roar. He vanished in a flash of white light while the echoes of His farewell faded away.

There were three,
But four will rise,
On dragon wing,
To uncharted skies.

– FROM "DRAGON HOPE" BY REYNA

Kitfox looked on anxiously while Xy and Dimitri exchanged furious blows. He yearned to rush in and help Xy, but Thera and Shazza held him back. He knew they were only trying to keep him safe from Hyperion, but their interference was aggravating. None of them knew exactly the Shadow Dragon would do if any one of them was to jump into the fray. For all they knew, the dragon would simply stand by and watch, but they did not want to risk it. So Kitfox was forced to watch as his beloved dueled with her greatest enemy.

It was torture.

A stupendous roar instantly brought everything to a sudden standstill. Everyone's gaze turned towards the bridge just as a regal, white dragon swooped in. Kitfox gaped at this new dragon, for it made Hyperion look tiny and unthreatening. The white dragon took to the air and vanished with a flash of light and a second spectacular roar.

Kitfox returned his gaze to the two Dragon Keepers. Judging by the looks on their faces, they were in silent conference with their dragons to figure out what had happened. Upon hearing Hyperion's furious growl, he decided to eavesdrop on Xy's exchange. She loosed a ring of laughter before he could focus on the connection.

"What is it?" Kkorian begged. "What happened?"

"Khatahn-Rhii brought the battle on the bridge to an end!" She cheered. "Every one of his," she accentuated the word as she stabbed a fan in Dimitri's direction. The Shadow Keeper glared daggers at her in response. "brainwashed soldiers has been cured and the hordes of undead are now at peace, never to rise again!"

Hyperion emitted a growl so furious it sounded like an explosion. "It took divine intervention for you pathetic meat sacks to win the bridge!"

"And it took you cheap tricks to even amass an army to begin with!" Kitfox snarled back.

The dragon's eyes began to glow red in fury. Immense pain suddenly racked Kitfox's entire body and he collapsed in a heap with a howl. Shazza and Kkorian dropped to their knees beside him and Thera was quick to retaliate the attack. She hurled a glowing pebble at the enormous dragon and uttered a string of Kinös Elda. The pebble struck Hyperion's shoulder and exploded with enough force to nearly knock him clean off his perch.

The attack on Kitfox ceased and he lay on the floor panting and shaking. Shazza began whispering spells of healing, but they did nothing to stop him from fading out of consciousness. Before the darkness took over his mind, he could have sworn he heard the violent clashing of metal meeting metal.

Pyrex wove his way through the massive columns, checking the work of his comrades. Even in the pitch black of the immense cavern, he could see their progress clearly. Many of the pillars were now only as thick as his thigh. Yet the Wakari were not ready to let them break, so their song had change to strengthen sections of the stone and weaken others. The few remaining pillars would be down to the same size within the hour. Then, and only then, would the Wakari evacuate to safety. Their song would change after that, once again weakening the stone until it crumbled and gave out, plunging the palace of Bakari-Tokai into the water on which it had been built.

Pyrex smiled as he turned his head to look at the Sentinel perched on his shoulder. "Go. Tell them we are almost ready."

The homunculus' little, silver head bobbed as if in understanding. The creature took flight a moment later, soaring out of the massive cavern.

A groan escaped Amorez as she reclined against an undamaged section of the bridge's low wall. Aidana was beside her, easing the pain of many of her wounds, especially the stump that was once her left arm. How the Elder Feykin still had the energy to work spells was beyond her, but she was grateful for the attention.

While Amorez recovered, Blood Fang and Black Kat took charge. Though he limped from the angry gash in his right thigh, the Demon still maintained a ferocious appearance, and people were too intimidated to argue his demands. He ordered those who could still stand to assist the wounded, "Bring them fresh water and bandages."

He also made sure to keep a close eye on those who were once under Dimitri's mind control. Almost all of them were in total shock over what had happened. Amorez and Blood Fang both listened as one soldier spoke to Zhealocera of how everything had gone awry.

Apparently Dimitri had attacked in the absolute dark, when no celestial bodies were visible in the sky. He had seized control of the city by dawn and named himself king. Then forced the soldiers of the Royal Army and Navy into the palace courtyard, where they had come face to face with Hyperion and the other Shadow Dragons. After that, the soldier's memories were a complete blank.

It shocked Amorez that Dimitri had managed to claim the city in less than half an hour. We're going to have to improve the defenses if we ever decide to rebuild this place.

She suddenly felt one of the dragons pressing against the back of her mind. It only took her a mere heartbeat to learn that it was Zenith. A small smile touched her lips as she allowed him access to her mind.

There is a Sentinel perched on my snout. Amorez cracked up at the tone in Zenith's voice. Aidana gave her a quizzical look, but she just waved it off. He is telling me that the Wakari are just about ready to topple the supports holding the palace aloft.

Thank you for letting me know. Amorez said, and her gaze fell on the palace. Hyperion's red force field was still in place, pulsing like a tiny star. She frowned. Have you told Xy about it?

Neither she nor Kitfox are answering.

Kitfox? Why would he be able to speak to– Courtesy of Zenith, several images of her daughter and the Demon flashed in her mind. Realization suddenly hit Amorez like a ton of bricks. She pursed her lips as she stared at the palace with renewed worry. That explains a lot.

I can try to send the Sentinel in to relay the message.

Amorez nodded. Do it. An idea suddenly came to her, and she called for Blood Fang's, Black Kat's, and Aidana's attention. In whispered tones, she quickly told them of her plan. They readily agreed. Hold on. You'll have three more to send in.

Zenith hesitated, uncertain if her choice was a good one. After almost a minute, his reply echoed back to her. If that is your wish.

My fans met the cutting edge of Dimitri's dual sword in a burst of crimson sparks and the metal rang like bells. I followed that attack with a series of quick blows. Dimitri's scowl deepened with every hit that managed to break through his defenses and draw blood. They weren't many, but, for me, they counted.

Finally, he had had enough and uttered a spell to shove me away. The gust of air knocked me off my feet, and the wind was knocked out of me from the impact. Ignoring the jolt of pain and my inability to breathe, I rolled a few times and managed to get back on my feet.

And just in the nick of time. Dimitri had crossed the distance between us and held his sword ready for a kill. I danced out of the way, feeling the rush of air across my face as his sword passed by. Before he could recover from his foiled blow, I twisted around him and landed a hard kick to his lower back. He loosed a yowl and hobbled forward a few paces. He retaliated with a blast of fire, which I deflected with a wall of ice. The fire and ice met in an angry hiss that blanketed the balcony with steam.

I stood on guard, waiting for the fog to blow away. Seconds ticked by like hours. I let them. I needed the respite, no matter how short it was. The initial energy I had when this bout started had dwindled to almost nothing. My fans had turned heavy and my shoulders burned from the exercise. I would be lucky to escape this battle unscathed.

I chanced a glance towards Kitfox's direction, hoping to get a glimpse of him through the steam. All I could make out were shadows in the roiling cloud. I truly hoped that he was okay. Whatever Hyperion did to him to cause him so much pain had sent me into a blind rage. I had nearly succeeded in landing a killing blow to Dimitri in the first few seconds that we fought. But his reflexes proved to be much faster than I had thought, and I had been unable to finish the cut.

A muttered spell and the sudden clearing of the steam brought me back to the current situation. My grip on my tessens tightened, and I forced myself to look away from my teammates to face Dimitri again. But he was nowhere to be seen.

No! I went cold. Frantically I searched every nook of the balcony for the Shadow Keeper, but found no trace of him. I even looked to Hyperion to see if he would betray an answer to his Keeper's mysterious disappearance, but the dark dragon only stared at me, bemused.

A whisper of Kinös Elda from behind caught my attention, and I reeled about. I had only managed a quarter of a turn before Dimitri's spell struck me on the right side of my body. The air rushed from my lungs and I spun heels over head in the air. It felt like an eternity before I collided with the stone banister of the balcony, busting through it, then tumbling further and further. I landed in a broken heap at the foot of one of the many trees in the courtyard, and there I lay, staring up at the leaf-heavy branches, struggling to breathe and wishing for the world to stop spinning so madly.

Every bone and muscle, every sinew within me, was afire with indescribable agony. My lungs burned, both from the lack of breath and a few broken ribs. At last I was able to breath and, through the shallow breaths and lightheadedness, manage a healing spell. The pain melted away, leaving me whole once again, but my exhaustion grew substantially the longer I maintained the spell. All too soon I was forced to cut off the stream of magic before I gave in to my fatigue. Pushing myself up to a sitting position, I reclined against the tree until a wave of dizziness passed. I placed my palms against the bark and drew in strength from the tree's essence, sighing in relief as much of the weariness left me.

My first coherent thought was: where are all the soldiers we locked out here? Taking a quick survey of the gardens, I saw no sign that they had ever been out here. I began to believe that those soldiers were nothing more than the product of a reflection spell. Was Dimitri so confident in his victory that he left himself unguarded?

Then I searched for Dimitri, finding him atop the balcony, squaring off against Kkorian and Shazza. I was amazed to see that Dimitri could fend the duo off so easily. He was moving so fast that Shazza could barely keep up with him and he somehow dodged several shots fired from Kkorian's pistols. I knew there was no way he could ever be that strong or fast by himself. Even if he used a spell on himself to enhance his physical abilities, he would have been tapped out by now and quickly growing weaker. Instead he was just getting stronger and faster.

That left only one culprit.

"Hyperion." His name escaped me in a growl.

Laying both my hands flat against the tree, I drew in more energy; I was going to need it for what I was about to do. When that tree was dangerously close to withering, I moved on to another and repeated the action again, and again. A total of five trees were nearly drained dry before I felt ready. By then, my hair was standing on end and I felt like I could soar to Bedeb.

Turning towards the guard tower upon which Hyperion sat, I focused and compressed all the energy I gathered into a tiny ball at the tip of my index finger. I kept the ball about the size of a pebble as I pushed every last drop of the excess energy into it. By the time I was done, the ball looked like a miniature, blue sun swirling on the tip of my finger.

I took a deep breath and glared up at the Shadow Dragon. As loud as I could I shouted, "Hyperion!"

The dragon's head jerked, and he looked down at me with a fire in his eyes. The moment I could see the crest of his brow ridge, I hurled the miniature sun at him as fast as I could, propelling it forward with a spell. He never even saw it coming.

The ball of energy struck him almost directly between the eyes and exploded with such force it rivaled Zenith's Galactic Tsunami. Hyperion bellowed a deafening roar of agony and reared. That proved to be his undoing, for his hind foot slipped off the apex of the tower, and the rest of his bulk twisted and followed. He howled as he plummeted, colliding with parts of the palace and knocking loose enormous chunks of masonry, which rained down on him. His impact with the ground rumbled like a thousand thunderstorms and threw a billowing cloud of dust several meters into the air. The entire palace and surrounding gardens were rocked violently, and I desperately held on to the tree to keep from falling.

Out of the corner of my eye, I saw Dimitri fighting to remain on his feet during the quake. He failed miserably, and slipped off the balcony crashed into the thorny bushes at its base. I could not help but smile at his pained cry.

A low rumble echoed far, far overhead.

All work on the massive pillars stopped, choking the cavern in near silence. Pyrex looked up, into the perpetual darkness, and a deep frown crept its way across his face. It sounded as if a colossal explosion had rocked the land, causing the supporting pillars below too much stress than what they could handle in their current condition.

A turbulent snap nearby confirmed Pyrex's suspicions: The impact had caused too much of a tremor, and pillars were giving out now.

"Run!" He screamed. "Get out of here, you fools! Go!"

Every Wakari immediately dropped their tools and bolted for the tunnels that would lead them to safety. Pyrex lingered behind longest, making sure each and every one of his clansmen was evacuating. Then he ran after them, singing as loudly and clearly as he could in hopes of softening the granite just right to fall away from their escape route and prevent it from crushing all of them. Several others lent their voices to his, and the cavern filled with song and the patter of many hustling feet.

Behind them, cracks shot through the enormous pillars like lightning. Chunks of the cavern's roof began to rain down, striking the stalagmites and exploding like thunder into rubble. Then the first pillar toppled, colliding with its neighbor hard enough to jar it loose. Both of those collapsed into the next, creating a massive domino effect.

The hatchlings asked me, "What is it to pray?" I told them that praying is speaking to the higher beings known as the Five Souls. One of the reasons to speak to them is to ask for guidance, another is to ask the Gods to watch over the spirits of the dead.

The dragons found the idea of gods to be strange. Then I told them about Khatahn-Rhii, the dragon-shaped God of Wind and Autumn and the inspiration for their creation. They liked Him very much.

– FROM "THE DIARY OF AMOREZ" BY AMOREZ RENOAN

Amorez stood with Blood Fang, Aidana, and Black Kat, ready to pass through the force field the moment Zenith created a passage. But the Dragon of the Heavens seemed distracted and hesitant to let them pass beyond the barrier. In fact, both he and the silver Sentinel upon his snout just kept staring at a distant point far beyond what any of them could see.

"What's wrong, Zenith?" Amorez surprised herself with how her voice was so calm despite being impatient.

"I feel a… distortion." Zenith did not look away from the point of interest as he spoke. His answer brought a fearful frown to Amorez's face. "It is almost as if space itself is collapsing in a single, miniscule point."

"What could possibly cause that?" Asked Black Kat.

"An exceptionally talented Sorcerer could manage it," Aidana replied after a moment of thought, "but not for more than a few seconds before they killed themselves from the energy drain."

"It has been much longer than a few seconds." Zenith muttered.

A pained roar from Hyperion won all of their attention in an instant. Amorez watched the enormous Shadow Dragon as he suddenly reared, lost his footing, and plummeted. With his downfall, the protective barrier he projected vanished with a rush of air. Without a moment's hesitation, she and the others burst forward, drawing their weapons and fearing the worst.

The ground continued to shake and rumble even after several minutes, and it showed no signs of letting up any time soon. Suddenly remembering the Wakari's plan to sink the palace, I jumped into action. I shoved myself away from the tree and hurried towards the balcony as fast as I could. With a simple spell, I jumped and landed neatly on the balcony beside Shazza.

"This place is coming down. We have to get out of here now." I explained, rushing to help Thera get Kitfox on his feet. Despite Thera's magic touch, the Demon was still too weak and shaky from Hyperion's attack to stand on his own.

"Here, let me take him." Shazza said, handing her bow to Kkorian. The pirate grunted and nearly lost his footing when the full weight of the weapon hit him. He made a face at Shazza's back as she bent to pick Kitfox up. "You owe me, fox boy."

Kitfox growled something that sounded like a death threat, and Shazza chuckled.

"Come on." I said with a smile. I hopped up on the banister, managing to balance for a moment despite the growing shaking. Then I uttered another spell and jumped off, landing gracefully in the gardens a few meters away from the palace. Shazza landed right beside me with a slight grunt, and the two of us looked back at Thera and Kkorian. The Feykin grabbed Kkorian around the waist and, ignoring his yelps, shoved him over the edge. She spread her ebony wings wide and managed to control the descent to the ground despite the weight in her arms.

An arm's length from the ground, Thera released Kkorian and pumped her wings hard several times to regain altitude. Before she could land, a terrifying rumble from deep beneath our feet rocked the land and a long fissure burst into existence a few meters away. Thera remained in the air while the rest of us bolted for the bridge.

After a few meters, I realized Kkorian was struggling to keep up with Shazza's bow in his arms. To help him manage the load, I cast a spell to force the bow to hover in the air a short distance from the Dákun Daju. The pirate somehow managed to keep a grip on the back of the bow as it took to the air, and haul himself up on it. Even though we were out of breath, the image of him riding on the bow with his coat and hair flapping madly behind him made us all burst out laughing.

Our laughter died the instant we saw four figures coming towards us from the other end of the bridge. Unable to tell who they were at such a distance, our escape from the crumbling palace ground to a halt a few meters before the main gate. We prepared for a battle, but with most of us being either weaponless or injured, the outcome could not be prophesized.

Several tense seconds ticked anxiously by. The shaking grew louder and ever more violent. Several new cracks broke the surface. I remained planted to the ground, ready at any moment to launch a counter attack at those who approached. A flash of silver suddenly streaked through the air, heading right for Thera, and I began to work a spell. Before I could utter the words, one of the four rapidly approaching called my name.

"It's Amorez's team!" Cried Thera as she dove towards them.

Relief washed over me, and I burst forward with renewed determination to escape. I hadn't even gone a meter when something snared me around my left ankle and jerked me back. I gasped as I crashed to the ground. My head bounced against the soil, and stars danced before my eyes. Before I had any chance to recover I felt myself being dragged across the ground by the invisible tether. Somehow, I managed to clear the fog in my head and trace the tether towards its origin. There stood a bruised and torn Dimitri, glowering furiously.

I shot him a look of pure hatred and tried a spell to cut the tether. Dimitri must have bewitched the line to prevent its destruction for all I managed to do is create a few dancing sparks in the air. I cried out for help and my friends quickly sprang into action. When they were just an arm's length away, Dimitri bellowed a spell and all four of them were sent flying from a violent explosion of fire and air. Just as I began a spell to save them, a wall of crackling, red energy sprang up between us. I shouted a curse unto Dimitri and he merely sneered back.

"You and I are not done yet." He growled and jerked the invisible line. I winced as a heated pain similar to rope burn sprang to life around my ankle. "You will pay for what you did to my dragon."

"Ha!" I shouted, getting to my feet as fast as I could. "I did everyone who died here today a justice by taking that overgrown bastard down!"

"Xy!" Amorez called from behind me. I spared her a glance over my shoulder, finding her dangerously close to the energized barrier. She was a mess of dried blood, gore, and dirt. And her left arm was missing from the middle of her bicep down. There was a look of absolute terror written on her face. "Xy, I can't force the barrier to drop."

I nodded in understanding. I glanced back at Dimitri, then at the shaking land all around. Several more fissures had sprung to life, some large enough to swallow the trees and statues that dotted the yard. Finally, I returned my gaze to her. "You should leave."

"What?!" Shouted Kitfox. I looked to him, seeing him half supported by Blood Fang and trying to escape. His amber eyes swam with a mix of hurt, fear, and anger. "I'm not leaving you here alone to fight that... that..."

"You have no choice." I said. As if taking a cue, a deep crack exploded into existence right between us. Shards of stone and clumps of dirt were sent flying in all directions. A thunderous rumble bellowed from somewhere on the opposite side of the palace, and a dust cloud appeared over the trees seconds later. "You have to go. Now."

"But.."

"Please, My Love."

He growled his displeasure at the situation, but I could tell his resolve was about to cave. "I'll only leave if you can promise me that you'll kill that bastard so we can be together again."

I smiled through a sob. "I promise, you and I will be having dinner together tonight."

Kitfox nodded and wiped a tear away. Finally he gave in, allowing himself to slump heavily against Blood Fang.

Another fierce jolt of the ground forced everyone into evacuation mode. Weapons and the injured were swiftly gathered and they began to leave. They paused a moment to wish me luck and mutter curses unto Dimitri, and then they were gone.

I took a deep breath and forced myself to face my greatest foe. Dimitri stood with his arms crossed and a bored look on his face.

He scoffed and uncrossed his arms. "About time you finished with all that useless touchy-feely crap."

My hands found their way to my belt by instinct, and a cold jolt of panic swept through me when I realized I had lost my fans. I swore silently and scanned the area for a sign of my weapons.

Dimitri loosed an infuriating laugh, drawing my attention back to him. He freed his dual sword from its sheath and flourished it in spirals at his sides. "Still think you can beat me without your precious war fans?"

"Let's find out." I balled my fists and sunk into the fighting stance Zhealocera had taught me long ago. Dimitri snickered and settled into his own stance. Our eyes locked and slowly, we began to circle each other drawing closer and closer. My mind raced, trying to anticipate when and how he would attack and how I would fend him off without a weapon or shield.

When we were only about two meters apart, Dimitri twitched; feinting right, but striking from the left. I had anticipated his deception and somersaulted beneath the blade. He recovered quickly and struck again, sweeping his sword to and fro a hand's width above the ground. I was forced to back flip to avoid it, but as I did, I grabbed handfuls of dirt. Once back on my feet, I hurled one handful of dirt towards his eyes, whispering a spell to guide it true. The instant the earth hit his face and exploded in a small cloud of dust, Dimitri recoiled as if touched by a hot iron. In that instant, I sprang forward and tackled him to the ground. His dual sword flew out of his hand, landing too far out of reach for what I had planned. I resorted to punching him in the face several times, managing to break his nose and fracture his jaw before he kicked me off.

I landed on my back with an 'oof' and forced myself to get up quickly. I scrambled to where Dimitri's dual blade lay, determined to snatch it before it ended up in his possession. His hand caught my ankle and jerked me back, leaving only inches between my outstretched hand and the weapon. He dragged me even further away and I screamed in fury. Dimitri sneered as he pinned me directly beneath him. I spit in his face and jerked my knee up to the junction between his thighs. I smirked as his face flushed red and contorted with pain.

Through gritted teeth, he snarled at me, "You wretch!" And he followed it with a hard punch to my jaw, then another to my clavicle, which gave way with a loud snap. I cried out in agony as he laughed.

The ground shuddered roughly, jarring both of us and knocking him off me. He rolled to all fours, covering his ears as an angry rumble echoed nearby. I used the short respite to heal as much as I could before it was too late. I swore as the energy drain of healing my shattered clavicle hit me and left me lightheaded. The noise of the collapse finally settled and I forced myself to get up. Dimitri had recovered, and began rushing towards his weapon. I was on my feet and chasing after him a heartbeat later.

He got there first.

Picking the weapon from the grass, Dimitri turned and aimed it straight for me. Realizing I could not stop in time to avoid the weapon, I twisted and hoped it missed. I gasped as cold steel sliced through my leathers and buried itself deep in my left side, just beneath my ribcage. Still grasping the hilt firmly, Dimitri got to his feet and laughed victoriously.

"We're not done yet." I quietly growled. He seemed not to notice as I grasped the blade with both hands and muttered, "Hyerjam."

The blade shattered like glass.

390

Before Dimitri could react, I jerked the shard free from my side with a wordless holler and planted it firmly in his neck. I backed away slowly, taking the fraction of the blade with me. His red barrier dropped and I heard a chorus of twelve shrieks echo from all around. He made a sick, gurgling noise and blood gushed from the wound and his mouth. His eyes went wide and his body grew rigid, as if he had been shackled to a board. A white light suddenly burst from the wound and red crystal began to creep over him, consuming him like a ravenous beast.

I chucked the shard away and turned my back on him as another angry rumble rocked the platform. Clutching my wounded side, I began to move away as fast as my tired and sore body would allow. The rumbling grew louder and louder, reaching a terrifying crescendo. Suddenly it went silent and the ground stopped shaking.

I froze where I stood and dared a glance back at the scene. As I did so, a deafening crack ripped the air. A split second later the entire platform began to crumble into the bay, spewing billowing clouds of dust into the air. It had started at the easternmost edge, but was rapidly moving towards me.

I swore and took off running as fast as I could, trying to ignore the searing pain in my side. No matter how fast I pushed myself to go, the landslide was faster still. It caught up with me before I had gone twenty meters. I resorted to spending the last bit of energy I had on a quickening spell and managed to pull ahead of the collapse.

I flew passed the palace gate and kept going, pushing myself well beyond my limit. The landslide continued to chase me, quickening as it reached the cobblestone bridge. Even with my magic, I was too slow to outrun it and found myself running over sideways sections of the bridge.

The landslide finally came to a stop several meters ahead. I leapt off the last crumbling bridge section and on to firm ground. Completely drained of energy and breath, I collapsed. I stared at the sky, trying to catch my breath as my eyelids grew heavy. I knew I should get up, for people were calling my name, but the ground was so soft beneath me. All I really wanted to do was close my eyes and sleep....

"Why did I agree to help Amorez?" Artimista scoffed at my query. "I didn't. I agreed to help my brother. He was the one eager for the challenge to create everlasting homunculi. Why Amorez sought him out, I cannot say. Though, I will admit I enjoyed her company, as well as the others. They had proven themselves capable warriors."

– FROM "THE UNSUNG" BY J'VAC TAIG (TRANSLATED BY B'REG KUNGA)

K itfox sat alone on the cold, hard ground; one arm resting on a bent knee. He reclined against the dingy, stone wall of a peasant's abandoned home. He did not about the dampness or the stench of mould upon it. Nor did he care that it was dismally dark and nippy. He was too miserable to care about anything right now. All he wanted was to see her smile again. To hear her laughter; her voice. To look into her beautiful eyes and tell her that he loved her.

But he could not do that now.

He cast his gaze around the room, trying desperately to find something to take his mind off the grief... if only for a moment. The room was small; measuring about three meters wide and two long. A threadbare rug adorned the center of the trampled clay floor, and a half crumbled hearth formed the wall opposite him. The adjacent wall held a shabby, wooden door with rusty hinges that complained each time it was opened.

Inevitably though, his attention returned to the still form on the sleeping furs beside him. He sighed, and buried his face in his arms.

Three long days had passed since Bakari-Tokai's collapse into the bay. Three miserable days without the love of his life by his side. Three days spent mostly alone, wallowing in a mix of guilt and grief. Despite being swamped with things to do to restore the world back into order, the others had taken the time to drop in and check on him and bring him food. They would leave soon after; returning to help organize the survivors and refugees in what little remained of Bakari-Tokai.

He should be helping.

He really wanted to.

But he simply did not have the will.

His ears twitched, catching the sound of footsteps prodding around nearby. He silently hoped that he was not about to have visitors; he was in no mood to entertain them.

"This city will take years to rebuild, maybe even decades." This voice – Kitfox recognized – belonged to the Hume Healer, Jaxith. "Even then, Bakari-Tokai will never be the same."

"The whole world will never be the same." Said a gruff-voiced man. "We've lost so much and gained so little… hardly seems worth it."

"Don't say that!"

"Well, it's true!"

"So you're telling me we were better off under that dictator's rule? Have you forgotten how his dragons brainwashed thousands of soldiers and turned them against their own friends and families? He could have done the exact same to any of us who opposed him. How is that better than what we have now?

"Yeah, we lost a city. It was a steep price. But we gained friends and allies amongst people we never even dreamed of! Look at the Wakari, for instance. They hid underground for nearly five centuries, yet here they are, aiding us in our most desperate time.

"Yes, the world will never be the same. It should never be the same after all the sacrifices made here. In the wake of destruction, a new and peaceful world has been born. We should strive to keep it that way forever."

An awkward silence consumed the two. After a minute, the gruff-voiced man agreed. "But you didn't have to preach it to me."

Jaxith chuckled. "Sorry, man."

Together the two shuffled away, talking about nothing of particular interest to their Demon eavesdropper.

Kitfox's gaze once again returned to the still form beside him. "They have no idea just how much was really lost." He whispered. But Jaxith is right; the world will never be the same again.

Amorez hesitated outside the rickety door of the old peasant's hut, all too aware of the miserable Demon within. She would have been content to leave him be, and return to her work securing the Shadow Dragons or helping to set up a new governing body. Thernu, however, had forced her away from those duties, saying a visit would do her some good. So Amorez had made her way across the refugee camp, only to stop outside the hut and stare at the door.

She felt like she was intruding. After all, it had been nearly two hundred years since she and Xyleena had grown apart. Amorez did not want to suddenly pop back into her daughter's life and meet the man she had taken for a mate. Sure, she had heard great things about Kitfox, and had been impressed by his sacrifices for Xyleena. She wanted to meet him, really she did. She just felt awkward about it.

Amorez took a deep breath, steeled her nerves, and pushed the door open. She immediately silenced the cursed wail of the rusty hinges, and passed over the threshold. To her surprise, she was not greeted by the angry growl she had been warned to expect. In fact, the only sound in the room was that of slow and steady breathing. So she moved towards the middle of the tiny room, summoning a dim light orb as she did. The light scattered the shadows of night to the far corners of the room. Amorez took a moment to allow her eyes to adjust to the blue glow. At last she could see the room in its entirety.

Like a constant protector, Kitfox, reclined against the moldy wall beside his beloved. His eyes were closed and his arms were crossed over his chest, which rose and fell in steady breaths.

Amorez looked away from the sleeping Demon, to the still form atop a thick pile of sleeping furs. Her skin was as pale as snow and her body placid, almost as if Death had placed a kiss upon her. Many had actually believed the young Dragon Keeper had been killed in the final battle, but Amorez and a few others knew the truth. Xyleena's body had become so exhausted from the continuous saps of energy used in spell craft that it needed time to recover. How long exactly remained unknown. Amorez truly hoped her daughter would revive soon.

With a sigh, she turned her gaze once again to the Demon. His eyes were open, glowing slightly as he stared at her. There was no anger or hatred in his amber orbs, only weariness. Suddenly, she felt even more awkward being there.

"Sorry, I didn't mean to wake you." She softly whispered, knowing his acute hearing would pick up her voice. When his ears twitched, she knew he heard her. She continued, turning away from him as she spoke. "I was just checking on you and Xy. I'll leave you to rest now."

"You don't have to leave." He muttered to her back. She looked at him over her shoulder, surprised that he would allow her to stay. His gaze, however, was no longer upon her. He was looking longingly at Xy as if begging her to awaken from her sleep. "It would be... nice... to have company for a while."

Amorez slowly turned to face him completely. Unsure of what to say, she settled for sitting on the threadbare rug. She silently watched Kitfox watch Xy, wishing she knew what to say to cheer him. Nothing she could think of seemed empathic enough, which is why she did not want to be here in the first place.

Amorez sighed. "I'm not good at this."

Kitfox tore his gaze away from his beloved to look at the older Keeper. "Good at what?"

"Dealing with people." She shrugged. "I've been hiding from the outside world so long that I have forgotten how to interact with them."

"Where have you been keeping yourself anyway?"

"Various parts of the world, mostly secluded places like the mountains around Pletíxa."

"Why?"

She sighed. "Because almost everyone I met would go on and on about my being the 'savior of the world.' I got tired of listening to them and having them regale me with my own exploits or ask a million questions. I would suggest you and Xyleena find a secluded spot to live for a few years so that you do not have to deal with the same thing."

Kitfox nodded. "Thanks for the advice."

"Tell me something," his ears perked up at her words, "how long have you and Xy been together?"

"Romantically? About four months or so. But I have been on this adventure with her since Atoka."

"So, quite a long time?"

He nodded.

"I've been told by quite a few people that you are very honorable and have been willing to sacrifice yourself for her on several occasions."

"Yeah…" He muttered so softly Amorez barely heard him.

"Perhaps you would like to know that Blood Fang has nominated you for the role of the Demon Representative on the new High Council of Ithnez." His ears went flat against his head as she spoke. "You do not like the idea?"

"Honestly, I have no idea what this High Council is that you speak of, much less if I am even suited for the job."

Amorez nodded, secretly impressed by his modesty. "Let me tell you a little about the new council. Maybe then you can make up your mind on whether or not to accept the nomination."

Kitfox slowly nodded in agreement.

"In the wake of the destruction that has happened here, many believe that a council should be set up to oversee the affairs of each race so that one does not become more powerful than the others and a harmony is maintained. The details are still being worked out, but the council will basically be made up of five representatives, one from each race. Each representative will be voted into the position for a duration, which lasts a total of five years.

"During those five years in service, the representatives will work together with each other and the five governments to resolve issues facing each race on a day-by-day basis. After the five years are up, another representative will be voted in. The same representative may be voted into the office again – to serve one other five year period – but after that he or she will have to step aside.

"The first four have been nominated, and you are one of them. The others include Pyrex of the Wakari, Vitaani of the Dákun Daju, and Thera of the Feykin. The Humes have yet to nominate one of their kind because there is no ruling family at the moment. Some seek to coronate Xyleena as High Queen because she has Djurdak's blood, thus making her the only living person with royal blood. I doubt she would want it though."

"You're right," mumbled a groggy voice. Kitfox and Amorez rushed to Xy's side in an instant. She looked at them through sleepy, dragon green eyes and smiled. "I don't want to be queen."

Kitfox captured her mouth in a passionate kiss. Xyleena was taken aback for a moment, and then quickly returned his kiss. It lasted only seconds, but in those few seconds, Amorez could see just how much they loved each other. A smile touched Amorez's lips and she secretly prayed for their eternal happiness.

When the two lovers parted, Kitfox helped prop Xy up to a sitting position. Then he whispered something in her ear. She smiled and stroked his cheek affectionately.

Amorez cleared her throat, earning their attention. "How are you feeling?"

"A little tired, and absolutely ravenous."

Kitfox chuckled. "I'll get you something from the mess hall."

"Thank you."

Kitfox placed a tender kiss on her forehead. Then, with a nod to Amorez, left the house in a hurry. An awkward silence swept over the room as Amorez fought to come up with something to say. To her, it felt like meeting a total stranger and inviting them for breakfast.

Thankfully, it was Xy who broke the silence first. "How long have I been asleep?"

"Almost four days now."

"Wow."

Amorez nodded. "And Kitfox has not left your side for a minute until now." Xy look absolutely amazed at that bit of news. Amorez smiled and adjusted her position on the pile of furs. "He's a good man. Fiercely loyal, too."

"That he is."

"So," Amorez shifted her position again, "you are certain that you don't want to be High Queen? You are technically a princess and can claim it if you desire."

Xy shook her head negative. "I have no desire to rule. Besides, how would the people react? Overthrow one Dragon Keeper and replace him with another. No. All I want is to live a peaceful life with the man I love."

"Your father said something similar." Amorez smiled softly at the distant memory. She quickly pushed it aside; now was not the time to grow nostalgic. "Do you have anyone in mind who would accept the throne?"

Xy was quiet for a long while as she considered the question. There were quite a few people she knew of that would make wonderful kings or queens, but they all had one flaw: they weren't Hume. And only a Hume can reign over Humes; at least that is what she learned from her history professor. At that thought, a name suddenly popped into her head. A smile crept its way across her lips. "Noralani Ithnez."

Amorez gawked at her daughter in complete surprise. "I had totally forgotten that there was still one remaining member of the founding family!"

"Me too, until just a moment ago."

Amorez quickly got to her feet. "I have to go tell the others of your nomination. That way we can send a message to her to get her reply quickly."

Xy stifled a yawn and nodded.

With a hasty but fond farewell, Amorez turned on her heel and rushed out of the home.

I sat alone in the dark for only a few minutes before Kitfox returned. And he was not alone. Thera, Kkorian, and Shazza were all with him. The moment they saw me sitting up in bed, great big smiles appeared on their faces and they rushed forward to catch me in an awkward group hug.

Once they had settled down, and a fire was started in the hearth, they began to regale me with the activities I had missed in the last three days. Most of the city had been leveled by Hyperion's Tetra Vortex attack, and was no longer salvageable; almost ninety percent of the city needed to be rebuilt from the ground up. Amazingly enough, scouts sent through the city managed to find several survivors beneath some of the sturdier, collapsed buildings.

"Speaking of the Shadow Dragons," Thera added at one point late in the conversation, "you will be surprised to hear that – when their Keeper died – they agreed to surrender under one condition."

"Oh?" I quirked an eyebrow. "What was it?"

"That they do not get locked away behind the Dragons' Gate again."

"Interesting request." Muttered Kitfox.

"Agreed." Thera nodded. "But, since their surrender was accepted, we are now at a loss of what to do with them. Clearly we can't let them roam free. With their destructive nature, they could do untold damage. And we can't keep them locked within a magical barrier like we are now."

"I've been thinking on that situation." Replied Shazza. "I would like to speak to you," she nodded her head in my direction, "about it alone."

Kitfox snorted. "Don't trust any of us?"

"It is not that, Kitfox-fratim." Said the Dákun Daju. "If the Shadow Dragons are to be secured away from any who would seek out their power, it would prove beneficial to have fewer people know the secret."

I put a hand on Kitfox's arm, silencing any response. "Alright, Shazza, you and I will meet up later to discuss your idea. Until then, is there any other news I need to hear about?"

Our impromptu meeting went on for hours. Each of my teammates filled me in on things varying from plans for rebuilding Bakari-Tokai to the establishment of the new, and – at the moment – temporary, government. They also mentioned that neither diary had been found in what had been explored of the ruined palace, but the crystallized remains of Dimitri had been dug up. Amorez had been put in charge of dealing with him. Hopes were still high that the books would be excavated from the ruins and restored to their rightful places in the libraries.

Somehow, I knew the diaries were no more.

Xyleena had taken me by complete surprise when she threw that spell at Hyperion; a spell so powerful that it unseated the gargantuan dragon and sent him reeling off his perch. How she had managed such power when she was obviously exhausted amazed me. And I am certain that the scar Hyperion now wears will be an eternal reminder: Do not infuriate the Keeper of the Light.

– FROM "THE SECOND KEEPER" BY THERA ONYX

Nearly nine months had passed since the day Bakari-Tokai fell. For me and my group of friends, most of that time had been spent apart. Shazza had resumed her duties as Queen of Katalania and had even taken Kkorian with her. I had recently caught wind of their plans to marry in the spring, and I truly wished the couple well. Thera had remained with her family in Bakari-Tokai to assist in the rebuilding process. She had even risen to become the first Feykin to serve on the new High Council. I even heard that she had been promoted to the ranks of Elder Sorcerer; making her the youngest in Feykin history to achieve the honor. Kitfox had agreed to join the High Council as well, though it took quite a bit of convincing him it was worth it. He and Blood Fang had also remained in Bakari-Tokai to help smooth the transition to the new government.

As for me: I was dragon borne, on my way back to the city after being on a mission for the last eight months. The mission itself was kept top secret as it dealt with the Shadow Dragons and their Keeper. Only myself, Zenith, and one other person knew exactly what was going on, and all of us swore to never speak of it. With that work done, I could finally return to Bakari-Tokai and relax. I could not wait to get back and spend some quality time with Kitfox. I had missed him so much it had become unbearable to close my eyes; every time I did, I would see his face.

But he was not my only reason for returning. In just a few days, a grand ceremony was to take place in which Archbishop Noralani Ithnez would be crowned as High Queen. And I, being the only surviving member of the Za'Car bloodline and heir to the throne, was to lead the ceremony. I don't know whose idea it was to put me in such a position – probably Amorez's – but I was not looking forward to it.

What if I drop the crown? I asked for probably the one hundredth time. It was my major concern because I had heard the Wakari had sung the headdress from stone and it was apparently very delicate looking. The last thing I wanted to do was break it.

Trust me, Little One, you will not drop the crown. Zenith affirmed.

How can you be so certain? The dragon looked back at me over his shoulder, as if asking if I had really just said that. I sighed. *Yeah, stupid question.*

You will do fine, Xyleena. He said, his voice thick with amusement. Then he faced forward, into the oncoming wind, once more. *I promise.*

I fell silent, watching the horizon fade to indigo as the suns dipped ever lower at my back. Overhead, the first stars twinkled to life and Bedeb grew ever more prominent. The blue and green planet with its multifaceted rings looked like a rare jewel plucked from the deepest parts of the universe. Only I knew its dark secret.

With a smile, I returned my gaze to the horizon before me. *Zenith, how long do you think before we will reach Bakari-Tokai?*

With this headwind slowing me, maybe another two hours or so.

Alright.

I gaped at the torch and orb lit city below. Bakari-Tokai had changed much since I had last seen it. The rubble, which had once been wooden or clay houses and shops, was now cleared. In its place, stood several new buildings craft from various types of stone. Their designs varied from small houses to long strips of shops. Foliage of all sorts and sizes filled the spaces between buildings and lined the cobblestone roads. Some of the plants even had the same bioluminescence as the ones found on the Sorcerers' Isle.

At the very heart of the city, about two hundred meters west of where the bridge had been, stood two brand new plateaus, probably sung into existence by the Wakari. Both of them were hundreds of meters high and linked together through a thinner strip of land. Long stair-shaped paths connected the plateaus to the city below. A high wall with guard towers at certain intervals circled around the bases of the landmasses.

On the northernmost plateau, a flat piece of land wide enough to fit two dragons abreast was cordoned off with an ornate fence aglow with orbs of light. Some meters away, a fairly large building was still undergoing construction. From its skeleton, I could tell it was something akin to a dome-shaped temple. Its purpose was unknown to me, but perhaps it would serve as a mausoleum for all those who gave up their lives here.

The other plateau was home to the new palace, which was nearing the end of its construction phase. Though similar in size as the old palace, this one was much different. It had been built of Caledonia granite, and set in a rectangular shape with a section in the middle removed to serve as a safe haven for plants and fountains.

And surrounding it all was a pair of thick, stone walls that stood over one thousand meters apart. Both walls exceeded one hundred meters high and guard towers sprouted from them like spines along a dragon's back. Sections of the walls that ran through the waters of the bay were still being constructed. Giant machines had been developed to lower the stone blocks into place where they would be secured with mortar. They gave the city the look of great ingenuity.

"This is all so amazing!"

Zenith dipped his left wing to begin another slow circle above the city. As the loop started, he silently asked, *Where would you have me land?*

A presence that I had not felt in a long time brushed against my mind, winning a smile. I opened my mind to allow Kitfox's to meld with mine and shuddered at the feeling of completeness.

Land in the Dragon's Sanctuary. He said, his voice betraying excitement. *It is the flat area beside the cupola on the north rise.*

I see it. Replied the dragon, dipping low to start his descent. *I shall be there shortly.*

And I shall be waiting.

Zenith flared his wings wide, slowing his descent to a crawl. A few meters above the Sanctuary floor, he fluttered and tensed his hind legs to prepare for impact. He landed surprisingly lightly, given his bulk. Before he had even folded his wings, I spotted Kitfox sprinting towards us. With a hoot, I broke free of the riding straps and leapt out of the saddle. With just three long and quick strides, I was back in his strong arms and kissing him fully on the mouth. He eagerly returned the kiss, and many more, before we parted.

"Friendly greeting." Muttered Zenith. Kitfox burst out laughing, and moved to the dragon to retrieve the saddle bags. As he did so, I took in his appearance for it had changed since I last saw him. His hair was still long, but some of it had been tied back in braids adorned with jewels and feathers. Over his usual white trousers and loose tunic, he wore a long sleeved, navy blue coat that fell to his ankles. His feet were still bare, but a runic tattoo had appeared on the top of his right one.

"Admiring the view?"

My gaze jumped to his eyes, which were glowing slightly in the dim light. I smiled at his coy grin. "Maybe."

He snorted.

"What's with the feathers and such?"

"Oh! I was promoted to Alpha within the guild." He said with a wide smile. "The feathers and braids are to show my rank. The coat is to let people know that I am on the High Council."

"So you've been keeping busy."

"Very." He chuckled. He thumped Zenith on the forearm before coming to my side. "How was your trip?"

"Long." I said with a sigh. After a moment, I snaked my arms around his waist and pulled him in for another kiss. "I've missed you so much."

He hummed in my ear. "How about we celebrate your return?"

A smile touched my lips. "Sounds like fun."

The two of us bade Zenith good night. Then Kitfox took my hand and led me around the Sanctuary, across the land bridge, and into the palace.

The suns' light broke through the curtains to sweep across my face. Morning came too soon for my taste. After the rigorous celebrating of the last two nights, all I wanted to do was sleep. Kitfox, however, had other plans. His hand roamed along my side in a soothing massage, but he was not trying to relax me; quite the contrary.

"Don't tell me I have to throw water on you to get you up."

"Don't even dare." I mumbled into my pillow.

"Fine." I could almost hear him shrug. "I'll go tell Ithnez you're going to be late because yo—"

I bolted upright and nearly succeeded in knocking heads with him. "The coronation is today?!"

"Not for a few hours yet, but yes." He nodded.

I groaned and threw aside the blankets. Ignoring the fact that I was naked, I made my way to the bath to wash up.

"I already drew a bath for you, Love." Kitfox called after me. I looked around the opulent bathroom, admiring the craftsmanship of the stone and metal. A deep tub sat opposite a vanity, and steam rolled off the flower petal infused water.

"Thank you." I called back. After a moment, I backed up to look at him through the doorway. He sat on the edge of the bed, clad only in his white trousers, looking out the window as if captivated by a dream. "What time is it?"

He looked at me, amusement burning in his amber eyes. "Shortly after midday."

I cried out in dismay, then promptly jumped into the bath to wash. "Why did you let me sleep in so long?"

"Because you have been on an eight month long trip, probably getting little rest in the progress. So you were exhausted to begin with. And then I kept you up all night the last two nights by... uh..." he cleared his throat, "celebrating your return."

"So, in effect, it will be all your fault if I'm late."

He laughed at that. "I guess so." A silence followed, within which I took the time to rinse my hair clean of the lather I had worked up. "Say, which dress did you want to wear to the ceremony?"

"Where in the rules does it say I have to wear a dress?"

He chuckled. "Sticking to your armor, then?"

"No, but I'm not wearing a dress."

"Going naked then? I might enjoy that."

I snorted. "You wish."

He suddenly appeared in the doorway, holding two outfits aloft for me to see. One was a royal blue dress with long, flowing sleeves and a black bodice with silver embroidery. The other was a forest green silk tunic with dark brown trousers which gave the appearance of a skirt. Kitfox smirked. "Honestly, I like the blue."

"If it came with pants like the green one, I would wear it."

"Xy, you are a Sorcerer." He said, turning to toss the green tunic away. He looked back at me with a smile. "I think you can modify the dress to suit you without too much difficulty."

"Good point."

He nodded and retreated from the room. Moments later, he returned empty-handed. He went to a closet by the tub and pulled a thick drying cloth from the shelves within. "You might need that, unless you prefer to air dry." He flashed a cocky smirk and wiggled his eyebrows.

"Thank you."

He laughed and shook his head as he left the room.

I pushed the gold-inlayed door open just a bit, and peered into the room beyond. The lavish throne room was about fifty meters long. From my peeping spot at one of the side exits, I could see the entire room. Five elaborately carved columns spanned both sides of the rectangular room and violet standards emblazoned with the hierarchy's Coat of Arms fell from each. Several benches and a small rise for the throne had been moved into position. A violet carpet lined with gold tassels spanned the distance between the throne and the double doors that made up the entrance to the room. The space under the benches was left bare so everyone could see the glistening, marble floor.

The benches were quickly being filled by people of all ranks and races. A few Feykin stood at various points throughout the room, each casting a spell that formed a special mirror. Those mirrors reflected what was seen before them onto much larger mirrors stationed throughout the city below. That way, every citizen could witness the historic coronation of the new queen without having to procure tickets to enter the throne room.

In just a few minutes, the procession would begin.

"Xy!"

I jumped at my name and let the door close with a soft thud. Looking beyond the rulers and musicians gathered around me, I spotted Thera. I made my way to her quickly, for there wasn't much time to dawdle in conversation before the ceremony began.

"What's wrong, Thera?"

"Nothing's wrong." She said with a shake of her head. "I just have a favor to ask of you."

"What kind of favor?"

"There is to be a recess of the High Council for a few months, so that we may return home to gather what we need to work here. I was wondering if you would mind giving me a ride adragonback to Thorna."

I focused my thoughts inwards, seeking out the presence of Zenith, still napping upon the Dragon Sanctuary. Zenith, do you mind flying Thera home once the ceremony is over?

Not at all, Little One.

Thank you. "Zenith says he doesn't mind flying you home."

Thera sighed in relief. "Thank you so much, Xy. I'll see you after the ceremony."

"Sure thing."

With that, she took off for the double doors to the throne room. Someone else called for the musicians to start filing into the room. As the twenty or so of them marched away, I took my place at the front of the remaining procession. Palavant Serenitatis fell in line behind me, then the Captain of the Guard and the other royals. I was actually surprised to see Shazza among them, especially with how pregnant she was.

A trumpet blared, signaling the start of the ceremony. Silence descended, then a slow drumbeat resonated into the hall. I squared my shoulders, held my head high, and started the march into the throne room.

The double doors were held ajar by some fortunate pages, and I resisted the urge to smile at them as I passed by. The violet carpet muffled our footsteps as we strode towards the rise, atop which sat the throne sung from stone and two pedestals. The crown was set upon one of the pedestals, while the other held the Sovereign Orb and Scepter I was to use in the ceremony.

It felt like forever before I reached the rise. Once there, I stopped before the throne and turned to face the crowd. Instantly, my gaze picked Kitfox, Kkorian, Zhealocera, and Thera out of the crowd. Amorez, however, was nowhere to be seen.

The trumpets sounded again, and the beat of the drums changed. I averted my attention to the double doors, waiting eagerly for Noralani to appear. Seconds ticked by like minutes. Then, at last, she appeared in the doorway. Her auburn hair had been styled in flowing curls that hung loosely from a simple circlet upon her brow. She wore a dress of pale green silks and lace adorned with pearls sewn into the ivy-like embroidery of her bodice. Her hands were crossed before her, and the sleeves of her dress nearly touched the floor. She strode confidently towards the rise, keeping her eyes locked on me.

When at last she stepped onto the platform, the drumbeat died down and a hush fell over the crowd. I took a calming breath and wet my lips.

"Noralani Ithnez, descendant of the Savior, Aadrian, you come before this honored body today to inherit the High Throne of Ithnez. Are you willing to accept the crown and all responsibilities of the Office of Queen until the day you pass into Havel?"

A curt nod, then she answered. "I am willing."

"Please kneel." I turned away as she did so, to receive the Sovereign Scepter and Orb from Palavant Serenitatis. I turned to face Noralani, and set the orb in her left hand and the scepter in her right. Then I retrieved the crown from the silk pillow bared by the Captain of the Guard. Turning once more to face Noralani, I held the crown between us. I took a deep breath, and began the oath. "As queen will you solemnly and sincerely swear to govern the Peoples of Ithnez according to their respective laws and customs?"

She held her head higher. "I solemnly swear so to do."

"Will you to your power cause law and justice, in mercy, to be executed in all your judgments?"

"I will."

"Will you to the utmost of your power preserve, protect, and defend the peace and prosperity of the realm against all evils? Will you vow to reconcile conflicting interests and to further strive for the hopes and aims shared by all? Will you to the best of your ability adapt to the changes and demands of the People?"

"All this I promise to do."

"Then with this crown, I pronounce thee Queen." I set the delicate circlet upon her hair. "Rise now, Queen Ithnez, First Sovereign Lady of the Third Age." I moved to her right side as she slowly and regally stood. Then, to the people gathered in the space before the throne, I said, "All hail the Queen!"

A loud chorus of "Long live the Queen!" echoed off the stone walls. Then Noralani sat upon the throne. King Zrehla of the Southern Stretch came before her and swore his allegiance, followed by Queen Luea, Sovereign of Aadrian, and Palavant Serenitatis. Elder Ruwviti, Blood Fang, Shazza, and Pyrex also pledged the friendship of their respective races.

All too soon it was my turn. I took a knee before the throne and, with a hand over my heart, began to speak the words of my oath. "I, Xyleena Renoan, Keeper of the Light and renounced High Princess of the Second Age, vow to be faithful and true to you, our Sovereign Lady, Queen of this Realm and Defender of the People, and unto your heirs and successors according to law, until I pass from this world and into Havel. So mote it be."

The queen whispered back, "So mote it be."

And the crowd cheered.

I wish that I could tell you what Xyleena did and where she went that year that she spent alone. I know what the rumors say, and I can neither confirm nor deny them. I will, however, take a cue from Mother and Xyleena and say:

The key to the Gate,
Shall now lie in wait,
For the one to come,
To see Dark undone.

– FROM "THE SECOND KEEPER" BY THERA ONYX

I felt Zenith tense in preparation for the landing. Thera, too, grew rigid and held fast to the straps of the saddle. Zenith's massive wings flared to slow his descent. He grunted at the impact and bounded a few steps before coming to a complete stop. He folded his wings and he and I glanced about.

The Sorcerers' Isle was as unchanged as it was the day I left. Plants grew wild and untouched, leaving barely enough room for a dragon as large as Zenith to land on its shores. Behind us, the white-sand beach glared in the afternoon sunlight.

I thumped Zenith's neck affectionately as Thera untied herself from the straps. She gathered the few belongings she had and glided to the ground. Zenith glanced back at me, seeming to smile as I finally dropped from the saddle.

The dragon's mind brushed mine. Take all the time you need to say goodbye. I shall enjoy a long sunning.

I watched for a few minutes as Zenith strode to the beach and arranged himself to catch the most sun. Though I wasn't ready to admit it out loud, I was really going to miss the dragons' presences once I returned home. I wasn't sure if I would ever see them again. Had I made a mistake in letting them wander freely?

"Are you alright?" Thera's voice called me away from my inner musings.

I forced a smile as I faced her. "I'm fine."

412

She frowned at my answer, but said nothing. Instead, she turned to the forest and led the way to Thorna.

I watched as Thera pulled aside the curtain to her hut. An instant's hesitation and she entered. She uttered the spell to form an orb of light as I pushed the curtain aside. The room was as unchanged as the day we left it, only now a fine layer of dust had covered everything.

Thera sighed and wandered from room to room. I figured she was checking to make sure nothing had been taken during her long absence. While she performed her task, I muttered a spell and blew all of the dust out of the room. That done, I sat on the couch to wait for her.

The young Feykin reentered the main room some minutes later, carrying two cups of tea. I thanked her for the one she offered me.

"So, what will we do now?"

I could only shrug. "Shazza is back in Kamédan, catching up on the business of Katalania again. I heard tell she is just days away from giving birth." Neither of us could hide our smiles at that. "Amorez has once again vanished off the face of Ithnez. She'll probably hide there for the next few centuries until we need her again. Teka, Pyrex, and Zhealocera all left before I could ask them of their plans."

Thera nodded and quietly sipped her tea. "What about Kitfox?"

I sighed upon remembering his farewell upon the start of the High Council's break. "He's back in Zadún taking care of some business with his guild." And I didn't even have the heart to beg him to stay with me.

"We've drifted apart." Thera muttered. I nodded. In the days that followed Noralani's coronation, every member of the team, myself included, had grown very introspective and depressed. It was as if the ceremony signaled end of our adventure together and, maybe, the end of our friendship. In a way, I found myself wishing all of us were still together, battling to save the planet. Suddenly finding ourselves alone and without a purpose left us all feeling melancholy about the future.

I sighed again. "What do you plan to do now that the adventure is over?"

"I'm not sure really." She shrugged. "I have not had much time to decide, what with serving on the new High Council and all. I've learned so much in these travels and experiences that I feel my existence here is no longer adequate enough to hold any interest."

"You could write a book."

Her violet eyes stared at me, betraying no emotion. Suddenly she muttered a spell and a leather-bound book appeared in her lap. After a moment to brush off the cover, she handed it to me.

"What is this for?" I asked as I flipped through the blank pages.

"In case you get a crazy thought to do something."

I scoffed. "I think one Dragon Diary was enough trouble. Producing another would be insane."

"Amorez's diary is her story." Thera said with a wave of her hand. "This one might turn into yours. You don't really need to write anything; that is entirely your choice. I am simply..." She paused and a strange smile crossed her lips. "... giving you a path."

I laughed whole-heartily at that. It was the perfect conclusion to this adventure. "Long ago... No. It feels more like a lifetime ago, I came here asking for a path to take. You led me down one full of things I never thought possible. Now, I find myself being offered another path."

"Though one that will be safer."

"Honestly," I met her violet gaze, "I really don't want a 'safe' life."

"I know what you mean, Xyleena-sortim," Thera smiled sadly albeit knowingly, "but I get the feeling our adventures together are far from over."

"One can only hope."

It was late in the afternoon the next day that I found Zenith. He was curled up on the hot sands of the beach, enjoying a nap. He lifted his great wedge of a head to look at me as I approached.

"Are you sure you want to leave?"

"I have to, Zenith." I reached out and stroked thorny his muzzle. "There is still one thing I have left to do."

"And what is that?"

The conversation with Thera last night replayed in my head and I smiled. "I have to go home."

"I thought you were afraid to return." Zenith replied as he got to all fours. I nodded and climbed up to the saddle.

"Take me to Sindai. You and the others will be free to go your own way after that. I will face my fears alone."

"Are you sure you want to grant us freedom? You are stronger with all of us together."

"I know." I said with a sigh. "But you guys have been locked up for the last three or four centuries, I think it's time you got out and saw the world with your own eyes." A smile split my face. "Besides, with you all roaming the planet, I bet people would be too afraid to do anything to disturb the peace that we have worked so hard to obtain."

Zenith was quiet as he stared at me over his shoulder. I could tell he was concerned, but he could not sway me from my resolve. Finally, the dragon nodded.

"If that is your wish."

The sunset warmed the back of my neck and shoulders as I stared out over the open water. Golden yellow and fiery orange danced across the waves, creating a spectacular mirage for the island straight ahead. With a heavy sigh, I leaned against the pitted metal railing and listened as the ferry chugged along.

I wished for it to slow down, but I knew I would have to face this long-suppressed fear sooner or later. I couldn't turn back now, even if I wanted to. I had to return home.

The ferry docked and passengers eagerly disembarked. I remained, unmoved, at the railing. I guess I was hoping to delay the inevitable for as long as possible. Several minutes after the last of the passengers scurried up the cobblestone walkway to the Temple, the ferry captain approached me. He didn't say a word; there was no need to. It was time.

With deliberately slow steps, I walked the length of the deck and paused at the plank that spanned the distance to shore. I took a deep breath and let my eyes drift shut as I took the last few steps onto the island. I opened my eyes and peered down the beach, seeing beyond what lay in sight.

Without thinking, I began the trek along the beach. With each measured step, I drew closer to my destination and still arrived too quickly for my taste.

I looked around and nodded solemnly. This was the spot, alright. And someone had been thoughtful enough to mark it with an obelisk grave stone. I read the inscription under the name:

Here lies the Hero of the Hero
Who saved us all

Fitting. And a dragon was emblazoned beneath the epitaph. Ríhan would have loved it.

A sad, but gentle smile crept its way across my lips and I reached out to touch the pinnacle of the obelisk. No words were spoken; they weren't needed. I knew he was happy in Havel and wished the best for me in my life. But I wouldn't have been satisfied had I not faced my fears and returned to the spot where he had been murdered almost three years ago. This was my final goodbye.

I felt a tear roll down my cheek, and did nothing to abate it. As it vanished into the sand at my feet, I rummaged through my hip sack. I found the treasure I sought and touched the crystal to the pinnacle of the obelisk. A quick spell later, and the jewel was forever fused atop the grave.

With the ghost of a nod and a final pat on the pinnacle, I turned and walked away.

The Temple of the Five Souls had changed drastically since last I stood at the gates. Standards of white and gray fluttered in the late autumn breeze. The white marble walls, once dingy with years, had either been washed thoroughly or rebuilt after the destruction wrought by Dimitri. New statues guarded the yards, overseeing newly-planted flower beds. Even the cobblestone walkway had been re-laid. I barely recognized the place.

As I walked the path to the central building of the Temple, I noticed that only a few priests and knights were about. It was a far cry from the once bustling population of three years ago. No surprise. After Dimitri practically leveled the place with his fire storm, parents had been too afraid to send their children here. I could only pray that his defeat would signal a revival of the Temple's community.

"I was wondering when you would show up."

I froze mid-stride at the familiar voice. It couldn't be him! I swallowed past the lump in my throat and slowly looked over my shoulder. Kitfox smiled coyly at me as he leaned against a stone pillar.

"K-Kitfox?" Was I hallucinating?

"That's me." His smile grew.

My heart fluttered. He's really here!

"I was beginning to think you'd never show up."

I finally turned to face him completely. "H-how did you know where I was?"

"Simple." He flashed that sexy smirk of his. "A certain dragon we both know whispered it in my ear." I nodded in understanding and watched as he moved slowly towards me.

"Zenith?"

"I'm not telling, but yes." He whispered, gently wrapping his arms around me and pulling me closer. I couldn't fight the smile that graced my lips as I leaned into his embrace and held him tight. I could stay like this forever, just listening to his heartbeat.

Slowly and deliberately, his embrace loosened as he brought a hand up to cup my chin. With a gentle pull, he had me staring up into his rich, amber eyes. He searched for any signs of rejection and found none. I didn't fight him as he brought his lips down against mine in the barest of touches. A delightful chill ran the length of my spine as the kiss deepened. My hands moved of their own accord, roaming over his strong back and burying themselves in his hair to pull him closer.

A passing priestess cleared her throat, forcing us to break the kiss. Slightly breathless, the Fox Demon backed away ever so slightly and stared into the depths of my dragon green eyes. "Marry me, Xyleena."

My heart skipped a beat.

"Yes."

Dawn. The twin suns broke the horizon and painted the sky a medley of colors. Dew on grass and glass turned to jewels as the light refracted. The softest lick of wind woke the standards atop the pinnacles. A new autumn day had come. Yet I did not revel in the beauty of it.

My mind, it seemed, was too busy reliving the nightmarish adventure that spanned the last three years. Every time I had tried to close my eyes, another battle replayed itself in my head. I couldn't help but wonder if I would ever be at peace again.

Kitfox snored and mumbled something, breaking my train of thought. I glanced sideways at him and couldn't suppress the chuckle that escaped me. He was curled up and hugging his bushy tail as if it was me. And he looked so adorable that I wanted to make wild, passionate love with him then and there!

I'll let him sleep a bit longer, I thought. With a sigh and a shake of my head, I forced myself to look away. My gaze returned to the view through the window, then slowly drifted downwards. The leather-bound journal Thera had given me at our parting lay untouched on the desktop in front of me. I clicked my tongue and nodded, coming to a decision.

I leaned forward and turned to the first page. I dipped a quill in ink and smiled as I wrote the words:

Dear Diary,

Epilogue

She stood motionless at the window; a moon-kissed silhouette in the blackness of her surroundings. Cool, cyan eyes stared out beyond the glass, to Bedeb's rings where the Greatest Treasure was surely sealed away once again. She had no doubt they would one day soon be released to serve in their Keeper's revenge.

A sad smile constructed its way across her lips and a hand instinctively grasped the crystal vial strung over her heart. She hated to admit it, but she deeply missed Dimitri, even his annoying way to show how much he cared for her. It wasn't like a Dákun Daju to betray such emotions, yet she loved him nonetheless.

An infant's cry pulled her out of her reverie. With a tired sigh, she let the curtain fall back into place. Using her heightened sense of sight, she found her way to the baby's cot in the blackness. She gently stroked the boy's cheek before picking him up to coddle him. Her gaze returned to the window as the baby quieted.

"One day, Jítanath, you will wield the power of the Shadow Dragons."

Selena Inali Raynelif Drake is an American author best known for her paranormal mystery series, The AEON Files. Drake is a martial arts enthusiast, a Wiccan with Cherokee roots, and an award-winning artist. Her love for writing started when she was eight, and she has won a number of Editor's Choice awards and a Shakespeare Trophy of Excellence for poetry. Her works have been published in *Thrice Fiction Magazine, Emerging Authors 2018*, and *Emerging Poets 2018*.

She currently lives in Minot, North Dakota with her dog, Pipsqueak, where she continues to work on more books.

You can find out more about Selena by visiting sirdwrites.com

Glossary

A note from the author:

I realize that the language of *Dragon Diaries* is extremely confusing. Most readers will probably just glance over the words, but for those (like me) who enjoy learning new things, here is a little bit of a guide to the language known as Kinös Elda. Hopefully it will help.

Kinös Eldic Phrases

Tabiki ni heile. — Wall of fire

Esté imlít lerra rité mertuác jidó. Arx et cólaz ni Kohnbenai rahn. — This great world will die soon. As the acts of Darkness spread.

Meo resuko. — My diary

Meo namae wa Agasei DéDos. Esté buko wa meo resuko bó et tel né rité sterim et Nírigone Súl. — My name is Agasei DéDos. This book is my diary and the key to finding the Dragons' Gate.

Sortim — Sister

Kahs gözandí — Good morning

Ja lah shikenó — You are welcome

Iríjhon Resuko — Dragon Diary

Kahs gözandí, fratime. Eo ík Teka Loneborne. — Good morning, brothers. I am Teka Loneborne.

Aké la ja chee? — Why are you here?

Kíen la ja süm, Teka Loneborne? — Who are you with, Teka Loneborne?

Estéz karétez la meo micallaz, bó et kanójo wa Xyleena. — These men are my friends, and the girl is Xyleena.

It ja nan hakaní estéz tantúre? — Do you not understand these words?

Hoko bemum Thera Onyx — Please call Thera Onyx

Núl wa de ja du bemum meo po, Ujak? — What did you call me for, Uncle?

Meoja ker dumakunga — We have decided

Iríjhone Reshé — Dragon Keeper

Vero — Yes

De wa et nena ni Amorez — She is the (female) child of Amorez

Shíkai ja — Thank you

Gratíe — Thanks (informal)

Eo du capel ja nan lig Kinös Elda — I thought you did not speak Kinös Elda

It ja hakaní? — Do you understand?

Ja lah tarlé, Pox. Da du la ja? — You are late, Pox. Where were you?

Kíen la déoja? — Who are they?

Eo dur ir né et izvucí tig Tarik bó Valadri — I went to the river with Tarik and Valadri.

Siminea — Lion

Kahs nóc — Good night

Tanda — Hello

Tíc it eo lig "standard words" den Kinös Elda? — How do I say "standard words" in Kinös Elda?

Meo namae wa Dimitri Renoan. Kíen la ja? — My name is Dimitri Renoan. Who are you?

Eo ík Habanya-Ürg. Aké la ja chee? — I am Habanya-Ürg. Why are you here?

Eo nan lig Kinös Elda. Eo ík guídes — I do not speak Kinös Elda. I am sorry.

Meo namae wa Xyleena. Eo ík et Iríjhone Reshé — My name is Xyleena. I am the Dragon Keeper.

Na — Zero

San — One

Sku — Two

Teh — Three

O — Four

Ven — Five

Mé — Six

Im — Seven

Lin — Eight

Bin — Nine

Ra — Ten
Sanra — Elven
Skura — Twelve
Tehra — Thirteen
Ora — Fourteen
Venra — Fifteen
Méra — Sixteen
Imra — Seventeen
Linra — Eighteen
Binra — Nineteen
Skucóra — Twenty
Mehnt — One hundred
Shréva — One thousand
Kahs gozavé — Good afternoon
Tanda, Kínashe. Eo din ormá né alú sa amyíac — Hello, Kínashe. I would like to rent a boat.
Tic kahl wah — How much for
Nai — No
Nír irím bó kerím ska — Now go and have fun
Infé — Open
Tanda, Zahadu-Kitai. Núl cistrena ja chee? — Hello, Zahadu-Kitai. What brings you here?
Núl wa et shríldu ni esté? — What is the meaning of this?
Ja lah tído guídemavet — You are all forgiven
Tic la ja? — How are you?
Byö – Cousin
Eo rité res meo ligto. — I give my word.
Dasum meo… — Show me…
Dasum meo nishi. — Show me everyone.
Kahs gözandí, Xy-sortim. — Good morning, my sister Xy.
Nevoa cäipe — Fog disperse
Et Sleiku ni Sango — The Dance of Blood
Meo sortime, meo fratim, illam durus. — My sisters, my brother, live strong.
Iktanilla — Immortal
Silentium — Silence; Be quiet

Symbilla et Illa-Arnaxu sornipé; Ten Sutétim isila con strujaz ni ponet — Symbilla the Life-Bringer dreams; On Southern isle with golden streams.

Ja la mishi, nena. — You are lost, child.

Ja la nan mert. Iram ger. — You are not dead. Go back.

Ligam ni Skura bó inferom. — Speak of Twelve and enter.

Hyerjam — Shatter, break

Spells

Aero bíraw *(air-oh bee-raw)* — Wind gust

Daréta esso *(da-ray-ta eh-so)* — Thunder ball

Daréta suahk *(da-ray-ta soo-awk)* — Thunder bolt

Dasai nagarésayo *(da-sigh na-guh-ray-say-oh)* — Sight reflection

Dasum meo *(da-soom may-oh)* — Show me

Heile esso *(hail eh-so)* — Fire ball

Heile pricé *(hail pree-kay)* — Fire storm

Heile suahk *(hail soo-awk)* — Fire bolt

Hydíca semít *(hi-dee-kuh sem-eet)* — Ice spike

Hydíca tabiki *(hi-dee-kuh ta-bee-kee)* — Ice wall

Hydor esso *(hi-door eh-so)* —Water ball

Hydor sibatín *(hi-door see-bat-een)* —Water spear

Kósa sibatín *(koh-sa see-bat-een)* —Chaos spear

Levítum *(lay-vee-tum)* – Levitate

Medícté *(med-eek-tay)* – Heal

Nagaré *(nah-guh-ray)* – Reflect

Nan dasai nevoa *(non duh-sigh ney-voh-uh)* — Blinding mist (literally "no sight mist")

Nan vocé *(non voh-kay)* — Silence (literally "no voice")

Luminös *(loo-mihn-ahs)* — Illuminate, Light

Uerto palaso *(oo-er-tow pah-lass-oh)* — Poison arrow

Names and Places

Aadrian *(ey-dree-ahn)* (city) — Lesser capitol city of Mekora-Lesca

Aadrian Ithnez *(ey-dree-ahn ith-nehz)* (person) — The man who ultimately saved the human race from extinction and helped found the planet which bears his name

Adoramus *(ah-dohr-ah-muhs)* — Shadow Dragon of Light who was killed in the final battle between Amorez and Agasei

Agasei DéDos *(a-guh-sigh day-dose)* — The original dark Dragon Keeper and creator of the Shadow Dragons

Aidana Wovril *(ahy-deyn-ah wohv-ril)* — Feykin Elder and one of the Generals leading the Army of Light

Aissur *(a-soor)* — A major city on Katalania

Amorez Renoan *(ah-more-ez ray-no-ahn)* — The original Dragon Keeper and creator of the Dragons of Light

Aruvan *(ah-roo-vahn)* — The smaller, yellow sun

Atlidmé *(at-lid-may)* — God of water, death, and winter (giant serpent)

Bakari-Tokai *(buh-kar-ee toh-kahy)* — The grand capital of Ithnez

Bangorian Mountains *(bahn-gohr-ee-an)* — Prominent mountain range running the southern spans of the Mekora-Lescan continent

Bedeb *(bay-deb)* — Ithnez's ringed sister planet

Beldai *(bell-dahy)* — One of the twin cities on the banks of the Anakor River

Breccia *(bresh-ee-uh)* — Shaman of the Wakari Corundum Tribe

Cah *(kaw)* — A city in the Southern Stretch

Cosín *(coh-seen)* — A small town on the Southern Stretch

Dákun Daju *(day-koon da-joo)* — Extreme race of elven-like beings

Djurdak Za'Car *(jer-dak zuh-kar)* — Amorez's husband and the former high prince

Feykin *(fay-kin)* — Preferred name of the Sorcerers

Freya Latreyon *(fray-uh luh-tray-in)* — Wolf Demon and teacher to Xyleena

Godilai Locklyn *(god-il-lahy lok-lin)* — Dákun Daju warrior

Havel (ha-vell) — The name for the realm of the dead

Ithnez *(ith-nehz)* — The planet where the adventure takes place

Jetep *(jay-tehp)* — City of outlaws and mercenaries on the southwest coast of Mekora-Lesca

Jítanath Locklyn *(jee-tuh-nath lok-lin)* — Only son of Dimitri De'Dos and Godilai Locklyn

Jormandr *(johr-man-dohr)* — Gargantuan rock serpent that terrorizes the Wakari

Kamédan *(kah-may-dan)* — The capital of Katalania

Khatahn-Rhii *(kah-tawn ree)* — God of wind, evolution, and autumn (dragon)

Kinös Elda *(keen-ahs el-duh)* — The ancient tongue

Kkaia *(kuh-kay-uh)* — Dragon of earth

Kkorian *(kuh-kor-ee-an)* — Hume pirate

Kula *(koo-luh)* — Shadow Dragon of Earth

Kúskú *(koo-skoo)* — Dragon of Illusion

Luea *(loo-ee-uh)* — Queen of Aadrian

Magnathor *(mag-nuh-thor)* — Gargantuan sea monster which haunts the waters of the Myst

Míjin *(mee-jin)* — One of the Feykin Generals in the Army of Light

Monrai *(mon-rye)* — Major city located on the outskirts of the Myst

Nahstipulí *(nuh-step-oo-lee)* — Goddess of earth, life, and summer (Ixys, a black unicorn)

Nemlex *(nehm-liks)* — Major Katalanian trade city

Nexxa *(nehks-uh)* — Dragon of Venom

Nír'l *(neer-il)* — An elder Dákun Daju who is related to Dimitri

Noralani Ithnez *(nohr-aw-lawn-ee ith-nehz)*— Named after Aadrian's only daughter, she is the last surviving member of the Ithnez bloodline.

Pletíxa *(play-teeks-uh)* — An insignificant town on Katalania

Pyrex Akregate *(pie-rehks ak-rii-gate)* — Wakari Alchemist who helped bring the Shadow Dragons to life

Q'veca *(coo-vay-kuh)* — Menta trainer on the Sorcerers' Isle

Régon *(ray-gahn)* — God of Chaos and Creation

Rhekja *(rek-yah)* — Gazelle Demon and owner of the Bird in Hand Tavern and Inn in Monrai; member of the Schaakold-Vond'l guild

Ríhan *(ree-han)* — Xyleena's best friend

Rishai *(ree-shy)* — The larger, blue sun

Ruwviti *(roo-vee-tee)* — Elder Sorcerer and Thera's uncle

Sauqe *(sok)* — Tiny fishing town on Katalania

Schaakold-Vond'l *(shahk-uld von-dul)* — A high-powered Equine Demon guild

Seramahli *(sehr-ah-maw-lee)* — Major Wakari city, home of the Corundum Tribe

Serpehti *(sur-pet-ee)* — Another rival guild of the Tahda'varett

Symbilla *(sim-bee-ya)* — Dragon of Life

Sindai *(sen-dahy)* — One of the twin cities on the banks of the Anakor River

Tahda'varett *(tuh-dah-vahr-eht)* — Kitfox's and Freya's guild

Taypax *(tay-paks)* — Dragon of Death who was killed in the final battle between Amorez and Agasei

Thedrún *(thehd-roon)* — Dragon of Thunder

Thera *(ter-uh)* — Feykin Occultist from the Sorcerers' Isle

Thernu *(ter-new)* — Thera's mother

Thorna *(thorn-uh)* — A major city on the Sorcerers' Isle

Thuraben *(thoor-uh-ben)* — The capital of the Sorcerer's Isle

Valaskjalf Za'Car *(vuh-lask-jahlf zuh-kar)* — Current high prince of Ithnez

Visler *(vihs-lur)* — Silver, dragon-shaped homunculus; also called a Sentinel

Vitaani *(viht-ahn-ee)* — Dákun Daju General within the Army of Light

V'Nyath *(v-nee-ath)* — Dákun Daju General within the Army of Light

Vronan *(vroh-nahn)* — Largest city on Ithnez; houses a major trading port

Wakari *(wuh-kar-ee)* — Dwarf-like creatures that live far underground

Warinarc *(war-een-ark)* — A rival guild of the Tahda'varett

Wyrd *(weerd)* — Shadow Dragon of Undead

Xyleena *(zahy-lee-nuh)* — Heroine of Dragon Diaries

Zadún *(zah-doon)* — The capital city of Arctica

Zahadu-Kitai *(za-ha-doo-key-tie)* — Goddess of fire, rebirth, and spring (phoenix)

Zalx *(zahlks)*— Dákun Daju General within the Army of Light

Zamora Argatör *(zuh-moor-uh ahr-guh-tour)* — Amorez's alias

Zhaman Verrs *(zah-mon verz)* — King of Arctica

Zhealocera *(zee-low-ser-uh)* — Dákun Daju friend of Xyleena

Zhücka *(zoo-kuh)* — Feykin General within the Army of Light

Zön-Rígaia *(zohn-ree-gayh-yah)* — High powered Feline Demon guild
Zrehla *(zer-ey-luh)* — King of the Southern Stretch

Other Languages:

Bakari-Tokai *(buh-kahr-ee toe-kahy)* — 'City of Survivors' in the Dákun Daju dialect
S'vil-Tokai *(suh-vhil toe-kahy)* — 'City of Invaders' in the Dákun Daju dialect
D'go-Pahngíl *(dug-oh pawn-geel)* — 'Blood Fang' in the ancient Demon dialect

Made in the USA
Columbia, SC
15 October 2021